LIBERTY STREET

LIBERTY STREET

A NOVEL OF LATE CIVIL WAR SAVANNAH

———◆———

Lawrence Martin
Author of:

Sherman's Mistress in Savannah

Out of Time: An alternative outcome to the Civil War

Lakeside Press
www.lakesidepress.com/CivilWarNovels.html

Print format ISBN-10: 0-9978959-3-4
Print format ISBN-13: 978-0-9978959-3-3
Kindle e-book ISBN: 978-0-9978959-1-9
Kindle e-book ASIN: B0748W3CTX

DEDICATION

To my wife Ruth, who has cheerfully traveled with me to numerous Civil War battle sites, from Gettysburg to Vicksburg. Without her support in so many ways, this book would not have been possible.

ACKNOWLEDGEMENTS

———

I HAVE BEEN FORTUNATE TO belong to several writing groups in The Villages, Florida, in which most of this novel has, at one time or other, been reviewed and critiqued. The comments received helped improve both my story and syntax immeasurably. In addition, input from several beta readers was crucial to honing the final manuscript. No author can (or should) write without feedback, and to all who have contributed I offer a heartfelt Thank You.

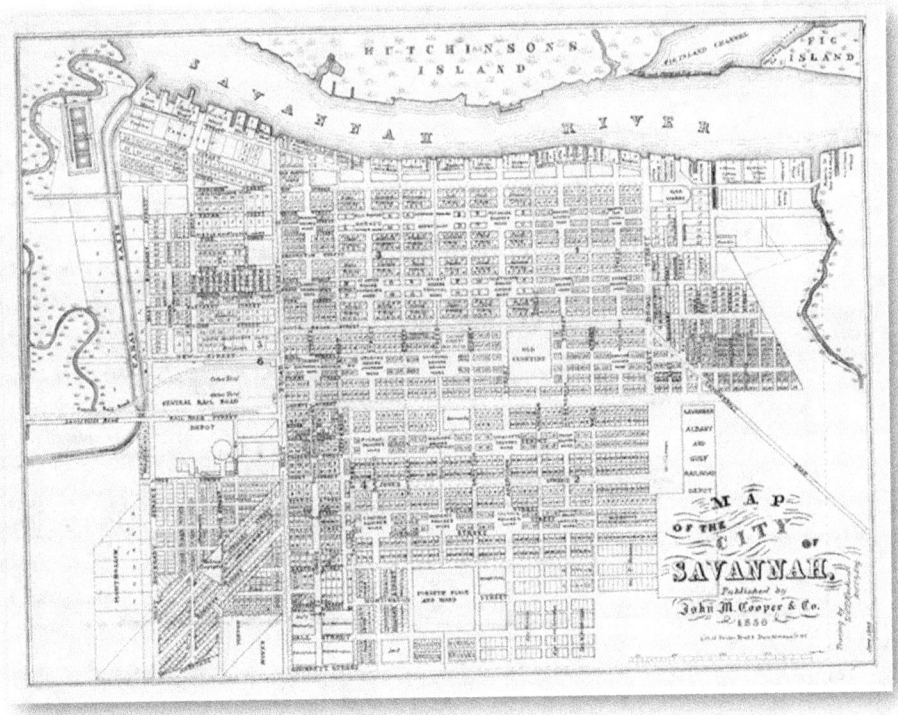

PREFACE

———

LIBERTY STREET IS A WORK of historical fiction. The framework is historically accurate, including dates and outcomes of battles, the general movement of troops, all messages and letters sent by General Sherman and President Lincoln, Sherman's Special Field Orders issued when his army occupied Savannah, and the plight of slaves toward the end of the war.

The story of Abigale Tate and her family, including their interactions with historical figures such as Mayor Richard Arnold, General John Geary and General Nathan Bedford Forrest, is entirely fictional. The character of Rufus Simms is fictional as well. These characters speak the language of the 1860s, some of which will sound offensive to modern readers. Also, words that today would be routinely capitalized, like Negro and Colored, are presented in lower case as they appeared in records of the period.

A number of historic documents are mentioned or briefly quoted in the novel, followed by a footnote reference to the Appendix. As part of the story I have created several letters, newspaper items and a book excerpt; these are not footnoted and all are fictional.

HISTORICAL NOTE

THE CIVIL WAR BEGAN APRIL 12, 1861, with the firing on Fort Sumter, Charleston, by Confederate troops. The war effectively ended April 9, 1865, with General Robert E. Lee's surrender at Appomattox to General Ulysses S. Grant. In the four years of fighting more than 700,000 soldiers died, about a third from battle wounds and two-thirds from disease.

Until near the end, a Union victory was not a sure thing. In the summer of 1864 President Lincoln thought he might lose the November election because of mounting battle losses. Then in September 1864, General William T. Sherman conquered Atlanta. With that victory northerners sensed the war's end was, in fact, near and that the Union would prevail. Historians credit Sherman's Atlanta campaign for turning sentiment in Lincoln's favor, and he easily won re-election two months later.

In mid-November 1864 General Sherman began his infamous march from Atlanta through the heart of Georgia. On December 21 his troops entered Savannah, without opposition. The Confederate forces under General William J. Hardee, whose numbers were no match for Sherman's 60,000 troops, had fled the city the night before.

Sherman stayed in Savannah until January 21, 1865, when he relocated to coastal South Carolina. Later that month, he led his army up the interior of South Carolina, with plans to eventually join General Grant's army in Virginia.

Savannah was fortunate, having avoided fighting that destroyed large parts of Atlanta, Charleston, Columbia and Richmond. For its residents, however, both black and white, the old ante-bellum way of life was forever changed.

PART 1: 1864

CHAPTER 1

———

— SAVANNAH, GEORGIA – TUESDAY, SEPTEMBER 20

AROUND TEN IN THE MORNING an envelope arrived to the townhouse at 27 Liberty Street, addressed to Mrs. Abigale Tate. Abigale, age twenty-four, was teaching at the Dayton Finishing School, so her negro servant Polly put it on a table in the front parlor.

Abigale's mother, Mrs. Henrietta Gordon, saw the envelope and felt sure of its message. She had received a similar message the year before, announcing her husband's death at Gettysburg. She retired to her bedroom and prayed.

Another daughter, Jane, age seventeen, was in her room reading a book about men and women and love.

Abigale came home for lunch.

"Mail be for you, Miss Abigale," said Polly, pointing to the table.

"Oh?" Abigale opened the envelope to find a one-page letter.

Dear Mrs. Tate:

I regret to inform you...Capt. Franklin Tate was mortally wounded on Sept. the first, in Jonesborough, Ga. He fought bravely and succumbed from a bullet to his chest. I do believe he passed without pain. We recovered the body and gave him a full military burial...

Abigale stared at the letter, then fell to the floor. Polly yelled upstairs: "Miss Henrietta, come quick! Miss Abigale sick!"

Mrs. Gordon ran down the stairs. "Oh, my God, she's fainted!"

Jane appeared. "Mother, what happened? What's going on?"

"The letter. The letter. Help me get her to the couch."

The three women picked up Abigale and laid her on the couch. Jane and Polly rubbed her arms while Abigale's mother read the letter. "I knew it," she said in a low voice.

Abigale awoke, looked at her mother.

"Oh, Abigale, I'm so sorry," said Mrs. Gordon. "I just read the letter. Are you all right?"

Abigale could only scream. "Let … me … die! LET ME DIE!"

— FRIDAY, DECEMBER 9

"Stop playing that funeral music!" yelled Jane.

"It's Chopin. Piano Sonata No. 2," retorted Abigale as she lightened her touch on the piano keys.

"I don't care who wrote it. It's driving me crazy."

"Girls, girls," admonished Mrs. Gordon, "must you always argue? Oh, if father were here, he would know what to do."

Abigale stopped playing, turned around on the bench to face her mother. "But father's not here. He's dead. Just like my husband. And just like we'll be soon, when General Sherman arrives."

"Don't say that," said Mrs. Gordon. "Abigale, you've changed so. I don't know what to do with you. You used to be a happy girl."

"I'm not a girl anymore. I'm a grown woman. Without a husband. Without a father. And with a brother God knows where, fighting in this damn war."

"Do you think Johnny will be all right?" asked Mrs. Gordon, as if Abigale somehow had the information at hand.

"We don't even know if he's alive," Abigale replied. "When was our last letter from him? Six months ago?"

"Mother, I'm going upstairs," said Jane. "I can't take this family much longer. My sister is a bag of melancholy, and you are in perpetual mourning. I feel as though I am growing up in a funeral home." With that, Jane climbed the townhouse stairs to her second floor bedroom.

"Polly," said Mrs. Gordon. "Go to the kitchen and fetch me some tea. Abigale, would you like some?"

"No thank you."

Polly left the room to do as asked.

"Abigale, I'm worried about Jane. She's only seventeen but puts on airs like a worldly woman. Do you know what I found in her room the other day?"

"I can only imagine."

"A book, with just a brown paper cover. I looked inside. It's called *The Art of Making Love — For The Modern Woman*. By some Frenchman, but it is our language. Where did she get such a thing?"

"Why didn't you ask her?"

"And have her snap at me? Oh, if only your father was here. Would you ask her, when you get a chance? I am afraid it is an evil influence."

"Did you read any of it?"

"Yes. To my dismay. It seems to convey a European viewpoint."

"Tell me. Nothing will surprise me."

"Well, he – this Frenchman – wrote that love between a man and a woman is all about physical attraction, that the woman wants the physical touch as much as the man, and that she won't be satisfied otherwise. And that was just the first page."

"Did you read more?"

"No, that was enough. I think the book is a manual for women seeking intimacy. Even, perhaps, before marriage. Only the French could write such a thing."

"Mother, you want some advice?"

"Yes, please."

"Leave Jane to herself. She is feeling the full blush of womanhood and is affected by our family misfortunes. As am I. One difference is that I have had what she now wants, and am more mature for it."

"What are you speaking of, I—"

"Tea is ready," said Polly, entering the room with a cup on a plate. She handed the cup to Mrs. Gordon.

"Thank you, Polly," said Mrs. Gordon. "Abigale, we can talk later, I am going upstairs to lie down. If you wish to resume playing Chopin, that is all right with me."

"Thank you, mother."

As soon as Mrs. Gordon left, Abigale lowered her head and sighed. Polly walked up to her, placed a hand on Abigale's shoulder and said, "Is you hurtin' Miss Abigale?"

Abigale looked up at her servant. "In ways I cannot express, Polly." She repeated her answer, but in a low voice and slowly, as if speaking only to herself. "In ways I cannot express."

"Sho' is a bad time."

"Polly, what are you going to do when General Sherman comes?"

"Ma'am?"

"He's coming soon. He's marching from Atlanta, and when he gets here he's going to free all the slaves. President Lincoln gave a proclamation to free all of you. General Sherman is coming to enforce it. If he doesn't rob and kill us all first."

"Ma'am, don't you talk like that. You and Mrs. Gordon have treated me right well. And besides, I gots no place to go."

"True enough, and I'll tell you a secret," said Abigale. "I have no place to go either. We are cut off, isolated here, surrounded by Yankees."

"How you knows dis?"

"Oh, everyone knows. Sherman is just outside the city. Do you know what he did to Atlanta?"

"Don't rightly know, ma'am."

"Burned it. Burned it to the ground. He may do that to Savannah."

"Don't know 'bout that, Miss Abigale. But I see what I sees in da Gordon house, and I know what might help you," said Polly.

"Oh, what?"

"You need to come to church with me this Sunday, hear our Reverend Simms. His sermon will make you feel better. He's got powerful speaking, he does."

"A colored church? A black church? Is that where you go every Sunday, on your day off?"

"Yes, ma'am. Ain't no secret."

"No, I suppose I knew that, just never thought much about it. This reverend, he's colored?"

"Yes, ma'am. Rufus Simms, a free colored man. He's got a nice-sized congregation. Third Ogeechee Colored Baptist. You heard of him?"

"No, I don't think so."

"You go with me, Miss Abigale. He'll make you feel better."

"I bet he's happy Sherman is coming."

"Don't know 'bout that. Maybe he'll mention it in his sermon."

Abigale was not partial to religion. Though raised Methodist, the war had left her disillusioned and disinterested in Sunday sermons. She had last been to church in August, when her mother dragged her.

"Do other white people go?"

"Usually a few shows up. You'll sit in the back. You won't be noticed or bothered with."

A colored preacher, thought Abigale. The idea intrigued her. *Why not go? I am willing to try anything to ease my despair.*

———

CHAPTER 2

— SUNDAY, DECEMBER 11

POLLY AND ABIGALE WALKED THE eight blocks to the Third Ogeechee Colored Baptist Church, in the section of Savannah known as Frogtown. The cool morning air and bright sunshine made the walk pleasant enough, except for trash strewn about the streets by local servants. Thankfully, there were no rotting animals. The negro work detail responsible for clearing the trash would show up Monday morning.

Abigale pondered what had become of her city. The war news was all bad. Atlanta had fallen in September, about the time Franklin was killed. In mid-November General Sherman began his huge army's march in a southeast direction. Reports of the march, which included pillaging, arson and wanton destruction of property, grew more frightening day by day. Now he and his army were just outside the city. Any day he will take us over, thought Abigale. Then what?

She also thought of Polly, sure to be freed when Savannah surrenders. Abigale had an affection for the woman, now thirty and with the Gordon household fifteen years, and hoped legal freedom did not diminish her loyalty or induce her to leave. Polly did most of the house chores, including cooking. Unlike many of Savannah's slaves she did not lack for nourishment. Big-boned and several inches shorter than Abigale, she was on the heavy side, with a full, round face.

Polly had married a decade earlier and initially she and her husband lived in the Gordon's basement. She had had no children and after about two years they separated, and though never legally divorced they were fully estranged. He was owned by a prominent Savannah family, the Caseys. Abigale did not know if Polly had another man, but doubted it.

Despite her foreboding Abigale enjoyed the walk, a chance to get outside and exercise. She wore an old deeply-pleated skirt and blouse, with a head bonnet. No new clothes had entered the household since shortly after the war began, and the women repurposed and resewed what they had. Polly wore an old unformed smock with skirt, and a kerchief for head cover. Both women had on jackets, Abigale's made of silk and trimmed with braid, her servant's of cheap pre-war cotton.

Initially, Polly stayed a few steps behind her mistress, as per custom, but Abigale insisted she walk beside her. "I want to ask about your church."

"Yes, ma'am."

"You go to the same church every Sunday?"

"Yes'm. Although Reverend Simms is not always doin' the preachin'. Sometimes others fill in for him."

"What's his regular job?" She knew that colored ministers, of which there were several in Savannah, had regular jobs to sustain themselves.

"He be a carpenter, I believe. He's a free man, though, do what he want."

"Yes, I understand." Well she did. Out of a Savannah population of 22,000, an estimated 7700 were legally slaves, with free blacks counting for another 700. "Free" meant they were not owned by anyone, though each free black person had to have a white "guardian," to represent them in legal matters. Still, they could move about, earn their own living and, if they had the means, even own slaves themselves.

"Does he own any slaves?" Abigale asked.

"Not as I knows, ma'am. He be a man of God."

Abigale pondered the statement. "Owning slaves is not God's way?"
"I don't rightly know, ma'am."

Abigale did not take offense, and let it go. If her servant had abo-
litionist ideas, they did not show in the household. Besides, everything would change in short order, when General Sherman arrived.
Polly would be liberated in name, but Abigale and her mother and
sister would still need her services and Polly would still need a job. So
perhaps nothing would change for her family. Unless, she thought,
Savannah is burned to the ground by that odious Yankee.

A few horse-drawn carriages passed by. The two women were
careful to avoid any clouds of dust kicked up by the conveyances.
Abigale's family did not own a carriage or she would have taken it to
the church, but she didn't mind the walk; it felt good to get outside.
She was thankful she had said yes to the invitation. It gave her an
excuse to dress up a bit, to feel more like she did before death and
destruction entered her life. For the first time in weeks she had an
agenda, albeit unusual for a woman of her background. She imagined what others might think of her going to church with Polly, and
then realized she didn't care.

After about twenty minutes they crossed West Broad Street
and reached the church. Abigale had seen the building before
but never paid much attention. It was of the second category of
Savannah structures, built of wood rather than masonry or brick.
Abigale noted it to be in some disrepair, with its white paint peel-
ing, several window shutters missing, and some wood planks need-
ing replacement.

The two women climbed a few steps and entered the building. A
single wood-burning stove adorned the stage, but the air remained
cool inside, the stove simply unable to warm the whole interior. In
wintertime, parishioners kept their coats on, making the services
tolerable.

Abigale noted a similar seating arrangement as in white churches, with two long rows of wooden benches, starting near the entrance

door and ending just before a raised stage. The benches could seat 300 people comfortably, and were now half full with negro parishioners. As more people entered behind them, Polly steered Abigale to the rearmost bench on the left, closest to the front doors. The bench was empty and Abigale sat on the end near the aisle. She felt a little awkward as the only white person present, man or woman, but her arrival didn't seem to cause any notice.

"Other whites be coming, Miss Abigale," said Polly, apparently sensing her mistress's discomfort. "We always have a few." The same could not be said of Abigale's First Methodist church, where no blacks were permitted to sit with the congregation.

"I goes up front, Miss Abigale. You'll see and hear fine from here. I'll come for you after Reverend Simms done with his sermon. That's when da service be over."

"If I choose so, Polly, I may go out earlier, so if I'm not here I'll see you back at the house."

"Yes, ma'am," Polly replied, and left Abigale to take her seat up front.

Abigale sat down and surveyed the room. The women mostly wore shawls, the men old jackets, some of them army issue. She wondered if they came from their dead masters.

After a few minutes a portly white gentleman entered the church and excused himself as he squeezed past Abigale to sit on the bench, leaving a space of two feet between them.

"How do you do?" he said, in a guttural German accent, and held out his hand. "I am Gustav Heinz."

She shook his hand. "Pleased to meet you, Mr. Heinz. I'm Abigale Tate. Mrs. Abigale Tate."

"Is this your first time, Mrs. Tate?"

"Here? At Ogeechee Colored Baptist?"

"Yah, yah."

"Yes, I came at the urging of my negro servant. She lured me here, I'm afraid. Said I should come listen to her Reverend Simms."

"Where do you live? On a plantation or in the city?" A fair question, since the city was surrounded by many rice plantations, run by women while their men were off fighting.

"Oh, close by, on Liberty Street," she said.

"I see. I see." He looked her up and down, nodding his head. This made her feel slightly uncomfortable. She turned away and tried to focus on the stage.

She was about to ask why he was staring at her, when he spoke. "You've suffered a loss." It was not a question.

Abigale jerked her head toward him. "What do you mean?"

Now she looked more closely at this figure and noted that perhaps he was not a gentleman at all. She noted unpressed pants and a frayed coat, and he had at least a two day's growth of facial stubble. She guessed his age in the late 40s, close to her father's age if her father had lived. By reputation most German-speaking immigrants, of which there were many in Savannah, were hard working and prosperous, and perhaps Mr. Heinz was too, but something about him suggested a lower middle class background. She smelled a faint body odor, but could not discern if it was sweat or cologne.

"Excuse me," he said. "I don't mean to pry. But I notice these things."

"Oh? What things?"

"For a beautiful woman, which you are, one whose life should be joyful, you do not show a smile. You introduce yourself as Mrs. Tate but wear no ring. And you came with no other family, at the entreaty of your negro servant. And alas, this is war time in America. Am I wrong?"

Though crude, his comment was somewhat reassuring. Even a ten-pound weight loss in recent weeks and a repressed smile did not dim Abigale's beauty. At almost five and a half feet tall, she was well-proportioned with a full bosom which, unlike other curves of the female anatomy, was not hidden by dresses worn in public. Unblemished skin, golden-brown hair and sparkling blue eyes added to her appeal. Gloom in countenance certainly did not diminish her attractiveness to men.

"You are very observant, Mr. Heinz. I am in fact a widow." Why, she wondered, is she even responding to him? Out of courtesy? Curiosity? Loneliness in a sea of black faces? Perhaps all these reasons. "My husband was killed just this year, near Atlanta. And what brings you here to this church, and to Savannah in war time?"

"Ah, before the war, long before the war," replied Gustav. "I came from Frankfurt, in Hesse."

"Hesse?"

"Ah, part of a loose German-speaking Confederation. One day we will all be united. Like your country, it seems." He gave out a short and sardonic laugh, as if responding to a private joke.

Abigale did not share his amusement, but remained polite. It was well known among educated Southern whites that Europe had long ago given up slavery, and that the South's adherence to the institution partly explained why no European country came to its aid. Had France or Britain entered for the South, the war would likely be over by now, and General Sherman would not be at Savannah's doorstep.

"I have been here since fifty-six," said Gustav. "Now proprietor of Savannah Gardens, boarding house on Broughton. You've heard? Fine establishment."

She had heard. Savannah Gardens was a boarding house in name only, a brothel for soldiers being its main function. There was even rumor that he employed one or two young black girls, a premium for white soldiers seeking forbidden fruit. *So Gustav is the proprietor!*

"Yes, I know where it is," she said, showing no surprise. She was careful not to say "what it is."

"Yah," he replied. "This war is terrible. Bad for business. Bad for the economy. Reverend Simms is a free black man. He speaks the truth and when I have time I come to listen."

At that point a tall skinny male negro came on the stage and bellowed out "Children of God, let us stand and pray."

"Is that him?" asked Abigale.

"No," said Gustav. "He is the choirmaster. First we have the sing-ing. *Then* comes the Reverend."

Abigale and Gustav stood with the others. Just then an elderly white couple came in and entered their bench. As they squeezed past first Abigale and then Gustav, the Hessian moved closer to her, to give the couple more sitting room, a totally unnecessary maneuver considering the bench was long enough to accommodate eight peo-ple. After the opening prayer, with everyone seated, she found him a foot closer than before.

Abigale pondered the irony of being made to feel uncomfortable by a white man in a black church. Should she just leave? For a minute she vacillated over what to do: stay or walk out.

A group of men and women came on stage, hymnals in hand, and the singing began.

No. I'll stay. I'm too damn curious about this Reverend Simms.

CHAPTER 3

———◆———

ACROSS THE ROWS OF PEOPLE Abigale saw Reverend Simms stride to the pulpit, attired in a flowing black robe fringed with a white collar that dipped down below his neckline. From the back of the hall he appeared light-skinned, though clearly negro from his dark, thickly-curled hair and general facial features. He was short and stocky, with broad shoulders, and clean shaven except for a small chin beard. Before speaking he stared left and right, then straight ahead. The first words he spoke surprised Abigale. They were not standard English.

"Our Fadduh awt'n Hebb'n, all-duh-weh be dy holy 'n uh rightschus name. Dy kingdom com.' Oh lawd leh yo' holy 'n rightschus woud be done, on dis ert' as-'e tis dun een yo' grayt Hebb'n. 'N ghee we oh Lawd dis day our day-ly bread. "N f'gib we oh Lawd our truspasses, as we also f'gib doohs who com' sin 'n truspass uhghens us. 'N need-us-snot oh konkuhrin' King een tuh no moh ting like uh sin 'n eeb'l. Fuh dyne oh dyne is duh kingdom, 'n duh kingdom prommus fuh be we ebbuh las'n glory. Amen."

There followed a chorus of "Amens" from the audience, along with stamping of feet.

Gustav leaned over to Abigale. "Gullah," he said. She nodded in agreement. By the time Simms had reached "N f'gib oh Lawd" she surmised it was the low country dialect of slaves imported from Africa. If this was to be Reverend Simms' choice of language, she saw little point in staying. *Another reason to walk out of here.*

"That's just to warm up the audience," Gustav chuckled. "Most of them know Gullah somewhat, especially those who spent time on the Sea Islands. He likes to start out that way."

"Loses me," said Abigale. "Will he speak in English?"

Before Gustav could respond Simms continued, his voice from the pulpit clear throughout the room. "My friends, what a glorious moment we are in. It's been a long hard road, it has. We have lost many brethren in the rice fields, to the plague and to the fevers and, yes, to the taskmaster. And our white folk have lost many of their own, to war and disease and more war. These have been difficult times. Is that right?"

"Difficult times!" the flock yelled in unison.

"Who among us has not suffered some loss, some pain, some hurt?"

"No one among us," they all responded, again in unison. This was not the first time Simms had asked these questions.

"But we see a light now. Yes, we do." He pointed to a man in the first row. "Do you see the light?"

"I do," said the first-row parishioner.

Pointing to a woman in the second row, Simms called out: "And do you see the light?"

"Almighty lawd, yes!"

Simms walked about twenty feet stage left and called on another woman, a middle-aged negro in the first row. "Do YOU see the light?"

"Hallelujah!" she yelled, and began gesticulating and making strange sounds with her tongue. At this the audience chanted "Amen! Amen! Amen!" The tongue-speaking woman had to be restrained by her neighbors, until she finally quieted down.

Simms strode back to the podium and turned to face the assembly. "WE ALL SEE THE LIGHT" he exclaimed. "The Lord is a comin' to deliver us, He is."

Abigale felt uneasy. She did not want to hear any more and stood to leave. Gustav reached for her forearm with one hand and raised his other hand to indicate 'wait a minute'. She was about to pull away and bolt for the door when Simms spoke again.

"And white folks see the light, including war widows and war mothers and war sisters. We have all suffered together, and now we can all see the light. White folk, dark folk. Don't matter. We are all children of God. Is that not so?"

"That is so! That is so!"

Simms smiled and lifted his eyes beyond the sea of black faces to the very rear of the hall. The reverend's gaze and the Hessian's gentle hand persuaded Abigale to sit back down. Gustav let go of her arm.

Abigale was thankful no heads turned in her direction. She would find another moment to make her escape. *Why did he mention 'war widows'?*

The sermon continued. "God has a purpose, he does. We must believe in God to make sense of the last four years. Why would God allow white folks to kill each other in such high numbers? So many deaths. The women folk left behind—those who've lost a father, a brother, a son or a husband, they may feel deep down that God is evil. But is God evil?"

"No!" roared the audience.

"Why would God allow black folks to suffer so, under the yolk of repression? Why would God allow our brethren to be shackled and whipped and torn asunder from their families? Must be an evil God. Is God evil?"

"No!" came the reply, from 300 souls.

Simms raised his voice to seek a louder response. "I say, IS GOD EVIL?"

"NO!"

"No, WHAT?" screamed Simms.

"God is not evil!"

"That's right! God is not evil. He has a purpose. This war has a purpose, as horrible as it is. It will free us. Our savior is coming!"

Abigale wondered how Simms could get away with such blasphemy. *My father and husband didn't fight to free the slaves! If Father was alive and heard this—he wouldn't stand for it, that's for sure. I bet this isn't the first time Simms has spoken such inflammatory rhetoric. Why didn't the authorities stop him? Where are the men in this city? Mayor Arnold and his aldermen? General Hardee and his army? How come only a few white people are hearing this? Can free blacks speak in public this way? In Savannah?*

She glanced over toward the elderly white couple. They seemed unfazed by the speech. Perhaps this is what they came to hear. She did not recognize them and wondered if they were visiting from up north. Then she realized no one was visiting from up north, at least not within the past two years or so.

"You say God is not evil, my friends," Simms continued, "and once again you speak the truth. There is a purpose in all this, God's purpose. We are all creatures of God, and I say this. Count your blessings. For whether you are enslaved by the white man's shackles or you are a prisoner of your own inner demons, there is light coming. There is light coming! DO NOT DESPAIR!"

What does he mean, prisoner of your own inner demons? Do blacks have inner demons? Is he speaking to me? How would he know? Polly! She must have said something to him!

Simms pivoted to New Testament scripture. "Jesus said, in Matthew, 'Ye are the light of the world. A city that is set on a hill cannot be hid. Neither do men light a candle and put it under a bushel, but on a candlestick; and it giveth light unto all that are in the house.' Our light is coming. It is coming."

Simms continued with more biblical quotes, each one powerful yet opaque, allowing him to fit it to the times. He never once mentioned Sherman by name, but didn't have to. Even the least literate among his flock knew, from countless conversations among their brothers and sisters and other kinfolk, that General Sherman was "the light," or was "bringing the light," and that when he arrived there would be a new order.

Simms' sermonizing went on another half hour, as Abigale wrestled with it all. He was infuriating and soothing, treasonous toward her culture and understanding of it as well. He spoke in generalities, yet his words seemed to touch her inner soul. Whenever she decided to leave, the next moment she decided to stay.

The parishioners intrigued her as well, especially when compared with her own Methodist congregation. Apart from race, she noted a striking contrast. Savannah's white Methodists sat in their pews dutifully, stoically, reciting scripture when called on, but without excitement or verve.

Here, when Simms swayed back and forth, so did all the negroes. When he threw up his hands to the Lord, they did as well. When he bellowed out a question, they yelled back the answer. And several times throughout the service, a man or woman would stand, call out "Hallelujah! Praise the Lord" and sit back down after the audience approved with a loud "Amen." Such a thing was unthinkable at her church.

Yes, she thought, verve was the right word. Compared to Simms' flock, the white congregation was sedate: no involvement, no *verve*. Her people attended Sunday service as obligation, lest they rot in Hell after death. Simms' people came to be entertained and uplifted; they attended for the here and now, not for any promise of a better afterlife. Her white church was duty. This black one was joy.

So despite initial misgivings, and the obnoxious Hessian beside her, Abigale decided to stay. As soon as the service was over she would question Polly about what she had told the reverend.

After the last "Amen" the audience rose to exit. Polly rushed to the back bench and before Abigale could speak, pulled on her mistress's arm and said, "Come, Miss Abigale, he wants to meet you."

"Who?"

"Reverend Simms."

"Why? What did you tell him?"

"That you be the nicest mistress in Savannah. He a free colored. He likes to meet nice white folks."

Abigale hesitated and Gustav chimed in. "Ah, you should go, Mrs. Tate. When General Sherman comes, will be helpful perhaps to have connections with the colored elite." He flicked his hand toward her, indicating she should go with her servant.

She did not reply. Instead, she looked down the aisle at the stage, then the opposite way, toward the church doors. Should she now run home? If she left, would Gustav follow her? Going with Polly to the pulpit would be a way of getting rid of him, at least, so she acquiesced. There was another reason; she *was* curious to meet the reverend.

Polly and Abigale fought their way down the aisle, past the exiting crowd, and climbed a few stairs to the stage. Simms was at the pulpit, conversing with several followers. Abigale noted that Simms was only an inch or so taller than herself. She estimated his age around thirty-five to forty.

Polly made a quick introduction. "This be Miss Abigale, Reverend."

He held out his hand and Abigale shook it.

"Nice to meet you," she said. *What am I doing?*

"The pleasure is all mine," he replied. "I hear nice things about you. Sadly, I have also learned of your losses. Please accept my deepest condolences."

"Polly told you?"

"Yes. It is indeed unfortunate."

Abigale gave her servant a disapproving look but said nothing. Simms exchanged a few pleasantries with the remaining parishioners on stage and they dispersed.

He sounds intelligent, she thought. Cultivated, even.

"Thank you for coming to my church," Simms said. "We welcome white folks who have an open mind. I see you sat with the Nelsons and Mr. Heinz."

"They are new to me," she said. "I did meet Mr. Heinz. He told me he comes to hear you often, that you speak the truth." How well did the reverend know Gustav? Was he a patron of Savannah Gardens? Why would she think that? She didn't even know if he was married.

Abigale looked back at the bench she had just left and saw Gustav sitting there, now alone, as if waiting for something. Or someone.

"Well, thank you," said Simms, "but I'm afraid the truth depends on whose viewpoint, wouldn't you agree?"

Truth and *viewpoint.* Abigale thought the words sounded strange coming from a colored man, free or not. She chose not to answer his question.

"How did you learn to become a reverend?" she asked.

"Ah, that is an interesting story. Perhaps you and Polly would like to come to my office for a few minutes? We can speak privately there. It's right behind the stage."

"Be fine with me," said Polly.

"Yes, for a few minutes," said Abigale. By then Gustav would be gone, she figured. And besides, there was something about this reverend that stoked her curiosity. *He doesn't seem like any negro I've ever met. If I closed my eyes he would sound like a white man. An* educated *white man.*

— *TUESDAY, DECEMBER 13*

GENERAL SHERMAN, ALONG WITH GENERAL Oliver O. Howard and several aides, stood on the roof of the Cheeves' Plantation rice mill, two miles from Fort McAllister. From this vantage point they could make out the ramparts of the low earthen fort, and easily spot its high-flying Confederate battle flag. Another mile beyond the fort lay Union ships at anchor in Ossabaw Sound, their masts also visible from the mill roof. Owing to the curve of the river, the ships and the fort were invisible to each other.

As Sherman gazed through his telescope he asked an aide, "What time is it?"

"Half past four, sir," replied his lieutenant.

"What's the delay?" Sherman's question was rhetorical, and reflected his mild anxiety for the moment. The sun would set in little over an hour, so there wasn't much time left. Two hours earlier Sherman had heard musket-skirmishing from the fort, and knew his troops were poised to strike. Three thousand Union soldiers surrounded the fort, under the command of Brigadier General William B. Hazen. *I personally selected Bill for this task. I'm sure he'll get the job done.*

Using semaphore flags, one of the ships in Ossabaw Sound signaled to the rice mill: "Has the fort been taken?" At that moment Sherman espied Hazen's troops emerging from the dark fringe of woods before the fort, with colors flying and moving quickly. Sherman instructed his semaphore man to signal back to the ship: "Not yet, but it will be in a minute."

Sherman's master plan to capture Savannah required he first take Fort McAllister, which lay just south of the city on the Ogeechee River. He needed the Ogeechee to resupply his troops. Trying to attack via the Savannah River was not feasible. Its mouth was fully blockaded with tons of debris dumped by Union forces in late 1861; clearing that river could take weeks.

Sherman could try to starve Savannah by laying siege, much as Grant had done at Vicksburg. But without fresh provisions, this was not a sound military option. His men were tired, ill-clothed and hungry from the long march through Georgia. For several days prior to reaching Savannah they had subsisted only on rice.

Fresh food, clothing and all manner of supplies lay aboard ships in Ossabaw Sound. To get those supplies, the ships had to travel up the Ogeechee River past Ft. McAllister. Union ships had tried to capture the fort several times in the previous two years, and each time were repelled by McAllister's cannons. The only sure way to take the fort was to attack by land.

Sherman certainly had the manpower. The Fort McAllister roster consisted of only 230 troops. All but two of the fort's big guns faced the river, and they could not be easily repositioned to repel a land attack. The numbers alone foretold the outcome of this battle. The only question in Sherman's mind was how long the fight would take.

The rear of the fort faced a forest whose trees had been leveled by the Confederates, to a distance of 300 yards. Any assault would thus be over an open plain. Hazen's men had to run the plain, then the deep ditches around the fort with their abatis and other obstructions. Once past those, they had to climb steep earthen walls to enter the fort. McAllister was well protected, but not against overwhelming numbers.

At 4:45 p.m. a "boom-boom" of cannon fire washed over Cheeves' Plantation.

"Hear that?" Sherman said to General Howard.

"Loud and clear, William. Hazen has engaged the fort."

White smoke obscured the movement of men but Sherman heard the loud reports, both cannon and rifle shot.

———◆———

Inside the fort, greatly outnumbered Confederates fought valiantly. One of the defenders, twenty-two-year-old Corporal Orville Bradley, a crack shot, was able to reload faster than most of his Division, and could fire his single-shot rifle twice a minute. Each shot required momentary exposure above the rampart, to sight the onrushing enemy. His last words were "I got two of 'em! I got two of 'em!"

"Orville's hit!" yelled a comrade. "Pull him down, pull him down!"

They pulled Orville down from the earthen rampart but it was too late. Too late for Orville, and too late for the soldiers still alive. The Yankees kept coming, over the abatis, over the ramparts. A fair number were killed attacking the fort, felled by rifle shot or mines planted in the ground, but so many came so quickly, the end was foretold. Within minutes of the first shot, bluecoats were inside the ramparts, fighting the rebels hand-to-hand – initially one-to-one combat, but within a minute, two-to-one, then three-to-one, then…it was over. The entire affair, from start to surrender, lasted a mere fifteen minutes.

Orville was one of sixteen McAllister defenders killed that day.

———◆———

"I hear no more gunfire," said Sherman. "That's good." Through his telescope he espied the most wonderful site: the Confederate flag being replaced by the Stars and Stripes. Then he saw his bluecoats on the ramparts, defiantly waving their rifles.

"Men, the fort is ours," said Sherman. "This is the prettiest damn thing I have seen in this goddamn war. Let's go to the fort. Get me a boat."

As Sherman climbed down the tower stairs he was already planning moves for the next few days. *Savannah is ours. It's just a matter of time.*

CHAPTER 5

— WEDNESDAY, DECEMBER 14

IN THE EARLY AFTERNOON, A colored boy came up the townhouse stoop at 27 Liberty Street and banged on the door. Polly opened it.

"What you want, boy?" she asked, always skeptical of folks who came calling without an invitation.

"These be for Mrs. Tate," the boy said, and handed Polly a bouquet of flowers with an envelope attached to one of the stems.

"Who give you these, boy?"

"They's come from Master Johnson's garden. Dat's all I know."

"You works for Master Johnson?"

"Yessum."

"Dat's good. You run on now."

Seeing no tip forthcoming, the boy ran down the stairs and into the street. Polly brought the flowers inside and called for Abigale. Jane came first.

"Oh, what lovely flowers. Are they for me?"

"No, boy said dey for Miss Abigale." *Abigale Tate* was written on the outside of the envelope, but Polly didn't read.

"Oh," Jane said, "let me see that."

"No, chile, dese be for Miss Abigale. I gets in heap of trouble if you mess with dem."

Jane was about to make a demand when Abigale and her mother walked into the living room.

"What's all the commotion?" Abigale asked.

"Dese be for you, Miss Abigale," said Polly, and handed her the bouquet.

Jane walked up to smell the flowers. "Ooh, a secret admirer."

"Who are they from, dear?" asked Mrs. Gordon.

"I have no idea."

"Well, open the envelope and read it to us."

Abigale wondered if she should open the note in front of them. *Oh, why not?*

The three women stood around Abigale, waiting for the answer. She pulled the envelope from the stem, opened it and read the message. Her face turned crimson and she crumbled the piece of paper.

"Abigale," said Jane, "what is it?" Jane reached for her sister's hand and pried away the paper. She read out loud.

Dear Mrs. Tate,

So nice it was to meet with you on Sunday. I hope you will return to the same church this next Sunday. Same bench, Yes? You are very lovely.
Your servant,
Gustav Heinz

"Who is Gustav Heinz?" asked Jane

"Who is Gustav Heinz?" asked Mrs. Gordon.

Abigale did not reply. Polly did. "He be dat German man who sat with her, I believe."

"Ooh," said Jane. "You *do* have an admirer."

"Hush your mouth," retorted Abigale. "He's a pig."

"A pig?" asked her mother, in a manner to suggest it was a literal description.

"Oink oink," teased Jane.

"Now I can never go back, even if I wanted to." *I was planning to return. Now what do I do?*

"You can go Sunday, Miss Abigale," said Polly. "We can seat you wi' da black folks up front, if you don't mind. We dun that befo.'"

Before Abigale could respond there was a loud knocking on the front door.

"Who now?" asked Polly. "We is gettin' busy." She moved to open the door.

"Could be Mr. Heinz," said Jane, "calling on my dear sister."

"Hush your mouth," scolded Mrs. Gordon.

In the doorway stood Joseptha Morgan, the next door neighbor, a widow about sixty years old. Her husband had died before the war, and now she lived alone.

"May I come in?"

"Of course," said Mrs. Gordon. "You look upset. Is something wrong?"

Joseptha entered the foyer as Polly closed the door. "I've just come from the market. The news is everywhere. Fort McAllister has fallen!"

"What?"

"It's true. Yesterday. Our boys were beaten badly. Who wasn't killed was captured. They say a dozen of our boys killed, maybe more. No one knows for sure."

Suddenly turning serious, Jane asked, "What does that mean?"

"Where is Sherman now?" asked Mrs. Gordon.

"They say the Union ships are up the Ogeechee. Bringing in supplies."

"Will someone tell me what this means?" yelled Jane.

"It means," said Abigale, in a monotone, "that Savannah is doomed." *Johnny, where are you? Please, please be careful. With luck our family will survive Sherman. We won't survive if you don't come back home.*

— *THURSDAY, DECEMBER 15*

DEEP IN THE WOODS SOUTH of Nashville, a Union soldier raised his rifle and aimed at the lone man on horseback. The horseman wore a grey uniform, but its officer insignia indicating he was a general would not be visible beyond a few yards. At that moment the horseman was riding alone, though to his rear rode dozens of other cavalry.

The man on horseback was none other than Nathan Bedford Forrest. Foolish Forrest, for riding without escorts, exposing himself to random sniper fire. Brave Forrest, for fearing nothing and no one. His reputation preceded wherever his men rode. Brave, cantankerous, headstrong, brilliant leader. Generals higher in command sparred with him, and feared his independence, but they needed and welcomed his abilities to lead men in battle.

In particular, Forrest had chafed under General John Bell Hood, in charge of the Confederate's doomed Nashville campaign. Less than two weeks earlier, Forrest had lost a battle at Murfreesboro, Tennessee, in part because of bad intelligence about Union troop strength. Now Hood's army was close to losing this campaign to Union General George H. Thomas. Forrest and his men were not directly engaged in the fighting, but were instead patrolling the area between Nashville and Murfreesboro.

Forrest's advance scouts had not reported any Union activity in this area, and he did not think riding unescorted was particularly risky. Forrest did not see the sharpshooter. Lt. Johnny Gordon, riding only twenty yards behind, did. The general's lieutenant let go the horse's reins just long enough to aim his rifle at the Union soldier and fire. The rifle's retort was loud and unexpected.

Forrest jerked his head back to see smoke coming from Gordon's rifle. "What the hell? What are you shooting at?"

Gordon pulled up beside Forrest, pointed his rifle at a soldier in blue slumped over a log some 100 yards to the right. Just then other riders caught up to them.

"Fine job, Gordon," said Forrest. It did not have to be stated that Johnny Gordon had just saved the life of his commanding general.

"Didn't expect any Yankees this far from Nashville," the general yelled out to horsemen now surrounding him. "There may be others over there. Dixson, take a party and see if there's more Yanks. I don't want prisoners, understand?"

"Yes, sir."

"We'll wait for you ahead. Gordon, you come ride by me. Need more fellas like you around."

On the same day her brother was saving the life of Bedford Forrest, Abigale decided to do some shopping. The newspapers didn't seem to know much about what was happening with General Sherman after the fall of Fort McAllister. Maybe the real, up-to-date news was only to be found in the town market on Ellis Square. It was only a twenty-minute walk from their home. She took Polly to help carry the groceries and set out around nine in the morning.

What a lovely city this once was, Abigale thought, with its squares and gracious oak trees. Now it showed decay. Most buildings and streets were in want of some repair. All port activity had ceased long ago. Early in the war renegade ships could break through the Union Navy's blockade, but none had done so since December 1861, when the mouth of the Savannah River was all but dammed with sunken stone and wooden pilings. The only rail line connected to Charleston, and was operated mostly for military purposes.

Even with the blockade and the shortages, the place kept much of its charm. *What will General Sherman do to Savannah? To us?*

Abigale and Polly passed many people on their way, and none seemed in a rush or exhibited any anxiety. There were rumors of people clamoring to get on the train to Charleston but she didn't know if that was even possible. All other routes north or south through Georgia were impossible because the city was now surrounded by Sherman's army. And the river was blocked, so there really was no escape route. It made eminent sense that no one seemed in a rush; there was, quite literally, nowhere to go.

Rice, some chickens and vegetables, were still being brought to the City Market from a few local plantations, for sale at reasonable prices. Reasonable, that is, considering the marked inflation of Confederate money in recent weeks. Abigale's family was among the more fortunate in this aspect; their father had hoarded silver and gold coins, and much silverware, anticipating a problem with the South's paper money should the war drag on. As long as the markets stayed open, they would not starve.

Several dozen stalls were in business when they arrived. The temperature was a cool fifty-five degrees. People were buying, walking between stalls, or just sitting on local benches, enjoying the morning sun. Abigale noted both negro servants and a fair number of citizens. She heard English, Gullah, German, and some English with a German accent. The accent made her think of Gustav, and she was relieved not to see him at the market.

They stopped at a stall selling rice, a necessary commodity to eat full at any meal. Polly could cook the rice plain, or mix it into a broth.

"Let's get a pound today," Abigale said. The old proprietor—he appeared old to Abigale, though he was probably no more than fifty—weighed out a pound.

"Twenty-five cents," he said. "Specie," by which he meant gold or pure silver, not confederate money.

"How much in Confederate?" she asked.

"I don't want paper," he said.

"I know, but Sherman isn't here yet. How much in Confederate?"

He thought for a moment. "Two dollars."

She had some paper money, which she wanted to get rid of, but thought that price way too high, so she handed over the requisite coin. She turned to go find another merchant, hoping to secure a chicken or two, and found herself facing a well-dressed, middle-aged man.

"Well, Mrs. Tate, nice meeting you here."

"Mayor Arnold, how do you do?"

"Fine, thank you. I am most happy to see you out and about. Please accept my condolences over Franklin. I trust you received my letter last September?"

"Yes, it was very kind of you."

Abigale did not expect to run into Mayor Richard Arnold, perhaps the most respected man in the city. He was also a physician, and still maintained his medical practice when administrative duties allowed. Her father had been a political ally during Arnold's previous terms as Mayor, 1851-1852, and 1859-1860. Arnold was very supportive of the family following Mr. Gordon's death in July 1863, visiting at least twice and arranging for a memorial service.

"The war is abominable," he said. "Our boys have suffered in the extreme, and now our great city is surrounded. I trust you know about losing our southern fort, McAllister?"

"Yes, I heard. What do you think will happen?"

"Wish I could predict, wish I could predict. All sorts of rumors are flying about. General Hardee has a small army in the city, but Sherman's troop strength is anywhere from 50,000 to 100,000. He could walk in without much of a fight, or we could end up like Atlanta, burned to the ground. I shudder at the thought. How's your mother, and that baby sister of yours?"

"They're fine, thanks for asking." Just then Abigale realized Polly was standing nearby holding a pound of rice. She didn't want to break off the conversation just yet, so she instructed Polly to go find a chicken vendor, and wait for her there.

"That negro's been with you sometime, hasn't she?" asked the mayor.

"Yes, about fifteen years."

"So how are you doing? Still in mourning, I presume?"

"I quit wearing black long ago, if that's what you mean," said Abigale.

"Well, that's fine with me. I perfectly understand."

Just then a troop of soldiers marched by in formation, heading toward the West Broad Street dock. Unknown to the Mayor, or any city official, General PGT Beauregard had issued orders to General Hardee that, if Hardee had to choose between saving Savannah and saving his army, to "save your army." This could mean only one thing: get out before Sherman arrives. And the only way to do that would be across the Savannah River, to South Carolina. This meant a bridge had to be built, and fast.

While the soldiers marched by, Arnold's eyes moved elsewhere, up and down Abigale's torso. She was not unaware of his gazing.

As soon as the soldiers passed, he said, "Would you like to get a cup of tea? We can talk some more about the happier times and your family."

Abigale sensed a subtle change. His roving eyes, his invitation, his body language. *Now that I'm a widow, I'm available. I know what he would like. He's showing it with his eyes. I should not be surprised. He's a man and men are like that. He's in his fifties, older than my mother! Is that to be my fate? But he's been a friend to my family, and I mustn't be rude. He is certainly no Gustav Heinz.*

"Oh, thank you Mayor Arnold, that is most kind. But I told mother we'd return home as soon as possible. She is, of course, terribly lonely since Father passed away. I fear these next few days may be decisive for us all, and our tranquility may be short lived."

"With God's grace we will survive, Abigale. Do give my regards to your mother, and to that darling little sister of yours. I imagine she's all grown up by now. Haven't seen her in over a year."

"Yes, I will. Thank you, sir."

Abigale left the mayor to search for Polly and some chickens.

———◆———

That night, at a campfire south of Nashville, General Forrest made it his business to query the young lieutenant. Though a junior officer, some might call him a boy for his youth and thin frame, but he was tall for the regiment, a shade over five feet ten. He wore a small goatee and thin mustache, one way young officers chose to show their maturity.

"Where you from, Johnny?"

"Savannah, sir."

"Learned to shoot there?"

"Yes sir. Since I was ten."

"How old are you?"

"Twenty-two. Been in since I turned twenty."

"We're losing the war, son."

Johnny did not expect such a blunt statement from his commander. He paused, then said, "Don't look promising after Murfreesboro, I reckon."

"We've given it a good fight. Just outnumbered by them Yankee bastards."

"Yes, sir."

"Tell me, Johnny, what are you going to do after the war?"

"Don't rightly know. I was a dock worker before I joined up. Savannah has a big port. No river business now, though, with the blockade."

"I know. And my intelligence tells me General Sherman is headed that way."

"I hope not, sir. Still have my mom and two sisters there."

"Your father?"

"Dead, sir. Killed at Gettysburg, year and a half ago."

"That's too bad. All for a bunch of nigras. Your family own any?"

"Just one. A domestic."

"How old is she?"

"Don't know. Late twenties I reckon. Been with us since I was a little boy."

"You had her?"

"Sir?"

"You know what I mean. Have you taken her to your bed?"

"Not really partial to black snatch, sir, if you don't mind my sayin'. Besides, she's a dumb nigger. And fat, too. I like skinny women."

"Fat or skinny, all the niggers is dumb, Johnny. Some are just dumber than others. They want freedom but don't know they'd be worse off. They can't read or write, so what the hell they gonna do? They sure are going to be sorry if they get their wish. You can bet on that."

Johnny sensed a bonding with his commander over the sorry state of slaves, and felt the courage to ask a question.

"Sir, do you really think there's no chance of us winning?"

"As much as a warm pot of spit freezing in July, I'd say."

"What about General Lee? He's still got his army up in Virginia."

"That be so, that be so. But when Thomas links up his army with Grant, and then Sherman joins *his* army too, they'll outnumber Lee three or four to one. Hard to beat them odds."

"Maybe if we all take to the woods, Indian-like?" said Gordon.

"Thought of that, I have. But we'd still be outnumbered. Meanwhile, they could rampage our cities, despoil our women—while we're out hiding in the bushes. Your sisters, they married?"

"One was. The last letter I got from home, learned her husband died in the fight for Atlanta, just the day before Sherman took the city. The other one's only sixteen or seventeen, I don't rightly know which, it's been so long, but she's a young 'un."

"Tell me they's pretty. I bet they are."

"They are very pretty, sir. Or they was when I left home. Probably prettier now."

"Well I'd like to meet them some day."

Johnny did not ask if the general was married, thinking it best to avoid personal questions. He also sensed what the General might have in mind, but didn't take offense. Southern gentlemen don't despoil Southern women.

"I do look forward to getting home, sir."

"You will, son, you will. What did your father do before the war?"

"He was a lawyer. We was comfortable."

"You didn't want to join him? Law's a fine profession."

"I worked in his office for a while, and he gave me some books to read. I got bored, couldn't take it. He said I wasn't suitable for the law, and I agreed. Got a job on the docks. When Abigale—that's my older sister—got married, her husband went to work in the law office. He was studying law when he enlisted along with my father."

"War is hell, ain't it?"

"Ain't fun if you get hit, that's for sure."

"Somehow, Johnny, we have to continue our traditions, our way of life. The bullies may defeat us with their guns and superior numbers, but we've got to carry on the battle. We've got to preserve our culture, our values. Wouldn't you agree?"

"Yes, sir!"

"I've got some ideas how to do that, once this war is over. Would you be willing to help in that type of endeavor?"

"Yes, sir. Anything you ask. What do you have in mind?"

"Not exactly sure just yet. But we hope to have many like-minded men scattered throughout the South. Like you and me, they'll want to preserve the culture, keep the nigras at bay, keep the Yankees from imposing their will on us. If we work together, we can accomplish much. But it takes leadership, and strong young men such as yourself."

"You can count me in, General. If I survive, you just come calling. Johnny Gordon, twenty-seven Liberty Street, Savannah."

"Good to know, son. I am pleased. Men like you are the backbone of this army. Now let's get some sleep."

CHAPTER 7

— *Friday, December 16*

AT THREE IN THE MORNING Mrs. Gordon carried a lantern to Abigale's bedroom door and knocked. There was no immediate answer. She opened the door, walked to the bedside and shook her daughter's shoulder.

Abigale awoke with a start. "Mother, what's the matter?"

"Where's Jane? She's not in her room."

"Not in her room?"

"No, I went in to get one of those headache pills she keeps. She's not there. Her bed's not been slept in. She's not downstairs either. Did she leave?"

"Leave? Why would she leave?"

"She's not happy here."

"Where would she go?"

"So you don't know anything?"

By now Abigale was on her feet, assuming charge of the investigation. "I'll ring for Polly. She may know something."

"Yes, please call her. We must find out."

Abigale moved to the corner of her room and pulled on a rope that hung from the ceiling of her second floor bedroom through small circular floor openings, all the way to the street-level basement. Each pull rang a bell at the bottom, a summons to the servant living there. They had not had to call for Polly in this manner for over a year. The last time was when Mrs. Gordon took ill with vomiting in the middle of the night, and needed help cleaning up.

"She never said anything to you about leaving?" asked Mrs. Gordon.

"Never. I still don't know where she'd go."

"I'm worried. Can't take any more losses. You children are all I've got."

Abigale did not respond. There was no need to. A few minutes passed and Polly appeared in the doorway.

"You rang for me, Miss Abigale?"

"Mother said Jane is nowhere in this house. Her bed has not been slept in. Do you know anything?"

"No ma'am. But if she not be here, I have idea where she might be."

"You do?" both women asked in unison.

"Not sure, but I seen her go out back once at night. To da stable. Figured she needed to be alone, and didn't bother her none. Maybe she be there."

"The stable?" asked Mrs. Gordon. "Why on earth would she go there? And if she went, why isn't she back already? It's unheated. Polly, you and Abigale go there now. I don't like this girl's shenanigans, but if she's there and not harmed, I'll forgive her. Here, take the lantern."

Abigale put on her robe and shoes and together with Polly walked downstairs and across the back alley. The moon was three-quarters full and with the lantern they had plenty of light to see their way. The stable had been built for a horse and small carriage, neither of which the Gordons now owned; both were sold after Mr. Gordon joined the army. Now the stable was full of old tools and horse blankets, and some discarded furniture.

The stable door was fastened from the inside, which meant someone was in there.

"Miss Jane, is you in dere?" yelled Polly. No answer.

"Jane, this is Abigale. Are you inside?" Still no answer.

Abigale began banging on the door.

"Leave me alone!" came a girl's voice from within the stable.

39

"Mother is very worried. What in heaven's name are you doing in there?"

"I'm fine, just need to be alone. Tell Mother I'm fine."

"We're not leaving until you come out."

A minute passed, then Abigale heard the low murmuring of another voice. A man's voice.

"Who's in there with you? Who is that?"

The door suddenly opened and Jane came outside, fully dressed but without a coat. She slammed the door behind her.

"Let's go," Jane said. "A body can't have privacy anymore."

"Who's in there?" demanded Abigale. She pushed the door open and stared into blackness.

"Never mind," yelled Jane. "Let's go!" She pulled on her sister's arm.

With a quick jerk Abigale pulled her arm free. "We're not leaving 'til I find out who's in here." Then Abigale turned to the darkness. "Whoever you are, come out or I will call the police!"

From the shadows a tall young man appeared, his features still obscured by the darkness.

"Ma'am," he said, "I didn't mean no harm. We was just talking."

"Who are you?" she asked. "Come outside, where there's some moonlight."

He followed her order. She saw he was wearing a Confederate uniform.

"Why, you're a soldier. Shouldn't you be at your post? What are you doing with my sister?"

"None of your damn business!" yelled Jane. "Let's go. Winston, go back to camp. I'll take care of this. We'll be in touch."

At that Winston scurried off at a fast walk. Abigale stood to face her sister. "You've got a heap of explaining to do." Then, to her servant, "Thanks, Polly. You've been a big help. You can go back to sleep now."

Back in the house there was both relief and consternation. Questions came fast from Mrs. Gordon, all variations of "You're only seventeen—what are you doing with that man?" and "How long has this been going on?"

Jane did not answer. "Leave me alone," she said. "I'm going to sleep."

"Jane, I demand to know—"

"Mother," interrupted Abigale, "let it be. Right now, we're all very tired. Let's all go back to sleep. We can deal with this in the morning."

"I suppose," said Mrs. Gordon. "All right, I'm going back to sleep. And you two should do the same. Let's have no more aggravation this night."

As soon as Abigale heard the upstairs bedroom door close, she turned to Jane. "Mother was deathly worried. Figured you had left home. Don't you at least have some concern for her?"

"I'm going to sleep," replied Jane. "As you said, we can deal with this in the morning." Jane proceeded up the stairs, lantern in hand, and Abigale followed. As Jane was about to close the bedroom door Abigale blocked it and forced her way in.

"Do you want to tell me about him? I think I'm a little more tolerant than Mother."

"There's nothing to tell," Jane said.

"Who is he? Where'd you meet him?"

"If you insist. Anything, to go back to sleep. I met him at the Colonial Cemetery. That's where they are billeted."

"They let you into his camp?"

"He was doing guard duty on the corner of Abercorn and South Broad. We struck up a conversation."

"Conversation? Then how did he end up here?"

"He asked if he could see me. Is that so bad?"

"Polly said you've been out back at least once before."

"Suppose so. Been seeing him about a month."

"How many times? Why didn't you leave a note on your bed? My god, you scared Mother pitifully."

"Didn't think you'd get up or notice. He's only here an hour or so, always after midnight, before he has to get back."

"So more than once?"

"I suppose so."

"How many?"

"Maybe three, four."

"But he's a soldier. How does he get away?"

"Others cover for him. He only comes in the middle of the night."

"So it's not just talking. Come clean, dear sister. I was not born yesterday."

Jane did not answer.

"Aren't you cold in there?"

"We have the horse blankets. And he keeps me warm."

"Do you know what you're doing?"

"He's got protection."

"Oh my God!" exclaimed Abigale. "At seventeen?"

"How old were you?"

Abigale did not answer.

Jane taunted her with possible replies. "Fifteen? Sixteen? When did you meet Franklin? Seventeen?"

"Eighteen."

"So, long before you got married. Somewhat of the hypocrite, are you not, sister?"

"I said we met at eighteen."

"You got married when you were almost twenty. It wasn't that long ago. Were you a virgin?"

"No."

"So it's do as I say, not as I do."

"But I knew we were going to get married. That was different."

"I don't think so. If I say I know I'm going to marry Winston, then I think it's the same."

Abigale was immediately struck by the logic of her young sister's argument. She could only get this skill from their father. They both had it.

"Excuse me," Jane taunted. "I didn't hear your reply. And by the way, just out of curiosity, since father was alive then, and we had a horse and carriage, just where did you two have your little trysts?"

Suddenly Abigale was on the defensive. She could have answered the question, explaining how she and Franklin made love in his home during the year before they married, always when his parents were away. Instead, she decided that any more personal explanation was futile. Jane had bested her in argument and logic.

"We were careful," said Abigale. "I just don't want you to be hurt," that's all.

"I said he uses protection."

"I know, but sometimes condoms don't work. They break. That's a simple fact. I don't want you to become pregnant and unmarried."

"Mama was pregnant with you when she got married."

Jane was correct, of course. Her mother and father married in January and Abigale was born in June, a fact not discussed in the household. Whether it was a faulty condom or none at all, the children never enquired.

"Mother's worried about you. I'm worried about you. He's a soldier and there's a war going on. Are you planning to marry him?"

"Hasn't been discussed. We just enjoy each other's company."

Abigale pondered the situation. The more she thought about it, the more she realized how close she was to losing her sister. Jane was of age and headstrong, and would go her own way, if not now then soon enough. This alone was not unacceptable, but what bothered Abigale more was the fact—and it was a fact, she felt certain—that if Jane didn't stop seeing this boy, her infatuation would come to no good end. She could think of several 'no good' ends: pregnancy without marriage; his court martial and disgrace (hanging?) for leaving camp without permission; a marriage doomed because it was based on lust and not love; his death in battle and *another* grieving sister.

What could Abigale do? Jane would do what she wanted, and if it wasn't with Winston it would be with the next Bill or Charles or Gaston she met at one of the local camps. There was no opportunity for normal socializing in Savannah, not with the war on and every young man either maimed or in military service.

"Now can I go to sleep?" asked Jane.

Abigale reached over and hugged her sister. "Oh Jane, Jane. I'm so worried about you."

———————

As the household awoke after a night of turmoil, and the women strived to stay busy——reading, or sewing, or tinkling at the piano— no one ventured to bring up recent events, lest it create unwanted conflict. Mrs. Gordon fretted over Jane. Jane wondered how she could achieve her independence. Abigale pondered what to do about Jane, about Gustav's unwanted attention, and whether to return to Reverend Simms' church on Sunday.

And Polly, too, pondered—what might really happen if General Sherman comes? Among all the negroes, whom she met at the market or when out on the street, there was general understanding that the famous Union general was close by, and would enter the city at any moment. It wasn't just Rufus Simms, but everybody saying the same thing: "He's a comin' soon."

It was Jane who broke the ice, by asking Abigale if she was going back to "that colored church" on Sunday. It was a taunting question, knowing that Abigale's not-so-secret admirer would be there. When Abigale didn't answer, Jane thrust the knife a little deeper: "I'm not using the stable tonight."

"Jane! Hush your mouth," said her mother.

"I don't sleep with pigs," said Abigale.

"Stop it! Both of you," scolded their mother. "I can't believe the language coming out of your mouths."

"I gots an idea," said Polly.

"Let's hear it," said Mrs. Gordon.

"I mention this two day ago, just befo' Miss Morgan came a knockin'. If da family all comes to church, I can get you together up front, so this man won't be anywhere 'bout. We've had white folk up front befo'."

"Me go to a colored church?" exclaimed Jane. "Let me eat cow dung first."

"Where do you come by such language?" asked her mother. "I didn't raise you that way. Oh, I wish your father was here. He'd put you in your place."

Abigale rose to the challenge. "*Would* you come mother? You should hear some of the blasphemy out of this black preacher's mouth. First he speaks Gullah, which you can't understand, then he talks our language. If we are invaded, which seems most likely, it would not hurt to be acquainted with this Reverend. You, too, Jane." *Somehow, Simms seems to understand me and my inner demons. Strange, he alone.*

"How far is it? I'm not walking to Frogtown," pouted Jane

"It's on the edge, not far. If all of us go I'll arrange for a carriage and driver," said Abigale. "I think we can afford it."

There was more back and forth, and in the end all agreed to go. Polly, through her network, would secure a bench up front for the four of them.

— SATURDAY, DECEMBER 17

Courtesy of the United States Army, the *Savannah Republican* was able to publish the list of Confederate killed and wounded during the brief Battle of Fort McAllister. They were all members of the 2nd Division, XV Corps, Army of the Tennessee. Only one was a native of Savannah: Orville Bradley.

"Oh my God," said Abigale, on reading the notice. "Mother, Orville Bradley was killed at Fort McAllister on Tuesday. Remember him? He and Johnny were such good friends."

"Oh, dear," she replied. "A nice boy. I think his mother still lives here, too. I wonder if she knows. That's such a tragedy. Do you think Johnny knows about it?"

"I don't think so. I don't see how he could. We don't even know where he is now."

Dear God, how many more? How many more have to die before this war ends? Will Johnny be one of them?

———◆———

In Savannah's streets life seemed as normal as ever, but all Savannah knew something big was about to happen after the fall of Fort McAllister. Possibilities ranged from total annihilation of the city, to the far less likely one of Sherman bypassing Savannah altogether and heading straight to South Carolina. In this latter scenario, wishful thinkers assumed there wasn't much worth capturing in the city except a bunch of cotton, so why would Sherman risk his troops?

The 'bypassers' were wrong. Under a flag of truce, on December 17 Sherman sent a written message to General Hardee, demanding "the surrender of the city of Savannah, and its dependent forts, and shall wait a reasonable time for your answer, before opening with heavy ordnance..."[1]

General Hardee had different plans. Savannah could be sacrificed, but not the army. He just needed a few more days to put his escape plan into action. He replied: "General...Your demand for the surrender of Savannah and its dependent forts is refused."[2]

CHAPTER 8

———

— SUNDAY, DECEMBER 18

GUSTAV ARRIVED EARLY TO THE church. He sat all alone in the back bench, waiting for more white folks to arrive, most of all Abigale. He placed his hat on the bench to reserve a space for her. Fifteen minutes later she walked in, with her family.

Gustave immediately stood, picked up his hat and motioned for her to enter his bench. But that was not her plan. Abigale, Jane, Mrs. Gordon and Polly all walked past him. Abigale nodded to Gustav so as not to be rude, but did not stop to make any introductions. The look on his face told her he was both surprised and disappointed.

In the front of the church the four women sat in the first bench. Polly had arranged for it to be held. The bench still had room for four more people, so just in case Gustav decided to relocate, Abigale arranged so she was at the far end of the bench, with Jane, her mother and Polly to her right. If Gustav did come down he would be sitting next to Polly the entire service.

She did not have to worry, for within a few minutes the bench filled out with four negro women.

"I can't believe I'm actually in a negro church," Jane whispered to Abigale. "What is our city coming to? If Winston saw me now I'd die!"

"Where is he, by the way?" asked Abigale. Jane did not answer.

As the previous week, there was music by the choir, then Rufus Simms appeared. He looked down to the front bench and acknowledged his white visitors with a head nod, then began with a Gullah prayer: a New Testament quote from Matthew 5:14.

"Oona jes like light fa de whole wol. Ain no way ya kin hide a city wa people build pontop a hill. An ain nobody light a lamp an den pit um ondaneet a bushel basket…

Jane gave Abigale a look to suggest, 'you dragged me here for this?'

"He will speak normally. Patience."

Just then Simms launched into his sermon. "What a glorious, a glorious day. Is it not a glorious day?"

"It is!" thundered his audience.

"Any why, my children?"

"The light is a comin'." That was of course the message in his Gullah recitation.

"I notice quite a few of our white brethren here today," said Simms, and his eyes scanned the hall's front and rear sections. Abigale turned her head around to look at Gustav's bench. It was now filled with seven white visitors, including the Nelsons from last week and four new people, three men and one women. She did not recognize the newcomers.

"You are most welcome," said Simms. "For as I have said, we are all God's children!"

"All God's Children" recited the audience.

"We are all equal in God's eyes."

"Equal in God's eyes."

Jane gave her sister another dispirited look. Mrs. Gordon did not flinch. Abigale considered that perhaps her mother just wasn't listening. Polly sat with a smile on her face.

Jane looked like she wanted to speak but remained silent. Abigale sensed her sister's uneasiness and reached for her hand. "Please," she whispered," just let him finish."

There was more of the same "light-a-'comin" speech from Simms, not once mentioning Sherman's name. He worked his audience up into a froth, then brought them down again with recitations and replies to his questions. This was not new material. They came to hear hope and that's what he gave them. But unlike previous years, or even previous months, this was tangible, real hope, for its source was at that point camped outside the city, 60,000 strong, and the congregation knew it.

Simms finished with a flourish—REJOICE! THE END IS NIGH!—then gave the benediction. As the parishioners got up to leave, he didn't wait for well -wishers to come on stage. Instead, he walked down the short flight and stood just in front of Abigale and her family.

"Again, thank you for coming," he said to Abigale. "And who are these other two lovely ladies?"

Abigale introduced her sister and mother. By this time there were other parishioners crowding around, seeking his advice or just waiting to thank him for the service. Simms excused himself from the throng and pulled Polly aside, out of earshot. He said a few words and she nodded her head, then he returned to the other negro parishioners, now in an informal line to speak with him.

Just then Abigale heard a familiar voice, a German-accented one.

"Ah, Mrs. Abigale Tate."

Gustav had bounded down the aisle to her bench.

"Oh, Mr. Heinz," she said facing him, as civilly as possible. "How do you do?"

"Yah, fine, fine. I see you came with others. Your family?"

"Yes, yes." Abigale made the introductions, but offered no background. "This is Mr. Gustav Heinz. He comes to hear Reverend Simms."

"Yah, yah. This reverend repeats himself, but still he has interesting outlook. Is never boring like so many others."

"Oh, you come often?" asked Mrs. Gordon. Abigale cringed. She did not want to encourage him to linger.

"As often as I can, when I am not busy." Same smell, thought Abigale. Must be his German cologne. Ugh!

Abigale was pleased to see Jane looking totally bored.

"Mother," said Abigale, "we really must be going." Polly pulled on her arm, and whispered in her ear.

"Oh?" Abigale said, genuinely surprised. Then to her family, "It seems Mr. Simms would like to meet with us after he is done with his parishioners." She moved her body so as to exclude Gustav from the invitation.

"Well," said Gustav to Jane and Mrs. Gordon, "I don't want to intrude. It was nice to meet both of you" And to Abigale: "And very nice to see you again. With that, he bowed and walked up the aisle.

"Nice man," said Mrs. Gordon.

"Can we go now?" complained Jane. "I'm hungry."

"Did you not hear? Mr. Simms wants to meet with us."

"Oh dear," said Mrs. Gordon. "I have nothing to say to Reverend Simms. He seems like an energetic negro, but I think we've heard enough. If you and Polly want to stay, I'll take Jane home in the surrey. You'll have to walk home, though."

Abigale analyzed the situation. She did feel better when Simms sermonized empathy for those with losses. She accepted his blasphemy as understandable; Sherman was coming, nothing could stop him, and why wouldn't the negroes rejoice? She would, in their situation.

Then there was his *manner* of speaking. It was soothing, in a way she had not heard since her horrible ordeal began. Her first visit in his office the week before had lasted only a few minutes, and there was more about him she wished to learn.

"Are you sure?" she asked her mother, seeking reassurance.

Jane beat her foot on the floor and scowled. "Can we go?"

"Yes, I'm sure," said Mrs. Gordon. "Jane, you come with me, we'll return home. Polly and Abigale wish to stay a little longer, meet with this Reverend. For the life of me, I don't know why." Turning to Abigale, she said, "I wish you had this much interest in our Methodist church."

Polly and Abigale sat down and Mrs. Gordon and Jane walked up the aisle to exit the church. By now the hall was almost empty, except for the few people still standing in line to greet Simms. Soon, Abigale knew, she and Polly would be the only ones remaining.

Outside the church, the one-horse surrey began its slow trot back to 27 Liberty Street. Across the street, unseen behind a large live oak, Gustav noted the absence of Polly and Abigale for the return trip.

———

"I'm honored that you have returned, Mrs. Tate," said Reverend Simms. "I am sorry your mother and sister could not stay."

"Thank you. They did have to return home."

"Our abode is humble, indeed, but our message is powerful."

The office furniture was old and worn: a table for a desk, some wooden chairs, a kerosene lamp. There was a potbellied stove but it had not been fired up. With her coat still on, Abigale did not feel uncomfortable.

"Are you in contact with General Sherman?" asked Abigale.

Simms laughed. "Whatever gave you that idea?"

Why did I ask him that? I sound like an inquisitor.

"Oh, we hear all the rumors, and you seem to know much about his coming. You may ignore the question."

"Not at all. I am not in contact with the Union army. They will come and liberate my people, that's true, but I do believe that's common knowledge."

Polly said nothing. Like a dutiful servant, she sat in her chair and conveyed no expression at the conversation before her.

"You seem to have a great deal of learning for a negro, if I may say so."

"Well, thank you. I owe that to my mother and father. As I explained last week, I was born free, on Jekyll Island. My father was a free negro, and a preacher. My mother taught in the local negro school. I learned to read, to write, and to think for myself."

"How did you learn of my husband and father?" Abigale knew the answer, but wanted to hear it from him.

"Miss Polly told me. She said she was worried about you."

At that Polly nodded, but remained silent.

"I understand what it means to lose a loved one," he continued. "Family is family, negro or White. We all suffer when loved ones die prematurely. I suggested she bring you to one of my Sunday services. It has not been for naught, I hope."

"No, not at all. Not at all. I see you have other white parishioners. How did you come about the acquaintance of Mr. Heinz?"

"Oh, he comes regularly, and contributes to our building fund. Only a few dollars, but every bit helps.

"And the Nelsons?"

"Ah yes, Margaret and Sam. They are retired missionaries my family knew on Jekyll. Whenever they come to Savannah they attend. Very nice people."

With such easy back and forth, Abigale felt comfortable asking the next question.

"And your family, Sir? Do they attend?"

He showed a faint smile. "My wife is ill, at home. A chronic illness, I'm afraid. And we have no children. Thank you for asking."

Chronic illness? What could that be?

There was more inquisition, all benign. She did not challenge him on his pro-Union rhetoric. Abigale explained how she had been a teacher, but was now on leave since her husband's death, although she did occasional work as a substitute. He explained that he was a carpenter by trade, and hoped to find more work when old and worn structures start to get rebuilt in Savannah.

"How did you end up in Savannah?"

"I had a small congregation on Jekyll Island. Only fifteen to twenty. When I learned of this position opening up, I applied and was accepted by the church board. My wife had misgivings about leaving

Jekyll and her family behind, but we both recognized better opportunities here, so came just before the war started.

"Was she ill when you left the island?"

"No, that has only occurred in the past year."

"Is she seeing a doctor? Do you know Dr. Arnold?"

"We have consulted Dr. Arnold, yes. Before his current term of mayor began. He thinks her problem may be related to a form of the typhoid fever, and has prescribed some medication, but she remains weak, I'm afraid."

"I'm sorry. I hope she gets well."

"Thank you."

I am getting too personal. Does he meet with other parishioners and divulge his private life?

After several more minutes of back-and-forth, Abigale said, "Well, Polly and I must be getting back. You've been most gracious. Perhaps we'll all get to meet General Sherman soon."

Simms did not comment, but rose to shake her hand, and Polly's, too.

The women exited the church and began their walk back to Liberty Street. Unseen, Gustav followed them from a distance, until they disappeared inside 27 Liberty Street.

— SUNDAY, DECEMBER 18

At three in the afternoon Susan Tate came to Liberty Street to meet with Abigale. She had sent a note the day before, announcing her intention to visit. In this manner she would show up unless Abigale replied that the date and time were not feasible, and stating the reason why.

Abigale could not refuse to meet with her former mother-in-law. Their last meeting was at Franklin's memorial service in September. They had not been close when Franklin was alive, a situation made worse by Abigale's 1862 miscarriage. Franklin had just joined the army, which meant a long wait for that first grandchild as Susan had no other living children. Another son had died at age four.

Susan's demeanor back in September – aloof, unfriendly – conveyed resentment and disappointment. Abigale remembered thinking at the time, *she has no use for me. I will never see her again.*

Franklin's parents used in live in Savannah but just before the war moved to Pooler, ten miles and two hours away by carriage. Abigale had only visited their Pooler home once, with Franklin, and they did not spend the night.

Now rumor had it General Sherman himself was near Pooler, deciding when to invade the city. Abigale wondered if Susan was forced out of her home. Her note came from an address on nearby York Street, home of a Tate relative. That made sense, but then the note gave no reason for the meeting. Abigale felt certain it was not a courtesy visit.

Abigale had told her mother of the impending visit, and when the knock came Mrs. Gordon answered the door. The two women hugged and exchanged pleasantries. When Mrs. Gordon commiserated over Franklin's death, his mother gave condolences regarding Mr. Gordon. Then Mrs. Gordon escorted Mrs. Tate into the living room, where Abigale waited. Abigale shook Susan's hand but there was no hugging.

"So nice to see both of you again," said Susan. "I have been in town a week now, staying at my sister-in-law's. The Yankees are everywhere around Pooler. I wasn't even sure they'd let me leave, but they did. I was afraid to remain in Pooler. Bluecoats everywhere. Where is *our* army?"

"Is your home safe?" asked Mrs. Gordon.

"They haven't looted it, as far as I know. My home is modest, so perhaps it will be untouched. If they break in they would find nothing of value. I brought our few family pictures and most of my clothes with me. They went after all the farms around Pooler, took all the livestock. Sherman is a bastard."

"Amen to that," said Mrs. Gordon.

"Please sit," said Abigale.

"Thank you," said Susan. "I have come to discuss an issue with you. Your mother may stay if she wishes."

I know what it is. I can tell. "Mother, perhaps we should speak in private. Would you mind?"

"Of course, of course," said Mrs. Gordon. "I shall be upstairs. Please call up if you need anything." She climbed the stairs, leaving Abigale and her ex-mother-in-law alone. Abigale sat in a facing chair. She wore her favorite house dress, a light blue blouse and skirt with a comfortably deep neckline, and only one petticoat underneath. Her visitor, by contrast, wore a coal-black long dress buttoned under the chin, plus a black shawl and hat. Susan appeared to have aged considerably in three months. *I believe she is close to fifty, but looks older. So thin and wan. Yes, that is the right word:* wan.

"What do you hear from Colonel Tate?" asked Abigale, referring to Franklin's father. "I trust he is well?"

"You know what they say, no news is good news. He's still up in Virginia with General Lee's army. But I didn't come to discuss my husband. I come because of what I hear – and now see – about you, dear Abigale."

She never called me "dear Abigale." She has come to criticize. It's the clothes.

"Savannah is a small city," continued Susan. "My husband's sister has a small circle of friends. They all know my situation, and have informed me what is going on about town."

"I see. I do not think you are speaking of war preparations."

Susan gave a little laugh. "That, too. Rumor is – did you know this? – General Hardee plans to escape with our army and leave the city unprotected?"

"No, but it would not surprise me. The rumor I heard is that Hardee is outnumbered ten to one. Did you come just to warn me?"

"No, no, dear. I came on a personal matter." Susan brushed the front of her dress and sat more upright. "These women I mentioned, they hear things, see things. You have been out and about much late-ly, it seems. And not once has anyone seen you in mourning clothes. It has caused gossip, which now comes back to me. Understand, you are free to dress as you wish, but it reflects poorly on me, and the memory of my son – your dear departed husband."

"I did wear black for the few weeks after the notice," replied Abigale. "But honestly, it depressed me. I thought I could honor his memory more by dressing the way he would have liked to see me, and the way in which I feel most comfortable."

"Umph. I must say, 'a few weeks' hardly fits our local tradition. A year is more appropriate. At least six months. I know of no widow who has not worn black at least six months."

I must stay calm and not upset her, but this is outrageous. "Mother Tate, you acknowledge I am free to dress as I wish. Please, why does it affect you so? I don't wish to offend. And you do not even live in the city."

"As I said, I have my own honor to uphold. People talk. I hear you go to market without proper dress. I hear you walk in Forsythe Park in similar fashion. And then I learn you have even attended a negro church, without any of the proper clothing for your situation. Abigale! That is unacceptable. Simply unacceptable."

"I am truly sorry if my activity offends you. I loved Franklin and would never do anything to disappoint him. But he is no longer with us, and I have my own life to live. It should not affect you."

"But, don't you see Abigale? It *does* affect me. And your poor moth-er, does she not feel the sting of gossip? When Colonel Gordon died, I know she wore black for a year. Has she no say in your behavior?

"I am not a child."

"Clearly not. Though I remember when you were a child, when we lived in Savannah. Your family always had a good reputation. Your father a prominent attorney, your mother an excellent homemaker. And you and your sister – you were good girls growing up. When Franklin fell in love with you, I was not displeased. I certainly would not interfere."

"Interfere? What do you mean?"

"Interfere with the union. He was in love with you, that was all my husband and I needed to know."

"Then you had a reservation? You speak obliquely."

"Not about your family, no. But there was always something about you, something I kept to myself."

"But you are going to tell me now, I fear."

"It is flattering in a way, and I am somewhat embarrassed to bring it up. But I suppose there's no harm now. I thought you were a touch too…how shall I say this…haughty."

"Haughty? I don't understand."

"Too smart for a woman. Smarter than my son. Quick, like your father. A certain way about you always suggested you knew you were so endowed, but worked to hide it so as not to scare away men. You are the smartest woman I have ever met, and that concerned me. What would become of a man in your grasp? The situation did suggest an eventual unhappy marriage, but I said nothing."

"But Franklin was no slouch. He was studying with Father to become an attorney."

"Yes, but you…you are something out of the ordinary for our sex. Were you not a woman, you would have been studying in that office as well. And no doubt be quite successful. But would you make a good wife, content to cook and clean and raise children? I had my doubts. I am being truthful."

"Mother Tate, there is so much supposition in what you say, I don't know how to respond. I can only say I don't think Franklin ever found me wanting in womanly attributes. Nor in the kitchen, nor the laundry, nor the marriage bed."

Abigale noted a smirk elicited by her reference to the bedroom. "If he did," she continued, "I was unaware. Either way, what does all this have to do with my wearing mourning clothes?"

"I sense you feel our traditions are beneath you. You are smarter than everyone else, so what we ordinary people believe does not matter. I hoped and prayed this quality would not interfere with Franklin's marriage. God has kept me from ever finding out."

I have had enough of this. "It is plain I cannot satisfy you," said Abigale. "There is really not much more I can say. I am sorry the gossip bothers you so, but these are not normal times. We are losing the war that claimed Franklin and my father, and Savannah is about to be occupied by the Yankees. We may be burned to the ground like Atlanta. And Sherman plans to free all the slaves. There may be social upheaval. Frankly, Susan, I think we have more important things to be concerned with than wearing mourning clothes."

"I was so hoping you would see the error of your ways, and follow our tradition."

"I am sorry. I cannot do what you ask."

"Then my visit has been for naught," said Susan, as she stood and prepared to leave. "I will give you a friendly warning, though. You may think society has changed because of this dreadful war. But people have not changed. Yes, our side is losing a valiant battle, but white people will still retain their morals, their traditions and their customs. Be very careful, Abigale. You are too free with your ideas, and could invite trouble."

"I appreciate your concern, and will consider your comments. I certainly do not wish to invite trouble."

With that, Mrs. Susan Tate said goodbye and left the home.

Abigale stared at the front door after it shut. *It is best Franklin left me with no children. She would make life even more miserable if I had her grandchild.*

CHAPTER 9

———◆———

— *MONDAY, DECEMBER 19*

AT HALF PAST MIDNIGHT, TWO men on horseback galloped up West Broad Street, the cloudless night lit by a near-full moon, their faces hidden under brown hoods cut with large round holes for the eyes and a wide oval for the mouth. Each man carried a flaming torch, the type made of tar and turpentine; once lighted, it could only be extinguished if fully immersed in water or sand. In each saddle, in a side pocket, rested a loaded rifle.

The two horsemen turned left on William Street. "There it is," yelled the man called Mike. They stopped in front of the Third Baptist Church and stared at the wooden structure. "Billy, you go to the other side. I'll take this side."

They parted and took up positions adjacent to a church window. Using the rifle butt, each rider shattered a window pane, then threw his torch, flame first, through the open space. Deed done, they retreated to the street.

"That ought to do it," said Mike. "We'll wait a minute, make sure it takes off. Giddy with excitement, Billy pulled out his rifle, shot in the air and shouted, "Whoo-hah!"

"Don't waste your ammunition," scolded Mike. Soon there was more noise, of burning wood, bursting glass and falling timbers. Flames were visible from the street.

"She's burning fast," said Mike. "That's good."

The noise awakened an old negro who lived across the street. He put on his pants and ran outside to investigate. "Oh my God, the church is on fire!" he yelled. "There's flames up to the roof!"

He spied the horsemen. "Hell and damnation!" he called out. "Did you do this?"

"Go back to bed, nigger!" yelled Billy, and raised his rifle.

"Don't shoot him!" said Mike. "We done our deed, let's go."

"Tell your people that's what nigger lovers get," said Billy, and pointed his rifle to the flaming structure. As they galloped off Billy brushed past the negro and hit him beside the head with his rifle butt; the old man fell to the ground, stunned but alive.

———————

While the church burned, Jane and Winston lay naked in the shed. She loved the feeling of him inside her, of his chest hair against her bare breasts, his tongue probing her mouth. She gave a low scream in ecstasy. Each jerk of his body gave her pleasure as she thrust up to meet him.

Their lovemaking over, he asked in a low voice, "Are you all right, honey? You're not cold, are you?"

"With you on top, no. Not at all."

He pulled himself off and lay beside her, under the two horse blankets. "I have some bad news."

"You have another girl. I was expecting that."

"No, not that. It's bad news for us two, but good news in another way."

"What do you mean?"

"I am meaning that we are evacuating tomorrow. Leaving Savannah."

"What? You're leaving?"

"Not just me. My whole outfit. General Hardee's entire army."

"But what about General Sherman? Aren't you going to fight the Yankees?"

"Orders have come down. We are outnumbered something like ten to one. To avoid capture, we're walking over to South Carolina."

"On water? I do believe there's a river between us and Carolina."

"They're laying a pontoon bridge over the river. Using rice flats."

"You're serious!"

"Yes."

"I'm coming with you."

He laughed. "You can't. Civilians don't travel with the army. And besides, even if they did, we ain't exactly married."

"Then let's get married!"

"I ain't ready for that, and you ain't neither."

She snuggled up closer. "Hold me."

He embraced her. "I'll miss you, but all us soldiers are pleased 'cause I really think we'd all be killed by Sherman's army."

She began to cry, softly.

"Don't cry, honey. I'll write to you."

"This is the last night?"

"Yes."

"Then I want you again," she said. She reached for his member and found it limp.

"Don't stop," he said, as he caressed her breasts and prepared to enter her a second time.

An hour later they emerged from under the blankets to dress, he to return to camp and she to her lonely bedroom. Despite their intimacy she felt awkward, not knowing quite what to say.

"You will write?" she asked.

"Sure will."

"Promise? I sure can't write to you, since you'll be moving around."

"I don't know where we're headed, that's for sure. Generals don't tell us, they just say get up, start marching this way or that way. And anything I write might not make it to Savannah until the war's over. Especially if the Yankees stay in charge."

They kissed one more time, pressing their bodies hard against each other. Then he stepped back and took her hands in his. "Stay warm."

"I will, Winston. And you stay safe."

Winston turned and set off for the cemetery. She closed the stable door and stood for a moment as his tall figure disappeared down the alley.

He won't write, because he's not in love with me. And I'm not really in love with him. I understand this situation, I really do. He wanted what I had to offer, and I wanted him just as badly. I enjoyed what we did. This is all new. I do like being with a man. How does Abigale go without? Mother? Polly? Aren't all women the same? Now I have to find another man.

———◆———

Early that morning, as the sun rose above the horizon, a boy about twelve knocked on Polly's basement door. He was part of an informal network of messengers that negroes relied on for information. And he had important news.

Polly opened the door, recognized the boy Moses, and said simply, "What?"

"Da nigger Miss Jones said to tell you the church burned down last night. She don't know mo' about it, but said you got to know as soon as I could get here."

"You seen it, boy? You seen it's burned?"

"Yes'm. Jus' came from there. Nuthin standing no mo. Dey say it happened middle o' the night."

"Oh, Jesus! Anybody killed?"

"Miss Jones don't say dat."

"Go to the others you gots to tell. Know you have more folks to tell."

With that Moses went on his way.

Oh Lordy. What's this world coming to? Could Moses be wrong? She knew he wasn't, no one would make up a tale like that. But maybe the church wasn't as bad as Moses said.

Polly dressed and entered the street. Negroes were already at work removing the trash and sweeping the sidewalks. She put herself close to one of them.

"What you hear?" she asked.

"'Bout what?"

"Anything 'bout the church? Third Baptist?"

"It burnt down."

"Who told you so?"

He pointed to his working partner, who then answered Polly. "Come up from West Broad. Dat's all dey is talkin' bout. Burned down to da roots. Don't know what caused it."

Polly returned to the house. *Now I gots to tell Miss Abigale. I'll wait till she comes downstairs.*

As soon as Abigale appeared in the dining room Polly relayed the news, quoting both of her sources.

"What are you saying? Burned to the ground?"

"Afraid it be true."

"Get your coat," said Abigale. "We're going to see for ourselves."

"Befo' your breakfast?"

"I'm not hungry."

Abigale ran upstairs to tell her mother she was leaving. Jane was still asleep and Abigale did not disturb her.

———◆———

Where there once was a church now lay a charred foundation, burning embers and blackened beams. Smoke twirled in the air. By the time the volunteer fire department arrived there was nothing more to save. Now the only thing standing was a lone brick chimney.

Miraculously no other building burned, because the church was surrounded by lawn and the night had been windless.

There were other people around, most notably Mayor Richard Arnold, who was just about to leave. He was accompanied by two other men, one an aide and the other a reporter for the *Savannah Republican.*

"Miss Abigale, what brings you here?" Arnold asked.

What does bring me here? What shall I say?

"Uh, this is my servant's church. She learned about the fire early this morning, and when she told me I thought we should go see for ourselves. Was anyone injured?"

"No, happened last night, after midnight. Building was empty."

Thank goodness!

"Well, is this Sherman's work?" asked Abigale. "Is he planning to burn the whole city?"

The mayor laughed. "Hardly. We've interviewed an old negro who saw the whole thing. Just two men on horseback. Arson, pure and simple. They told him that's what happens to nigger lovers."

"Nigger lovers?" she asked. "But it's a black church, my Polly's church. Why would they say that?"

"Well," interjected one of the men with the mayor, "apparently some white folks have been attending. Rumor has it this church's reverend has preached some inflammatory sermons. Would you know anything about that?"

"I'm sorry, who are you, sir?"

"Name's Jeff Biggert, and I work for the *Republican.*"

What am I getting myself into? She decided to deflect the inquiry with another question. "Are you sure, Mr. Biggert, this isn't Union men, advance men from Sherman's army?"

"Not sure of anything, Miss ... sorry, I didn't get your name."

"Oh, I do apologize," said the mayor. "Mr. Biggert this is Mrs. Abigale Tate, and her servant, I believe Polly, you said?" He looked to Abigale for confirmation but Polly spoke first.

"Dat so," said Polly.

"And the other gentleman with me is my secretary, Colonel Seth McGuire."

McGuire tipped his hat.

"Colonel?" asked Abigale, "Are you in the army, sir?"

"It's an honorific, ma'am. Just call me Seth."

Both men were younger than the mayor, and they looked at her the way most men always did, with penetrating eyes and a wish to do more than just look. Abigale decided she should leave this group and avoid any further questioning.

"Well, it's nice meeting you gentlemen. I think Polly and I would like to take a little closer look at what remains of her church."

With that she began to walk away. Biggert strode quickly beside her. "Excuse me, Mrs. Tate, would it be all right if I asked you a few questions?"

"Not now, sir. This is a most distressing day. Please let us be."

"Then perhaps your servant? You said she's a member of this congregation."

Polly was about to speak but Abigale grabbed her arm and turned to the reporter. "Not now, sir, please. Not now."

"Yes, ma'am. I understand." At that Biggert returned to the other two men and the trio walked to their carriage. As they did so, the mayor waved goodbye to Abigale. She watched them leave, then continued to survey the ruined church.

Other white and black milled about, the two groups avoiding each other as they surveyed the embers. Polly said hello to a couple of negroes, and they commiserated together. Abigale heard some Gullah language, but didn't enquire as to what was said.

She wondered if Reverend Simms would appear.

Surely he must have heard by now. Is he threatened, in any danger? Am I?

— *TUESDAY, DECEMBER 20*

WORD OF THE EVACUATION SPREAD quickly and confirmed what Winston had told Jane—all 10,000 of General Hardee's defense forces were to walk across a hastily-assembled pontoon bridge, into South Carolina. They would leave the city undefended against the massive Union army now surrounding it.

Jane insisted on going to watch the exodus. Abigale, too, was curious, but wary. "They're marching tonight?"

"Starting when the sun goes down, so everyone says," replied Jane.

Their neighbor Josephtha Morgan came over late in the afternoon, to announce she wanted to see the soldiers leave, and asked if anyone would like to accompany her. The fact of there even *being* a bridge that you could *walk over* intrigued everyone.

After some back and forth discussion, mainly over the question of safety at night, Jane and Abigale agreed to accompany Josephtha to the riverfront. Polly would could along as well.

Mrs. Gordon decided to stay home. "If they were coming *into* Savannah, I'd go watch and cheer," she said. "But leaving? Why bother?"

The three woman started for the river just before sunset. The bridgehead was located where West Broad Street ends at the Savannah River, a twenty minute walk from Liberty Street.

A few blocks from the river they met a wall of soldiers, all waiting to cross the bridge. Civilians could not continue further. They were shunted east to Broughton Street, and then north on Barnard Street to the wharf area. There, between massive three-story warehouses, the gawkers could find a place to look out over the low-lying pontoons, situated end-to-end across the river. That they formed a true bridge was shown by the hundreds of soldiers filing across on foot, along with numerous wagons and horses.

"What a sight!" exclaimed Jane. "A full evacuation, just like Winston said."

"Better to have them escape than be slaughtered," sighed Abigale.

"It's something I never hoped to see," offered Joseptha. "What will become of us now?"

The torches carried by the marches, and some moonlight, gave enough glow to appreciate the one-way march, although not enough to reveal features of any individual. From her vantage point Jane tried to pick out Winston, by his silhouette if not his face, but found the troops indistinguishable.

The soldiers and animals disappeared from view once they reached Hutchinson Island, a landmass splitting the river. Another pontoon bridge crossed from Hutchinson over to South Carolina, but was not visible from the Savannah side.

Remarkably, the march itself was silent, no singing or yelling, lest the Yankees get wind of the evacuation. To further confuse the enemy, Confederates continued cannon fire in the general direction of the Union troops, to make them think Hardee's army was still positioned to fight the invasion. Soldiers manning the cannons would be last to cross the pontoon bridge, at which point it would be dismantled.

Abigale surveyed the crowd around her, mostly women of all ages, along with a few middle-aged men. If there were any young men left in the city they would not show here, lest people wonder why they, too, were not on that bridge. She noted a faint smell of sulfur in the air, mollified by the cool temperature. Everyone wore coats or shawls. Nearby a baby wailed, and its mother said, "shush, shush, don't cry." Abigale wondered if its father was marching across the bridge.

"Frau Tate?" The question came from directly behind her, the German accent sending a shudder down her neck. Abigale turned to face a middle-aged, portly man whose body features she well recognized.

"Gustav?"

"Yah, Yah. I see you are curious like the rest of us."

Jane also turned, but Gustav but did not acknowledge her at first. Then Abigale, out of ingrained politeness, said, "You remember my sister, Jane Gordon?"

Gustav faced Jane. "Oh, yes, of course, at the church last week." He held out his hand and she took it.

"Please to meet you again, sir," Jane said. A child's greeting, learned at home and not easily unlearned.

"And my neighbor, Josephtha Morgan."

"Am pleased to meet you as well, Mrs. Tate's neighbor."

Why did he refer to her this way? And is he following me, or is this just a coincidence?

Gustav waved his hand toward the departing soldiers. "Yah, this is good. I'll tell you why." Gustav paused for effect.

"Oh, why?" asked Joseptha.

"Because there will be no wasting of the blood. The city will be, how you say, spared, and my humble boardinghouse will not be burned. Now there is no reason to burn. I am most happy to see this."

The women did not respond to his analysis, but turned back to follow the mass of soldiers still streaming quietly across the bridge.

"Well," Gustav said, raising his voice to gain attention, with the 'Well' coming out 'Vell', "it was nice meeting you again. And I assume you know about the tragedy with Third Baptist?"

It was a question and Abigale felt obliged to respond, not to be rude. Turning around, she said, "Yes, we saw the ruin. Do you know who did it?"

"No idea. The newspaper said two men on horseback. Could be anyone. Where will you go now to worship?"

There are no bounds to his brazenness, thought Abigale. To this point Polly had not spoken, or been acknowledged by Gustav or the women. Now was the time. "Polly has not decided," Abigale said. "And you?"

"I myself am not a religious man. I have little use for religion. I go to Third Ogeechee Baptist only to hear Reverend Simms. And I have just learned where he will administer to his congregation."

"You have?" asked Abigale, with more surprise than she wanted to show.

"Yah, yah. Just found out this afternoon. He will preach at *First* Ogeechee Colored Baptist, guest of Pastor Patterson. Until his own church is rebuilt."

"Polly, did you know that?" Abigale asked.

"No ma'am, dat be news to me. I heard of Mr. Patterson, tho. Lots of folks goes to him also."

"I am curious," Abigale said, "how did you find this out ahead of Polly, who is a member of Mr. Simms' church?"

"Yah, I meet lots of people who visit Savannah Gardens, some know more than others, they tell me. No secret, I just learn first."

Abigale could not help wondering who 'they' might be. Rufus Simms himself? Reverend Patterson? Since the two preachers were negroes, she thought it unlikely they visited his 'boardinghouse'. Not just because of their position, but also because negroes had their own brothels in Frogtown, and were not welcomed at white establishments.

She also considered that Gustav was making up this information, to get her attention. Either way, the news would be confirmed shortly. She decided to ask no more questions about the plans of Reverend Rufus Simms.

Gustav looked at his pocket watch. "I really must be going. It will be hours before all the troops are over the bridge, and I must get back to my establishment. So, good evening." With that he left the women and began his walk up the steep incline from the river, toward Bay Street.

"He seems like a nice man," said Joseptha.

"Abigale thinks he's a pig," said Jane.

"Be nice," said Abigale

"Well, it's true. You said that."

"I find him crude," countered Abigale. "And his boardinghouse is a brothel."

"Oh?" asked Joseptha.

"How come you never mentioned that before?" asked Jane. "And how do *you* know?"

"I don't gossip. But it's common knowledge. He may be nice outwardly, but I know what he's interested in. If not for business, then personal pleasure."

"You can't put men down for that," said Jane.

How did I end up in this twisty conversation? I should shut my mouth now. Joseptha is a gossip.

"Think what you want," said Abigale. "I don't think he's a particularly nice man. There is even rumor he has negro women in his employ."

"That's interesting," said Jane.

"Well," said Joseptha, "if that's true, the Yankees should become his best customers. I understand they love the nigras."

The women watched the marching soldiers for another half hour, then walked home, unfollowed and unmolested.

CHAPTER 11

— TUESDAY NIGHT, DEC 20 TO WEDNESDAY MORNING, DEC 21

"WHAT'S GOING ON?" ASKED SAVANNAH Alderman Henry Brigham. "Why do you need us at City Exchange nine o'clock at night?"

"Gentlemen, the situation is dire," replied Mayor Richard Arnold. "General Hardee has begun his evacuation."

"How can that be Richard? I hear guns in the distance. Surely we are being defended."

"Surely not," Arnold shot back. "Hardee began evacuating a couple of hours ago. The gun fire is to cover their retreat. Go down to Anderson's Wharf on West Broad after you leave here. You'll find a pontoon bridge over to Hutchinson Island, and then another bridge to South Carolina. That's why I called you in now. It's just nine. By three o'clock in the morning our troops will all be gone from the city and you won't hear any more confederate shelling. The ironclad *Savannah* has been scuttled and Fort Jackson by now should be empty of all soldiers. The only troops remaining in Savannah will be the sick, the infirm, and those who faked illness to stay behind. Probably many of them, I'm afraid."

"How do you know all this?"

"Hardee met with me twice, Monday night and again this morning. He showed me the order. It's from General Beauregard. Hardee is to defend Savannah, but if it's between Savannah and the army, save the army. They are needed in South Carolina, where Sherman is sure to go next. He says Sherman has well over 62,000 battle-ready troops. They were resupplied after we lost Ft. McAllister. Hardee has but 10,000."

"What did he tell you to do?" asked George Wylly.

"Pray."

"Pray? You're the doctor, Richard. Surely you have a better remedy."

"Yes, Richard, what do you propose?" asked Christopher Casey, a middle-aged, paunchy alderman. He puffed on his cigar as if this affair didn't concern him as much as the others.

"We must meet with General Sherman. His troops are very close to the city, and poised to enter. They will come right to our doorstep as soon as he realizes our troops are gone. Sherman may have already given orders to burn the downtown, but we must implore him not to. If we can just get him in peacefully, so he can see what we have, see that he is truly welcome and will not be snipered, I trust they will spare us."

Henry C. Freeman, unmarried and with no close family, spoke up: "Sherman has burned everything so far: Atlanta, Milledgeville, farms, homesteads. He's torn up the railroads. The man is a monster. You have read the papers. We should join Hardee and get the hell out, I say."

"A lot of that's hearsay, we don't know what he plans to do here," said the mayor. "We really have nothing strategic of value except the cotton."

"Maybe hearsay," said Casey, "but I do hear a lot of people say it. A plantation owner came into the shop just yesterday. His place near Millen was pillaged, then burned to the ground. He saw it all from a redoubt. Nothing he could do. He skedaddled here with his wife and two children. I don't think he made any of it up. He said it was like that all around Millen; plantations that owned slaves have been stripped bare, the slaves gone and in most cases the houses burned.

And we know for a fact Sherman uprooted all the citizens of Atlanta before burning it to the ground. Sherman's been on his goddamn march since middle November. It's now December 20. That's five weeks of burning, pillaging, stealing, raping."

"It's war, Chris. And we're out of bargaining chips, or fighting chips, or any chips."

"We should get in line with Hardee," blurted out Freeman

"And your wives and children?" Arnold asked of the other aldermen. "What of them? And your property? I'm not talking about your slaves, they are no longer your property, at least not after Sherman gets here. How many of you even own slaves?"

Four of the eight raised a hand.

"Well, if not already, they will be free by tomorrow morning. Unless you don't understand Lincoln's Emancipation Proclamation." He pronounced the document with sarcasm: e-Man-ci-PA-shun Pro-CLA-ma-shun.

"But what of your homes, your horses?" continued Arnold. "Give it all up? I say there is a better way. I say as the last of our troops cross over the river, that we rush to meet Geary, catch him before he has a chance to do any damage. I propose to formerly surrender the city."

"How can you 'surrender'? Last I heard that's a military tactic."

Arnold ignored the comment. "As painful as it may seem gentleman, we have no other choice. I will go alone if I have to, but I sincerely wish us to be unified in this matter, to represent the city government. We may be vilified by the citizens, at least in the beginning, but soon they will come around and be thankful if we can save Savannah."

Freeman did not respond and the others murmured agreement. None of them really wanted to march across a wooden pontoon bridge into the marshes of South Carolina.

"Excellent. Then we are agreed," said the mayor. "Let's meet here at one o'clock. All the carriages are gone, taken by the troops. So we will have to go out on our own horses. Anyone not have a horse?"

There was no reply in the negative. "Excellent. That will make eight of us altogether. I have some knowledge of where the enemy is camped, out on Augusta Road. We best ride from here to Anderson's Wharf together. As soon as the last troops enter the bridge, we'll head out to meet them. I think we'll find Union blue in no time and they can take us to General Sherman."

———————

The night was cold and rainy. At one hour past midnight the city officials rode their horses down Bay Street to West Broad, then to the pontoon landing. Another thousand troops were milling about, waiting their turn. Straw had been placed on the pontoons to minimize the sound of footsteps. General Hardee was already in South Carolina. The ranking officer, a colonel, approached Mayor Arnold.

"Dr. Arnold, are you planning to cross over?"

"No, we are going to search for General Sherman after you leave, to negotiate something. How many are going across?"

"We estimate about ten thousand altogether. We're leaving a whole lot of guns and ammunition behind. General Sherman should be happy with that. Wish we could help you, Dr. Arnold, but orders are orders."

"I completely understand, Colonel."

An hour later ties to the first set of pontoons were cut, letting them drift away from the bank. No more troops would be crossing the river. Arnold and his party then rode south on West Broad Street and turned right on Augusta Road. Arnold carried a white flag and a letter of surrender in his saddle bag. In the rain the horsemen spread out some distance and became separated. Arnold and four others turned down a narrow lane, while the remaining three aldermen stayed on Augusta Road. Just when the separation became apparent the Augusta Road group ran into a roadblock manned by a dozen union troops.

"Who goes there?"

"We are here to surrender Savannah," said O'Byrne.

The Union Captain approached with a torch. Riflemen on each side stood ready to shoot

"Yeh? Who is we? Dismount or risk being shot."

They all dismounted, not sure what else to do but raise hands in the air. "We are Mayor Richard Arnold and seven of his alderman. Can you take us to General Sherman? We want to surrender Savannah."

"I only see three. Three ain't eight. Where are the others?"

"They split off, took another road. The mayor is with them, but they will find us shortly."

Surrounded by blue coats, the three hapless aldermen were marched 200 yards beyond the roadblock, to a small tent city.

"Wait here." A bluecoat entered one of the tents and awakened General Geary, who promptly came out in coat and hat. He did not seem pleased.

"I am General Geary. Which of you is the mayor?"

O'Byrne explained the night's events, that the mayor was temporarily separated from them, but that their intent – unanimous – was to surrender the city.

"Well that explains the silence over the past half hour," said Geary. "Not a word nor any response from Hardee's boys. Skipped to South Carolina, heh? So who's defending your city?"

"No one, sir. The only Confederates you'll find are those too ill to leave. That's a fact."

"Well, which direction did your infernal mayor go?"

They gave him an idea, and he dispatched half a dozen soldiers to find Arnold and bring him to camp. Half an hour later Arnold and the others rode in, surrounded by blue coats on horseback. In his right hand the mayor carried a white flag on a short pole.

Geary yelled out. "Flag's not needed. Got your message. Mayor Arnold, I presume?"

"General, I am Dr. Richard Arnold, mayor of Savannah. Thank you for meeting with us." He dismounted and bowed, as if he meeting a European potentate. "I have in my hands a letter of surrender for General Sherman."

"Sherman isn't here now. I'm in charge."

"Yes, sir," replied the mayor. "Sir, General Hardee has left the city and we are defenseless. We ask of you, protection of the lives and private properly of the citizens and of our women and children. We have no troops, no one to fight you. I think you will enjoy our beautiful city and our hospitality. You will see it is well worth preserving." With that, Mayor Arnold handed his letter General Geary, who read it quickly.[3]

"So Hardee has escaped over the Savannah River, and you will offer no opposition?"

"His entire army, General. As I wrote, we are utterly defenseless. The city is yours. Sir."

"Excellent, Mr. Mayor," said Geary. "Now you and your men can lead us into Savannah. If it's as you say, no harm will come to your city."

———◆———

Just before sunrise Mayor Arnold and his aldermen led a 1000-strong Union division up West Broad Street. Heads poked out of second floor windows, believing and not believing. The troops encountered a black freedman on the street, perhaps slightly inebriated, bowing profusely and yelling "Praise the Lord, Sherman is come!" Near the end of West Broad the marchers turned right, to enter Bay Street. When they left camp the sky was still dark with a wet drizzle. By the time they reached the corner of West Broad and Bay the sun was lighting up the morning sky.

It became apparent with daylight that looting had been going on all night. Word of the evacuation spread fast, and shops were being vandalized by lower class whites, but also some blacks, as well as Confederates soldiers who had stayed behind. Some of the looting was motivated by hunger, but there was no way to separate out the desperate from the despicable. Several times Geary dispatched a small contingent to put a stop to the looting. Each time Arnold chimed in with "Thank you General, we are so glad you're here." In truth, Arnold was glad. He knew what chaos might ensue without the Federal presence.

Two blocks from Bull Street a shot pierced the air, then a scream. Geary turned his head briefly, then kept riding. He knew the sound -- a Union rifle. Arnold, just a few yards to the side of Geary, was very curious but said nothing and kept riding. A few minutes later a union captain galloped past the marching columns and trotted next to his commanding general, saluting smartly. They exchanged a few words and the young officer rode off. Geary then spoke, with a hint of sarcasm,

"You have one less looter to worry about, Mr. Mayor."

The troops stopped in front of the Customs House at the corner of Bay and Bull Streets. Geary and Arnold climbed to the base of the spire to reach a spacious four-sided balcony. From there the general could survey the city in all directions, as his aides raised the American flag and lowered the Confederate one. Alongside the stars and stripes they also raised the flag of Geary's Twentieth Corps. A complete transfer of power had just occurred with no shots fired (save against looters).

The sun was now fully above the horizon. The city was, Geary confessed to Arnold, just as he had heard: a grand and beautiful place, full of small parks or squares, handsome buildings, and a series of capacious warehouses fronting the Savannah River. In them were thousands of bales of cotton -- cotton that would no longer be of service to the Confederacy. They climbed back down to Bay Street and orders were given to encamp on the nearby squares. Geary then sent orders for the rest of his division to deploy.

"Where the hell is Sherman?" Geary muttered to himself.

Even as events were unfolding, the *Savannah Republican,* one of the city's two daily papers, apprised of Hardee's evacuation and the Mayor's desire to personally surrender the city, published a most timely editorial, counseling "obedience and all proper respect on the part of our citizens," [4]

CHAPTER 12

— *Thursday, December 22*

Late in the morning Abigale looked out the front window and saw several blue coats ambling down her street. Each man carried a rifle and back pack, and as a group they seemed jaunty, in no hurry to get wherever they were going.

Nothing inside the house had changed but outside was a whole new world. The Confederate army was gone, and Savannah was occupied by the enemy. The *Savannah Republican's* December 21 front page editorial told citizens what was coming;[4] it did not mention that the paper itself would immediately cease publication. The *Morning News* would soon cease printing as well.

One didn't need a newspaper to learn the city had been invaded, or that it was, to this point, a peaceful occupation. Abigale felt overwhelming relief that Atlanta's fate was not to be Savannah's. Intense curiosity overcame her and without much thought said to Polly, "Let's go to the market. I want to see all this for myself."

Mrs. Gordon did not want to leave the house, at least not now. She was still waiting for the newspaper that would not be delivered, because it was no longer being published. Jane also did not want to join Abigale, stating rather archly, "I'd rather go out on my own. I feel safe."

Abigale knew what Jane wanted—to search for someone to replace Winston. The very thought made her wince. *Nothing good can*

*come of this. But what can I do? Tell her not to leave the house? Insist mother
quarantine her? Mother has given up on Jane. If only daddy was alive! He'd
know what to do.*

Abigale could only offer her sister weak advice. "Take, care, Jane.
Be careful. These boys are hungry, they've been marching for weeks.
They're not Southern boys. They don't share our values."

"Don't worry about me," Jane replied.

———

Polly and Abigale entered Chippewa Square, where they saw a few
Union soldiers setting up campsites. This was not a massive camp like
in the Old Colonial Cemetery, just a few tents for what would like be
a sentry post. Other citizens and negroes were out and about, and
no streets were closed or off limits. The occupation that had com-
menced only thirty hours earlier was, so far, largely peaceful.

Exiting the Square onto Bull Street, Abigale saw a carriage coming rapidly toward them. As it came beside Abigale and Polly the pas-
senger instructed his negro driver to stop, and he got out. He looked
to be in his fifties and was smartly attired in a three-piece suit, fedora
and cravat. His dress, along with the carriage, indicated he was part
of the city's elite.

"Abigale Tate!" he said. "My, my, so nice to see you." He spoke in a
British accent, and took a deep and exaggerated bow after the greeting. He did not mention Polly, who stood behind her mistress.

"Mr. Green?"

"Yes, yes. Charles Green. I haven't seen you in a while. How are
you doing? Of course, I heard about Franklin. What can I say? I am
so sorry. But you seem to be holding out well."

"Thank you. Well, you seem to be in a hurry."

"I am, I am. Haven't you heard? General Sherman is in town!"

Abigale waved her hand toward the troops in Chippewa Square
and said, "Yes, it seems so. Since yesterday."

"No, no, he himself arrived only within the past two hours. He was in Port Royal when General Geary entered the city. He arrived back by boat last night. And I just met him at the Pulaski Hotel."

"You met the infamous general?"

"Yes, yes, very nice man. He's going to stay at my home! He's agreed."

"Your home? On Madison Square?"

"The one and same, that's what I offered him. And he's accepted. I'm on my way now to greet him when he arrives."

Green was a cotton merchant, among the most successful in the city. As a British citizen he considered himself non-partisan to the conflict, though by virtue of owning cotton stored in Savannah, he was at risk for losses.

As to his house, it was by far the most expensive in the city. Built in the 1850s, by architect Charles Norris, in the "Gothic Revival" style, Green had spared no expense. The house even had indoor plumbing. Abigale had been inside twice before, for Christmas parties when her father was alive.

"And will your family be staying there as well?" she asked.

"My wife and children are safe in Virginia. I brought them up a few months ago, and returned to oversee my holdings. Can't be too careful with this conflict."

"Well, that is interesting," she said. "May I enquire how you knew the general would be at Pulaski House this morning?"

"I learned from Major Howard yesterday that Sherman was coming back from South Carolina. I told him my plan, and he said Sherman would stop at Pulaski House as soon as he arrived. I think he was planning to stay there. So I went on my own initiative, introduced myself, and made him the offer. He is, quite frankly, desirous of some luxury after marching through our fair state."

"And no cost to the Union, I assume?" asked Abigale.

"Free, of course. Though I do have a motive, which should be no secret."

"Which is?"

"You'll remember, the house is full of art and antiques from mother England. With Sherman there, the property will be protected. And I will feel safer."

"You will be staying in the house, then?"

"Yes, yes. Just two rooms. The general and his staff will have the run of the place. That's my plan and he's agreed." Green exuded glee, as if he had just closed on a successful business deal.

Abigale did not share his glee. "Franklin was killed near Atlanta last August," she said, showing no emotion, simply stating a fact. Her severe non-sequitur seemed to catch Green off guard, as he frowned and cleared his throat.

"Yes, yes, I read that. That is indeed tragic. I am so sorry."

"Thank you."

"Well, I must be getting to the house. It was very nice seeing you again." He bowed once more, climbed into the carriage and instructed the driver to proceed.

Abigale watched as the carriage moved down Bull Street and around the square. When it was no longer visible, she turned to Polly. "Was I nice to him?"

"You was very nice. Why you aks?"

———— ◆ ————

Jane chose to visit Forsythe Park on her afternoon walk, a thirty acre expanse south of Liberty Street. The choice seemed sound. For one thing, she would not run into her sister who was headed north with Polly, toward the markets. And for another, if there was to be any large encampment in the city, other than Old Colonial Cemetery, it would be Forsythe Park. The southern end of the park, with its wide expanse of lawn, was always being used for military purposes by the boys in grey. Surely the boys in blue would now want to occupy it.

Forsythe's northern end was a favorite of gentry, with its tree lined walkways and large baroque fountain. Jane stopped for a minute at the fountain, around which were several people standing and talking, or just staring at the spouting water. Then she walked around it and continued south toward the open field. Two bluecoats passed her by. As they did so one of them whistled, in the manner of men who see a pretty girl. For some reason—she wondered why—they did not stop to ask her any questions, but kept on walking. As did she.

The southern end of the park was indeed busy. Hundreds of soldiers were engaged, some drilling, others constructing tents and building fires, and still others sitting at various tasks: whittling, cleaning a rifle, playing checkers. A few men were busy setting up a perimeter, which consisted of stakes in the ground connected by rope, in effect a makeshift fence. Clearly, this half of the park was now coopted by the Union army.

"May I help you ma'am?' asked one of the fence builders.

"I was walking toward Park Avenue," she fabricated. "Is the path blocked?"

"Afraid so, ma'am. You'll have to go out to the street and continue south that way."

She studied the soldier. He looked to be in his early twenties, thin with hollow cheeks, and unwashed. But not, she thought, unappealing.

"Could you make an exception? I am in a hurry."

His fence-building partner came up to join the conversation.

The first soldier explained, "This woman says she wants to walk through our camp, to get to the end of the park."

"Miss—"

"Gordon," she said, "Jane Gordon."

"Miss Gordon, this is a new Union Camp. No civilians is allowed. And certainly no women."

They don't seem interested. What's the matter with me?

"Oh, no," she said. "I understand. But tell me, all of you are sleeping under the stars tonight? Here in Forsythe Park?"

Both men laughed. "Ma'am," said one of them, "this is like a fancy hotel compared to where we been sleeping the past month."

"Well, thank you for your time. I'll be on my way."

She made a slight curtsy and turned toward the fountain. It was only three in the afternoon, and she decided to look elsewhere. *If I cut across Gaston, I can reach Old Colonial, without running into Abigale. Soldiers must be camped there as well.*

———◆———

Abigale found downtown Savannah most interesting – and depressing. Compared to her last visit, there were twice as many people out and about. Many of them were Union soldiers, and a large number of what appeared to her to be homeless negroes. They came with Sherman, she knew, from the plantations up north. *Where, she wondered, are they going to live, and who's going to feed them?*

Despite the new influx of humanity, there was peace and order, and commerce too. The markets were open, and the same amount of haggling as always. This time soldiers were also buying.

In fact, Abigale was surprised at the peace and civility. The soldiers were not behaving like a conquering army as much as one resting between battles. Considering all the fighting the troops must have experienced, she surmised they were just happy to have no imminent battle, no opposing army in their midst. She thought of asking a few soldiers about their march from Atlanta, but quickly decided against it She fantasized meeting the man who killed her husband, though of course there would be no way to know from a simple greeting. Still, she decided against it.

After an hour of walking and sightseeing, buying a few items for the kitchen, and denying the outstretched hands of a few beggars, they headed home.

"What do you make of it all, Polly?"

"Make of what, Miss Abigale?"

"All this. The soldiers, all the negroes in town, the activity. We've been taken over by the Union army. Yet everything is peaceful."

"Well, dat's sure good. I didn't know what to 'spect, tellin' the truth. They do seem a nice bunch."

"What do your people tell you?" Abigale enquired. "About freedom and such? What do you hear?"

Abigale was aware that Polly had a loose news network, colored folk who would report on the latest information, whether it was Sherman's imminent arrival, a church burning, or something more common like the latest marriage or death. In this way Polly was up to date on local affairs, at least those that affected her class.

"Nuthin, fo sure. Dis Gen'rl Sherman just gettin' here, so people waitin' on him, I guess."

"I see," said Abigale, and she asked no further questions.

CHAPTER 13

— *Thursday, December 22*

Within an hour of taking up residence in the Green Mansion, Sherman had his first visitor: Mr. A.G. Browne, of Salem, Massachusetts, United States Treasury agent for the Department of the South. Browne had been waiting in Hilton Head until the city was seized by U.S. troops.

"What brings you here, Mr. Browne?"

"I am here to claim possession, in the name of the Treasury Department, of all the cotton and rice your men have captured. And may I say, magnificent march, General. Magnificent! The whole country is marveling."

"Well, these items were fairly won, Mr. Browne, and I must say, I am first beholden to the army, so they can be fully provisioned."

"I understand, I understand," said Browne. "But these goods were won by the *United States* Army, and rightly belong to the treasury. I must assure that whatever is not vital to your army, befalls to the U.S. I'm sorry General, but that's my job. I will of course defer to you in all things military, but must file my report soon."

Sherman was not going to be outfoxed by a government bureaucrat. "I have marched 300 miles in thirty days, risked life and limb of 60,000 of our finest troops, and just arrived in town. I have 10,000 poor negroes to get fed and housed, and a civilian population that hasn't yet come to grips with their defeat, who may yet turn outwardly hostile. I am in possession of southern cotton and guns and god knows what else, and there is as yet no accurate inventory of all that. And the first greeting I get is 'give me all your goods'? Is that what I am hearing, Mr. Browne?"

"I *am* sorry, but I am just doing as instructed."

"Well, you *are* sorry, sir. I am not ready to surrender possession just yet. The quartermaster and commissary will manage these spoils for now. After proper inventories are prepared, whatever we have no special use for, I *will* turn over to you, but not before."

"Yes, sir" said Browne, deferentially. "What is your estimate?"

"Oh, I estimate that the warehouses store at least twenty-five thousand bales of cotton, and in the forts probably hundred and fifty large guns."

"You mentioned 10,000 negroes? I did not see many on my way in. Where are they hiding?"

Sherman laughed. "They're not hiding. I'm keeping them out of the city, in various locations. I could have had three times that many, from the plantations. We tried to stop them from leaving, but once they were freed they all wanted to follow my army. Now I've got to keep them fed. Just another responsibility."

"Well, your capture of Savannah is the main enterprise. I have an idea, as Christmas is upon us in a few days. The *Golden Gate* is this very afternoon to sail for Fortress Monroe, Virginia. If she has calm weather off Cape Hatteras, she will reach the fort by Christmas day. Might I suggest that you send President Lincoln a welcome telegram offering him as Christmas gift this bounty? He likes such peculiarities, you know. Once the ship reaches Virginia your message can be sent to Washington over the telegraph wire."

The idea intrigued Sherman, and warmed him to this Mr. Browne.

"I like your idea." Sherman sat at his desk and wrote out a brief message, offering the city to Lincoln as a "Christmas-gift."[5]

"There, that should do it."

Brown read the missive. "Splendid. Mr. Lincoln *will* enjoy this." Browne pocketed the note. "Well, General, it's been a real pleasure meeting you. I'm going to the ship now, and will see that this is handled with special care."

With that, Browne left the mansion on his horse and reached the *Golden Gate* but an hour before she sailed.

———

When Abigale and Polly arrived home it was half past four, an hour from sunset. Mrs. Gordon was distraught.

"Where have you been?"

"I told you we were going to the walk around, go to the market, and such. You said you didn't want to come."

"Jane's not with you?"

"You know she went out alone."

"Did you see her?"

"No, not at all."

"Well, where is she?"

"Mother, I fear we're going in circles. She'll be home soon, I'm sure."

"I'm worried about her."

As am I, thought Abigale. She really had no basis to reassure her mother. Anything was possible.

"Please, go out on the street, and see if you can find her."

Abigale didn't argue with her mother, though she felt a search was futile. Jane could be anywhere. Still, she put her coat on and left the house, walking first toward Barnard Street, and then back toward Drayton Street. There was no sign of Jane. Twilight set in and she returned home.

"Mother, we'll have to wait and see. She'll be home, I'm certain," she said, while thinking the opposite. *I have no reason to be certain of anything with that girl.*

Fifteen minutes later came a loud knock on the door. Mrs. Gordon jumped from her chair and ran to open it. There stood Jane, accompanied by two bluecoats.

Mrs. Gordon hugged Jane and began crying. "Where have you been? Come in. Who are these men?"

"Pardon, ma'am, said one of the soldiers, I am Sergeant Hendricks and this is Sergeant Smithfield. Are you the girl's mother?"

"Yes, who are you? Why are you with my daughter?"

Abigale came to her mother's side. "Mother, invite them in. I'm sure they will explain everything. Please, sirs, come in."

They entered the foyer, where the light was now much brighter than outside. Without a word, Jane walked into the living room, then ascended the stairs to her bedroom.

"Ma'am, we were ordered by our colonel to escort your daughter home. It seems there was some, uh, misunderstanding, and some of our boys got a little rowdy with her."

"What are you saying?" demanded Mrs. Gordon.

"Sir," said Abigale, in as stern a manner as she could muster, "please be specific. Tell us what happened."

Sergeant Hendricks told the tale. Jane had started a conversation with one of the sentinels, reminding Abigale what she had done with Winston weeks earlier. Apparently it had been a friendly conversation at first, but when she showed no interest in leaving, and much interest in staying, the sentinel tried to sneak her into the camp, throwing his army coat over her shoulders as they made their way to his tent. They made it to the tent, but then all hell broke loose, when other men discovered she was there. They came into the tent also, or at least two of them did. There was hollering and hooting, and before long two officers, Colonel Ryan and his aide-de-camp, Captain Broderick, came by and discovered Jane inside the tent, at this point with several men.

The colonel ordered her out, and made inquiry as to who she was. She refused all identification, though it seemed, from her clothes and bearing, that she was well-bred. The colonel had to threaten her with staying overnight in the female prison if she didn't identify herself. Just as he ordered her taken away, she spoke up and revealed her name and address.

"So he ordered us to bring her here, and not to leave until a responsible relative took charge. He said she looked awfully young, and had no business carousing with the troops. Sorry, ma'am, but that's the full story."

Mrs. Gordon looked him in the eye and asked, "Was...she...violated?"

"No ma'am, as far as our understanding is, this all happened very fast and she was not violated."

"Thank you," said Mrs. Gordon.

"Thank you," said Abigale. "You have been most kind. Can we get you something to drink?"

"No ma'am. We do request that you sign this order, showing that we did bring her to the proper address. It's army procedure." He held out a piece of paper, with simple writing indicating Jane's name and address as she related them.

"I'll sign it. I'm her older sister. My name is Abigale Tate."

"That'll be fine Miss Tate. We do see that you live here as well."

Abigale signed the paper and returned it to sergeant.

"Well, we have to be going. We need to report back to camp."

"Again, thank you. Thank you very much."

As soon as they left, Mrs. Gordon collapsed in Abigale's arms, and begin sobbing.

"It will work out, mother. Don't cry. It will work out."

CHAPTER 14

—

— *Friday, December 23*

ABIGALE MADE UP HER MIND. She would confront Jane with questions, and demand answers. She felt her family disintegrating, and not just because of Jane's loose ways. Her mother was a recluse. Her brother was god knows where, and always in danger of being killed by disease or bullets. She realized the basic problem. *Our men are gone. We are adrift, alone.*

She found Jane alone in the dining area, and sat down next to her. Jane turned to her older sister and gave a look that made Abigale uncomfortable, as if *she* was an intruder. But there was no turning back.

"I know you don't want to discuss this with mother, but I'm your older sister, you can tell me. What's this all about? At your age, I could not even imagine bringing a young man to the shed late at night and making love to him."

"I really don't want to talk about it."

"You must. I'm not leaving until you do."

Jane stared at her for a few seconds, then replied, "Where were we supposed to embrace? In my bedroom?"

"Jane, I understand. This activity would have been inconceivable were daddy alive. You would be too scared to even try something like that. Daddy might have killed him. No, I understand. Our anchors are gone."

"I have a secret, sister."

"What is it? You can tell me." For a moment Abigale felt she might be making some headway.

"I like men."

This was not what Abigale expected.

"So do I, but—"

"So, Franklin is gone. What are you doing about it?"

"About what?"

"Don't you want a man in your bed? Don't you miss him?"

"I miss him every day, you know that."

"That's not what I mean. Do I have to spell it out?"

"Please do," Abigale said, fearful of what Jane might say next.

"Don't you want a man caressing you, kissing you, inside of you!"

"Jane!"

"You said to spell it out. I'm not a child anymore! You and mother make me feel like I'm in a nunnery."

"That's your perception. We just don't want you to be hurt."

"And you didn't answer my question."

"Of course I would prefer to have a husband, and I will one day. But I won't go around sleeping with every man who happens to occupy a street corner."

"Not every man, just Winston."

"And what was that affair yesterday? What were you doing in the tent of Union soldiers, for god sakes?"

"We were having fun, just joking around. Nothing happened."

"Nothing happened because you were rescued. Why did they have to escort you home?"

"I was against Army regulations. They wanted to arrest me! Can you imagine? For talking to some soldiers?"

"Arrest you? That was just a threat because you wouldn't tell them where you lived."

"Well, that's what they were going to do, so I told them."

"You embarrass us, Jane Gordon." *I shouldn't have said that.* "I mean, think of mother. She's so fragile. She doesn't need a daughter building a bad reputation. Don't you think of her?"

"I wouldn't want to do anything to hurt her. But I can't go on living in a nunnery!"

"This house is *not* a nunnery. Why do you keep saying that?"

"Because nuns, that's what they do. Pray all day and never sleep with men. That's what you and mother do. Pray all day that things will change for the better, and sleep alone every night. That's a nunnery."

"Where do you get these ideas? You're only seventeen."

"If I hear that one more time, I'll scream."

"How come you don't have any friends, or at least you never bring anyone over here? What about other girls your age?"

"Are you talking about Brenda?"

"Well, she was your closest friend until a while ago. Where is she?"

"Married."

"Married? To whom?"

"Some young boy in Augusta. Remember she moved there?"

"No, guess I forgot."

"She found a boy who didn't make it to the army. Has a limp or something. But he can perform in bed."

"Jane, please, enough of this. How do you even know that?"

"She told me, in her last letter, couple of months ago. You want to read it?"

"Definitely not. I don't understand your urges, I really don't."

"And I don't understand why you don't have any."

"How do you know I don't?"

"Do you?"

Abigale had not planned on a personal inquisition from her sister, and did not like the discomfort it engendered.

"Jane this is about you, not me. I wasn't escorted home by soldiers. Can we have a truce?"

"You started it. I was just minding my business."

"So Winston is gone, and the Union boys are not receptive. Now what are your plans, if I may ask?"

"Find another. That's more than you are doing."

Abigale held her head down in disappointment. "This conversation is getting us nowhere. We are at sea without our sails, nay, without our mast."

"Now you're the poet?"

"Just be careful. Please, for mother and me, please just be careful."

———

With the arrival of Sherman and his 60,000-man army, there were suddenly two Savannahs: the military and the civilian. The former dominated in sheer numbers, triple Savannah's population (black and white), though most of the troops were camped outside the city limits.

For Sherman, it was an interlude from the fighting and pillaging. Now he had to regroup, prepare for the next phase of his army's march, which would be up the Carolinas. Preparation required orders, the first of which came on December 23. Special Field Orders No. 139 stipulated "possession of all public buildings, all vacant storerooms, warehouses, &c, that may be now or hereafter needed for any department of the army." Private property – homes and goods – would not be affected.[6]

CHAPTER 15

———

— *SATURDAY, DECEMBER 24*

THE KNOCK ON THE DOOR came from a young black man. Polly opened the door and spoke to the man briefly.

"Who is that?" asked Abigale, from the parlor.

"It be message for me, Miss Abigale."

Polly and the messenger talked for another minute, then he left and she closed the door.

"Who was that?" asked Abigale, as Polly returned to the parlor. "You look concerned. What's the matter?"

"Benjamin be ill, very sick."

"Benjamin?"

"He be my husband. You came to da wedding."

"That's right. I thought you were separated?"

"Dat be de case. But nevah divorced. They aks me to come."

"Who asked you?"

"Be Benjamin hisself. According to Sebastian, who just come to da door. I gots to go, Miss Abigale."

Polly married Benjamin Carter when she was twenty, he twenty-one. Legally she was Polly Carter, though the Tate-Gordon family never called her by any name but Polly.

Benjamin was owned by Mr. and Mrs. Lamar Casey. Slave weddings were common on the plantation, where a master may own dozens or even hundreds of negroes, who all knew each other.

There, marriage did not present a logistical problem, unless the owner decided to sell one of the pair. City marriages were different, since the husband and wife were likely to be owned by different families.

When Polly and Benjamin wed in 1855, neither the Caseys nor the Gordons wanted to sell their slave to the other family, which meant the couple had to live apart. They could buy their freedom, but neither one had any savings, as they were not paid wages. However, as their owners' houses were only a few blocks apart, it was agreed they would have unlimited visitation to each other's quarters, where they could function as man and wife. As a practical matter, this meant they could sleep in the same bed four or five nights of each week, and spend most of their Sundays together.

The Casey house, on Habersham Street, was a much grander home than the Gordons' row house. Mr. Lamar Casey had been a banker before the war, and remained wealthy throughout the conflict. On the day Sherman arrived he owned an estimated ten percent of all the cotton in Savannah's warehouses.

The Caseys also owned four domestic servants, and considered Benjamin their most valuable. He tended to their horses in the barn, and was adept at fixing things, like carriage wheels and balky door jambs.

The Carter marriage seemed to go well enough the first two years, but then began to grow cold. Benjamin came over to be with Polly less and less, and she began to nag about why he seemed to be avoiding her. He would always say "I gots work to do," or "They keeps me very busy."

Their domestic turmoil was *sub rosa* to the Gordons and the Caseys. As long as servants did the required work, and didn't complain, the families had no reason to concern themselves with their servants' personal affairs.

In the third year of marriage word came out that one of the Caseys' slaves, a young woman named Corey, was pregnant with Benjamin's child. There was no hiding the fact, and it bothered the Caseys not at all. Young women in slavery were expected to have children, who would then be owned by the family that owned the mother. So the Caseys kept on both parents, unconcerned that Benjamin and Corey were not husband and wife.

When Corey was four months along, Lamar Casey mentioned to Marshall Gordon, in a joking manner, that his Benjamin was fathering a child with Corey.

"What does your Polly think about that? Nigras is something, aren't they?"

"I know nothing about it," was all Mr. Gordon could reply.

That evening Mr. Gordon asked Polly if it was true that Corey was carrying her husband's child. His question arose out of natural curiosity, not just as a slave owner but also as a lawyer; he wanted to hear from the aggrieved party.

"Yes, it be true Mista Gordon," Polly said, and then she immediately began wailing, so badly that Mrs. Gordon had to walk her down to the basement and have her lie down. Once in her room, in bed, Polly told Mrs. Gordon she'd be all right, and asked to be left alone. Polly was able to return to work the next day, and no one said any more about her predicament.

Shortly after Corey gave birth to a boy, Abigale asked Polly why she didn't get a divorce. Polly replied something about "too messy. Let him be. He be da boy's father, wedder I gots a divorce or not."

Hearing about this conversation, Mr. Gordon offered to do the divorce papers for free, but Polly never took him up on it. And Benjamin never asked either. So they stayed married, and fully estranged.

The knock on the door was the first Polly had heard anything about Benjamin in two years.

"I understand he's ill, Polly," said Abigale, "but shouldn't that other woman—I forget her name—be the one to comfort him?"

"Dat be Corey. She da woman."

"Yes, Corey. Now I remember."

"She no good, dat girl. I owes it to him to go see. He aks for me."

"Do you want me to go with you?"

"Be nice, for sho. Ifn' he gonna die, I gots to see him once. Lord knows where he gonna end up."

So around ten a.m., the day before Christmas, Abigale and Polly walked over to the Casey home. Abigale knocked on the gilded front door and was greeted by a servant, who said she could come in, but Polly must wait outside.

"We've just come to see Benjamin," said Abigale, and the servant directed them to the horse stables out back.

There they found Polly's husband laying on a bed of hay. Corey was at his side, along with a six-year-old boy, their son. Immediately Corey stood up. "He aks for you, why I sent the message. Says you gots to come. He wants to say somethin'."

Polly leaned down, rubbed Benjamin's sweaty forehead and held his hand in hers. His face was gaunt, eyes sunken and wide with the terror of fatal illness. On seeing Polly, he managed a faint smile.

"Benjamin, Benjamin," was all she could say. "Oh, Benjamin."

"Pol….ly. I'm, I'm….sorry. I just had to tell you befo I go to the Lord."

"What you be sorry fo?"

"I…I just wanted a child. I…I'm sorry. Forgive me."

Benjamin's words hit Abigale hard. *He wanted a child! Oh, my god, I'm going to cry. This is so painful.* She did her best to stifle the tears, then took a step back to distance herself from Polly and Benjamin.

"Don't you be sorry," said Polly, "jus gets well." Polly began sobbing, softly at first, then louder. She laid her head on his breast. Standing to the side, Corey pulled the boy toward her, so his back was to his father.

"We be goin' to the house," Corey said. "Stay here ifn' you want."

Polly didn't move. Abigale nodded, and Corey and her son left the barn.

A minute later, from outside the barn, came a loud call. "Abigale Tate, is that you in there with Benjamin?" Abigale was pretty sure the caller was Mrs. Casey.

"Yes. Mrs. Casey?"

"Child, you shouldn't be in there. He has the fever. No white folks should be in there."

"Polly," said Abigale, "I'm going to speak with Mrs. Casey." Polly nodded her head against her husband's chest, indicating she understood.

Abigale knew Lucretia Casey as the second wife of Lamar and a prominent matron, now almost fifty. When Mr. Gordon was alive the family had attended parties in the Casey mansion. Mrs. Casey was still the neighborhood's matriarch and influential in whatever social circles remained during the war.

Outside the barn Lucretia seemed mildly reproachful. "I didn't expect to have you come with your servant. When Corey told me Benjamin wanted to see Polly, I sent for her. Didn't know you would come too. He's got the fever. You really shouldn't go in there."

"I see that," replied Abigale. "He looks very bad. Has a doctor tended to him?"

"Child, we are not primitives. I had Dr. Smithers see him when he took ill four days ago, and he's been back one more time. Says Benjamin has the typhoid, not much to do. We will miss him."

Then, without warning, Lucretia put her arm on Abigale's shoulder. "Oh, I'm so sorry. Do forgive me. I did hear about Franklin, and must express my condolences. I believe we did send you a note at the time."

"Yes, that was kind of you. And how is Mr. Casey?"

"Involved as ever. Now he is in a turmoil, not knowing what this Sherman fellow is going to do about all the cotton in the city. And we've just learned one of the Union generals wants to billet in our home. All the generals are finding quarters in the city. They plan to be here for some time, looks like. Lamar says we have no choice, after Charles Greene gave over his house. It might actually help protect our property, so Mr. Casey's not protesting. In fact the more he thinks about it the more he thinks it's a sound idea."

"I haven't heard anything about that. No one's asked to billet with us."

"Perhaps you don't have the room, dear." Abigale chose not to take offense at this remark, snide though it seemed to her.

"Frankly, that's not our major concern," said Mrs. Casey. "The general and his staff—he may bring one or two aides—will be courteous, I'm sure. No, the major concern is the cotton. Lamar may be out of luck with this Union takeover. But we'll survive. We are just thankful Sherman didn't burn us down. You never know with these damn Yankees."

Abigale wished to turn the conversation back to Benjamin. She did not know this Doctor Smithers, but had no reason to doubt his diagnosis. Still, she wondered, would not a second review be of some benefit? Perhaps there was some risk to the idea welling rapidly in her mind, but she had to try, for Polly's sake. No, for her own satisfaction. Yes, that was it. *For my own satisfaction.*

"I would like Dr. Richard Arnold to examine Benjamin."

"What? The mayor?"

"Yes. He's a fine medical doctor."

"Why, Abigale, I don't believe that's necessary. Dr. Smithers is a competent practitioner, and besides, dear, it's the day before Christmas, I don't think you will be able to engage the mayor. He has official duties, you know."

"I would like to call for him, if you don't mind."

"I don't want to seem impolite, dear, but I don't think Lamar wants to spend any more on Benjamin. There is a limit to—"

"I will pay Dr. Arnold's fee."

"Well, I, I— "

"Please, Mrs. Casey, may I ask your servant to go to his office and home. They are in the same building, and if he is not there, then surely he will be found in the City Exchange."

"You do seem determined. I will not stand in your way, if that is what you wish. But you must make it clear it is you who are making the request, neither I nor Lamar. I think a written note should be sent, signed by you."

"That will be fine," said Abigale.

"Do not be surprised if he declines to come. There is not much imperative to attend a dying negro."

"All I can do is ask." *He will not decline a request from me, if it is in his power to come.*

"Very well. Come into the house. I will go fetch Sebastian and tell him to do your bidding, and a pen and paper to scratch out your note. And please, for your health and the health of your family, don't go back in that barn."

Abigale followed Mrs. Casey inside the mansion. She marveled at the wall tapestries, the art work and ornamentation. The rooms were not as richly decorated as in Green's mansion, but sumptuous nonetheless.

Abigale was directed to an ornate writing desk. Using a dip pen, she wrote out the following note.

Dr. Richard Arnold.
Please, sir, come as soon as possible to attend to one Benjamin Carter, slave to Lamar and Lucretia Casey, 145 Habersham. He is very ill. I am here with his wife Polly, our house servant. I will cover all arrangements, and be forever thankful for your assistance.
Sincerely,
Abigale Tate, daughter of Col. Marshall Gordon

She thought the note well-crafted, promising nothing more than to "be forever thankful." *If he considers that I may have some* other *obligation, the disappointment will be all his.*

She folded the paper and gave it to Sebastian, along with the address of Dr. Arnold's home and office. "And if he's not there," she told him, "then follow the path indicated by his servants."

"Yessum," said Sebastian, and he ran off for his second errand of the day.

Abigale found Mrs. Casey in the sitting room. "Thank you. I must go back and tell Polly what is happening."

"Don't you go in there," she admonished once again.

"I will just go tell Polly, and then with your permission return here, to await Sebastian, with what news he may have."

Abigale left the house and re-entered the barn. She had already been in once, she figured, and another visit wouldn't make any difference. She found Polly still at Benjamin's side, but now sitting upright, his hand in hers; they were conversing in low whispers. Abigale could not make out the words, and thought perhaps they were speaking Gullah.

"Polly, I've sent for a physician I know, Dr. Richard Arnold. You met him with me at the market last week. He may or may not come right away, there's no way to know. Sebastian is delivering my note."

"Dats right nice, Missus Abigale," she said, without looking up from her husband. "You hear that Benjamin, they's gettin' a doctor for you? Youse gonna be fine."

Abigale did not tell Polly about Dr. Smithers' prior visits or his dismal prognosis. "Polly, do you want to stay here? I asked Sebastian to return after he delivers the note to let me know the response."

Polly nodded.

"That's fine," said Abigale. "I will wait in the house with Mrs. Casey, at least until Sebastian returns. Then I will be going home. You may stay as long as you like."

Abigale returned to the comfort of the Caseys' sitting room. The two women chatted for a while, about the war and the occupation. Events of the day showed that not much had changed in the relationship between slaveholder and slave, but then again it was only two days since Sherman entered the city. Both women acknowledged that he would soon make some proclamation affecting their lives. "Then we'll see," said Mrs. Casey.

After fifteen minutes of idle talk, Mrs. Casey left Abigale to "attend to a few things."

In another half hour Sebastian returned, with welcoming news.

"Da doctor say he will come, but maybe not for a couple 'ours, he gots chores to attend to."

"Did he give you a note?"

"No ma'am, just told me to tell you dat."

"Did he say anything else?" asked Abigale.

Sebastian hesitated a moment, and smiled.

"Well, did he?"

"Yessum, he aks me to describe you."

"Describe me, how?"

"Yo age, yo hair, yo face. He may think you not be you, I wondrin'. Well, I say a few words about what I see and he move his head up and down, den say, dat's her, dat's her. Yo must be good friends or somtin'."

"Yes, Sebastian, we are friends. My father and the mayor go way back. Way back."

Abigale thanked Mrs. Casey for her hospitality and allowing Sebastian to deliver the note. On leaving the house she passed by the barn and this time, from the doorway, told Polly she was walking home.

———

Polly did not return to Liberty Street until just before sundown. Abigale rushed to meet her in the foyer.

"What happened? Did Doctor Arnold come? Is Benjamin all right?"

"He be dade."

"Dead?"

"Yessum."

"Did Doctor Arnold arrive?

"In time to tell us what we just knew. Put that thing on his heart and said, he dade."

"I'm so sorry, Polly."

"Be da Lord's way, I rekon."

"Was Corey there?"

"She be dere. Her son done took it real hard."

"Did Dr. Arnold say anything, ask where I was?"

"He did. I told him you back to da house. He say give you dis note." Polly handed over a folded piece of paper, which Abigale opened and quickly read. The hand writing was scribbled but legible.

> *My dear Mrs. Tate,*
>
> *Sorry I could not be of help in this unfortunate situation. Mr. B deceased just before my arriving. There will of course be no charge.*
> *Your obedient servant,*
> *RC Arnold, MD*

Abigale was glad she had called for Dr. Arnold and felt better for it. At the same time she felt sad, sadder than she ever expected to feel from the demise of her servant's estranged husband. *Is our household cursed?*

— *Sunday, December 25, 1864*

Christmas came just four days after Union troops invaded Savannah. For the Tate-Gordon household, the holiday was anything but festive. They had a Christmas tree in the front parlor, a Georgia pine bought in the market, but it was sparsely decorated, with paper cutouts and ribbons. Underneath lay a few obligatory presents.

No one at 27 Liberty Street felt like celebrating, and except for these few artifacts of tradition, the day was like any other. Polly was off for the holiday, out with cousins in the area. She had no immediate family, but a large extended one in the Savannah area. In 1863 they had hosted their neighbor Josepha Morgan for dinner, but now she too was away with relatives in Pooler.

Mrs. Gordon stayed in her bedroom much of the morning. Abigale used the time to play more Chopin. She tried a few Christmas songs, but did not feel the mood and returned to classical repertoire.

Jane stayed in her room, reading a book given to her by Winston, before he departed for South Carolina. It came with a brown paper cover, on which there was no printed title or words. Winston told her many soldiers kept a copy, which they liked to share with reluctant girlfriends.

The first printed page stated in small print:

The Art of Making Love.
For the Modern Woman.
Prince Philipe Gusteau, Paris, 1862.
Translated from the French.

The author was a pseudonym and *The Art* was no translation at all, having been written and published in New York, then disseminated under the counter to enlightened men and women in the northern states. This was Jane's second reading. From the introduction:

> In my affairs with Parisian women I have learned much about the fairer sex. That this information is repressed and hidden by our society is unfortunate, but these pages are meant to unfold the truths of all womanhood. And make no mistake. Women are the same in London and New York and Moscow, as in Paris. Native cultures only alter the outward appearances, the dress perhaps, or the manners shown in polite society. Cultures do not -- cannot -- alter the inner soul of the intelligent woman, what they want and desire, how they behave in the uninhibited confines of the marriage chamber.
>
> ...women want to be held and caressed, which they sometimes mistaken for "love" or "affection." No! It is the physical need to be held and caressed by a man that they want. Yes, it is true that the man must care for his woman in the personal sense, to be kind and gentle and considerate. But all the "love" and "affection" expressed in ways other than physical will not satisfy -- nor should it -- the modern woman.
>
> The key is for the modern woman to understand that she has every much a right to physical satisfaction as her male companion, that she has the same physical needs as he does, and to work toward that mutual satisfaction. These pages will tell you how to accomplish that goal. For readers of my

work outside Paris, I trust the translation will not stint on
the details...

Without Polly in the house, the women had to prepare their own
meals, which meant trips to the kitchen. There was talk about one of
them cooking up a Christmas meal, but lacking agreement on who
would do it, and Jane making it clear she wasn't interested, the wom-
en decided to fend for themselves. Thus it was that they met in the
kitchen sometime mid-morning. All three wore their night clothes
and slippers.

"Merry Christmas," said Mrs. Gordon, as she hugged her two
daughters. "At least we have each other."

"Yes," said Abigale. "Do you think Johnny is all right?" *How would
mother know? Why do I even ask?*

"I'm sure he is, and he's having a very merry Christmas, fighting
the Yanks." Abigale did not think this was funny, and chose not to
respond.

"I suppose we should open the presents," said Mrs. Gordon.

The three of them walked to the tree and retrieved the gifts.
They were wrapped in old newspapers.

"Here, girls, for you," said Mrs. Gordon. Abigale and Jane dutifully unwrapped their presents: a hairbrush and pocket mirror for each.

"And for you Mother," said Abigale. "Jane and I pitched in and
bought this together."

Mrs. Gordon opened her present: an ornately carved box. She lifted the lid and the box played a simple melody, *Fur Elise,* by Beethoven.

"Oh, a music box, how nice. Thank you. It's lovely. Where did you
find this in Savannah?"

"At the old B&B Pawn Shop," said Abigale. "On West Broad. You
remember Mr. Pritzer, the owner?"

"Oh, yes, he's still around?"

"Still there. I went in last week, just to shop for something different, and saw it. Nice, don't you think?"

"Yes, dear."

"We're glad you like it, mother," said Abigale. *It's Christmas. Why do I feel so sad?*

———◆———

Around two in the afternoon there was a knock on the front door. None of the women was expecting a visitor or a message. Abigale instantly feared it might be another gift from Gustav or—God forbid!—the German himself. She asked her mother to open the door.

The caller was Sergeant Hendricks, one of the two soldiers who had escorted Jane home three days earlier.

"May I come in?" he asked.

Mrs. Gordon did not answer immediately, and Abigale, ever curious what he might want on Christmas day, spoke up. "Mother, ask the soldier in."

"Yes, of course, come in, sir"

What could he want now?

"May I speak with Miss Jane Gordon?" he asked.

"About what?" snapped her mother.

"I have a message from Captain Broderick, ma'am."

"You may give me the message."

"I see Miss Gordon," said the sergeant, pointing to just a few feet away, where Jane and Abigale stood. "I was asked to deliver the message directly, ma'am. It's a note, and I am to await a response."

"Let me see that message," said Mrs. Gordon.

"Mother!" interjected Abigale, "the message is for Jane. Let him give it to her. We will stay here. I am sure the sergeant won't object."

Mrs. Gordon motioned for Jane to come forward. "You heard my daughter. Please deliver your message."

Jane approached and the sergeant handed her an official-looking note, folded and sealed with a bit of wax.

"Should I open it now?" asked Jane.

"Of course," said her mother. "You will read it to us."

Jane did so, and began reading:

Miss Jane Gordon
27 Liberty St.
Savannah City
    I would be honored if you would accompany me to a dinner party on Sunday, January 1, 1865, at the home of Mr. and Mrs. Lamar Casey, 145 Habersham St. General John W. Geary, Military Governor of Savannah, will be hosting a private dinner party to celebrate the New Year. Upon your acceptance, I will arrange to escort you at 5:30 p.m. I hope you will be able to attend.
Yours,
Captain Jason Broderick
XII Corps., U.S. Army

"Yes!" exclaimed Jane, even before her sister or mother could make any comment.

"Jane," said her mother, "Do you know this captain? Who is he?"

By now Jane was swooning, speechless.

"Sergeant, I am her mother. She is not going to any party at the Caseys until I get some answers."

Abigale, just as curious, was less demanding. "Sir, my mother simply would like some more information. Who is Captain Broderick? We have not met him. And why is the party at the Caseys?"

"I understand ma'am. Captain Broderick is an aide-de-camp of General Geary, the military commander of Savannah while the army is stationed here. Both he and the general are billeted with the Caseys. He is having this dinner to thank them and several Savannah dignitaries for the smooth transition they have fostered."

His answer did not satisfy Abigale. "How would the captain even know my sister? This is most unclear."

"Abigale," said Jane, "leave the sergeant alone. I can answer that."

"Then please do."

"He was at the cemetery, when I was escorted home."

"He was going to arrest you, now he's inviting you to a party?"

"No, no. He was with that nasty colonel."

"Who is the colonel? I feel as though we are in some comedic farce," said Abigale.

"Oh dear," said Mrs. Gordon, now relegated to a bystander as Abigale took over the questioning.

"Ma'am, that would have been Colonel Ryan. Captain Broderick was with him at the time, on loan from the general, so that would be when they met."

"So there's a general, a colonel and a captain. And the captain is with the general?"

"Yes, ma'am. He's the general's aide-de-camp, or one of them. Colonel Ryan is in a different unit."

"Will he be at the party? Colonel Ryan, I mean."

"Don't know, ma'am."

"Abigale," said Jane, her voice raised, "Will you stop this inquisition? Please, enough."

"May I ask how old he is?"

"Who, ma'am?"

"Captain Broderick."

"Not sure ma'am. My guess he's in his early twenties."

"Do you know how old my sister is?"

"No, ma'am, I do not."

Abigale sensed that a quick affirmation of Jane's "yes" would be the wrong response. "Excuse me a minute," she said, then pulled Jane aside and motioned for her and their mother to come across the room.

Once out of earshot, Abigale spoke up. "Jane, you don't even know this captain. What's his interest in you?"

"Yes, Jane, please tell us," said their mother.

Jane glared at her sister. "Read this." She thrust the invitation in Abigale's hand.

"You just read it to us," said Abigale, who nonetheless perused the note. "It's just as you read it."

"He's a nice young man," said Jane. "He wasn't at all cruel like that old colonel, what's-his-name."

"Did you speak to the captain when you were being escorted out of the camp?"

"We said a few words. Not many. They didn't give me any time."

"Don't you think it's premature that he now asks you to a dinner party?" asked Abigale.

"And he's a Yankee," said Mrs. Gordon.

"Why don't you tell him you'll think about this, that you'll get back to him in a day or so," offered Abigale.

Jane looked hard at her sister, then her mother, then back at her sister. "Now listen to me, both of you. I am going. If you try to stop me, you will never see Jane Gordon again. Do I make myself clear? I have had enough of this nunnery life. This is an invitation to get away from here, if only for an evening. I am not a child any longer. You can't stop me. Unless you want to lose a sister." Then, without missing a step, she turned toward her mother and said, "Or a daughter."

"Oh, I don't want that to happen," said Mrs. Gordon.

Abigale was beat, and knew it. Further argument was pointless. She turned around and walked over to the waiting sergeant.

"Yes, my sister will attend."

"Excellent. I shall inform the captain."

"A question, sir, if I may ask."

"Certainly."

"Will there be other women there? I mean, your army does not come with women. So I am unclear as to the guest list."

"Yes ma'am. The Caseys will be there, it's in their home. And it's my understanding that local dignitaries will be accompanied by their spouses. How many, I do not know."

"One more question, sir. Could you please advise what time we may expect her to return home?"

"I will not be attending, but it's my understanding affairs of this nature typically end around nine thirty. So I would expect she should be returned home no later than around ten."

"That will be perfect, sir," said Abigale, feeling some relief. *At least she won't be spending the night.* "My sister will be ready. Please thank the captain for the invitation."

"Yes, ma'am." And with that he turned and left. Abigale closed the door behind him.

"Well," said Abigale, looking at Jane, "you seem to have caught the attention of another soldier."

"Oh, dear," said Mrs. Gordon.

———

CHAPTER 17

— SUNDAY, DECEMBER 25

THE *GOLDEN GATE* ARRIVED TO Fortress Monroe in Virginia just after midnight, December 25th. The *Golden Gate's* captain instructed the night adjutant to awaken the telegraph operator, as he had telegrams for the president: one from General Sherman and another from General Howard. Sherman's was the most pressing but they could be sent together. Sherman's handwritten missive was sent verbatim over the telegraph. It was promptly received by the war department's telegraph office and immediately transcribed in the hand of the receiving officer. The telegraph office was only a city block from the White House.

Sergeant Butler, on duty in the War Department, brought the message to the White House. He arrived to the front gate at 2 am and was received by the sentry on duty. Butler said he had a telegram for the president.

"Should I awake Mr. Lincoln?" asked the sentry.

Butler knew the contents. "Yes. It's a military matter."

Two aides later, Lincoln was awakened. He read the message, smiled and thanked his aide.

Mary Todd Lincoln was now awake. "Good news, I hope?" There were times before, when the news interrupting their sleep had been of a most depressing nature.

"Yes," he said. "General Sherman has Savannah, and he's offered it to me for Christmas!"

"Oh, that's marvelous," she said, and promptly returned to sleep.

Lincoln had known about Sherman's arrival to the vicinity of Savannah since December 12, from Navy messages sent from Ossabaw Sound. But he had not known the city was fully captured. What a glorious present! In the morning he would ask one of his aides to run down to the telegraph office and send Sherman's telegram to the New York Times. He also thought of an apt reply, which he would pen later that day.

———

Christmas 1864 at the White House was more festive than any since Lincoln took office. He had been re-elected largely because of Sherman's timely victory in Atlanta, and now Sherman had captured Savannah, and without bloodshed. Confederate John Bell Hood had been beaten in Tennessee by General George H. Thomas. All that really remained in the way of total Union victory was Lee's army of Northern Virginia, and Grant was closing in. The war would be over soon, that was certain.

Lincoln had a number of visitors for Sunday's Christmas Brunch, and he was glad to share the exciting news. He expected, as usual, to be buttonholed to do this or do that, and political battles were already looming about post-war reconstruction. The first three years had seen a series of less than competent Union generals come and go—George McClellan being the biggest disappointment—but now that he had Grant and Sherman in command, Lincoln was no longer second-guessed about military strategy.

The loss of life had been appalling, something neither side expected in 1861. But now Lincoln felt confident the war would soon end. Reconstruction was on his mind. Surely, rebuilding the South should not be nearly as difficult as fighting the war. His nemesis faction was the Radical Republicans, men who wanted the south punished for the war, and wanted the negroes to have instant equality. He would have to rein them in, and let the south gradually adjust to losing its economy and over 200,000 fighting men.

Lincoln was known for listening and weighing each argument, not being overly swayed by one faction or another. His cabinet had come to respect that quality, including the Radicals among them, or members who sided with the Radicals. Three of this group came for Christmas brunch: Salmon P. Chase, Chief Justice of the Supreme Court and ex-Secretary of the Treasury; Edwin M. Stanton, Secretary of War; and William H. Seward, Secretary of State.

Just before the buffet opened, the men stood and talked in the intimate Green Room. Lincoln was ebullient. With evident excitement he showed them Sherman's telegram, and a draft of his reply. They did not share his level of enthusiasm.

Chase spoke first. "Mr. President, this is indeed good news. General Sherman has done a masterful job in Georgia, but what about the negroes? Have they been totally freed? And have any signed on to fight for the Union?"

"Excellent questions, Salmon. Sherman is a highly competent general. I think he appreciates the will of this administration."

Stanton guffawed, a not so subtle counter to Lincoln's confidence in Sherman.

"Yes Edwin?" Lincoln acknowledged. He was used to the War Secretary's disagreements, which made him a valuable cabinet member.

"I don't think Salmon is questioning the General's military ability, only his attitude toward the negroes." Salmon nodded agreement, and Stanton continued. "Sherman is known to resist placing any of them in his army. And there is great concern that the negroes he *has* freed in his march may be wanting of life's basic necessities. If we are ever to rehabilitate the South, with its four million ex-slaves, the time to start is now. Sherman has won a masterful victory, I agree, but that may be his only concern, not the position of the Southern black people."

"Hear, hear!" interjected Chase.

Lincoln looked at Seward, to see how he might weigh in.

"Well, I agree," said the Secretary of State. "How can I not? Your Emancipation demands we do something beyond our military victory."

"So there we have it, I suppose," Lincoln replied. "I understand, gentleman, and I am well aware of your attitudes toward the issue. You would want all blacks to be equal at once, to vote, to have commerce with us. But let's be realistic. They have a long, long way to go."

"We must start somewhere," interjected Stanton.

"Yes, and we have, with legal liberation. General Sherman has done that in Georgia, and will soon do the same action in the Carolinas, of that I have no doubt. But let us be realistic. True *equality* is altogether different than a legal proclamation. It does no good to legislate against human nature; then you have achieved nothing and lost the respect of the legislation. The sooner we win the war, the sooner we can begin the long road of rehabilitation. And, at some point, equality. I am afraid it will not come in our lifetimes. Don't you agree?"

"Yes, Mr. President," said Seward," but perhaps you could send Edwin to talk to General Sherman, to see where he does stand. We know he's going to South Carolina very soon, and I'm not suggesting replacing him, of course not. But we need to make sure he is not alienating the very cause for which we have fought so hard."

"It's my understanding," replied Lincoln, in a tone of exasperation, "that the very cause was and is preserving the Union. We did not go to war to end slavery. The South went to war to preserve it. That's altogether different."

There was no response and the president continued. "Edwin, perhaps you should go to Savannah, talk to General Sherman. Would that be feasible?"

"Yes, of course, Mr. President. I could use a touch of warmer weather for my aching bones. I shall make the arrangements. It will have to be by sea, of course."

That night Lincoln finished his reply to General Sherman, which he would post the next day, and also sent a copy of Sherman's telegram for publication in the New York Times.[7]

In his thank you note Lincoln also acknowledged the December 1864 Union victory by General Thomas over General Hood's army in Tennessee.[8]

CHAPTER 18

— MONDAY, DECEMBER 26

ABIGALE'S APPOINTMENT WITH REVEREND SIMMS was scheduled for three o'clock and she was on time. The large masonry structure housing the First Ogeechee Colored Baptist Church was near the city's main market. In front of the church she noted a small group of soldiers on the front lawn, seated in between two tents, talking and playing board games. She assumed they were assigned to protect the church from whomever destroyed Third Baptist.

Polly had instructed her to go to the pastor's office in the back, and not use the front entrance. Abigale was glad for this direction, as she didn't want to engage with any of the soldiers. Behind the church she saw a lone soldier, but he seemed more a sentry for the whole rear area than a specific church guard. She walked up a brick path directly behind the church, past a small garden and came to a door marked "Pastor."

She knocked. Simms unlocked the door, opened it and welcomed her with "Come in, come in. I was expecting you." He relocked the door and showed her to a comfortable couch, then moved to his chair behind a large mahogany desk.

"Rufus, this is a much nicer office." She noted a Persian rug on the floor and two walls lined with bookshelves.

"Yes, but of course it's not mine. It does belong to First Ogeechee Colored Baptist Church, Pastor Clarence Patterson presiding."

"So he lets you use it?"

"Only on Sunday afternoon and Monday. I hold my service Sunday afternoon, and after the service come in here to meet with parishioners. And since Pastor Patterson is off on Mondays, I can use it then as well. I'm here today to finish paperwork."

"So I am paperwork?" joked Abigale.

"As I recall, Polly said *you* requested a follow up to our previous discussion. I was happy to oblige."

"That is true. Christmas was not a time of merriment in our house, as you can imagine. On top of everything else, Polly's estranged husband died on Saturday. I walked over with her to see him just that morning. She was alone with him that afternoon, when he passed. There is much sorrow in our household."

"I understand. Polly came here this morning and told me about Benjamin, but her concern was really more about you. She insisted I speak with you. Though you are not a member of our church, as Polly's mistress I count you as one of our flock."

"Is that like a flock of birds?"

"You do have a sense of humor, I must say."

"Sir, it is a sense of cynicism, I believe. Born of the times."

"You educated well," Simms replied. "Few of my congregation can even read."

"The Drayton Finishing School. I did complete the final level. And my father was an attorney, so I am used to having books around."

"And yet you retain that lilting southern accent, those drawn out words. So different from the north. I am not offended."

"Offended? I don't understand? Why should my accent offend you?"

"It does not, coming from your lips. But from the lips of others, it often portends a degree of bigotry. Of ignorance. Forgive me, it is an association hard to part with. But in you, the accent is somehow becoming. Charming is a better word."

"Well, thank you. That is fortunate, because I have no intention of changing, even if I could."

"And I would not want you to. As to books," said Simms, "Pastor Patterson has quite a few." He pointed to the bookshelves. "Feel free to browse, if you wish."

"Thank you. What are your plans for Third Baptist?"

"Did you come to inquire about our rebuilding?"

"Among other things."

"We are planning to rebuild, and soon, I might add. That will be my next construction project. Savannah's negro ministers have volunteered to help in fund raising, and the Union government will be providing assistance with security. I trust you saw the soldiers camped in front?"

"Yes, most surprising."

"After we explained the burning to General Sherman, he was appalled. He has positioned soldiers around all the black churches. We are unlikely to be assaulted again, at least not while Sherman is here. As for my own church, we should start rebuilding soon."

"Is Mayor Arnold investigating the culprits? I understand it was arson."

"Ostensibly."

"Ostensibly it was arson?"

"No, no. You are very quick, madam. Ostensibly he, or rather the police, are investigating. I imagine the mayor has more pressing matters at this point, with the occupation. I have met with police authorities, but do not expect any justice. A proper investigation would require many questions of people not sympathetic to a colored church."

"I heard the perpetrators wore hoods."

"Yes, in the manner of cowards."

"Any idea who they were?"

"None, as to specific names. Since they rode quickly, like young men, and carried rifles, my hunch is they are rebel deserters, hiding out somewhere."

"Well, the times are certainly favorable for rebuilding, with General Sherman in town and the other ministers behind you. Your congregation has followed you here, to First Baptist?"

"Yes, those who can make it, and you are welcome to come as well. For the near future my services will be held Sunday afternoons at two, so perhaps not as convenient."

"The time is not inconvenient, though we did remain house-bound yesterday. In your sermon, are you still preaching the light is coming?"

Simms let out a laugh. "No, the light has arrived. I do remind them that they must be patient, that new laws will be written and they must wait. It's too soon to know how the change will evolve."

"And do you still speak in Gullah?"

"Only the first part. I grew up learning Gullah, and many of my congregation do understand the dialect."

"I almost walked out when you started that way."

"Well, I am glad you did not."

"Did you mean those things you said at Third Baptist, when I was there?"

"I said a lot of things, Mrs. Tate. The people are largely unedu-cated, and I speak to them in a way they can understand. But I don't believe I misspoke. Anything in particular?"

"Yes, you said war widows and war mothers and war sisters have all suffered, together with negroes. That we are all children of God, something like that."

"Yes, have we not suffered together?"

"Well, white folk are born free, as are very few negroes. And most of us do read and write. Why did you include our suffering with the negroes?"

"Why not, if I may ask? Your dead are as dead as our dead. We are all human, of the same flesh and bone. When Polly first told me of your losses, I cringed. I felt the pain you must feel every day. The killing is so senseless. So utterly senseless. Doesn't matter if it's negro or white in the grave. We all have family ties, kinfolk that help define who we are. In some ways, white folks' losses are more severe."

"Why is that?"

"Slavery as an economic policy is not sustainable. Your losses are for a lost cause."

"Policy? Sir, I am not an expert on these matters, as you may be, but we don't think of it as a policy. I do believe it is written into the constitution of the country we were once part of."

"Mrs. Tate, you are the smartest woman I have ever met."

Abigale blushed. *That's exactly what Susan Tate told me. The same words! Why do I come across that way?*

His comment brought back memories of dinner table conversations with her father, when he would give some viewpoint, and she would take the opposite one, and they would spar in a friendly manner. Her younger brother seldom took part. All her family knew, but never stated outright, that she was the smarter one. If not a woman, she could have been a lawyer. The thought nagged at her but she quickly put it aside.

Simms continued. "Call it what you wish, slavery's basis is economics. Free labor. Yet for so many young men to die trying to maintain the institution makes no sense. The northern states gave up slavery years ago, and they still operate under the very same constitution. Europe abandoned slavery decades ago. The world is changing. Slavery could not be sustained indefinitely in the South."

"Why not?"

"Do you really want this discussion? I am happy to oblige, but have fear of boring you."

"You are decidedly not boring me. Do you want me to return the compliment? I will. You are the smartest negro I have ever met. Please, continue."

"Very well. If there was no Civil War, and the South went about its business as usual, slave economy and all, it would have fallen further and further behind as the North continued to grow in population and prosperity. Held a decade or two later, a war that has taken four years would probably be over in four months, so great would be the disparity between the two sides. Have you been to New York?"

"I have not been out of Georgia, except once to South Carolina."

"It is an amazing city, forty times the size of Savannah. So energetic. Factories and warehouses everywhere. New York trades with Europe, and has more ships in one port than all of the South had before the war. Slavery makes southern white men lazy. They lollygag while their brothers in the north use paid labor to build factories and buildings and, dare I say, weapons, the likes of which the South could never match. The past four years, the South has been fighting to maintain the unmaintainable and—" Simms stopped in mid-sentence.

"Yes?" she asked.

"I apologize. I must sound so strident about the futility of the fighting, and that is disrespectful of you, and your losses. Very sorry. Forgive me."

"You speak ... you speak like you attended school up north. Such big words. I have not met many men who speak so clearly. I don't understand how—"

"How I came to sound so educated?"

"For want of a better word, yes. You belie what I was taught to think of the negro."

"We are not all illiterate. As I explained before, I had the advantage of educated and loving parents. I was reading the Bible at age five. The newspaper of our little island when I was six. I read any books we could find. Did you ever hear of Frederick Douglass?"

"No, can't say as I have."

"He's probably the most literate negro in America, a free black from Maryland, though he now lives in Washington. He has called for the abolition of slavery for years, written essays, and even advised President Lincoln in the White House. And he's not that old, in his late forties. Douglass writes and speaks clearly. I heard him once on a trip to New York. It was eye opening for me, that a colored man could be so eloquent and inspiring. I introduced myself afterwards and shook his hand. You know what he said?"

"Probably that you should leave Savannah."

Simms laughed. "I wasn't in Savannah then, still on Jekyll Island. He said, 'Rufus, don't give up. We shall prevail. Don't give up.' His words have guided me ever since."

"Your parents, are they still in Jekyll?"

"Sadly, they are deceased. Natural causes."

"So they were not slaves?"

"No, both free. My grandfather was white."

"Really?"

"A plantation owner. My grandmother was one of his slaves. Their child was my mother, a mulatto. When she was of school age, he saw to it that she be taught to read and write. I admit to some advantage there."

So that explains it! "And she married a free colored?"

"Yes, now I believe you know the whole family genealogy."

"Did you ever meet your grandfather?"

"No, he died when I was an infant."

"If I may ask, why did you stay in the South? Why not migrate up north, to be with Mr. Douglass and his kind."

"A fair question. This is my home, in spite of the war and the way our people have been treated, I feel comfortable here. In the north I would feel uprooted. And here I can have a more positive effect on my people."

"A missionary among your own people."

"Never thought of it that way. There is something of the poet in you, Abigale. May I call you Abigale?"

She nodded.

"And you may call me Rufus."

Abigale felt a need to shift the conversation back to the present situation. "Do you really think things will change now that the Union looks like they're going to prevail?"

"Not right away, no. The South won't give up its traditions so easily. They will lose the war because they're tired and worn out, weary.

There are just not many men left to fight. But the poison, it's still there, and will be for a long time. Of that I am certain."

He is so self-assured. Father was like that.

"It's just tragic that you and other white folks have had to suffer these losses over and over. Polly said you had the melancholy. She didn't use that word, but her description fit my understanding of the condition. I have studied the melancholy, and know how it can affect people. I try to mollify it when counselling some of my parishioners."

"The melancholy? Yes, I have heard that term also. I would call it a feeling of despair. Have *you* ever had that feeling?"

She didn't expect to be asking so many personal questions. Family history, yes, but not inquiry into his soul. Did she have the right? Yet the question came easily. How would he answer?

To her surprise he just stared at her, then turned around to gaze out the room's solitary window behind his desk. Ever curious, Abigale waited for a response.

Turning back around, he said, "Yes, I have."

His face had changed. Now it showed sadness, a certain pensiveness, and perhaps, she thought, he was even close to tears. She would ask no more.

"Two sons, deceased," he said.

"Oh my God! I'm so sorry."

"Thank you. I often do not understand God's way, and for a long while did think Him to be evil. But I've reconciled."

"They passed from illness?"

"One son, Rufus, Jr., when he was less than a year old. And the other when he was nine. Both ill with the fever."

"So you have tasted despair."

"I have drunk fully from the cup, yes."

"Then you *do* understand, perhaps."

"Life is short, and we must take what comes."

"And now your wife is ill?"

"Not ill, as with fever, but weak. She is able to do some things, but not everything a wife normally does."

His wife is no longer his lover? Will he reveal more? "You are opaque, Rufus."

"I have already divulged more than I should. These things are not a secret, but a pastor's personal life should never intrude when counseling others. It is a matter of ethics."

"Ethics?" Abigale let out a small laugh.

"Why do you find that funny?"

"Sir, you are too formal. I have lost a husband and father. And did I neglect to mention, a child aborted in my womb but two years ago, when my husband was at away at war, and therefore no chance to have another until he returned. Which he never will."

"I am sorry. I knew nothing of that situation."

"You have lost two sons and, if I may be so bold, perhaps a wife's affection. Now I see we are both sufferers of the melancholy. You have no doubt heard the phrase, 'Misery loves company'?" She laughed once more, a forced laugh.

"I came here to help ease my pain," she continued, looking him hard in the eyes. "Now I see you are perhaps also needful of such help."

"Your boldness is astonishing, Abigale. And refreshing, I will admit. But the truth is, I am no longer miserable. I have reconciled. Which you should do as well."

"How?" Before he could answer she added, "So you met with General Sherman?"

His eyebrows arched, reflecting surprise at her pivot. Abigale sensed he welcomed a change in topic.

"Yes, very briefly, as I mentioned earlier, about the church. I met him along with some of our negro ministers, this past Saturday, just two days after he arrived. He is approachable, and understands the concerns of our race. I do believe Mr. Lincoln wants to right the wrongs my people have suffered, and Sherman is one of his emissaries."

"It is difficult for me to be dispassionate about the man. While Sherman was attacking Atlanta his soldiers killed my husband." *Let him justify that fact.*

"And if you were to confront him, he would not deny your allegation. He would not boast of it, but would not shy away either. This general is very single-minded. His goal is to end the war and preserve the Union. He would have much preferred there *be* no battle for Atlanta. I am sure he would rather be home with his own family than sitting in Mr. Green's mansion, plotting his next move through the Carolinas."

"That helps me not."

"I understand. But talking about the losses does help most people. It is a matter of showing not sympathy, but empathy."

"Empathy?"

"Putting yourself in someone else's shoes, then showing them you understand their situation. No amount of talking can bring back the dead, but those who feel what you call despair can learn to cope. They have to be counseled, which is what I do."

"Then I will stop being a wiseacre child. You may counsel me."

"It takes time. Do you read the Bible?"

"Not any longer."

"There are verses in there that can help most folks. However, I sense you may be skeptical of what the Bible has to offer."

"Try me."

"'The Lord himself goes before you and will be with you; he will never leave you nor forsake you. Do not be afraid; do not be discouraged.' That is Deuteronomy, thirty-one eight. There are many other such uplifting passages."

"You would do better with my mother, who reads the Bible regularly."

They both gave a low chuckle.

"And she has the melancholy?"

"I suppose she does, as well my younger sister Jane, who doesn't read the Bible at all."

"Abigale, the despair you describe, or what I call the melancholy, is natural. People who don't have despair over something like this are not fully human. You are human. You are a most sensitive soul, if ever I met one. A beautiful and intelligent woman with a full life ahead of you. You have everything to live for."

His insight gave her a warm feeling, and she sensed some lifting of her despair and cynicism. Perhaps there is some solace in the Bible, she thought, at least when quoted by this man, who seemed to be wise, patient, and understanding. Could she continue meeting him here?

There followed a lull in the conversation and they simply looked at each other, one gaze more piercing than the other. Then a new feeling came upon her, one she tried to suppress: physical attraction. The realization was sudden, and scary. *This is most unnatural. I should leave now.*

After a full minute of silence, she said, "You are most kind, Mr. Simms."

"Rufus. We agreed, remember?"

She started to cry. *I don't like this feeling. I should leave.*

Simms got up and closed the window curtains, turning the brightly lit room into a dusky twilight. He pulled out a handkerchief, walked over to the couch and sat beside her.

"Most kind," she repeated, between quiet sobs. She took his handkerchief and dabbed at her tears.

He took her hands in his.

"I really must be going," she said, half-heartedly, her head bent down.

"I would like you to stay."

"Why?"

"Look at me, Abigale." She did, and began shaking, as if a chill had just entered the room.

"I will not force myself on you," he said. "That is not the Lord's way. That is not my way. You must be strong, and be sure."

Simms pulled her toward him and gently moved one hand up and down the back of her neck. "You have the nicest hair."

She did not move away, nor show any reluctance. Then he kissed her, lightly at first, and she did not resist. He kissed her again, harder, more passionately. She relished the sensation, of being held by a man, and returned the kiss and the passion. Then he moved her hand to his thigh and she felt his hardness.

What am I doing? This is so wrong. He is not my kind. My kind? What is my kind? He is a man and I am so in need of love. Oh God, help me!

She pushed away and stood up.

Simms stood also, now a foot away, his eyes on hers. "What's the matter? I trust you are not offended."

"Offended? Not at all. I am flattered by your attention. I need some time to think, to reflect on our discussion."

"I know this, Abigale. You desire me as much as I do you. No matter my color. You want what I can give you."

"Sir...Rufus...I am...I am just not ready for intimacy. I am still in mourning. You are married. You are..." She paused, not wishing to finish the sentence.

He finished it for her. "A black man."

"I must go, really I must," she said, and walked toward the door.

"Wait, I'll unlock it." He opened the bolt. "Will I see you again? Ever again?"

"Please, I need some time to think, to reflect."

"My door is always open for you. Do not think me presumptuous, please. We can help each other." He leaned over and kissed her on the forehead.

She opened the door and he stepped back, so as not to be seen from the street.

"You will return," he said.

Now in the doorway, Abigale replied, "Was that a question?"

"No."

"Goodbye, Rufus."

———◆———

CHAPTER 19

— *Monday, December 26*

Savannah Gardens was always open, but its main business did not typically start until after 8 p.m. That's when the local men showed up to
pay three dollars for a stint with one of Gustav's ladies. Now almost
all his customers were Union soldiers, except for a few Confederates
unfit for military duty or who, through cowardice, deserted Hardee's
army before it evacuated.

One of those cowards was Ignatius, whom Gustav first met two
days after Hardee's army skedaddled from the city. Being a new customer, Gustav asked for his name.

"Just call me Ignatius. You don't need my last name."

"What you do here? You are young, strong, have Savannah accent.
I smell a Confederate soldier," Gustav challenged. "You should be
with your troops in Carolina, Yes?"

The not-too-bright Ignatius replied, lamely, "I was sick that night.
Couldn't go."

"Yah, yah, I understand," said Gustav, feigning the understanding-
uncle routine he liked to use on dumbbells. "You know, Mr. Ignatz—"

"Ignatius."

"Yes, Ignatius. You know, the Union army doesn't like deserters,
whether they wear your gray or their blue."

"I ain't no deserter, Gustav. Watch your tongue."

"Of course not, of course not. I think in all honesty you are a smart
young man, and perhaps could use a few extra dollars, is that not so?"

"What you talking about, old man?"

"I have a proposition."

"Let me hear."

"First things first. Tell me, do you have any schooling? Can you read, write?"

"I ain't illiterate, if that's what you mean. Did the eighth grade."

"Good, good. My proposition requires an educated man, just like yourself. Not difficult job, but must have what we in Europe call "Gehirnen.""

"Greenin', you say?"

"Smarts. Brains. Ah, sometimes my English not best way to say things, I use German."

"I get your meaning."

"Good. I need you to scout a certain individual, without being noticed, and report back to me her movements about the city. I will give you the home address. I want you to watch the house until she leaves, then follow wherever she goes and report back to me. Of course, if you are noticed and questioned, you will say nothing about me. At the same time, I will know nothing about your illness the night of the river crossing. We have a deal?"

"That ain't no proposition. I got to watch this house all day. For what?"

"Ah, yes, I forget sometimes these important things. Bring me useful information and I will reward you with three dollars. Or one of my lovelies. Your choice. But don't come to me with nothing. I want to know her whereabouts, as well as you can follow. Without of course, being discovered."

"That's more like it. She one of your honeys? Looking to see if she's cheatin' on you?" Ignatius let out a laugh and Gustav smiled.

"Ah, yes, as I said, you are a very smart man, Ignatius. Remember, you know nothing about me or our agreement, if ever asked, under any circumstances. And I will know nothing about you. On the other foot, as you people in Savannah like to say, if I hear you've mentioned my name, well, General Sherman is my good friend. He would like to know we have one of Hardee's boys who missed the bridge. I do believe he is still at war with your countrymen."

Gustav loved his veiled threat, thought it most clever, but noted Ignatius seemed puzzled.

"Voar?" Ignatius asked. "Oh, oh, *war*. That's some accent, man. Yeah, we's still at war."

This fellow is a dunce. He does not think to ask how Sherman, who only just arrived, could be my good friend.

"So, Ignatius, we have a deal?"

"Well, right now, I ain't got nothing better to do during the day, so give me her name and where she lives. I can find some work on her street, I guess, make it look like I'm busy."

"Excellent. We'll give it a few days. This is a busy time of year for her and she should be out and about."

Gustav provided the relevant information, careful to distinguish between Abigale and her younger sister, a difference he hoped Ignatius could discern from a suitable distance. He liked the teen-age girl also, but his interest was in Abigale. He harbored a vague suspicion – so far without any evidence – that she must have a secret lover. Someone so secret that she would not want anyone to find out. He liked knowing such secrets, especially if they could provide information for *erpressung*: 'blackmail'.

The deal consummated, Gustav congratulated himself on maneuvering the witless deserter to do his bidding.

———

Four days after General Sherman entered the city he issued Special Field Orders No. 143 for 1864. They made clear, in case anyone doubted, that he was in full command of the city. [9]

———◆———

— MONDAY, DECEMBER 26

POLLY'S SISTER LIVED ON LOWRY Plantation, only six miles west of West Broad Street. Benjamin's unexpected death interrupted Polly's plan to leave Savannah December 24, on the plantation's hay wagon. There was no transportation Christmas day, so she got a ride the next day, leaving around two p.m. That gave her ample time in the morning to visit Reverend Simms, and explain Abigale's need to see him.

Lucy, her husband Digby and son Sam lived in one of the Lowry's slave shacks adjacent to the rice fields, which were now flooded and non-productive. The Confederates had opened the flood gates just days before Sherman's troops arrived, as one way to slow down the invasion.

The plantation held forty slaves at its peak but was now down to just twenty, the rest having run away, to where no one really knew. From contact with the hay wagon driver in early December, Polly knew Lucy was still around. "Tell her I'll be dere Christmas week," she said.

The hay wagon pulled into the slave quarters just as the sun was setting. Lucy, now twenty-six, was home but Digby was not. Digby wasn't really her husband, not in the eyes of legal Georgia, since no marriage certificate had ever been issued. They had had a slave ceremony a few years back, jumping over a broom and singing a Gullah hymn, which meant they were married in the eyes of the other slaves.

Lucy cried out on seeing Polly and ran to hug her. "I so sorry. I heard about Benjamin."

"Nuthin to be sorry for. Da Lord took him, just like he gonna take me and you one day."

"You always was a strong one, Polly. Come in."

Sam held tight his mother's skirt. Polly picked him up and gave a big hug. "Sam, you is getting' big. You treatin' your momma nice?"

"I is four," he said. She carried him inside the shack.

Inside was a 400-square foot space, its floor raised on bricks to keep out snakes and other vermin. A stove and chimney occupied one corner, and two beds lay against a side wall, with a small table and chair in the middle of the floor space. Polly had stayed here before and knew what to expect. She was always happy on arriving, to be with her sister, and always happy on leaving, to return to the luxury of Liberty Street.

"Where be your Digby?"

"Lord knows dat," said Lucy. "He keep a talkin' about joining dem Yankee soldiers, spending lots of time w' dem. Sleeping in da' camp, tending dere horses and such. Ain't seen him since yesterday morning."

"He wasn't home fo' Christmas?"

"Just da morning. Said da Yankees needed him for cookin' and servin'. Dey's celebratin' Christmas too."

On previous visits Polly had slept on a corncob and Spanish moss mattress laid on the floor. She saw no mattress this time. And no Christmas tree. Liberty Street always had a Christmas tree. She did smell the sweet aroma of soup cooking over the fire.

"I be sleepin' here?" she asked.

"Heavens no. We got you your own place. Half the black folks done left. You gonna be next door. Empty now, but dere's a bed and stove inside. Hope you ain't gonna be lonely over there."

Polly was thrilled. She didn't expect any privacy during the week. "Where'd they all go?"

"Lord knows. When da Yankees come close, they just took off, figured no one gonna stop 'em. They's right, too. Digby thinkin' of leaving, but don't know where we'd go. We's gonna wait it out, see what happens. All kinds of noise and talk and such."

"Same thing in Savannah. No one knows much. But I see you gots what to eat, dat's good."

"We gots food. The Yankees don't mess wi' us. True to tell, dey don't seem to care much about us."

"What's happenin now? You workin' the fields?"

"Ain't no fields to work. Dem all flooded. Truth to tell, sister, we is freer now den ever. But don't know what's happenin. Jus don't know. What 'bout you? I heard Miss Abigale's husband done got killed."

"Mighty sad, mighty sad. They's a sad bunch, they is. Still treat me good, but the house is cold. I gots her to go see Reverend Simms, to cheer her up."

"Ummm."

"I walked over dere with her. She sat through the service. And she been back, too. She don't much care for the sermons, though. He keeps a talkin' about the light and such, how we gonna be free."

"So she burned the church down?" Lucy let out a big laugh at her joke. Everyone on the plantation knew about the fire.

"Taint funny, Lucy. The next mornin' I took her to look at what's left. Taint funny. They could a killed somebody."

"Well, it would be us niggers they be killing, if anyone. Thank the lord the Yankees done got here, or we'd be all gone. What else you got there?"

"Where?"

"Back in Savannah. That nigger hater ain't back home, is he? He's the one ought to have been killed."

"You mean Johnny Gordon?"

"Dat be the one."

"Ain't heard nothin' 'bout him. Still fightin' I guess. Just me and the women. The mother, and dat brat of a sister, Jane."

"You got yo' hands full, taking care of dem. What you gonna do now youse free?"

"Free?"

"As a bird, sister. It be the law of Mr. Linkum, and the Yankees here to make it so."

"Don't mean nothin'. Everyone seems to be just talkin'. Even Miss Abigale aks me that same question. Jus like you said, where I'm gonna go? Where you and Digby gonna go? We gots no schoolin. No money. What free be to me and you?"

"Soup's ready, sister. Let's eat."

Polly found the soup delicious and they consumed every drop. Sam practically drank his bowlful like a slurping dog. A little rice was thrown in to give bulk, but after the meal Polly still felt a bit hungry, and wished Lucy had served some bread. *But I don't need no more food. Be good to lose a few pounds this week.*

There was a knock on the door, and a voice outside. "Singin' beginnin' now, Miss Lucy."

"What's that?" asked Polly.

"It be Christmas, we go sing outside, until the cold run us off."

The women and Sam left the shack and gathered with half a dozen other negroes around a brisk log fire. The air was a crisp fifty degrees, but no wind. Without printed music, or accompanying instruments, they sang many songs, including *Silent Night, Oh Come All Ye Faithful, Deck the Halls*, and *Hark, the Herald Angels Sing*. Polly knew some of the words, and hummed what she didn't know.

———◆———

That Lucy, Digby and Sam remained together through the war was a matter of luck, and laziness. The slave trade, or rather the price of slaves, had plummeted with each Yankee victory, and by October it was almost zero. No one wanted to buy slaves if they were going to be emancipated soon.

The laziness was on the part of Master Lowry, an old man who did not delegate, yet was himself too frail and disinterested to start wheeling and dealing slaves. "That's for the younger men," he was heard to say on more than one occasion.

So Lucy and Digby stayed in the plantation's rice fields, at least until shortly before Sherman arrived. Now it would be weeks before the fields could be drained, replanted and harvested.

In fact, Polly arrived at a most unusual time. The principal crop at Lowry's was now Union soldiers. At least 1000 were camped on the 700 acre property, mostly around the homestead and available dry land, and there was nothing Lowry could do about it.

The soldiers awaited orders. The slaves awaited their emancipation. Mr. Lowry and his family awaited deliverance from the uncertainty of having their property temporarily confiscated. The one good thing about it being Christmas was that no one expected much to happen during the holidays. They could sit back and relax, enjoy the quiet period.

———

The next morning Polly awoke later than usual, around 7 a.m. She dressed, found the outhouse and after cleaning up walked over to Lucy's shack.

"How'd you sleep, sister?" Lucy asked.

"Good 'n deep. Tired from yesterday."

"Well, we got some vittles for you. Genuine grits."

Polly didn't much care for grits but, being hungry, did not complain.

"Got word Digby's on his way back from da' Union camp," said Lucy. "Dey got runners to deliver da news. Don't know what time but afore lunch I'm told."

"Were you expecting him?"

"I don't expect nothin'. He comes when he comes. As I said, he does work for da' troops. If dey tell him to skat, he skats, comes home."

"Is he joining the army?"

"Don't think they take black folks. That's what I hear from da others."

The two woman and Sam sat around the small table, consuming their grits and some small biscuits.

"Didn't know you had bread in da' house," said Polly. "Could a had some last night."

"Just a little. I saves it for—"

The front door burst open, as if by a strong wind. Polly jerked around to see the figure of Digby, filthy in overalls and bib, exuding a strong barnyard smell. He carried a canvas bag in one hand that appeared to be heavy from the way it stretched to the floor boards.

"Digby!" Lucy screamed. "You scared the bejeezeus out of us, jumping in like that. Which you got in the bag? Say hello to Polly."

"Daddy!" Sam jumped up from his chair and ran to his father's legs. "Is this for me?"

Digby dropped the bag, lifted his son and gave him a hug. "This is for all of us." He put Sam down, carried the bag over and placed it on the table. "This is gen-u-wine pig. Courtesy of the third Union Cavalry."

"Lord a' mighty," cried Lucy, "we eats tonight. What else they pay you with?"

"Just this." He reached in his pocket and pulled out a silver dollar.

"We is gonna get rich off them Yankees, we is," said Lucy. "Is you joinin' up?"

"They don't take colored soldiers. Orders of Gen'l Sherman. I knows our kind fights up north, but this general, he don't want any. But they's lookin' for laborers. I just might get a chance to go with 'em to Carolina."

"Jus' you?" asked Lucy. "What about us?" She pointed to Sam.

"Too soon to know much mo'. But marching with the army no place for a woman and child."

Polly could sense tension over the subject, but said nothing.

"Come, have some grits," said Lucy. "You must be hungry."

"I got vittles at the camp before leaving. Got to go roast this pig, salt the meat away for later. We'll have some tonight. How you doin', Polly? Haven't seen you in a long time."

"I'm doin' fine, Digby."

"We got lots to talk about," he said, then picked up the pig and went outside.

Polly could only wonder what he meant by 'lots to talk about'.

———◆———

CHAPTER 21

— *TUESDAY, DECEMBER 27*

ANOTHER KNOCK ON THE DOOR, another message for Abigale. She thanked the messenger, a young black boy who looked to be about twelve.

"I was asked to wait for a reply, ma'am." He stood on the porch, just outside the doorway, while she opened the envelope and read the note:

> **Abigale Tate**
> **27 Liberty Street**
>   *I respectfully request the honor of your company to the home of Mr. and Mrs. Lamar Casey, Friday, December 30ᵗʰ, 6 pm. A dinner party hosted by General John W. Geary, Military Commander of Savannah. Please affirm and I will make all arrangements for your safe travel, etc.*
> **Your obedient servant,**
> **Mayor Richard Arnold, M.D.**

This is the same dinner party Jane was invited to. What is going on here? I will decline, of course.

Before saying no, she first decided to learn more about this party and that meant going to the source.

"I will have a reply shortly, within a day's time," she told the messenger, trying to hide any indication that she might accept or reject the invite. "I must check on some things."

The boy nodded and returned to the street. She closed the door, retrieved her coat from the closet, then yelled up to her mother that she was going for a walk. Within minutes she was on her way to the Casey residence on Habersham Street.

She noted a white fellow cleaning the street, his face covered with a scarf against the cold. But it wasn't that cold, so she figured the scarf was to keep from inhaling dust, and thought no more about it. She reached the residence in about fifteen minutes.

Fortunately, she found Mrs. Casey at home. "Come in, come in dear," said Lucretia. "What's on your mind?" She ushered Abigale to the living room and a comfortable chair.

Once seated, Abigale wasted no time explaining her reason for coming. "Over the last two days we have received invitations to a party in your home, one from a young captain inviting my sister Jane, and one from the Mayor, inviting myself."

"The mayor's invited you?"

"Yes."

"You are half his age. No, less than half."

"He was close to my father, as you know."

"Well, dear, I assure you it's nothing more than a social invitation. I doubt he has designs. Since his wife Margaret died in 1850 he could have married a dozen women, but chose not to. He is very devoted to his politics, and to his medical practice when he's not running for mayor. Anyway, it's a party Lamar is throwing for our new house guest, General Geary, plus the mayor and his council."

"General Geary is your house guest?"

"Yes, I thought I mentioned it to you last Saturday, when you were here."

"You said a general, but didn't give his name.

"Oh, then that's because I didn't know at the time. He's the general in charge of the city."

"Yes, I know. The one our very mayor surrendered to."

"The same. Now our dear military commander. And he's staying in our home."

"At the point of a gun?"

"Oh no, no, nothing like that. You are a bit dramatic. These Union men, they are gentlemen. No, by request, though if we had refused, who knows?"

"And this Captain, Broderick, I believe his name is?"

"A fine young man, from Pennsylvania of all places. He is the one inviting your sister?"

"Yes."

"Well, Captain Broderick is the general's aide, so I suppose he's entitled to come and bring a guest. He is staying with us as well. It's Lamar's idea to have the party, so the general and our civic leaders can meet in a more social setting."

"What does he hope to gain, if I may ask?" *He wants his cotton saved, I'm sure.*

"He just wants to be on the good side of both sides, if you know what I mean. The occupation promises to be peaceful, and he wants it to stay that way. Come and join us. You will have a grand time."

"You know I cannot."

"Oh? Why not?"

Abigale thought carefully before answering. "Because I am still in mourning. It is too soon to celebrate, let alone celebrate a Union victory, and with a man twice my age."

"Arnold's wealthy, you know. A doctor and a politician. You cannot best that combination."

"I'll send mother."

"Henrietta? Your mother?"

"Why not? She's forty four, much closer in age to the mayor."

"Dear, whomever the mayor wants to bring is fine with me. And I don't want to be too personal here, but I don't think Henrietta has been out of her house since your father died."

"I'll ask her. Now that I have a better understanding. If she agrees I will ask the mayor. I should hope it would make no difference to him. This is a better idea the more I think about it. Mother can keep an eye on my sister."

"Your sister needs an eye kept on her?"

"In a manner, yes. We know nothing about this young captain."

"As I said, he's a nice man."

They talked some more, nothing substantial, and all the while Abigale plotted something bolder than just sending her mother to the party with Mayor Arnold.

———————

"Oh dear," said Mrs. Gordon. "Lucretia wants me to attend her party? I haven't been to their house since before your father was killed. What will I do there?"

"Mother, there will be solders at the party, including the general in charge of Savannah. I will find someone to escort you, if you agree to go."

Abigale considered the possibility Arnold would balk at taking her mother and so was careful not to mention any specific name. If her plan didn't work out she would just say all the soldiers were spoken for, and her mother would lose nothing. However, that would wreck another part of her plan, so she needed to act quickly and carefully.

"And besides, mother, Jane will be there. Don't you want to keep an eye on her?"

"Yes, dear, that is true. Well, if you can work out the details, then I will go."

"Excellent, mother. Give me a couple of days. I will let you know."

Abigale could not trust the next step to a written note. She would have to see the mayor in person. *He should be in his City Exchange office, working on occupation policies. Getting in should not be difficult.*

———◆———

Abigale stopped before the stone-faced Exchange building. Along with the Customs House and Christ Church, it was one of Savannah's grandest structures. She walked up to the second floor office and in the outer room encountered a male secretary.

"Who should I say is calling, ma'am?"

"Mrs. Abigale Tate."

"Do you have an appointment?"

"Yes, but it's probably not recorded. He sent me a note, said to come right away, so he's expecting me."

"Let me see if he's busy." The secretary knocked, then entered the mayor's office and closed the door behind him. In less than half a minute Arnold was out to greet her.

"Abigale, what brings you here? Come in, come in." He motioned his secretary to return to work and ushered Abigale into his office.

She gave a quick look around the room. Fourteen foot high ceilings, molded cornices, a picture of George Washington on one wall and a large map of Savannah on another. And something else caught her eye, sitting upright on its own floor stand. "I've not seen your office here before, but I notice the United States flag. Is that new?"

"Yes, yes, we have an agreement. We are now under the command of the United States, so all artifacts must reflect that position. I must say, you are very observant. I trust you got my invitation?"

"Yes, that's why I came to see you."

"Good. General Geary will be there, so this is a very important gathering. The Caseys have invited me and my aldermen and their wives, plus I believe his aide de camp. A small party. I understand your family knows Lucretia and Lamar, so it will be very cordial."

"Richard – may I call you Richard?"

"By all means, by all means."

The mayor sat on the front edge of his large oak desk while Abigale stood in the middle of the room. She planned for a quick visit.

"I do appreciate your thoughtfulness, Richard, but wanted to explain in person. I am still in a period of mourning. True, I don't wear black, as you know, but I fear it is way too soon to participate in festivities such as a party with the Union general. Especially considering the circumstances of Franklin's death. I hope you will understand, and I wanted to tell you in person."

She could see true disappointment on his face. Lest it gain momentum and lead to her eviction, she quickly added, "But I have an idea."

"You do?"

"Yes, mother would love to go. She has not been out of the house for quite a while, and though you have not seen her lately, she is quite the woman when dressed up. I think you will find her very attractive and entertaining, and you two have so much in common."

"Please, please sit down." Richard motioned her to a high-backed, thickly upholstered chair. He rubbed his chin, which to Abigale meant her proposal was under consideration.

"Just so you know, Richard, I have discussed this idea with mother and she will be delighted. And of course I will forever be in your debt for such a gallant action."

"To be honest Abigale, I have been lonely since my wife died. I was planning to go with or without you. I fully recognize our age difference, but find you compellingly attractive, and thought you would enjoy a night out at the Caseys. But I understand your concern and will honor your wishes. I will be delighted to escort your mother. You may tell her so."

"Excellent!" Abigale was ecstatic. "You are wonderful, Richard, I shall be ever so grateful. I will await mother's report of this grand affair, and only wish I could participate freely and happily. But perhaps another day." *I will give him something, without giving him anything.*

———

The pieces of her plan were coming together nicely, but there was more work to do. *I will see this through, but where to find Rufus?*

As it was Tuesday, she assumed he would not be at Pastor Patterson's First Ogeechee Colored Baptist church. But what about his own church, Third Ogeechee Colored, or what was left of it? She would take the chance.

The church site was about a mile from the City Exchange. Her legs felt strong and she found walking the city invigorating. In fact, it was somewhat of a novelty, for now there were so many more people in the business district compared to a week before. Many were wandering negroes, from the plantations, who somehow managed to find shelter at night and food during the day. Others were soldiers in blue. Still others were well dressed white folk she didn't recognize.

And something else new caught her eye: tall ships docked on the river. With the river cleared of debris and the blockade lifted, shipping was returning to the port, at a rate quicker than she thought possible. And now new people – not just soldiers and plantation slaves – were coming in. Would Savannah begin to prosper with the Yankee victory? Perhaps so, she thought, perhaps so.

She walked briskly over to Williams Street. When near where the church used to stand she noted several workmen around the charred foundation. Was he one of them?

Yes! Oh good fortune.

Like the others, Rufus wore carpenter's overalls. He held a saw in one hand and seemed to be examining a pile of lumber. Now came the difficult part: getting him over to her, speaking with him privately while out in the open, and without raising the slightest suspicion among his co-workers.

Abigale stood on the sidewalk in front of the church and approached the first workman she encountered.

"Would you please ask Mr. Simms to come see me for a moment? Please tell him it's to enquire about his work on my horse barn."

The message delivered, he came promptly over to her. Now they were out of earshot of the other workers.

"Hello, Abigale. Horse barn?"

Abigale moved her arms as if measuring a shelf or a dresser. But her words were not about shelves or furniture or carpentry. She spoke quickly, explained her plan, her idea for a meeting, the exact time and circumstances. It was a one-opportunity circumstance, she explained, but a grand opportunity, one he should most welcome.

If he did not agree – or perhaps he had an unbreakable commitment for that day and hour – there would be no meeting. Then she would be alone, at home, during the Caseys' party.

He had a few questions, a few doubts, a few what-ifs. She addressed them all.

Yes, he could do the carpentry work. Yes, the date and time were acceptable. Yes, he would follow her instructions.

CHAPTER 22

— TUESDAY, DECEMBER 27

LUCY AND HER FAMILY INDEED ate well thanks to Digby's enterprise: roast pig, potatoes, and some cider he also managed to sequester from the army camp.

"We is so stuffed," said Polly, "I wouldn't a know'd we is slaves. Look at lil' Sam playin w' them bones. He is sure a cute one." The boy was banging pig bones on his plate, to some innate rhythm.

"Sam, cut that out," yelled his mother.

"No, let him be. Dat's good," said Polly. "He got rhythm, be a musician some day. Keep banging Sam. I likes it."

The boy obeyed.

"Glad you liked the pig," said Digby. "Gots more salted away for later in week."

"Yeh," said Lucy. "Gots what to eat, dat's for sure. But we still be slaves, sister. These be strange times. Massa Lowry hisself a prisoner I hear speak, or at least he ain't a running things no mo'. But dese troops, dey ain't staying forever, ain't dat right Digby?"

"That is right. So right. They don't give a rat's ass about us, north or south. When they leave, who knows what will be? One thing sure, tho."

"What dat be?" asked Polly.

"As soon as they can get them rice fields drained, we'll be back at 'em. Unless we leaves out of here."

"You keep talking, and I keep saying, where we gonna go?" asked his wife.

"Same place as the other coloreds what followed Sherman here. I hear tell thousands left their plantations, now they scattered around Savannah."

"Are they goin' with him when he picks up and leaves?"

"Could be. We'll see. If they do, I might go with 'em."

"You said that yistaday. What about me and Sam? He's too young to be a marchin' in the winter."

"I'll think of somethin'."

"Let's me know before you done go off again."

Digby did not reply, and Polly filled in the lull. She remained curious about his comment the day before. "Digby, which you want to talk to me about?"

He paused before replying. She figured maybe he was thinking about what to say.

"Polly, what you gonna do, now that you are free?"

"I sure ain't a gonna go marchin' to Carolina with a bunch of them Yankees."

"You staying with that family of yours, then?"

"They been good to me. Why not?"

"What they paying you?"

His question caught her off guard. She knew he knew the answer – zero in dollars – and sensed he might be trying to provoke her. She didn't feel like arguing with her sister's husband, but needed to offer some response.

"Don't get no wages, you know that."

"Then you ain't nothin' but a house nigger."

"Digby! Watch yo' tongue. Don't talk to my sister like that."

"Shut up, Lucy. Don't mean no disrespect, Polly, but you act like a slave, that's how they gonna treat you. You need to go back and demand your wages."

"Yeh, you knows what happens then," said Lucy. "Then they wants you to pay for your bed and vittles, and you end up the same – dead broke. That's what I hear gonna happen when we go back to the fields. Lowry gonna pay and take it right back for this shack and what we eats. The white folks, they gonna get you, one way or t'other."

Polly had not thought much about the economics of slavery, but now her sister seemed to make sense. "So what's the use?" she asked.

"I'll tell you the use," offered Digby. "They pay you, and like Lucy says, then they take the money fo' your food and such. But then you ask for more, see? They say no, then *you* say you gonna pay *less* for your bed and food."

"You mean argue money with da white folks?"

"Dat's what I mean."

"And if'n they still say no?"

"Then you walk."

"Walk? To where?"

"I mean leave, go find a job somewhere else."

"What you mean, Digby?"

"If you never gonna demand your freedom they ain't gonna give it to you. No proclamation, nothing, don't matter. Now with Sherman here, they can't lock you up or keep you from walkin'. They still gonna need you, you house nigger."

"Digby!"

"That's all you are. Sure, they treats you nice now, maybe, but wait til that brother gets his ass home. He ain't gonna treat you any different than befo' the war, probably worse. You know why?"

Polly shook her head.

"Cause he lost the war! His side lost. And he's gonna blame it right on you and your colored face. He's gonna blame the colored. You just watch out. He ain't gonna be friendly. If you are lucky he will take a bullet wherever the hell he is."

Polly started to cry. Cry because she knew there was some truth in his words. Cry because she just lost her husband, estranged though they were. Cry because Liberty Street, with all its luxury compared to the Lowry slave shack, was a fountain of moroseness. Cry because she was 'free' and it didn't mean a damn thing; if any-thing, it gave choices that bewildered her. *What's gonna be?*

"Digby, see what you done?" admonished Lucy.

"I done nothin' but told the truth. I ain't gonna stay around this plantation and be treated like a slave no more."

CHAPTER 23

— *TUESDAY, DECEMBER 27*

"YOU BACK ALREADY?" ASKED GUSTAV.

"You got my money?" replied Ignatius.

The two men stood in the foyer of Savannah Gardens, close to 8 p.m.

"If you have some information to tell me?"

"A day's worth," said Ignatius. "Your honey sure do like to walk. Nearly wore me out."

"Tell me."

"Let me see the money."

"I said the money or one of my girls."

"You said "my choice, Gustav. "I had one of your girls last night. Now need the money."

Gustav unlocked a drawer, removed some coins, then relocked it.

"I have the coins," he said, and showed three silver dollars to his spy. "Now, tell me."

"She left the house and walked over to this address, a fancy mansion on Habersham." He handed a slip of paper to Gustav. "She stayed about half an hour."

"Just a half hour?" *Not enough time for a lovers' tryst.*

"No more, just as I said."

"Good, will be easy to see who lives there. Someone of wealth, for sure."

"Then she walked downtown to the City Exchange. I stayed across the street. Again, there about a half hour."

"Umm," said Gustav. "That's the mayor's office. Also keep property records there. Please, continue."

"Then, and by now my legs is getting tired—"

"Maybe that's why you didn't walk across the bridge," said Gustav, and immediately regretted his comment. *Dummkopf! Let him speak, don't stop him with insults.*

"Ain't funny, you old man. Her next stop might interest you."

"I do apologize, Ignatius. Please, please continue."

"She walks over to where they burned that church last week, Baptist something or other. You know, that nigger church."

Gustav's eyes widened in anticipation. "Yes, I am aware of it. Please, go on."

"They had a bunch of darkies doing some construction there. She goes up to one of them, says something, and then he goes and fetches another darkie, who comes over to her. They talk maybe ten minutes. She uses a lot of hand motions, like she's describing some piece of furniture or something. Then he gets back to work and she leaves and walks home."

"Are you sure she went home?"

"Sure as my name is Ignatius. I followed her from a distance, saw her enter the house. Just where she started in the morning. Twenty-seven Liberty Street."

"Good, good."

"I ain't done yet. I'll show you I earned my dollars. I walked back to the church and played dumb."

Not hard to do, thought Gustav, though he had to admit Ignatius was delivering.

"What did you do?"

"I asked if there was any job I could do, that I was looking for work. The first darkie I asked told me to see another one – the very man who your woman talked to for ten minutes. I walked over and introduced myself, and asked his name. He said he was Rufus Simms, pastor of this burned down church, and how could he help me. I'm looking for work, I said, which was not untrue."

"What did he say?" Gustav could not believe his good fortune in finding Ignatius, and assigning him at the right time to this task.

"He said he was sorry, but all the men there were volunteers, and they had no money for wages. I sort of figured as much. Then he asked me if I had any information about who might have scorched his church. I said I was sorry, I had no idea, which is also true, and I thanked him and left. Stopped to get some chow and now I'm here."

"Very good job. You do deserve your dollars." Gustav deposited the coins into Ignatius's outstretched hand.

"Do you want me to keep following her? At some point she may get suspicious."

"Good point. Let's hold off for a while, let me think on it. Umm, if you happen to see her out and about, maybe see where she goes, but don't spend your day waiting at her house. If you have some information obtained this way, let me know, we negotiate."

"Negotiate?"

"Not three dollars every time. No, no. But maybe a little something for more information. Very informal. Savannah is a small city, you see her, where she goes, yes, I would like to know. But do not be noticed."

"I don't think she noticed me at all."

"Good, good. Now, would you like to spend those dollars on one of my lovelies this evening?"

"No thanks. I'm going to get me a beer."

— *Wednesday, December 28*

Unlike any Southern city so far invaded, Savannah had fully capitulated, ensuring peace if not immediate prosperity. This result could be attributed to the confluence of two remarkable situations:

General Hardee's complete evacuation of troops, and Mayor Arnold's attitude and level of cooperation. Though some damned the mayor for cozying up to the conquerors so readily, he had an easy reply: "Where resistance is hopeless it is criminal to make it."

To facilitate a return to normalcy and set an agenda for the coming months, Mayor Arnold arranged a special town meeting the evening of December 28. Among the resolutions passed were a formal acknowledgment of Union victory, specific praise for General Geary, and a request that Georgia's governor convene a constitutional convention to reverse the call for secession.[10]

CHAPTER 24

— *Friday, December 30-evening*

Jane felt giddy on entering the Caseys' spacious home. A real party, she thought, with guests and food and servants to wait on us. And no gloom. She hated the moroseness that hung about her own home. Yes, the party was on behalf of the 'hated' Yankees, but so what? Her escort was a Yankee, a rather handsome one at that.

She had visited the house years ago, and remembered some of the rooms and furniture, particularly the giant oak table in the dining room. It seemed impossibly big back then, but now she thought it merely large. It sat the fourteen guests comfortably—eight men and six women.

The women included herself, her mother Henrietta, Mrs. Casey, and wives of three aldermen. The men included General Geary and Lamar Casey seated at opposite ends, and along the sides, intermingled with the women, Captain Jason Broderick, Mayor Richard Arnold and four aldermen. Two black servants stood behind Lamar, ready to serve the guests.

Lucretia Casey arranged the seating. Thus did Henrietta sit between Mayor Richard Arnold and Jane, Jane between her mother and Captain Broderick.

"Let me propose a toast," said Lamar, standing with wine glass in hand. "To our own Mayor Arnold and General Geary, for the way they handled the situation last week. I won't mince words. Working together, they saved our city from destruction, needless destruction. No one is happy with this war, and anything we can do to lessen the carnage, the better off we'll all be."

Glasses clanged and clinked.

Jane cringed but tried not to show it. *I'm no dummy, no matter what mother and Abigale think. I've lost my father and brother-in-law to this war. Let's not kid ourselves, Mr. Casey. And why is mother smiling? Is it for show? Is she not bothered being in the presence of these Union soldiers?*

Geary rose to speak. He came dressed in full uniform, as soldiers did not go to battle carrying civilian clothes.

"My goodness," whispered Jane to her date, "he is tall."

Broderick nodded, then whispered, "Yes, six feet five inches. Taller even than our president."

"Let me second that, Lamar," said General Geary. "War is hell, as my commander likes to say, and to be feted in your fine home a week after we arrived, is probably a first in the annals of war. I too wish it were all over. I would much rather be with my wife, to know her comfort, and be free of this conflict. I am not here to make any speeches, but want you to know we do appreciate your hospitality, and will do everything possible to make our stay short and unintrusive."

More clanging of glasses. Jane took a small sip of wine. *He does not look at mother or me. Does he know about father? About Abigale's husband? Did Mrs. Casey tell him?* She decided to let go of these thoughts, and enjoy the evening. She, too, would have wine, drink freely, unless her mother tore the glass out of her hand.

Geary and Casey took their seats, and Mayor Arnold immediately stood up. "Well, I'd like to say a few words."

"Just a few," said Alderman Henry Brigham, a comment that brought laughter around the table.

"Thanks, Henry, I'll get you later." More laughter. "This is serious business, this war, and I, too, am thankful Savannah has been spared the destruction that has befallen Atlanta and other southern cities. General Geary was receptive to our entreaties when we met in the middle of the night last week. And General Sherman has continued a policy of rapprochement, so we are optimistic. I say, let's toast to Savannah's bright future!"

Applause, and shouts of "Hear-hear!"

As soon as the noise died down, and the mayor took his seat, Lucretia Casey rose. "You men aren't going to get off so easily. Now it's a woman's chance to speak." All were silent.

"I say…let's eat!"

"Hooray!" someone yelled. The servants retreated to the kitchen and in a few minutes returned with the first course.

Jane enjoyed the food, the mingling and most of all the red wine. Her mother didn't seem to notice, or if she did, chose not to comment. Mostly Henrietta talked with the mayor, and across the table to Alderman Brigham and his wife, a comely woman who looked older than her spouse by ten years.

Jane and Broderick started off with small talk, as befit a first date. Inevitably, the question arose from the captain. "You said your brother is in the army. How about your father, what does he do?"

"He's dead. A colonel with Robert E. Lee. Killed at Gettysburg."

"Oh. I'm sorry."

Your army killed him. "Thank you. You weren't at Gettysburg, were you?" She sincerely hoped not.

"No, fortunately. I was in Virginia that summer, in the Shenandoah Valley. My regiment never got orders to march to Pennsylvania."

Strange, she thought, she didn't feel animosity toward him over her father's death. He's a soldier. Daddy could just as well have killed him in some god-forsaken battle.

With the succession of courses – soup, chicken, a rice dish – conversation between the captain and his teen-age date grew freer, not war talk but personal information. He grew up in Scranton, went to a military academy, has two sisters. Jane is the youngest child, has one brother and one sister, and so forth. She gave her age as eighteen – not quite true, but almost – and he gave his as twenty-two.

He is smart, courageous, handsome.

She fell for him, she wanted him, a feeling that felt natural.

Same as I felt with Winston, this yearning. I know this is a normal desire. It is mother and Abigale who are not normal.

The wine helped. She felt a slight bit tipsy, so when Broderick told a funny story, it seemed natural to touch his arm, and say, "Oh, that's funny!" Just a light touch, but a message clearly stating 'I like you'.

There were other brief touches during the meal, eliciting no notice by the other diners. At the height of the wine's affect she let her hand fall on his thigh and rest there a moment. Their eyes hooked, conveying in her mind desire, both ways. *I know he wants me.*

Jason caressed her hand under the table, then gently removed it from his thigh, all the while looking into her eyes. He leaned over and whispered: "You have lovely eyes, Jane."

"Thank you." *We have communicated. I have him. But when. Where? Oh, I hate this stuffy dinner party!*

"Let me see how my mother is holding out," she said, and turned her attention to Henrietta and Mayor Richard Arnold.

"Is your meal good, Mother? This is the best we've eaten, I fear, in a while."

"Yes," Henrietta replied. "Mayor Arnold was just reminding me of dinners we had when your father was alive, with food this good."

"Agree," said the mayor, his voice slightly raised, so Jane could hear above the table chatter. "You were just a little girl back then, maybe seven or eight. Cute as a button, I might add."

"You flatter me, Mr. Mayor," said Jane.

"Oh, you can call me Richard."

"Oh, well," said Jane, "I will, then. Richard, I do have a question I've been meaning to ask you."

"Go ahead."

"Do we allow brothels in Savannah?"

Heads turned, at least the few that could hear her question.

"Jane! What kind of question is that for Mayor Arnold?"

"Mother, he said I could ask a question. He's the mayor, he should know."

"Richard," said Brigham from across the table, "the young lady has asked a question, a not unreasonable one I might add."

By now everyone turned to look at Jane, though not all heard the preamble.

"What's that?" someone called out, from four people away.

"This young lady has asked our mayor if we allow brothels in the city of Savannah," explained Brigham. "And the mayor is about to answer." All heads turned to the mayor.

"As we are now under military command," proclaimed Arnold, in a faux-speechifying voice, and looking toward Geary's end of the table, "I will defer to the military commander on matters of morality."

"Not so fast, Richard," replied Geary. "I'm not getting involved in that one. I will say, though, that our soldiers are forbidden to visit houses of ill repute. That's the official policy. On the other hand, I will also say we do nothing to stop them, or to punish our soldiers who go to these places, unless they miss roll call. So, Mr. Mayor, the question remains for you to address. Please, you may leave me out of it."

Jane had started something that now had a momentum of its own. Had she suddenly disappeared, or taken leave to attend to personal hygiene, the question would still be hanging above the table, wanting an answer.

"Well," said Arnold, "I see I am on the docket for this one. Like the good general, we have an official policy as well. Brothels are illegal. But, also like his army, we cannot police every establishment year round. So, truth to tell, if there is such an entity in our city limits, I would not be surprised. I hope that answers your question, young lady."

Applause. "Spoken like a true politician," someone offered.

Mayor Arnold leaned across Henrietta to speak in a whisper to Jane. "Why did you ask that?"

"Abigale says Mr. Gustav Heinz runs a brothel. Does he?"

"We'll talk later," Arnold replied, and he returned to his upright position.

"Oh my," said Henrietta.

"Henrietta," asked Arnold, "where *is* that other lovely daughter of yours tonight?"

"Home alone, I'm afraid. Still mourning. Poor child."

— *Friday, December 30-evening*

Rufus knocked on the back door at twenty seven Liberty Street and Abigale quickly opened it.

"Come in. Did you have any trouble, anyone see you?"

"Not as I know. Left my horse two blocks away at Gideon's Stable, just as you suggested. I take it no one is home."

"Mother and Jane left about forty-five minutes ago. That's when I placed the lantern in the back. This is all very clandestine. And working too well, I fear."

"Why do you fear?"

"Just an expression, Rufus. I hope for the best and expect the worst."

"And I hope for the best and expect the best. A better philosophy."

"Here, give me your coat. How far did you have to travel? I don't even know where you live.

"About a mile from here, actually. In Yamacraw. You ever been to the Free Colored District?"

"No. No reason to. Strange, isn't it? Never even thought about where the Free Colored live."

"We have houses like you do, though not nearly as fancy. Frame construction, just two rooms. Mine's right on corner of Zubley and West Boundary Street. You should come visit sometime."

"And meet your wife? No thank you."

"I believe we are starting on the wrong foot."

"Agreed. Did the men at the church suspect anything?"

"No, your performance was brilliant. Told them you hired me for a small carpentry job."

"And your wife? What did you tell her, if I may ask?"

"She is used to my going out at night, to see parishioners, or work late in the church. I have not told her anything."

"I suppose there is nothing to tell. It is all very platonic."

Rufus did not respond.

"Come, let's sit down. You comfort me with your conversation. I fear going crazy without someone to talk to, someone who understands and can sympathize."

"Remember, it's empathy, not sympathy."

"Yes, of course. Empathy. Empathize. It rhymes."

They moved to the couch, but as soon as Rufus sat down Abigale pivoted to a side chair.

"Abigale, did you invite me over just to talk?"

"Yes, and because I trust you. I do not fear you, though you are a man, and could, I suppose, overpower me. I do not fear that."

"Then you know my wish is to have you."

"Please, that is not my purpose. I wish you to accept that for now." She regretted saying "for now."

Rufus did not question what she meant. "So it is more of therapy, for the melancholy?" he asked.

"No. It is more of two like-minded friends helping each other through difficult times."

He laughed. "Like-minded? I don't think there could two more un-like-minded creatures in God's universe."

"Why in heaven's name do you say that?"

"Why? Just look at this situation. First, man and woman. The two sexes don't think alike. Men create war, women create life. Big difference, there. Then there's race. I'm of the slave race, you are of the master class. How you came to accept someone like myself on any equal footing remains a mystery."

"A mystery to me as well," she said. "I felt repulsed by your sermons, at least at first. They were alien to my culture, the way my parents raised me. The war has upended all that. Upended everything."

"All to the good."

"Yes, I can appreciate you have a different perspective."

"You use such big words."

"Sorry. Around you, I tend to get pedantic."

"There you go again. Platonic, perspective, pedantic. You do like your p's."

They both laughed.

"Here's another P for you," she said. "Polly. Now she is free, though what that will mean I don't know. She doesn't read or write. What will she do? Strange, though, as I think about her."

"What?"

"Until her husband died, and I saw her at his deathbed, I always thought she was happy, certainly happier than us Gordon girls. Now I have my doubts. His death brought out something in her, an inner misery I never before appreciated. Now I wish she could be free in ways other than what's written on a piece of paper, but I fear that's not possible."

"You mean free to take care of herself, to be her own person?"

"Yes, you put it well. Would you like some tea?"

"Yes, that would be nice."

Abigale set a kettle in the fireplace to boil water. "Mother made some Christmas cake, I'll go get some."

She returned from the kitchen with two pieces.

"I think we may be leaving crumbs as evidence," he said. "And you will have to explain why you ate such a big piece of cake."

"Oh, that won't be a problem. Mother knows I love her cake. And I of course will clean up any crumbs. They won't be home for at least two more hours."

"And what if they return early?"

"You are here to measure for shelving in the barn."

"At night?"

"You work all day to rebuild your church."

"You think of these things, I suppose. I would prefer to be long gone when they return. I think you are naïve in these matters. Very naïve, in fact."

"How so?"

"A colored man alone with a white woman of the upper classes, in her home, at night? My brethren have been lynched for far less. I would rather not make myself vulnerable. A word from you that I forced myself in the house, or assaulted you, and I would not see the morning sun."

Abigale did not respond, but thought on his comments. He had a valid point, but at the moment she held a more pressing thought: how to end the evening. By giving herself to him? Or by keeping her distance, an evening of dialogue only?

The former would separate her forever from her heritage and culture. She might as well move up north and join a congregation of abolitionists.

The latter would deny her true needs, for love and affection, especially the affection of a person she admired more by the passing minute. And if family came in while they were embraced? Yes, the noise of their arrival should give Rufus time to exit through the back alley. But what if they heard no one approach, perhaps due to their own lustful sounds, and Jane and her mother entered with their escorts? He could be killed, she banished or worse. All these thoughts came in an instant. *Was it right to invite him? I am so lonely.*

"You seem deep in thought, Abigale."

"You scare me with your comments, Rufus. Not seeing the morning sun if we are discovered? I am not that kind of person."

"Of course not, which is why I came at your invitation. But others can contrive, invent, anything to damn the colored. You are a like a child playing with fire, putting yourself in my sphere."

"Your sphere? Whatever do you mean?"

"You are like an innocent girl who has come upon a swamp, and is oh so curious to wade into it, to see if it's really full of snakes and scorpions and alligators. You are totally unprepared for what may happen, but your curiosity is getting the best of you. So you wade in."

"My, you do have a literary bent, Rufus. Perhaps I am not so innocent. Perhaps I enter with full armor."

"Or none at all."

"The tea is ready." She poured the boiling water over tea leaves in the cups, and handed one to him.

"Thank you. This is good and hot."

Abigale remained standing, and walked over to the fireplace. "It is true this meeting would have been inconceivable until recent events. Something has changed, and now it doesn't seem so strange after all."

"But you are anti- negro at heart, no matter your opinion of me. You would subjugate us, whip us, destroy us, you and your countrymen."

"Why do you lump me with them? You are being most unkind."

"I am only speaking the truth. I have no illusions. The one thing that binds us, maybe the only thing, is that we are man and woman, with physical and emotional needs. You have so much as admitted that. But look what must be overcome! Centuries of white attitudes about slavery, race, economic servitude."

"Rufus! Stop lecturing me. And stop blaming me for all that. I don't deserve it. And I have changed. I am changing."

"True. Your invitation speaks to that. And also, I might add, your concerns about Polly. But it is not so easy to undo what one has learned from childhood."

"You want to label me a negro-hater, no matter what I say or do?"

"No. No. I only want to make you aware of how deeply rooted are the prejudices we – my race – must overcome. Even by people as enlightened as you are."

"I am more enlightened now, as you put it, than before I met you."

"But still shackled by your culture. Hence the ruse to get me here. The back door entrance. The fear of being found out. All necessary because of the prejudices."

"I don't deny that. But now that we are alone, I feel liberated from that culture."

"Then come over here."

"What?"

"Come over here," he said. "You are a woman, I am a man. By your words, alone now, race is not an impediment. Please, sit next to me. Let me hold you."

"No. I fear that will repeat last week, in your office."

"Yes, of course. Come over here. Now."

"Please Rufus, don't command me. Please don't."

"It is not a command, but a request. Come here, sit beside me."

She did not move, except to put her cup on the mantle lest it fall from her hands.

"Rufus, don't do this."

"Then ask me to leave."

"I don't want you to leave. Not now." *Why does he challenge me so?*

"Abigale, go open the back door and I will walk out."

She did not move.

"No? Then come, sit beside me."

She kept her position, stared at him, knowing full well she revealed indecision, borne out of fear and desire. Fear *and* desire. *He knows it!*

He stood up, walked to the fireplace. She did not move, nor flinch.

"Look at me, Abigale." She raised her head and he kissed her. She did not push him away, nor resist. She could have, but did not.

He put his arms around her and kissed again. He put his tongue in her mouth and she accepted it, relishing its smooth sensation. She shook and he held her, and she felt his manhood.

I can stop this now, I should stop this now. O Lord, help me to decide. Help me to decide.

———◆———

Henrietta and Jane returned home together in one carriage, accompanied by Captain Broderick. Mayor Arnold stayed behind at the Casey mansion, to speak privately with Major Geary.

On the way home, Henrietta sat opposite her daughter and the captain, who held hands.

"Mother, are you upset Mayor Arnold didn't escort you home?"

"Heavens no, I'm actually glad. It was easier to say our goodbyes at the Caseys, than on the porch of my own home. He's a nice man, but not for me. Too political."

"In what way, Mrs. Gordon, if I may ask?"

"Oh, Mr. Broderick—"

"Please, call me Jason."

"Yes, of course, Jason. I mean he's got priorities serving the citizens, and now cozying up to our conquerors. It's no wonder he never remarried. Probably too busy. Not the kind of man a mature woman would want."

"Mother, he's very nice. I hope I didn't scare him away with my question."

"I'm sure you did not, honey. Don't you worry. I'll be fine. Did he ever answer your question about that man Gustav what's-his-name?"

"No, the mayor sort of avoided me after the dinner. As I expected. He's probably in cahoots."

Broderick laughed. "The mayor?"

"Well, if it's true the brothels are illegal, how do you explain it?"

Broderick did not offer an answer. The carriage pulled up to the house and the driver jumped down to assist the women. Jason told him to wait, that he would return in a moment.

At the foot of the stairs leading to the stoop, Jane asked her mother to go inside alone.

"I'll be up in a minute, Mother. I just want to say goodbye to Jason."

"Yes, dear. Don't be long." Henrietta climbed the stairs, entered the house and shut the door.

Alone, the two young people kissed in the dim light of the stoop's lamp, a more passionate kiss than might be warranted on a first date. Then they spoke rapidly, about a next date, where and when, and with each decision Jane nodded yes. Another deep kiss, and Jason returned to the carriage. He waited a moment until she entered the house and the front door closed.

Jane found her mother in the living room, being debriefed by Abigale.

"So," said Abigale, "mother tells me you and the young captain got along splendidly."

"He's a nice man," said Jane, with as little emotion as possible. "But mother and the mayor are also compatible, I believe."

"Jane was quite the belle tonight, though she upset the apple cart a little, if I may say so."

"Oh, how so?" asked Abigale. "Please, tell me."

Henrietta recounted Jane's question and the mayor's response, and how "the whole table joined in."

Abigale laughed. Looking at Jane, she said, "Good for you. Sometimes being very young helps. I don't think I would have been brave enough to ask that question."

"And what did you do tonight, all alone?" asked Mrs. Gordon.

"Oh, I read, and played the piano a little. The time did pass."

END OF PART 1

PART 2: 1865

CHAPTER 26

— THURSDAY, JANUARY 5

SAVANNAH WAS SPARED THE DESTRUCTION visited on the rest of Georgia, at least that 60-mile-wide swath cut by Sherman's troops as they marched 300 miles from Atlanta. General Hardee's timely departure, coupled with Mayor Arnold's ready submission, made for an unusually peaceful transition during time of war.

But politics and military probity could not feed the masses, and food, or the lack thereof for the poor citizens, including thousands of negroes who migrated off the plantations to join his troops, remained perhaps Sherman's biggest headache. As *The New York Times* reported on January 5, 1865, "There is absolute want of the necessary means of subsistence. Rice abounds [but] they cannot subsist entirely on rice."[11]

Thus was borne the idea of sending an emissary to the north, one Julian Allen, to trade rice for other food stuffs. As the plan unfolded, it would gain momentum, and go a long way toward feeding the hungry of Savannah.

The aristocracy and upper class were affected as well, but never to the point of hunger or shelter. Their old Confederate bills were no longer of value, but they found other means to pay: hoarded coins, family jewels, silverware, simple barter, even IOUs. Thus places that catered to the moneyed classes still flourished, especially if, like The Pulaski House Hotel, they could also serve the occupying army. Built in the late 1830s, the hotel occupied the corner of Bull and Bryan Streets, across from Johnson Square. Now Savannah's finest hotel, it was one of the first places Sherman stopped on his horse ride into town, since he intended placing his headquarters there.

Sherman changed plans when Charles Green made him a better housing offer, free use of his mansion on Madison Square. Pulaski House management had no remorse over losing the general, since there was no guarantee the U.S. government would pay for all the rooms he needed.

The hotel saw its business actually increase with the Occupation – mainly from Union officers who could afford the nightly rental. While many officers found lodging with wealthy Savannahians, a few chose the hotel for its greater privacy. And some used the hotel for one-night trysts with ladies of the town.

Pulaski House did not rent rooms to the free Colored, an uncontested policy since none of that group ever tried to find a room there. The hotel did rent to unaccompanied women, a policy dating to its inception, when traveling female singers and actresses came to town for performances.

Since the naval blockade there were no out of town entertainers, of either sex. There were, however, occasional women who rented because they needed a place to stay after a divorce, or because they had sold a home and were planning to move elsewhere. Or, as suspected by management but never questioned, because they had chosen the hotel for a night of private business. As long as the customer impressed as a lady and not a tramp, and paid the $3 hotel fee, she secured the room.

Thus when Abigale showed up at the desk, asking for a room, no questions were asked by the young male clerk, except "how many nights will you be staying?"

"One," she said, "until the workmen finish the painting in our home. Too much fumes to stay there tonight. I would like to see the room first, before registering, to assure it meets the standards of a young lady." She stated her request in a straightforward manner, to impress that she would not rent anything less than first class.

"Yes, ma'am," said the clerk. "I can give you a key if you wish to inspect one of our rooms. "Do you have your bags with you?"

"I will be returning in the evening, and will bring my suitcase then. That is, of course, if I decide to rent the room. First floor is preferred."

"Yes. Here is the key to room 115. Just down the hallway to your right. I trust you will find that one to your liking."

"Thank you."

Her plan was to make sure the room was suitable and suitably private, then pay the fee, then inform Rufus, who was waiting outside. They would return after sundown, around 6:30, she arriving first. He would come a few minutes later, knock twice and she would let him in. Besides arriving in the dark, layers of clothing would help assure anonymity on entering the hotel. By 9 p.m. she would be ready to return to Liberty Street.

Guests filled the lobby, many in uniform. She saw no familiar faces. Key in hand, she walked down the long corridor toward room 115, somewhat surprised by the size of the place and that it had so many rooms.

She felt a sudden doubt. *What am I doing here? Is this a wise move? What if someone recognizes me?*

On the way she passed the wing's lavatory, one for men and one for women: an indoor outhouse, fancied up and cleaned several times a day.

She unlocked the door to room 115. Inside she found a double-sized bed, a dresser, wash basin and a well-padded chair. The room was quiet and appeared quite comfortable.

This will do nicely. I will pay the fee and let him know.

She exited the room and turned left toward the lobby. Just at that moment she saw a young girl exit the lavatory and walk toward her. They made eye contact.

"Jane?"

"Abigale? What are *you* doing here?"

"I could ask the same."

Jane approached her older sister. "No secrets. Captain Broderick has a room here. It's the one place we can meet with any privacy."

"Are you spending the night?" asked Abigale.

"Of course not. Just the afternoon. I'll be home soon. How about you?"

"Me?"

"Yes. Are you moving out, taking up lodging here? I see you have a room key. A short stay?"

I could say I was following her to make sure she was not in any danger, but that would be a lie and she would know it.

"This Captain Broderick, he is the man who escorted you to the Casey party? I must say, you don't waste any time."

"Abigale, I have no secrets. I am of age. I am not going to waste my life—"

"Like I am?"

"I didn't say that. But maybe you've quit resisting normal female desires. Coming or going? Here, let me help you. Is this your room? Where is your suitcase?"

I can't continue with this. Oh, my God! Why did I arrange for such a public place to meet him?

"I have no suitcase. I…I just wanted to be alone for a while. I did not intend to spend the night here." *What am I saying? She's not stupid.* "Now, I've changed my mind. I'm not checking in. I'm going home."

"Oh, don't let me spoil your plans. Who is it? The mayor? General Geary? The general didn't have an escort at the Caseys' party. Or maybe that handsome alderman, what's-his-name, the one with the ugly wife."

Good. At least she doesn't suspect Rufus.

Abigale re-opened the door to room 115. "See? Empty. Satisfied?"

"What time does he arrive?"

"Stop it, Jane. There's no one here." *Thank goodness.* "I'll see you at home. I don't think we should upset mother, who I assume knows nothing about your trysts. So we'll keep this little meeting a secret."

"Suits me. You're the one with the secrets, it seems."

Jane returned to the hallway and walked to the room harboring her lover. Abigale shut the door and walked back to the registration area. She told the clerk the room felt too drafty, that she wouldn't be staying there after all. He offered her another room. She said no, she decided to sleep at home after all, and would open all the windows to dissipate the paint fumes. She returned the key and left the hotel.

Rufus sat alone on a park bench. She walked to the bench and motioned for him not to get up. She stood beside him, haughty-like, as if talking to a servant and not her lover. There could no public display of affection. She explained the previous fifteen minutes.

"Well," he said, "better you saw her before I arrived, than after."

"Yes, that was a little bit of luck. But the hotel is not feasible. Too public. A dumb idea."

"Yours, I believe?"

"Do you have a better one?"

"Actually, I do," he said. "Can you come with Polly to the service this Sunday, at First Ogeechee Colored Baptist?"

She nodded.

"Good. Will see you there. We'll talk then. Now best you start walking."

Abigale left Rufus and ambled down Bull Street. Along the way soldiers and colored people abounded, outnumbering white citizens. She noted a faint aroma of manure, from the horses but also, perhaps, from the mass of humanity that really had no lodging at all.

— Friday, January 6

While still in Tennessee General Forrest made Johnny Gordon his aide-de-camp, which meant the young man rode beside him, and helped set up his camp every night. Since the Battle of Nashville the cavalry had traveled across Alabama and into Mississippi where, in Verona, some of Forrest's men were captured in a surprise Union raid on their camp. Now the remaining force bivouacked in western Alabama, undaunted, resting, and getting ready for the next battle.

After dinner, Forrest invited Johnny to sit with him outside the general's tent. The winter sun dipped below the tree tops, turning cool air to cold. They wore coats and sat on small folding chairs, a luxury available to all the generals.

In moments like this Johnny knew what to expect. The general had a habit of asking him questions, about life in Savannah, his upbringing and attitudes on topics like slavery and religion. Always, Johnny sensed, Forrest seemed pleased with what he heard. Still, Johnny felt some discomfort – what if he didn't like my responses? The best thing to do – the only thing, he figured – was just to tell the truth, which should be easy since he had nothing to hide.

"Pretty sky, with the sun setting," said Forrest.

"Yes, it is."

"Johnny, what do you know about Fort Pillow?"

"I know you were the general in charge, and we won, took over the fort. That's pretty well known, sir."

"Yes, the battle took place last April, couple of months before you joined our outfit. What else do you hear about it?"

"You killed a bunch of niggers."

"Me alone? You heard that?"

"Well, not exactly. I guess your troops, the men who attacked the fort."

"And who told you that? Did you read that in some paper?"

"No sir, ain't read nothing much about this war. It's just what other soldiers say. You have a reputation, sir."

"For what, may I ask? Don't be afraid to say something not good. Won't hurt me. I trust you to be honest with me."

"Oh, no sir, nothing bad at all. A reputation for being fearless, and a great leader. And a great horseman. That's your reputation. I hear nothing bad at all."

"Well, thank you, but I am still curious. In all the scuttlebutt you hear around, did anyone make any criticism of the Fort Pillow battle, of the way I conducted that raid?"

"No sir, not as I heard."

"Well, that's good. But let me give you a warning. When you return home, and you meet any northern sympathizers, you may hear that we massacred unarmed blacks at Fort Pillow. You may hear that I am a war criminal or such. The truth is, those soldiers guarding the fort, both the colored and the white ones, were fighting us like in every other battle. I gave them several chances to surrender, and they never accepted them. If they had accepted, there wouldn't of been a battle. But they didn't, the fools!"

"Well," said Johnny, "guess they deserved what they got."

"They were trying to kill us. We killed back when we had to. And we won, by God, we won! I fought a fair and honest battle. But the Yanks, they can't abide by the killing, except when they do it to our side. So that's my warning. If you hear about some massacre at Fort Pillow against unarmed and defenseless soldiers, it's all a lie, you understand?"

"Yes, sir."

"Good."

CHAPTER 27

— *Sunday, January 8*

The First Ogeechee Colored Baptist Church lay about the same distance from Liberty Street as Rufus's own church. His service began at 2 p.m., well after congregants for Reverend Patterson's morning service had departed.

Abigale knew what to expect. 'The light is here'. 'We are saved'. Now she could listen to his words from a different perspective. This fire and brimstone preacher could put on an act when necessary, but she knew the real Rufus Simms: a sensitive soul, an educated man, an extraordinary therapist. *Why couldn't he be white? Or me negro? No! Banish that last thought.*

Gustav came with a lady friend, someone she had not seen before. Abigale estimated her age in the mid-forties, possibly newly arrived from one of the ships in the harbor. This is good, she thought; at least he won't make any overtures this afternoon.

After the service Abigale remained on the front bench with Polly while parishioners chatted with Simms until, finally, they were the last two in the sanctuary. Simms motioned for her to come on the stage.

"He wants to see me in the office, Polly, do you mind waiting a few minutes here in the church? I won't be long."

"Glad to. Glad to see you mo' happy now, that he be able to help you."

If only she knew. "Good, it'll just be a few minutes."

Alone in his office, she sat in the armchair, he at his desk. They did not embrace, it being the Lord's Day, lest temptation win over.

"How is Polly doing?" he asked.

"Well as can be expected. She had a rough time at her sister's. Said Lowry Plantation is a mess, no one knows what's going to happen with the colored folks. Sounds pretty chaotic."

"I'm sure it is. Every plantation within ten miles of Savannah is housing Yankee troops. I'm surprised your house hasn't been taken over."

"We're just lucky, I guess. Or maybe no one wants to stay with three women."

"I would stay with the lucky part."

"So I am here, Rufus. When last we met you said you had a plan. I'm most curious to know what it is. I don't see a lot of options."

"A very simple plan, actually. Can you come for counseling on a regular basis?"

— WEDNESDAY, JANUARY 11

Unknown to Simms, or indeed to any Savannahians, or even Sherman's own generals, was the grief heaped on Sherman from Washington, over his treatment of negroes. Word had filtered up about the huge number of colored joining his army's march south, and about his disdain for this wretched mass who did little more than slow the march's progress. One of Sherman's generals even kept a group of negroes from following his division over a creek near Savannah, causing panic when they were set upon by Confederate cavalry. Many jumped into the creek and drowned.

News of that incident and Sherman's refusal to use colored soldiers made its way up north, prompting letter warnings by his confidants in Washington. In reply to one of the letter writers, Salmon Chase, Sherman replied "I mean no unkindness to the negro," and went on to justify his handling of the thousands of colored who followed his troops.[12]

In fact the colored, including Simms and his fellow preachers, *did* view Sherman as friendly to their cause. But the Washington elite and hardline radicals wanted hard evidence, and they didn't have any. To assess the situation Secretary of War Edwin Stanton made a trip to Savannah aboard the steamer *Spaulding*, arriving unannounced early on January 11. His first meeting with Sherman took place that same morning.

After much discussion they agreed to convene a conference of all the negro ministers for the following evening. Twenty invitations went out.

———◆———

Abigale arrived to Simms's First Ogeechee Colored Baptist office at half past one, the appointed hour. Earlier in the day came the elderly widow Shields for half hour, then Mrs. Wainwright dressed in mourning clothes, followed by Mrs. Wiggins with her troubled nine-year-old boy – all in need of some counseling. Thus did a pattern of visiting parishioners precede Abigale's appointment.

And, as if ordered by Cupid, there came a steady rain that made the front-lawn soldiers tent-bound. The lone trooper who guarded the back of the church huddled in an alley doorway, not visible to Abigale as she strode up the back walk.

To complete the obfuscation, Abigale wore extra clothes and carried a large umbrella, shielding her youth and beauty. And she had splurged on a carriage, so as not to arrive dirty.

"Well," she said, entering his office and taking a seat, "we couldn't have asked for better conditions."

"Yes, I have already counseled three families today. You are but one among several."

"Reverend Patterson didn't object to using his office on Wednesday?"

"No. As I explained, he is in Pooler all day. Won't be back until tomorrow morning."

"My, the Lord works in mysterious ways," said Abigale.

"Yes, and what the Lord giveth he taketh away," replied Simms.

"Don't be so pessimistic. How much time do we have?"

"You know, your southern accent is charming."

"So I've been told," she replied.

"Yes, by me. When I hear others speak with that slow lilt, I think the person is ignorant. But it becomes you. Strange, isn't it?"

"And what happened to your accent? Coming from Jekyll, even more southern than Savannah. You speak like a Yankee."

"Ah, my own. Very affected. I work hard at it. Don't change. Stay natural."

"Well, thank you, kind sir," replied Abigale, every syllable extra-long and clothed in sarcasm. "And your next appointment?"

"Oh, yes. My next appointment is at three. Glad I could squeeze you in."

"Funny. Along with your intelligence and affected accent comes humor."

"You don't think my poor, ignorant brethren have that sense? The funny bone?"

"Well, I've never known Polly to make a joke."

"Her life doesn't permit it."

"For a negro, she's had a good life, at least until recently."

"Why, what's happening?"

"Her husband's death, of course, even though they were estranged. And some words with her sister's husband at Lowry Plantation, she told me about."

"Like what?"

"He's got her thinking about what she's going to do with her freedom. Made her anxious. Asked me about it, as if I know."

"Did she make any demands?"

"Demands? Of course not. What could she demand?"

"Wages."

"Wages?"

"She does the domestic work. And a lot more."

"And we feed and house her."

"True, but if she fed and housed herself, then you would have to pay her."

"That wasn't discussed."

"She's a good woman, that Polly of yours. Don't let her go."

"You mean keep her in bondage? That's a strange request, coming from your lips."

"You know well what I mean. Keep her happy, accede to reasonable requests, treat her like a human."

"As we have all along."

"There is some good news," he said, changing the subject, and handed over a piece of stationary, which she read:

Reverend Rufus Simms, c/o First Ogeechee Colored Baptist Church

You are cordially invited to attend a <u>SPECIAL MEETING</u>, Thursday, January 12, 1865 with Secretary of War Edwin M. Stanton and Maj-General William Tecumseh Sherman, at Army HQ, Bull and Macon Streets. Meeting time is 8 p.m. Estimated to last two hours. Subject: The negro situation in areas under United States Command. Please review the attached list of questions we will cover, and be prepared to select a spokesman from among those able to attend this meeting.

Respectfully, Edwin M. Stanton, Secretary of War, United States of America, On board the *Spaulding*, Savannah Harbor.

"You just received this?"

"Around noon. From one of the soldiers. There's another one for Reverend Patterson. It's gone out to all the local negro ministers."

"That's impressive. How did they know you were here? I mean Secretary Stanton."

"Oh, they have spies everywhere. I imagine they can find anyone they need to on fairly short notice. Savannah's a small city, not like New York."

"Does that go for ordinary citizens as well? Women?"

"I suppose, if they are up to any mischief."

"Should I be concerned?"

"Did anyone look twice as you came around the church and entered my office?"

"In all honesty, no one turned a hair. Bad weather certainly helped."

"Yes, and to the soldiers, you are just another parishioner seeking my advice."

"A white parishioner? Seeking a colored minister's advice?"

"The soldiers are from the north. Perhaps they are more accepting of such oddities."

"Possibly. Getting back to your invitation from the war secretary, appears that Mr. Lincoln means to deliver on his promise."

"Yes, I'm truly excited. For the first time in history, our government seems to care what we think."

"Well," she said, unbuttoning a collar button of her dress, "perhaps it's time to get you excited about something else."

CHAPTER 28

— *THURSDAY EVENING, JANUARY 12*

THE NEGRO MINISTERS' CONFERENCE TOOK place in the second floor library of Green's mansion. Twenty black ministers came, ranging in age from 26-year-old James Lynch to 72-year-old William Bentley.

Simms knew of Charles Green's mansion—who in Savannah did not?—but had never been inside. Even by northern standards it was spectacular in scope and detail, the most expensive house in the city. Designed by famed northern architect Charles Norris, the house sported a covered porch on three sides surrounded by ornate ironwork, beautiful "oriel" windows in the gothic style, and numerous original adornments on the interior, including walnut woodwork on the main floor, elaborate crown moldings, marble mantles, matching chandeliers and large mirrors in gold leaf frames from Austria. Green liked to boast of one unique feature: the only private home with a curved stairway leading to the second floor.

The spacious library had a ten-foot high ceiling made of ornately carved wood. Dark red vellum covered the four walls, each adorned with pictures of the English countryside. In one of the pictures, men dressed in formal evening wear rode horses through a field, while their dogs ran beside them. Titled "Hunting with Hounds," it caused one minister to quip, "Looks like they be hunting for us."

To avoid influencing responses, Stanton and Sherman did not mingle with the ministers beforehand. Instead, they entered the room just before eight p.m., and sat together at one end of a long table. Stanton's adjutant, Edward Townsend, who served as secretary, sat in the middle. Half the ministers also found seats at the table, with the others standing or sitting against the walls.

Townsend took detailed minutes, including each question and answer, which the war department would later publish in a New York newspaper.[13]

"Gentlemen, I am Edwin M. Stanton and to my right is Major General William Sherman, who I trust needs no further introduction." Most of the ministers nodded in Sherman's direction.

"I want to thank all of you for coming. As you may know, I arrived just yesterday from Washington, on the *Spaulding*. The war has created tremendous hardship for most Savannahians, your congregants included. Our government is determined to listen to your concerns and do what we can to ease the transition from slavery to freedom. First, let me ask, how many of you were slaves until General Sherman's army marched to Savannah? Please raise your hand."

Nine hands went up.

"And those of you who did not raise your hand, how many were ever in bondage before?"

Another six hands.

"And how many were born free?"

Five hands went up.

"Well, if my addition is correct, that makes twenty. Five born free, and fifteen with experience of slavery. You men are the fortunate negroes. You can read, write, care for your families. How can we help your congregants and the great humanity of negroes who are newly made free with the general's arrival? I know you all have ideas, and I've asked you to appoint a spokesperson to answer the questions, to help speed along the meeting. I promise that anyone may speak or dissent if they wish. My purpose is just to get your thoughts recorded, so my government—now *our* government—can begin some action. Gentleman, have you appointed a spokesperson?"

All eyes turned toward a middle-aged, strongly-built man seated to Stanton's left. He rose from his seat to speak. "Sir, my name is Garrison Frazier. I am sixty-seven-years old, and the brothers have appointed me as their speaker. They do feel my views fairly represent their own, and I am honored to be chosen. I have been in the ministry for thirty-five years, but do not currently have a congregation, as the demands are too great for my health. But I have kept up with affairs, and done a fair amount of reading over recent events."

For over an hour Frazier answered Townsend's questions in a clear and direct manner. Perhaps the most seminal response came early in the session, when Townsend asked how the government could help the colored to take care of themselves. Frazier's answer was "to have land, and turn it and till it by own labor…We want to be placed on land until we are able to buy it and make it our own."[14]

— MONDAY, JANUARY 16

Following his meetings with Secretary Stanton, and the responses from the January 12th meeting with the negro ministers, Sherman issued Special Field Orders, No. 15 for 1865.[15] The very first paragraph seemed a godsend to the ex-slaves: "The islands from Charleston south, the abandoned rice-fields along the rivers for thirty miles back from the sea, and the country bordering the St. John's River, Florida, are reserved and set apart for the settlement of the negroes now made free by the acts of war and the proclamation of the President of the United States."

Unlike most of Sherman's military orders, these were complicated and impractical, in part because they were designed to serve different agendas, and would not even be legally binding after the war.

To Stanton, they were a way to empower the newly-freed slaves and satisfy the radical Republicans back in Washington.

To Sherman, they were a method to move the masses of negro women and children out of Savannah. A proviso whereby their menfolk would enlist in the Union army looked good on paper, but Sherman knew they were not necessary to the war effort. In his mind, the war would be over before the first negro could be fully trained and put in uniform.

To the ex-slaves, the orders meant they could have access to the abandoned coastal plantations, and thus the ability to become self-sufficient. Just as important, if not more so, the orders showed this new government listened to the Colored, and cared.

CHAPTER 29

———◆———

GUSTAV HEINZ CAME TO SAVANNAH in the 1850s, after his wife died, to seek a better life. He had worked as a hotelier in Germany and knew something about the business. When a cheap boarding house came on the market he bought it, and called the place Savannah Gardens, thinking the name would attract customers.

He loved to tell the story of how he changed Savannah Gardens from an under-performing boarding house to a successful brothel. Local bartenders and patrolmen who covered his street – the latter paid off to look the other way – had heard his account more than once, always accompanied by Gustav's laughter and a caricature of his own accent.

> One night a customer asked me for "a woman" and I asked "vat do you vant vith voman? For to clean your room?"
>
> "No, no," he said. "I thought this is where you come for women. This is Savannah Gardens, isn't it?"
>
> Ah, light, how you say, go off in my head. It explode!

After "explode" Gustav would invariably let out one of his belly laughs before finishing.

> I say to him, I am so sorry, Mister, dis is not that kind of establishment, and I return his money. Then I vow I vould lose this customer but gain others. So I go about my vork.

Gustav decided to aim for the lower-end market, for two reasons. His establishment was not in the best neighborhood, and there were many more customers for the cheaper women. Savannah Gardens soon became the place to go if a man desired a woman but had little money or self-esteem. He initially charged clients two and a half bucks an hour, of which the woman kept fifty percent.

Gustav could not possibly run this business by himself, and in the first week of operation he hired Miss Sophie. Previously she was a madam at Pulaski Commons, from where she had been fired for drunkenness. Sophie then found religion and never drank again. About age forty-five, she carried a stout figure, at 160 lbs. and five-foot-four inches tall. Her hair sat in a bun atop a full and pretty face with just a hint of middle age around the eyes. Gustav found Sophie sober, sassy, bosomy and perfect for the business. He paid her twenty dollars a week. She was unmarried and had no close family. He tried to seduce her the first week and she promptly rebuffed him. "I work for you, hands off. Understood?" He did, and she remained his most loyal employee.

———————

With Sherman's arrival came additions to Gustav's list of boarders. In the first days of the occupation many Union soldiers came looking for rooms, and Gustav managed to fend them off, finally realizing that the army could confiscate his place *en toto* if it wished. When a young captain and a lieutenant next showed up asking for rooms, Gustav made an offer.

"My rooms are all filled with women, yah, that is my business." In his broken English he followed with, "But proud to have you two stay for free, while in Savannah, if you keep others out. So I can continue my business." He made no offer of free women, thinking that would be too costly. Free lodging proved feasible, since he did have a spare room used for storage, one that could easily be converted into a small bedroom.

The officers agreed. "Then we have a deal," said the captain. "A roof over our heads is more important than the nature of your business. You don't bother us and we won't bother you."

"Good, good. Just keep others out. Have no more rooms."

True to their word, when more soldiers arrived with enquiries, the officers shooed them away, with "this place is spoken for."

Gustav also hired a young negro girl, eighteen-year-old Sarah, comely, well-proportioned and healthy. He found her newly-freed the day after Sherman arrived, at a plantation abandoned by its white owners. With Sarah having no money and nowhere to go, he offered her a job as a domestic, to "clean and sweep." She readily accepted, completely ignorant of the nature of his establishment.

Her cleaning position lasted but three days when he made his second offer: far more money if she would entertain "a few white soldiers." To his surprise she agreed, on the one condition that they all use "protection." He marveled that a negro girl would even know about condoms. They were seldom used in brothels, but Gustav accepted her demand. It meant he had to buy some, but knew condoms were available in a local apothecary.

For the first few weeks the arrangement worked well. She was servicing two to three men a night, those who were eager for "something different," and earning real wages for the first time. Most clients were Union soldiers, but Gustav felt sure some were Confederate deserters.

— *FRIDAY, JANUARY 20*

Half past nine on this cold night Gustav heard screaming from Sarah's room. He ran to investigate.

From outside her room he heard the loud voice of his customer: "You bitch! You goddamn bitch!" The words echoed throughout the second floor of Savannah Gardens. They were followed by a girl's scream and another "Goddamn bitch!"

Sophie came running to the room and stood behind Gustav. They opened the door and saw the customer, a large, naked man, easily six feet and over 200 pounds, slapping Sarah. Gustav ran to restrain him. The brute pivoted away from Gustav and raised the palm of his hand to hit Sarah again. Before he could strike Sophie shoved the man from behind, He lost balance and fell face down on the floor.

"Get out of my hotel. Leave!" yelled Gustav.

The customer sat up, buck naked, holding the side of his head with one hand. "That bitch bit my ear off!" He removed his hand to show the ear. Gustav saw a noticeable gap in his earlobe.

"He done raped me," said Sarah. "Cause I told him to use protection I give him. He say no, I say yes or no sex, and he grabbed me, held me down, forced himself. I bit his ear. I bite his dick if I get a chance!"

"You didn't give me a chance to come, you bitch. So you can't say I raped you."

"Mister, please, put on your clothes, leave, no trouble. Please?"

"Fuck you, you piece of shit, I want my money back. I ain't paying for no black whore that bit my ear off."

"Sophie, go get the captain, the lieutenant, quick." The soldiers' room sat in the building's rear, so they could enter and not interfere with Gustav's business.

She returned in a minute. The brute was now almost fully dressed. "Not in their room, Gustav. They must be out for the evening."

"Oh, shit. Go, look for Sergeant O'Riley, quick. Ve got troubles." By now several women crowded the doorway, along with a couple of their clients.

The dissatisfied customer finished dressing, all the while pointing to Sarah. "You black bitch, you whore. Knew I shouldn't have taken a chance with no teenage nigger."

"Mister, I'd vatch your tongue," said Gustav.

"Vatch? Vut is vatch? You dumb immigrant." He swung for Gustav, hitting him squarely on the jaw. Gustav fell to the floor.

"You goddam cocksuckers. I'm out of here," and with that the man fled the room and ran down the stairs.

Sophie knelt down to Gustav, found him dazed but moving, and yelled for someone to fetch a basin of water. Within minutes both the water and Sergeant O'Riley arrived.

"Gustav," said O'Riley, "what the hell happened?"

"Crazy customer," said Sophie. "Raped one of our girls, she bit his ear, he hit Gustav."

"Oh Gustav," Sophie moaned. She sat down on the floor and gently lifted his head to her lap. "You poor man."

"Everyone in the hallway, leave us be," yelled O'Riley. "Back to your rooms. I'm in charge now. Move on."

Gustav stirred, his head cradled in Sophie's arm, his nose close to her right breast. He nuzzled himself into her chest while she stroked his head.

"Oh Gustav, you tried to do the right thing. There, there. I understand."

O'Riley asked a few desultory questions, which seemed to focus more on Gustav's injury than Sarah's rape, of which he did not seem concerned. "Maybe that's what you get for hiring a nigger whore."

"Don't say that sergeant," protested Sophie. "We treat her well. Her customer, just an animal. Refused to use protection, though we pass it out free."

"Do you know his name?"

"Jim," said Gustav. "That's all I know. Said his name was Jim."

"Likely an alias," said O'Riley.

Sensing futility, Gustav wished the matter to drop. "Let it go," he said. "Please, no police report. I have a respectable business."

Gustave turned to face Sophie, his back to the police officer. "Go out with Sergeant O'Riley." Gustav scratched his palm with three fingers, meaning give the sergeant the usual, three dollars.

When they left he looked around, did not see Sarah anywhere. He could only wonder where she might have gone. He hoped she didn't run away.

She is still very good for business.

———————

At the moment of mayhem inside Savannah Gardens, bliss reigned in a certain room at Pulaski House Hotel, at least until Jason confirmed what Jane already knew.

"Tonight's the last night," said Jason. "We leave tomorrow. I'm afraid it's definite."

"Take me with you!"

"I wish it were possible, but even you know better."

"I don't want this to end. This has been the happiest few weeks of my life."

"All eighteen years of it?"

"I have a secret to tell."

"I'm listening."

"I'm only seventeen. My birthday is June fifteenth."

"You are very mature for a teen-ager. A naughty teen-ager." He lightly spanked her buttocks.

"Oh, don't go. Desert. Run away. Take me with you. We'll go to California, start a new life together."

"How about you stay here and wait for me."

"Till the end of time. Think you could return in a week?"

They laughed, hugged, kissed. Both were spent from the night's lovemaking, but fondled nonetheless.

"You'll write?" she asked.

"Of course, but I don't know where I'll be, and if you write back, I may not receive your letters."

"You said you were going to Carolina."

"Well, that's true, but General Sherman doesn't tell us what part. Charleston, Columbia, or straight through to North Carolina. We, or at least I, don't know."

"I'll wait for you."

"Don't go prancing that gorgeous figure of yours before any of the troops we're leaving behind. They're a bunch animals."

"Like you?"

"Like me. Think you can wait?"

"Jason! What do you take me for? We Gordon girls are tough. My sister Abigale went without her husband for almost two years, and she didn't as much as look at another man. I am not a flirt. I will wait for you. Just don't end up dead…or worse."

They kissed again. Then she dressed and he escorted her home.

They stopped at the foot of the stairs leading to her front stoop, hugged and kissed once more.

"Don't come up the stairs," she said in a whisper. "I don't want anyone to hear us."

"I don't want to let you go."

"I know. Come back soon. I love you." Jane turned, ran up the stairs and entered the house.

Abigale was waiting. "It's almost nine o'clock," she said. "Mother's asleep. Been out with Jason?"

"Of course. I told you I'd be late tonight. He's leaving for Carolina in the morning, with all the army brass. Unlike you, I have nothing to hide. We made love one last time, at least until he returns, which I hope will be soon."

"The war could yet drag on."

Jane did not answer.

"You are using protection?"

"So," retorted Jane, "who was that man you were meeting at Pulaski house? I don't think you ever told me."

Abigale had lost all big-sister clout after her aborted meeting with Rufus. Now she was the one with secrets, the one being coy. How ironic, the change, she thought.

"Jane, I'm going to bed. See you in the morning."

———————

Sophie found Sarah curled up under the lobby desk, wrapped in a blanket. When the girl refused to budge, she called for Gustav.

Gustav bent down to talk to his employee, still semi-hidden under the desk. "Sarah, please, come back to your room. We have taken care of that brute. He is vamoosed, will never return. Police are looking for him."

"You don't pay me enough for what I have to put up with," she said, between sobs.

"Ya, Ya, we pay you well. What more do you want?"

"Another dollar."

"Vhat?"

"Another dollar, Mr. Heinz."

"Each customer?"

He could make out her head nodding. Gustav stood erect. "Oh, my back. I should not bend down."

Sophie grabbed his arm, led him to one side of the room. "Better agree, for now, Gustav. If we have any more trouble, can always let her go. Say yes."

"Mein Gott. What a business this is. She make more demands than all the other womens."

"She's still worth it. Tell her yes."

Gustav walked over to the desk, bent down to speak to Sarah. "Yes, you return to work. One more dollar."

CHAPTER 30

— SUNDAY, JANUARY 22

SHERMAN LEFT TOWN WITHOUT FANFARE on January 21, accompanied by most of his generals and junior officers. All week his troops had been ready to enter South Carolina, but rains delayed their movement. As soon as the rain slacked off the bulk of the army crossed the river, on newly-constructed pontoon bridges.

Sherman established transient headquarters in Beaufort, near Hilton Head, with plans to move up toward Columbia. But first he would feint marching to Augusta and Charleston, in order to make the Confederates keep troops in those cities. His real goal was always South Carolina's capital city.

Savannah remained occupied with a small contingent Union troops under command of General Cuvier Grover. Most were concentrated in the city, to make sure Savannahians did nothing to augment the now-feeble southern war effort.

The most notable changes in the city were a drop in military population and re-opening of the port. Ships were coming and going, reestablishing trade, and northerners visited to check out business opportunities.

There were still many colored to house and feed, and black churches and other property to protect. While many ex-slaves began moving to coastal islands, to take advantage of Field Orders No. 15, Savannah still retained a sizable colored population.

Less troops meant less protection of colored property, though that was of little concern to the white citizens. Soon a real shock would invade their sensibility: a shift from white to black soldiers in the city. Sherman had no negroes in his 60,000 man army, but the new and slimmed down military command deemed it fitting and proper that this southern stronghold should have a taste of colored military.

———

While most Savannahians accepted defeat, and chose to get on with their lives, a small group vowed to protest to the end. Not an open retaliation – that would be quashed by the remaining military. Their protest had to be secret and anonymous – another hooded night ride.

St. Timothy's Protestant Episcopal Colored Church in Savannah was a modest church, an old wooden structure. Its congregation numbered around 200. Before Sherman's army moved to Carolina, a single soldier stood guard at night. Now, with most of the blue-coats gone, no one guarded this particular church, making it an easy target.

Under the dim light of a quarter moon, just before midnight, two men rode in on horseback, carrying lighted torches and rifles.

"We found ourselves a good one," said one of the pair, as he broke a window pain and threw in his torch.

The dry wood burned fast. From the street, the two riders watched in fascination.

"Burn, burn!"

Before any alarm could sound the church was fully consumed by fire. By morning of January 23, all that could be seen were smoldering planks and a charred chimney.

— Monday, January 23

News of the fire reached General Grover just before sunrise. He rode with two aides to survey the ruin. One of the aides, Major Stephen Sanford, was also a good friend. Grover and Sanford both hailed from

Portland, Maine and were avowed abolitionists before the war. They fought for Union, but also for emancipation. For them, this cowardly act was doubly despicable: destruction of property without purpose, and performed by cowards.

"Not on my watch," said Grover. "Not again. Stephen, I want you to get to the bottom of these church burnings. Sherman didn't do a whole lot to find these men. I want it a priority. Do what you have to do."

"Yes sir," said Sanford. He didn't have to say "sir," but it came out naturally.

———————

CHAPTER 31

— *WEDNESDAY, FEBRUARY 1*

AT NINE A.M. THERE WAS a knock on the door of twenty-seven Liberty Street. Polly opened the door to greet another soldier.

"Lordy, Lordy, what be this time?"

"Good morning. I am Lieutenant Gideon Smith. I have a message for Mrs. Abigale Tate."

"Come in. I goes fetch her."

Polly returned with her mistress a few minutes later.

"Yes? I am Abigale Tate."

The lieutenant bowed, an affectation Abigale thought unnecessary.

"Mrs. Tate, I bring a formal request from Major Stephen Sanford. He is conducting an enquiry into recent church burnings, and would like to interview you on the matter. It is a routine interview, looking for any information that may be helpful to find the culprits. He is flexible with your schedule, and offers you a choice of this afternoon, or tomorrow afternoon, at two p.m."

That's flexible? Why me? How did he get my name? What's this really about? I'm sure the lieutenant doesn't know. Can I say no?

"Excuse me, sir, you went so fast. What did you say your name is?"

"Gideon Smith, ma'am. From Delaware. I'm with the army."

"Yes, I see that. Do you know why your major wishes to interview me? I know nothing about those horrible fires."

"No ma'am, I am only delivering the request. He is making a broad enquiry into the events, and meeting various people. I am also instructed to accompany you to the interview, once you have picked a day.

There is no point in resisting. I doubt this has anything to do with Rufus. It's probably just what the man says - an enquiry about the fires.

"Well, I am teaching tomorrow, so today is better for me."

"Excellent. I will be by at one thirty to accompany you to the church building."

"Oh? In a church?"

"Yes, ma'am. Second Ogeechee Colored Baptist, a negro church. They've volunteered him space to use for the interviews. He likes it better than army headquarters."

———◆———

Much to Abigale's surprise a one-horse carriage came for her. Surprised, because she had expected to walk the distance, no real challenge considering her recent outings. Then she realized that walking the city for appointments, especially unaccompanied, was a little unusual among her class. Either the army didn't expect women to walk alone about town, or this major wanted to make sure she appeared as promised. Probably both reasons accounted for the carriage.

An elderly negro drove the carriage. On the way she sat next to the lieutenant but they barely spoke. After a short ten minute ride the carriage pulled up to the Houston Street church. Smith helped her down to the street, then escorted her inside the building. As soon as the door opened she heard something totally unexpected, piano music from the far end of the church: a Chopin mazurka. She wasn't sure which mazurka, but he played it with some expertise.

"This way ma'am," said the lieutenant. He walked her down the aisle to the church's stage. There she saw the piano player, dressed in uniform. When they made eye contact he stopped.

"Sir, I have brought Mrs. Tate, as instructed."

Abigale pointed to the piano player. "Lieutenant, *he* is the major who wants to interview me?"

"Yes, ma'am. Major Sanford."

What's going on here?

"Thank you for coming," said Sanford, now standing. "Please, come up to the stage. My office is up here." Addressing Smith, "Lieutenant, please summon the stenographer."

"Yes sir."

Sanford appeared to be about thirty, tall, perhaps five foot ten. Like most officers, he had a beard. She noted two other features, one pleasant and the other less so. The pleasant one was neatness. His uniform and the way he wore it were neat, as if he might appear on stage, before a full audience, prepared to give a recital. This was in contrast to the utter sloppiness adopted manifest in so many soldiers, including officers.

Then there was the faint aroma of cigar smoke. She knew the smell because her father smoked cigars, a habit decried by all the women in her house. She searched for the source and saw the vile cylinder of tobacco slowly burning in dish on the piano top.

Sanford ushered her to the long table in the middle of the stage. Thankfully, he left the cigar in its place. She sat down, and he took a seat opposite. On the table she noted several books and a legal ledger.

"I am sorry for the formality, but my inquiries must be recorded for the war department. Our stenographer will be here shortly."

"I didn't expect to be interviewed by a Chopin expert."

"I am hardly an expert. You recognize the piece?"

"Yes, I have played it."

"You have? I am impressed. I wasn't aware southern women had such refined upbringing."

"And I wasn't aware Union soldiers knew anything about music."

He laughed. "Touche, madam. I see we will hit it off well. Music is my passion. The army is a diversion, a lengthy one, I'm afraid.

I've been in since sixty-two. Before that I worked as an attorney, but played for relaxation. Whenever I get the chance, I brush up, as it were. And you?"

"My father was also an attorney, and I grew up playing Chopin. Were you in the Battle fought over Atlanta, last summer?" *Why do I always ask? I can't help myself.*

"Oh, here is our stenographer, Sergeant Jackson." A young army sergeant bounded up the stage, introduced himself to Abigale, and took a seat next to her.

"Robby, we were just chatting. Let me know when you're ready."

"Yessir, just give me a minute," said the sergeant.

Turning to Abigale, Sanford said, "Not directly, to answer your question. In North Georgia I functioned as quartermaster, arranging logistics. Did not fire a shot."

That's good. It will make my interview less painful.

"Why do you ask?"

"Major Sanford, something tells me you know why."

"Ready sir," said the stenographer.

"Hold on for a minute, Robby. We haven't started the interview just yet." Turning to Abigale: "About your husband?"

"So you do know."

"Yes, it's not a secret. We are acutely aware of the losses the war has caused. And I will not make any excuses. But we are not barbarians. My immediate task is to stop the violence against black churches, and I need your assistance. I trust you will cooperate."

And if I don't? "Well, then, major, you may proceed with your inquiry. However, I can summarize my responses before we begin. I know nothing about who perpetrated these acts."

"I accept that, but you never know where information will lead. Robby, let's begin. First question. How well do you know Gustav Heinz?"

Abigale did not expect this question, first or last. Was Gustav a suspect? "Not well at all, and I have no wish to improve on that position. I sat next to him the first time I visited the church that burned down. Or rather, he sat next to me. Later he sent me flowers. His interest in me is not reciprocated, I assure you."

"Could you share with me, in a general way, any notes Mr. Heinz may have sent you?"

"Only one, with the flowers, hoping I would attend the same church again."

"And did you?"

"Yes, but with my mother and sister, and our servant Polly. So I was well protected from his aspirations. We sat the greatest distance possible from his bench."

"So he has not provided you any information about who might have torched the Third Ogeechee Colored Baptist Church?"

"None. As I said, I've avoided him. Has he told you something different?"

Sanford did not reply, but asked another question. "How well do you know this negro minister, Rufus Simms?"

"My servant introduced me. She goes to his church and thought I would be inspired by his sermons. At the time I was feeling low, very low in fact. I am sure you can understand."

"Yes, of course. Did his sermons help?"

"Sort of, yes, I suppose, though while there I did not appreciate his prediction about your side winning the war."

Sanford smiled.

How much does he know about us? I have to assume little or nothing, though Gustav must have said something to pique his curiosity.

"I want you to think about that second visit to the church. Can you describe for me the other white folks who were there?"

She dimly remembered the two missionaries, and a few others. She described what she could remember.

"Did you meet with Mr. Simms after the service?"

"Yes, with my servant Polly. Why do you ask?" *He's getting a little too personal. I am sure Gustav told him. I cannot lie. And if I object to the question it will only raise suspicion.*

"In that meeting, did he express any fears of personal danger, or threats to his church?"

"No, none at all. These are questions that could be more directly asked of the minister himself. Why are you asking me these things?"

"A good question, Mrs. Tate. I see your father's influence. Sometimes people forget details, or don't remember them fully. We have of course interviewed Mr. Simms, but it is useful to hear all parties. So please bear with me."

"Again, sir, the answer is no. He never expressed fear or threats."

"And you have met with him at his new temporary location, the First Ogeechee Colored Baptist Church?"

Sanford's questioning seemed achingly close to her true relationship with Rufus, but she felt prepared. "Yes, he has assisted me in dealing with what he calls my melancholy."

"I accept that." *Why did he say he accepts it? Does he doubt me?*

"Have any threats been made on your person, by anyone, as far as you know?"

"As far as I know?"

"Yes, by written note, or even verbally."

"No."

"I'm going to show you a note we received yesterday." He handed her a piece of paper containing block letters.

YOU YANKEE BASTARDS. GIVE UP. GET OUT. AND TAKE THE NIGGER LOVERS WITH YOU. THE WHITE BITCH, THE GERMAN, THE MISHINARIES. GET EM OUT WILE U CAN.

Her hands trembled reading the note.

"You've not seen this before, or anything like it?"

"No....No. May I ask how you came by this note?"

"My men found it on the front lawn of this church, attached to a rock. Presumably thrown during the night."

"And you think I am the white....?" She could not finish the sentence.

"It would seem so."

"And why, do you think?"

"Perhaps your relationship with this Mr. Simms?"

"Just because of my going to hear his sermons?"

"Mrs. Tate, we believe these arsonists are Confederate deserters, lashing out at losing the war, a war that has freed their former slaves. We think they will stop at nothing to cause mayhem, even at the risk of getting caught and hung. So far they've only caused property damage. Lives could be next. I would be very careful in your associations."

Is this a fair warning? Really, how much does he know?

He continued. "It is not my wish to interfere with your personal life, but I must warn you of the old adage, where there's smoke there's fire. Your association with this minister is probably not a good idea."

If he knew the true relationship it should be obvious in his countenance, but I see no trace of a smirk. He is either ignorant of my affair or a superb actor, as well as pianist.

"So you have interviewed Mr. Simms?"

"Yes, twice."

"And what did he say?"

"I am not at liberty to divulge anyone's comments. He is an intelligent man, is aware of the dangers, and is of course cooperating."

"Did you ask him about me?"

"Frankly, only after we received the note. That is why I summoned you. For now I have no more questions. While I prefer to conduct my interviews here, my regular office is in the Army headquarters on Bay Street. If you learn of anything new, of course feel free to contact me."

"I will, sir. Are we done?"

"Yes, unless you'd like to play one of the mazurkas. I would love to hear another pianist."

She could not resist. "I see you have the music."

"Yes, for a few of them."

"Would you mind removing the cigar from the piano? I am not a fan of the tobacco smell."

"Of course, of course," said Sanford. "It's a habit, but I can certainly forgo it for the moment. I do apologize."

They walked to the piano and she sat on the bench, while he stubbed out the cigar and threw it in a trash bin near the interview table. He then sat on one of the chairs to await her performance. She thumbed through some well-worn sheet music, settling on a mazurka in A minor. She played the two-and-a half-minute piece flawlessly.

Sanford applauded. "Bravo." You play well, Mrs. Tate. We should play a duet some time."

She turned to look at him and said, "Thank you. I really must be going." She stood, they shook hands, and Sanford called for his lieutenant to escort her home.

———◆———

The carriage rumbled over rutted roads, jarring its two passengers. Abigale didn't mind the ride; she was deep in thought over what had just transpired.

What's going on? Am I a fool? How could I let myself get into this situation? What should I do now? He is smart and talented. And not career military. Is he married? I must find out more. I must redirect. Yes, I've got to redirect.

"Lieutenant?"

"Yes ma'am?"

"Your major is a very good piano player. Do all your officers play music? *An inane question, just to get him talking.*

"Not as I know, ma'am. He's the only one I know of."

"Where is he from?"

"New York, I believe."

I cannot ask if he is married. Too obvious. I saw no ring.

"He's a rising star in this outfit," offered the lieutenant. "Very smart. Friends with the general, too."

"General Sherman?"

"Oh, no ma'am, General Grover, our military commander of Savannah."

"How long do you think the Union troops will stay in Savannah?"

"Have no idea, ma'am. Guess we'll be here until orders tell us otherwise."

"You are very young for an officer. May I ask how old?

"Twenty, ma'am."

"That's young. Do you like it here, in Savannah?"

"Well, it beats dodging bullets."

"Where do you stay?"

"As a junior officer, I get to bunk in the Pulaski House with two other lieutenants. So that's pretty good luxury for us."

"And the major, where do people of his rank stay?"

My questions are natural, just routine conversation.

"He's in the hotel also, but has a private room. Majors, colonels, generals, get private rooms."

"Are you married? Have a girlfriend?"

"Not married, ma'am, but have a girlfriend at home, in Philadelphia. We do plan on getting married, when the war's over."

"Well, I hope that's soon, and you get to go home."

And the major? I will find out.

———◆———

Back home Abigale met with expected questions about her interview. Jane expressed curiosity about the captain and right away asked, "Is he married?"

"How should I know," replied Abigale, "and what difference does it make? He's looking for the culprits."

"Does he know who they are?" asked Mrs. Gordon.

"He thinks they are Confederate deserters, but doesn't know any names. Thinks they could strike again. We have several black churches in Savannah."

"Oh dear," said Mrs. Gordon.

Abigale did not mention the threatening note. She would keep that to herself.

CHAPTER 32

— THURSDAY, FEBRUARY 2

ABIGALE WAS UNSURE WHAT TO do next. Her situation with Rufus now appeared untenable, fraught with two main risks. First, the distinct possibility of physical harm from men so far unknown to the authorities. She doubted these thugs knew about her true relationship with Rufus; their crude note, lumping her with the missionaries, certainly did not hint at knowledge of any intimacy.

The second risk was one of lost opportunity. Involvement with Rufus precluded a normal relationship with another man, someone who might be truly eligible. There was no real possibility of domestic life with a black man, no matter what his qualities. He was her part time therapist, reliever of boredom and secret lover. Their relationship could never advance, never go public and certainly never end in marriage. It was both limited *and* limiting. To find a new mate, she had to be free.

That meant terminating the affair, but how? A letter would be incriminating. Yes, she could give Polly a note to deliver at the next church service, but anything written could be found by someone. She could ask Rufus to burn the note after reading it, but what if Polly lost it, or it ended up in the wrong hands? No, a written missive was not a good idea.

She could go herself to First Ogeechee Colored Baptist on Sunday, and ask to meet with him privately after the service, but that would be awkward. People would notice – the culprits, perhaps – and there might not be enough time to explain all that needed explaining.

There was one sure way to communicate her intention – keep her regular appointment for Monday, when he occupied the office of Reverend Patterson. She would go, they would talk, they would not make love and she would end it then and there.

That is a good plan. Really, the only one. And he will understand.

— MONDAY, FEBRUARY 6

Abigale walked to First Baptist on Montgomery Street, and along the way she felt more vulnerable than on any previous visit. The day was sunny and cool, with many people outside, and she worried about being recognized. A scarf and wide-brimmed hat hid her most of her face.

Near the church she found only a single guard walking the street; there was no campsite on the lawn as before. Around the back of the building she saw no guards.

She knocked on the rear door. *I'll say hello, walk in, and tell him first thing.*

A tall, very dark man opened the door. Not Rufus!

"Yes, Miss, may I help you?"

"I…I'm sorry, I was told this might be the office of Reverend Simms."

"This is my office. I am Reverend Patterson. He is not here today."

"Do you know where he might be? I was to meet him in reference to his church they are rebuilding." *That sounds plausible.*

"I really do not know. You might try walking over to Third Baptist, where he often works on rebuilding his church. I am sorry, I did not get your name."

"Abigale Tate, Mrs. Abigale Tate. Thank you. I will go look for him. It's about the building fund, and I was told he might be here."

"He does conduct services in my church on Sunday afternoons. But this is my office."

"Thank you. I'll be on my way."

Patterson closed the door and Abigale turned to leave. Very strange, she thought. *Does he even know Rufus has used his office, that I have been supine on his couch? If Rufus is at the construction site, I won't be able to talk with him, certainly not to break up our relationship.*

While walking around the church she looked to see if Rufus might be hiding somewhere, trying to signal her. Perhaps he, too, was surprised to find Reverend Patterson in the office, and was waiting for her to arrive.

Turning the building's rear corner she spotted a man across the street. A short man, he walked slowly, in what might be called a shuffle, as if he had no real destination. He looked vaguely familiar, and she paused. Then realization set in – she had seen him in the streets at least twice before.

The same man. He's following me! This is not a coincidence. One of the arsonists, who wrote the note? Am I going to be attacked?

She walked briskly away from the church, down East Bryan Street. Fortunately the crowded street crossings made it easy to casually glance around without being obvious. He continued to follow, from a block away.

Let him think I don't recognize him. I'll handle this. I know just what to do. Please God, let him keep following me.

———

She found the building on Bay Street, a three-story brick structure no longer used to handle cotton exports. Now it served as military headquarters for the occupying forces. The only sign announcing its new occupants was a Union sentry posted outside. Just before entering the building she took a quick glance down the street and saw her follower, now about half a block away. *Good.*

Inside, just a few feet from the door, she came upon a sergeant seated at a large desk.

"May I help you?" he asked.

"Yes. I wish to see Major Sanford. I understand this is his office."

"This is the army headquarters. We have several offices here. Do you have an appointment?"

"Yes, sort of. It's very important that I speak to him. Now."

"I cannot interrupt the major. Give me your name, and when he's free I will tell him you came to see him."

This direct approach was not working, she realized.

"Sergeant, do you have a piece of paper, and a writing instrument, so I could pen a note for the major?"

He handed them over. She quickly wrote a short message and signed her name.

"Please hand this to him immediately. If he knows you held this note one second too long, those stripes on your uniform will be in some jeopardy. It is about the church burnings." *Father taught me when to be bold.*

The sergeant stared at her for a moment, then without further delay or comment, stood and walked through a rear door.

She looked around and did not see much activity. She expected more.

Within a minute the sergeant returned. "He will see you now, Mrs. Tate."

He ushered her down a long hallway to a room in the rear. Like all the rear offices, it had a window overlooking the Savannah River.

Sanford stood facing the window, his back to the door. She noted many papers on his desk, and wondered if this is what majors do when they're not fighting– shuffle papers. She also noted a lighted cigar, and the same aroma as at the church.

He turned and said, "I read your note. Please, tell me what you know."

"I think one of your church culprits is following me. Now."

"Now?"

"Yes."

She explained the situation, omitting anything about her abortive visit to First Ogeechee Colored Baptist.

He had a few questions, and expressed some concern for her safety were she to continue strolling down Bay Street, but she reassured him that, with proper coverage, she could do what had to be done. Thus Sanford wasted no time in assigning two soldiers to follow her outside. Within ten minutes she was back on the street, ostensibly walking home. She glanced behind her. *Good, he's still following.*

A block down Bay Street she did an about-face and walked directly toward the man, while her two escorts across the street pretended to pay no attention. Soldiers were still common in occupied Savannah, so their presence did not raise any alarm.

As she came closer the mystery man bent down to tie a shoe, which she took as a ruse so she would pass by. Instead, she stopped in front of him.

"Why are you following me?" she asked.

"Ma'am?" he replied, in a squeaky voice.

Vermin. "You've been following me!"

He stood up, looked in her eyes. "Ma'am, I ain't following you. This here's a public street."

She pointed her finger at his chest, without touching. "You are following me! Why?"

He turned to walk away, but now it didn't matter. He was identified.

Within a minute the two soldiers had him by his arms. "Sir, you will come with us," said one of them, adding, "If you resist I'll break this arm."

Abigale followed the trio and in a few minutes was back in the army office. The apprehended man was sequestered in another room, closely watched by the two guards.

"Well, Abigale, looks like you may be right," said Sanford. "My men found this in his coat pocket." He held out a dirty gray hat, army issue. "Confederate hat. At the very least this guy's a deserter, so we have every reason to be suspicious. I suggest you go home, but return

215

tomorrow, so we can follow up on this. I should have some answers for you by then."

"Return here?"

Sanford paused for a moment. "Ah, no. Why don't you come by the church, say, two p.m.?"

"I'm sorry, which church?"

"Yes, there are a lot of them around. Second Ogeechee Colored Baptist, the one with the piano."

———

Sanford entered the interrogation room and closed the door. A single window provided light, and it was cracked open a bit to allow some fresh air. The prisoner sat behind a table, his guards standing.

"I am Major Stephen Sanford, United States Army. What is your name?"

"Ignatius Gardner."

"Your age?"

"Twenty six. What am I being arrested for? I ain't done nothin'. Walking a city street ain't no crime. I want a lawyer."

"Mr. Gardner, from what I gather, we have two reasons to hang you. One, as a Confederate Army deserter. Two, as one of the men who burned two black churches here in Savannah."

"What?! Are you are crazy? I ain't burned no churches!"

"What outfit were you in, in Hardee's army?"

"I got sick the day they left over the river. I ain't no deserter neither."

"Did you go see the army surgeon?"

A pause.

"Did you?"

"No."

"I thought not. And you sure don't look sick to me now."

"I recovered."

"Let's see. Desertion – hanging offense. Church burning – hanging offense. Stalking a citizen – a year in the stockade. However, given your hanging offenses, you won't be in the stockade that long."

"I ain't burned no churches, I tell you. Why do you keep accusing me? And I ain't no deserter. I was deathly sick the night they left."

"Here's what you're going to do. First, give me your full name, your rank and outfit in the Confederate army, then the address where you are staying in Savannah. We'll go search your place. Next, a full account of why you're following that woman. Who are you working with? Where are the others? I could hang you in the morning, but would rather not. It's up to you. You better not leave anything out. Do I make myself clear?"

———◆———

CHAPTER 33

— MONDAY, FEBRUARY 6

AN HOUR'S INTERROGATION OF IGNATIUS yielded no confession about the church burnings. Each question that might implicate him in the crime was met with denial and surprise at being asked. As to his stalking Abigale, Ignatius convinced Sanford he did not know the woman. Instead, a single name kept surfacing to explain his motivation: Gustav Heinz.

When Sanford's men returned from investigating Ignatius's apartment, a one-bedroom flat in a rundown boarding house, they reported nothing to implicate him in the arson: no hood, torch or riding gear, and no written communication from other deserters. His landlady said she'd never seen him on a horse, and that whenever he was out at night he usually came home drunk.

They did, however, find his Confederate uniform, dirty and wrinkled. "He seems to be a bum, sir," said the reporting sergeant. "A confederate deserter and a bum."

"Well, a whoring bum, as well," replied Sanford. "Both of you, go to Savannah Gardens and get the proprietor, named Gustav Heinz, bring him in now. You can threaten to close down his business if he resists. Tell him we have full military authority to close all brothels. He'll understand."

———◆———

Gustav was brought to army headquarters around 6 p.m. On the way over he kept asking his soldier escorts, "Vat do they vant vith me? I do nothing wrong." As instructed, the soldiers only told him he was "wanted for questioning."

The soldiers ushered Gustav into the interrogation room and seated him across from Major Sanford. After Sanford introduced himself Gustav asked the same v-riddled question. Sanford paused a moment to make sure he understood the question, then proceeded.

"Mr. Heinz, we have reason to believe you may have knowledge of some criminal activity. I need to ask you a few questions. This city is still under military rule, so I have the authority to hold you if I have to."

"My boarding house is legitimate business, everyone—"

"This has nothing to do with your brothel. I am speaking about the church burnings. We think you know who did it."

Sanford noted an expression of relief on the German's face. *That means he's probably innocent, which is what I assumed. Now he'll be happy to tell me about Ignatius.*

"Mein Gott, I know nothing about those awful acts of vandalism. Why you called me here for that? I could have told your soldiers. I know nothing. Now, may I go?"

"A few more questions, please. Who is Ignatius Gardner?"

Gustav's expression changed from relief to consternation, clearly revealing he knew the man. After a short pause, "I believe he's a customer of my establishment."

"Just a customer?"

"Ya, I have many customers."

"Do you talk to your customers?"

"Sometimes."

"Did he tell you about the church burnings?"

"What would he tell me?"

"Did he tell you who did them?"

"Nein, he never mentioned anything about the churches. I don't think he is a religious man."

Sanford chuckled at the comment. "Do *you* know who set those churches on fire? Or have any idea?"

"Again, I know nothing about such crimes. I am an honest man. If I know anything, I tell you right away. Alas, I know nothing. I tell this over and over."

"Ignatius is a customer of your boarding house?"

"Yes, I already say so. Occasionally, he comes."

"Then why do you pay *him*?"

"What are you talking about? Pay him? My customers pay me."

"I can hold you forever, your business will probably close in a day without your presence. I know it is a cheap brothel, only one manager around. If you want to return there tonight, I suggest you cooperate."

Sanford noted his prisoner's look of despair. *I have him. He will cooperate.*

"What did this Ignatius fellow tell you?" asked Gustav. "That I paid him some money?"

"That you paid him occasionally to follow a certain woman about town."

There was no response. Gustav stared down at the floor.

"Is that true?" asked Sanford.

"It was innocent gesture. I meant no harm."

"Who is the woman?" Sanford demanded.

"What woman?"

"The woman you paid him to follow."

"Who did he tell you?"

"I want YOU to tell me. Or we stay here all night. And you don't see Savannah Gardens again. Except when the building is sold at an army auction."

In a barely audible voice, Gustav replied. "Mrs. Abigale Tate."

"Louder. I couldn't hear you."

"Mrs. Abigale Tate."

"How do you know her?"

"I met her in the negro church, Third Ogeechee Colored Baptist, before Christmas."

"How do you know where she lives? Ignatius said you gave him her address."

"I followed her home after the service. But I don't myself chase after her."

"Then why are you are paying Ignatius to follow her?"

"I find pretty women, like to know more about them. It is my, what you say, fetish. But I mean no harm."

Sanford did not know if Gustav had said 'woman' or 'women'.

"You've done this before?"

"Once or twice. I mean no harm. I get charmed by women, like to know more. I mean no harm."

The man is an actor. Perhaps he was planning to abduct her? No, that is unlikely. More probable he wanted something to blackmail her with. If so, what could that be?

"What could you learn that made it worth your money to find out?"

"I don't know. That's why I pay. I am telling the truth. She is a fine woman. Does not deserve a rogue like me. Ich bin ein niemand."

"Come again?"

"Sorry, I get nervous, talk in German. I am a nobody. Mein Gott, I tell you the truth. Now please, let me go. My customers start arriving soon."

"What did you learn from Ignatius about her?"

"That she likes to walk. She walks all over Savannah. Visits many peoples."

"Anyone in particular?"

"No one in particular. Friends, churches, City Exchange. He does not follow her inside these places. None of my business."

Except you make it so.

"Ignatius noted her visits to First Ogeechee Colored Baptist Church. You met her at Third Ogeechee Colored Baptist Church. What was that about?"

"I don't know, except the preacher from Third Ogeechee Colored, this Mr. Simms, moved his service over to First Ogeechee Colored while his church was being rebuilt. First, second, third, the colored have several Ogeechee Baptist churches. Maybe there's a number four? I don't know."

"And you went to First Ogeechee also?"

"No, no. I only go to Third Ogeechee Colored, before it burned down. Mein Gott, I get confused, First, Third."

"But he moved over, and she later visited that First Ogeechee Colored Baptist church. You paid Ignatius to learn of this, correct?"

"Yah, he moved there. But for what purpose, I don't know."

"For what purpose he moved there?"

"No, no, no. For what purpose she visited him. I don't know."

"So her visits to First Ogeechee Colored Baptist were to see him? Not someone else? Not just for Bible study?"

"I don't know. Perhaps."

"Perhaps what?"

"Perhaps she went to visit him. I don't know."

Sanford glared at his prisoner. At first Gustav stared back, then lowered his eyes.

Perhaps he doesn't know. Or perhaps he does. No matter. He's innocent of the fires. But a lowlife, nonetheless.

Sanford pushed his chair back and stood. "Mr. Heinz, I must say, you are unworthy specimen. A real fimble-famble. Lucky for you, you are in this country. In your native country the nobility would probably have you hanged."

Gustav bowed his head, did not reply.

"Look at me, Mr. Heinz."

Gustav complied.

"I don't know how long we will be in Savannah, the army, I mean. But if I hear you ever again bother this woman, or arrange to have her followed, you will end up in my stockade so fast your head will spin, your brothel will close, and the good people of this city may never see your face again. For which they will be better off. Do you understand?"

"Yes."

"Good. Then tell me, what did I just say?"

"That if I bother – or follow – Mrs. Tate again, I will disappear."

"Well summarized, Mr. Heinz. Now you may go."

— *TUESDAY, FEBRUARY 7, 1865*

Ignatius was kept overnight in the stockade. The next day, finding no evidence that he took part in the church burnings, and nothing more damaging than his agency work for the German, Sanford had to release him.

Ignatius was brought back to army headquarters for a final debriefing. Despite the hanging threat, Sanford didn't much care that Ignatius was a Confederate deserter. He was far more interested in his potential as an informant.

"You're free to go, Mr. Gardner, but of course if we hear about you harassing our female citizens again – Mrs. Tate or any other – we will lock you up and throw away the key. Rest assured Mr. Heinz will never again ask for your services, but just in case, be aware."

"I ain't never goin' near that German ever again. Bad business. And you can be sure I'll get my pussy somewhere else than his rathole."

"Well, then, you're free to go, but…we could use your help."

"Oh, really? How so?"

"You know the value of information. We need information about the arsonists."

"I done told you I know nothin'."

"And we believe you. But being a Confederate, it's possible you'll hear something about these men, who they are, or when they'll strike next."

Ignatius did not respond.

"If you learn of such things, and your information is accurate, there is a reward. Have you seen our posters? Probably not. They only went up yesterday."

"I ain't no snitch."

"This isn't snitching, Ignatius. This is revealing information about outright criminals. It is not about blue versus gray. These people aren't fighting for anything but destruction. They wish to destroy property in your city. Do you want Savannah turned into a lawless frontier town? Help us find these men and bring them to justice."

Sanford reached into a leather case, removed a large piece of paper and laid it in front of Ignatius.

"You can read?"

"'Course I can read. I ain't dumb."

"Then you see the reward?"

The poster read: WANTED. SAVANNAH CHURCH ARSON-ISTS. $100 PAID TO PERSON OR PERSONS PROVIDING INFOR-MATION LEADING TO THEIR ARREST AND CONVICTION. CONTACT ARMY HQ, 138 BAY ST.

There was a pause, then Ignatius said, "One hundred dollars. But they got to be convicted first?"

"Well, yes. Otherwise people could be turning in anyone, just to get the reward. No, we need the actual culprits. The perpetrators, who will be convicted in a court of law."

"You don't hang 'em first?"

Sanford could not resist a smirk. "Only if they're deserters. No, we won't hang 'em until we can prove they did it. You lead us to the actual arsonists, and we'll get the evidence. I'm sure there's plenty of it, once we know where to look."

"If I knew, which I don't, and I informed, my life wouldn't be worth two bits, let alone a 100 bucks."

"Your name won't be revealed. At least not by me, and you only need to tell me."

"What if'n you ain't around? Ain't you moving back up north soon?"

"Eventually, yes, but not anytime soon. Probably not for at least a few months. We certainly hope to find them before then. You'll help us?"

"Well, I understand where you're comin' from. If'n you hear from me again, I'll have something to tell ya. If I don't, don't look for me around this place."

"Fair enough," said Sanford, and the men shook hands.

CHAPTER 34

— *WEDNESDAY, FEBRUARY 8*

SANFORD RETURNED TO SECOND OGEECHEE Colored Baptist to interview one or two more people about the fires, and to play the church's upright piano. Abigale came in the afternoon, as requested, this time without an escort.

She heard him playing from the vestibule, and was at first reluctant to interrupt. But the sergeant at arms told her to walk to the stage, that he was expecting her. When she was half way down the aisle he stopped playing, bounded down the stage stairs and shook her hand. The auditorium was empty except for the one soldier up front, now out of earshot.

"What did you find out?" she asked.

"Not much, except I can almost guarantee, you'll never be bothered by that scoundrel again. He was hired by the German fellow, Gustav."

"I suspected as much. Why?"

"Can't say for sure. I think it's because he runs a brothel and has a sick mind when it comes to women. You can fill in the details."

"Should I be worried?"

"Not at all. As long as I am around."

"Are you leaving anytime soon?"

"Not as far as I know. But we think the war is going to end soon, and then who knows?"

"And when it ends, where do you go? Where is your family?" *Innocent enough question. But I've got to know more.*

"Some in Maine, some in New York."

"Well, you must be enjoying our warmer winters."

"Yes, can't complain about the weather. Feels like June where I live."

"Your family must miss you greatly." *Now he'll tell me.*

"Come, let me hear you play the piano. It's so good to listen to someone else. I get bored hearing only myself."

"I…I didn't bring any music."

"I have lots of sheets. Play anything you like."

"Are you sure?"

"Absolutely. Have you ever played a duet, where one person plays the left hand and the other the right hand?"

"As a child, with my teacher."

"Well, play a couple of pieces by yourself, then pick out something we can play together. I prefer the treble clef myself."

She laughed. "So that makes me the bass clef girl."

"We'll see. It should be fun."

He took her arm and ushered her up the stage stairs. She sat at the piano and thumbed through the Chopin mazurkas, settling on two. While she played Sanford sat at the table used for interviews. After each piece he applauded.

"Now, find a duet. How about that last mazurka you just played?"

"Yes, that will work. She moved left on the bench and he sat next to her, their bodies almost touching. She felt excited but willed her concentration on the keyboard.

"I'll count, he said. One-two-three-four."

They began playing, a little out of rhythm for the first few measures, then together, the two musical clefs in harmony. The piece lasted only two minutes.

"That was fun," he said.

"Yes, yes it was."

"Let's do another."

After a few more pieces a sergeant came down the aisle, and called out, "Sir?"

"Yes, sergeant?"

"Your next appointment is here, sir."

"Thank you. Tell him to wait, I'll just be a minute."

"Well, Abigale, back to work. They stood and he took her hand. "I would like to see you again. General Ryan is hosting a dinner tomorrow night for his staff. Would you join me?"

Should I ask if he's married? No. I'll find out in due course. But this is too quick. And where is Rufus? I can't ask him that. He'll want to know why I care.

"Oh, Major Sanford, that is such short notice. Thank you, but I am busy tomorrow night." *Don't ruin this opportunity.* "Perhaps another time."

"Yes, that would be nice. I will check my calendar, see what evenings I may be free next week."

I must know before this situation goes any further. "Excuse me for being inquisitive, Major—"

"Stephen, call me Stephen."

"Yes, Stephen. Excuse my probing, but I really don't know much about you. Your family situation. Are you not married?"

She hoped for a 'no' but it was not forthcoming. Instead, he turned his gaze up the church aisle, where his sergeant and the visitor were waiting.

"Abigale, this is not the place to discuss my background, or as you put it, my family situation. Perhaps if you could come to headquarters tomorrow afternoon, we could chat then?"

"Are you sure? I don't want to bother you if you're busy."

"I am sure. You'll come on official business, with more information about the church fires. You will be ushered right in."

— THURSDAY, FEBRUARY 9

Oh her way to his office Abigale felt glad she had been direct with the major. She could not deny strong attraction to him, but wished not to start another relationship with a married man.

She entered the headquarters building and met a different sergeant. "Please tell the major that Mrs. Tate is here."

"He's expecting you, ma'am. Come this way."

In the office Sanford was effusive. "Thank you for coming. I was afraid you might change your mind."

"Your piano playing intrigues me. I wish to learn more about you."

"As I do, you," he said. "Please, sit down."

She took a chair and he sat behind his desk.

"So, you are married?"

"Was. She died last year."

"Oh, I'm sorry. Why didn't you tell me at the church?"

"Have you seen a grown man cry? It was not the place to discuss my past."

It is wrong to feel happiness at another's loss, but I cannot help the feeling.

"From what did she succumb?"

"They say consumption. Some type of illness. She is buried in Brooklyn."

"Do you have children?"

"No. She had two miscarriages."

"How old was she, if I may ask?"

"She died at twenty-six."

"And so you did not remarry?"

"Hardly. I entered the army. Not the place to find beautiful, talented women such as yourself."

"Sir, you flatter me."

"Abigale, your questions are not unimportant, but I am not proposing marriage. I am just asking if you will have dinner with me some night."

"I understand. But I have lost a husband and father to this war, killed by your compatriots. And I have recently suffered from what some call the melancholy. I wish to spare myself more loss, more disappointment, should something ever develop between us. I am perhaps too wise in the ways of this world, though I have scarcely ever even stepped foot outside Savannah."

"So you cannot date a Yankee soldier? Do you fear my kind more than the men who fought for the Confederacy?"

She laughed.

"Why do you laugh?"

"Men are men."

"What does that mean?"

"You are what you are."

"You speak in riddles. Will you have dinner with me?"

"I would love to, but please, not right away. I will be busy for the next week or two with family matters, but then I should be free. Perhaps then you could come to my home, for dinner, meet my mother and sister. We have an old upright and you could play after dinner."

"I would be delighted. You will let me know, then?"

"Yes, as soon as I am free of other obligations."

"Madam, I await your invitation."

What am I doing? Inviting a Yankee officer to our home? What will mother say? Jane will be delighted. Perhaps he knows her lover, Captain Broderick. Yes, it's the right thing to do. I shall have no more excuses. I am done with mourning, done with the melancholy. I am almost twenty-five, for God sakes. But first I must find Rufus, talk to him.

—————

CHAPTER 35

— *Sunday, February 12*

ABIGALE WAITED UNTIL SUNDAY TO start her investigation. As soon as Polly returned from church she asked, casually, "How was Reverend Simms' sermon? Is he still preaching the light is coming?"

"Oh, he didn't preach none today. They's had a replacement fo' him."

"Really, where is he?"

"Da new preacher say he went to Jekyll Island, that his wife is ill, needs salt air. We did a prayer for dem."

"Is that the first you heard he had moved?"

"Sho nuff."

"Do you know where he lives, in Savannah I mean?"

"Only that it's out in Yamacraw, wi' the free colored. Why you aks, Miss Abigale?"

"I want to go visit, see if he's home."

"Go to Yamacraw?"

"Why not? Is it not safe?"

"Fo' a white woman? Not a place ta go alone."

"You'll go with me?"

"Well, you sho can't go by yourself."

"You ever been to Yamacraw?"

"Sho 'nough, when I was little. But ifn' you aint free, no reason to go."

"But you are free, now."

"I spose, but the free colored befo' Sherman came, they still more uppity. Got dere own houses and such. None of da slaves done that as I know."

"Well, uppity I can deal with. Doesn't sound dangerous to me."

"Well, if I goes wi' you, we'll be fine. But why do you want to go ta his house? If he's in Jekyll?"

"Well, maybe he's home now. Maybe someone in the neighborhood knows more. Can you find out, from your friends, where he lives? Someone must know."

"Dat's true. I gots people I can aks. Why I be aksing, though?"

"You just want to check to see if he's all right. That's a fair reason. No need to mention my name."

"Yes, ma'am, I can do dat. I know he sho' done helped you, and you gots to talk wi' him. He's got a way wi' the women folk."

Abigale accepted the statement as innocent of innuendo, as spontaneous from a loyal servant, and did not reply.

— MONDAY, FEBRUARY 13

Polly made enquiries and learned only that Rufus lived on the corner of Zubley and West Boundary in Yamacraw. No one knew which house number.

Monday was cool but sunny, and at 11 a.m. Abigale and Polly set out on foot for the Yamacraw neighborhood, its southern border only a half mile distant across West Broad Street.

They soon entered the free-colored section. "I ain't been over here in years," said Polly. "Better than slave shacks, dat's da case."

"I looked at a map," said Abigale. "The intersection is this way."

They arrived at the sought-for corner. There were four houses at the intersection, each a small frame structure, with a short stoop and front porch, and a tiny front lawn. Looking up and down the dirt streets, Abigale saw no brick structures, certainly none of the town-houses so prevalent in Savannah. The wood on all the houses needed painting and patching, and she wondered if the roofs leaked.

A few colored walked the streets, but none close by. On the porch of one house, near the corner, sat an elderly woman. They approached her, and from the lawn Polly enquired as to where Mr. Rufus Simms lives.

"Right next to me," she replied, and pointed to the house next door. "But he ain't home. Gone to the islands. With his wife."

"Do you know when he might be returning?" asked Abigale. She noted a suspicious look on the woman's face.

"He owes you some money?"

"No, no, nothing like that. I am helping with his church building fund, and want to go over some things with him." A plausible lie, she thought.

"Well, I don't rightly now. But when I sees him, I'll tell him youse looking for him. What be your name?"

"Oh, just say Abigale and Polly came looking for him."

"A white woman and a colored," she said. "Lordy be. Which one you be? Let me guess. You be Abigale. Polly more a black folks' name."

"Yes, that's right. Please tell him we came by, to enquire about his church."

"Too late. Done burned down."

"Oh, we know. We came to discuss the rebuilding."

"Don't know when it be finished. But I'll tells him you came by. May be a while befo' he comes back, though."

"That's fine. Thank you."

They turned to begin the walk home, stopping in front of Rufus's house. "So that's it," said Abigale. "Number fifty-two West Boundary. Remember that address, if we ever have to return."

"Fifty-two," said Polly.

They walked up Zubley toward West Broad. "Well, da walk be good," said Polly. "But I don't think we know mo' than before we set out."

"No, this was worth it. Thank you for coming with me."

Why didn't Rufus let me know?

— TUESDAY, FEBRUARY 14

"Polly, how would you like to take a boat trip with me?"

"Where dat be?"

"To Jekyll Island."

Abigale assumed Polly would be surprised, though she didn't know in which way – resistance or anticipation. Polly had never been on a boat. For that matter, Abigale had been on a ship only twice, both daytime excursions on the Savannah River. She'd never been out in the ocean, or around the Sea Islands.

"You still looking for Reverend Simms?"

"That's why we are going. You will go with me, won't you?"

"All your runnin around to da black folks' country, you sure do need me. Don't think any white folks live down dere."

"Actually, that's not so. The Union army has some soldiers stationed on Jekyll."

"How long be da boat trip?"

"I checked with the docks. They have a packet going to the Islands twice a week. We can leave tomorrow and come back on a Friday boat."

"Dat be passed on wi' Mrs. Gordon?"

"It will be fine with Mother. She and Jane can do without your services for a couple of days."

"And where we be stayin? I don't like to sleep wi' no alligators."

Abigale laughed. "Polly, tell me, have you ever seen an alligator?"

"Sho have. Big and ugly. Lots of teeth."

"They have a boarding house on Jekyll. It's actually run by colored, so shouldn't be a problem you staying there."

"He know youse comin?"

"No. I have not written. For all I know he might not even be there."

"Oh, he be dere. I hear his wife took for da worse, he wouldn't be leavin' and travelin'. Maybe not a good idea you showin' up."

"What do you mean?" *How much does Polly know? She is uneducated, but not dumb.*

"Can I aks somethin'?"

"Sure."

"Why yo be wanting to go?"

"I've got to talk to him. He helped me so much in my time of sorrow. I am much improved. I've got to just speak with him, if only for an hour or so."

"Well, dat makes some sense. As long as dere be place to lay my head, and food for da table, I'm on my way to Jekyll Island."

"Good. I will get the tickets. We leave tomorrow. I'm told it can be windy and cold at sea, so pack heavy clothes."

"Sho nuff."

Abigale waited until dinner was finished, while Polly was clearing the table, to tell her mother and sister. They were surprised by both the timing and the purpose.

"You're leaving *tomorrow*, with Polly?" asked her mother, followed quickly by Jane's "You're going there to look for that *colored* preacher?"

"Yes, mother, the way the ships run, tomorrow is the best time."

"And...?" asked Jane.

"Yes, that's my reason for going."

Though Polly worked for Henrietta Gordon, and not the children, Mr. Gordon's death had left Abigale in charge of the household, in practice if not formally stated. Abigale knew this and did not expect any real resistance, at least from her mother.

Jane was more vocal, and probing. "You visited that preacher some afternoons, for help with your melancholy."

"Yes, you knew that."

"And he left town suddenly?"

"His wife was ill, so I was told, and he took her to Jekyll for better air."

"Well, sister, you seem to have been helped by his treatment, whatever it was."

"Yes, I just need to talk with him. It's been a while."

Jane looked at her mother. "Mother, do you have any questions for Abigale?" The expression on Mrs. Gordon's face, at least to Abigale, was one of resignation.

"No, dear," she said.

"Well, I do," said Jane. "Perhaps you could leave us to talk."

"That's not necessary," retorted Abigale. "We can go in the living room."

The two sisters got up and walked to the living room. Rather than sitting, they stood before the fireplace.

"I now see what I did not see before," said Jane. "It is a very clear picture, my older and wiser sister."

"What are you talking about?"

"The hotel room. The church visits during the week. Now, going to Jekyll Island. I have been blind to the truth."

"Which is?"

"Do you deny it?"

"Deny what."

"That *he* has been your lover!"

Abigale did not respond.

Jane's eyes widened and she smiled. "I am surprised and not surprised. You are not the prude I thought you were. But a colored man? What do you see in him? Did *he* use protection?"

"Think what you will, Jane. You are living your life your way, please let me live mine."

"Fine. Just don't lecture me about men."

"I've never lectured you about men."

"No? Let's see. Jane, do you use protection? Jane, do you know what you're doing? Jane, how can you flirt with every soldier you see? On and on."

"You are being unkind. I have had some concerns, as you are but at teenager, but—"

"In number of years only. I have never been married or pregnant, but feel I know as much about men as you do, if not more."

How to argue with her? She is so headstrong. "Jane, back at Pulaski House we agreed not to discuss our chance meeting, and we have both kept that promise. Can I now ask you to please keep your speculation entirely to yourself, to tell no one?"

"Yes, on one condition. If you agree, my lips are forever sealed."

"What condition might that be?"

"That you admit Rufus Simms has been your lover."

Abigale stayed silent.

"So you won't admit? Then I am at liberty to speak out."

"No, please do not."

"Then tell me."

"It is true. But our affair is over. That is why I must see him. To tell him in person."

— WEDNESDAY, FEBRUARY 15, 1865

The ninety-five-mile sea distance from Savannah to the Jekyll Island dock showed a nine-hour trip on the steamer packet's manifest, including a stop on the way at St. Catherine's, another of Georgia's Sea Islands. Abigale and Polly boarded the ship at 7:30 and set sail at 8 a.m. They were blessed by good weather. Abigale enjoyed the novelty of trip, being out on the water, the wind in her face, and observing a myriad of sea birds and an occasional porpoise.

The packet held sixty passengers, a mixture of soldiers, negro settlers going to Jekyll or St. Catherine's, and a few white men seeking business opportunities in the Sea Islands. With the war almost over, many northerners were migrating south to look for prospects. One man Abigale met on deck was convinced Jekyll would be a great place for rich Yankees to spend the winter, "when this infernal conflict is done with." His plan was to purchase land, or at least to see if there was land to purchase. "A lot of the owners have fled, so seeking title may take a while."

An hour out to sea and Polly became sea sick. "I don't like all dis rocking back and forth," she told Abigale. "I go down below and rest my soul." She came back on deck at St. Catherine's, then submerged again until the ship was in sight of Jekyll.

The Jekyll dock faced the inland waterway, across from the beach side of the island. As soon as they disembarked Polly felt back to normal.

"Glad to be off dat boat," she said. "I think I might walk home."

"On water?" asked Abigale.

"Lordy be, we is surrounded by da ocean."

"You'll be fine, Polly. A couple of days here and we'll be ready to get back on that ship."

They asked directions for the Du Bignon boarding house and one of the dock handlers pointed to an area close by, to "keep walking and you can't miss it."

From her research Abigale knew the boarding house was run by negroes who used to work the Du Bignon plantation. In fact, it was once part of that storied plantation. By the time the Federals arrived in 1862, the plantation was completely deserted. Ex-slaves took it over and set up the boarding house, aided by a few free colored who could read and write. They did not have title to the property, but so far had not been challenged by any member of the Du Bignon family. Their non-legal position was strengthened by the presence of Union troops, who would occasionally board there.

The two women approached the house, situated only a few hundred yards from the dock.

"Well, here we are," said Abigale. "It's smaller than I imagined. Maybe ten rooms? What do you think?"

"I think it be big enough. Happy I ain't the one doin' the cleanin' of the place."

Inside they encountered a middle-aged black man sitting behind a desk. He was thin but not wasted, and wore a short white beard. He looked them over.

"You just come off da boat?"

"Yes," said Abigale, "we will need a room for two nights."

The clerk pointed to Polly. "You a free colored?"

Abigale proceed to answer. "Yes—"

"Pardon me, ma'am, but I'm asking her. She may not know she be free. Lots of our folks think they still be owned."

"Free as a bird," said Polly, "now dat Mr. Sherman done come. We's travelin' together."

"Well, then" said the clerk, "reckon I got a room. Two twin beds. You'll share. Three dollars a night."

Abigale had never slept in a room with a negro, but did not resist. Rufus would be proud, she thought. *I really have changed.*

By now it was close to sundown, and Abigale had not noticed any place to eat while walking from the dock.

"I'm afraid we didn't bring any food," she said. "Are there provisions for a meal nearby?"

The man laughed.

"Ma'am, do it look like we're starving?"

He sure is uppity for a negro. Better watch myself. Abigale gave him a bewildered look.

"For an extra dollar for each of you, you get two meals. My wife cooks. We eat at six p.m. Other guests will be joining you."

"That will be wonderful," said Abigale, clearly relieved that she didn't have to go scrounging for their meals.

By the time they settled in to the room it was already half past five. "It'll be dark soon," said Abigale. "Too late to do any exploring, but we'll start off first thing in the morning. Find Rufus and maybe see some of this beautiful island."

"Dat be good."

Abigale felt excited, first the boat trip and now the prospect of walking around a new land, like one of the European explorers she read about in school: uncharted territory, natives. Perhaps danger?

"How you goin' to find Mr. Simms?"

"Oh, we'll ask around. We'll start with that hotel clerk. Polly, why don't you ask him? Say he was your reverend at your church."

They returned to the small lobby, ready for dinner. The man was still at his desk when Polly went up to him.

"At my church we had a preacher from dese parts, done left us. Dey say he back here. Rufus Simms. You knows him?"

"Rufus? Course I do. Everybody on da island knows him."

"Where he be staying?"

"Same place as always. Since his wife died, don't see him too much."

The words stung Abigale. She fought any outward emotion. "When did she die?"

"Been a week. Just shortly after they got here from Savannah. I went to the funeral. Real Sad. Sad, I tell you."

"What did she die from?"

"Oh, some say da fever. Others say, heartbreak."

"Heartbreak? Why's that?" asked Abigale.

"Don't rightly know. Just what some say."

Abigale felt a knot in her abdomen.

CHAPTER 36

———▸———

— *THURSDAY, FEBRUARY 16*

THE NEXT MORNING THEY OBTAINED directions to where Rufus lived on the island. He was boarding with his wife's relatives, about a mile from the dock. The path was a grassy lane wide enough for a horse-pulled cart. Cool morning air made the walk pleasant. They encountered only a few people, and no wagons nor horses. Perhaps it's too early, thought Abigale.

"Polly, did his wife ever come to church?"

"Not as I knows, Miss Abigale. Folks didn't know much about her, 'cept she was ill some way. Da fever or somethin', I don't know."

"I honestly didn't think she was that ill, from the way he talked. But you never know."

Their directions were fairly specific. 'After about a mile you'll come to a sign that says "Cartersville." That's the compound her family lives in. Turn right and you'll see a clump of houses about 100 yards down. The first person you see, ask for him'.

Abigale hoped the sign was still there. Other paths diverged from the lane, and it would be easy to get lost, or delayed.

In twenty minutes they came to the sign, hand lettered in crude fashion to read "Cartesvile." It was just before nine in the morning.

After a right turn and walking some more they came upon a negro woman washing clothes in a tub. "Looks like we're here," said Abigale.

Beyond the woman were a dozen shacks or small houses, smaller and more dilapidated than what Abigale had seen in Yamacraw.

"Sho nothing fancy," said Polly

"I'll say. Makes his Yamacraw look like a palace." They approached the washerwoman and Abigale motioned for Polly to speak.

"We's lookin for Rufus Simms, told he stayin' out here. We's from Savannah."

The woman seemed surprised and Abigale added, "Oh, I hope it's not too early."

Without warning, the woman half turned her head and yelled, "Rufus, you got visitors!"

Abigale didn't know where to look. The small shacks were on both sides of the clearing. Then a straw curtain parted from one of them and Rufus came outside. He looked unlike the Rufus she knew – now unkempt, eyes sunken, perhaps ten pounds lighter than when last seen, and more facial hair. He walked to where they were standing.

"Abigale?"

"Yes, Rufus. Polly and I have come to see you. We took the steamer yesterday. I'm so sorry to hear about your wife. We just heard last night, at the boarding house."

Rufus rubbed his eyes. "Well thank you. Excuse my appearance, but—"

"Oh, that's fine. Nothing to excuse. We're sorry to barge in so early, but we're leaving tomorrow, and I--we-didn't know how long it would take to find you, so we set out early. I would like to talk with you. Just a little bit, if you could make the time."

Rufus laughed. "Does it look like I'm busy? Let me wash up a bit, and I'll be right back."

"That will be fine," said Abigale.

The washerwoman stared at them, but said nothing. Polly said something to her in Gullah, and she replied in kind, and then Polly and Abigale walked a distance away and sat on a log.

In a few minutes Rufus came out.

"You say you came in last night?"

"Yes, that's right."

"Well, I've got to show you around. I'll take you to the beach. That's a nice place for solace, for talking, and thinking."

"Oh, that would be wonderful," said Abigale.

———

Abigale found the beach was surprisingly close, about one-third of a mile from Cartersville. The only other time she had actually walked on a beach was during one of the Savannah River boat trips; then the ship anchored off Tybee Island, and a small skiff took her and some friends to the beach. That was fun, and she looked forward to again walking barefoot on soft sand.

Even before the ocean came into view she heard the waves and smelled the salt air, stirring anticipation. *Why wouldn't people want to live here? That man on the boat yesterday, he knows what he's doing. Northern people will love it down here.*

They climbed over a sand dune and there it was – the Atlantic Ocean.

"Oh, Rufus, this is marvelous."

"Yes, it's quite nice. I've been a few times since Mabel passed."

That's the first time he mentioned her first name. "Polly, isn't this nice?"

"Sho nuf. Lots of water, dat's for sure." The tide was low and the beach wide.

"Can we take our shoes off, walk on the sand?" asked Abigale.

"Of course, said Rufus. That's what you're supposed to do."

"Come Polly, let's go walking."

"I leaves mine on. Don't want to get no chiggers or nothin'. Hear'd 'bout them things."

"Your choice, Polly. I'm walking in my bare feet." Rufus already has his shoes off.

"We'll leave them behind this dune," he said. "No one around to bother them."

The trio ambled up the beach, north toward St. Simon's Island across the sound.

Without having been asked, Polly stayed discreetly behind, allowing Abigale and Rufus to talk in private.

"Do you know why I've come Rufus?"

"Not really."

"First, I came not knowing anything about Mabel's illness, and I am profoundly sorry. I assumed she'd be alive, and…well, I came to end our relationship."

"It ended when I left."

"That's the other thing. Why no warning, no message?"

"Wasn't time. There were threats to my person, and I could not jeopardize Mabel's safety. Also, any written note would be a risk, you know that."

"Yes, I thought the same thing."

"So you really didn't have to make this trip."

"I'm glad I did. Your island is beautiful, and I needed this closure."

"Closure?"

"Yes, to talk to you in person. You helped me a great deal, lifted me out of my melancholy, as you like to call it. But for race we would be – could be – a couple."

"But for race," he echoed. It was not a question, just a statement.

"Rufus, for a brief moment, a while back, I thought we could move to New York, make a life there."

"You thought such only for a brief moment?"

"Yes. But it would not work. And for the life of me, I can't explain why not. Just deep, deep down inside, I knew it would not work, even if you agreed."

"I would not agree."

"I know. And I'm thankful. It makes things easier to know I was right."

"Abigale, look at me." He stopped, turned toward her, held her shoulders at a distance. Polly, now some fifty yards back, slowed her walk.

She stared into his eyes, waiting for whatever he needed to say in such an abrupt fashion.

"Abigale, what is it you want? You've come all this way for closure? To talk to me after I have just buried my wife?"

"I didn't know she died. I told you that."

"But she did, and you're here. And if she was still alive, it would be more awkward. What was I to tell her, 'my mistress just dropped down from Savannah to say hello'?"

"I'm sorry, I didn't think about that. I had no conception of where or how you lived on the island. You always said she was bed-confined, so I didn't even expect to meet her, if she were alive."

"Yes, we had an affair, by your own admission it's over, done with. But I don't understand why you're here. What do you want?"

"Rufus, let's keep walking, please. I don't want Polly to think we're having an argument." He let go of her shoulders and they continued to stroll the beach.

"I can answer your question."

"Please, do."

"I want to feel comfortable inside, and coming here, talking to you has allowed that. That's all I want. Call it a feminine thing, a need of the weaker sex, whatever you wish. You could leave me and Savannah and not think twice about it. I could not do the same, that is, break apart without a meeting. I went to your office to tell you, last month, at what was supposed to be our regular appointment. You weren't there."

"No, I had left by then."

"But Reverend Patterson was. Did he know you had been using his office?"

"Yes, of course."

"Then why was he there, when you were supposed to be?"

"Oh, that's simple. I sent him a note."

"But you didn't tell him any details."

"None. Just that I would not be in the office that day. I am surprised he was there, though. He's usually away on Mondays."

"Did he know about our meetings?"

"Not to my knowledge. Why all these questions? They seem of no importance."

"Oh, just more feminine guilt. I had to tell him I was looking for you, to talk about your building fund. He seemed to accept that."

"He's a good man. Helped me in time of need."

Abigale turned around to look for Polly, who was now some distance behind, and waved for her to join them. "Let's wait for Polly. I fear she's going to feel isolated. It is so beautiful here. How far does this beach go?"

"Only another mile. Then we come to an inlet, and across the inlet is another island, St. Simons."

"So we have Tybee Island near Savannah, St. Catherine's Island, where we stopped on the way here, St. Simon's Island and Jekyll Island."

"And lots of little islands in between the bigger ones."

"These are the Sea Islands I hear so much about? What General Sherman's order refers to, where he's going to give land to the negroes?"

"Yes, that order came out of the meeting we had with him and Secretary Stanton in January. Remember the invitation I showed you?"

"Yes."

"Stanton asked us at the meeting what would be good for the colored, and we all agreed, our own land."

"So they did listen, after all."

"Yes. The idea is a good one. Sadly, their plan is doomed to fail."

"Oh, why?"

"It was done for politics. To satisfy Washington. There is no title to the land. Colored who have moved to the islands are like squatters.

As soon as the white folks return to their plantations, they will be kicked off, or made to work for slave wages."

"Slave wages? I haven't heard that term before."

"You will. It's wages paid to people who were once slaves, and are still treated as such."

"Here on Jekyll?"

"No, thankfully, but on the other islands."

Polly reached the pair. "Sho' nice beach you gots here. I been watchin' the birds. Some of them dives straight down to da water, snatches them a fish and gobbles it up. What a sight to see."

"Polly, you can walk with us."

"If you have time," said Rufus, "We'll go to the end of the island, to the inlet, then walk back and have lunch."

"Oh, that would be nice," said Abigale. "We actually have all day. Our boat leaves tomorrow morning. But are you sure that won't be an imposition? To feed us?"

"No, we have plenty."

Abigale pivoted toward the breaking waves and walked into a thin film of surf. Simms followed, while Polly stayed higher up on the beach. "My shoes is stayin' on, Miss Abigale. You two goes and get soaked."

Abigale entered the water up her ankles. "Oooh, the water's cold. I thought the ocean would be warmer."

"Come back in August. You can go swimming then. The Atlantic is always chilly in wintertime."

"Rufus, if we join you for lunch, the people around you, won't they think it odd?"

"You mean a white woman coming in the middle of Jekyll to have lunch with a negro minister whose wife just passed?"

"You do have a nice way of summing things up."

"If they ask, I'll just say Polly, one of my parishioners, came to visit, to see how I was doing and report back to my congregation. And she brought along her mistress."

"You know I'm curious about these things, forgive me. But did a doctor see your wife before she passed?"

"No need to. None on the island anyway. She had seen doctors in Savannah. None could help her. One doctor said he thought she may have cancer, but never knew for sure. She lingered for a long time, then got worse. Knew she was dying, wanted to come home, to be around what family she has left."

So why did the clerk say she died of a broken heart. Should I ask? No. Leave well enough alone.

———◆———

Lunch was dried pork and rice. They ate outside, sitting at a small picnic table. Abigale met Mabel's sister, some cousins. Rufus' in-laws were deceased. Relatives did ask 'What brings you two to Jekyll?' and Rufus replied with the Polly explanation. No more questions were asked. Abigale was thankful for this, but also thought Mabel's family was rather incurious.

Afterwards, Polly asked where the facilities were, and she and Abigale trotted off fifty yards to a small outhouse, with the door only a thin white sheet. Polly went first, then told Abigale she would head back to Rufus, and "not to hurry."

When Abigale returned she saw neither Rufus nor Polly, so she went exploring around the clearing where the small houses stood. In the far end she heard voices, indistinct at first. As she got closer she realized they belonged to Polly and Rufus, speaking in Gullah. Not wishing to intrude, she returned to the picnic table.

About ten minutes later Polly and Rufus returned.

"Where'd you two go?" Abigale asked, lamely.

"Just talkin'. He speak da language better'n anyone."

"You mean that Gullah dialect?"

"That be it. Common on dis here island."

"Well, I don't understand a word."

"How was the facility?" asked Rufus, with a grin on his face.

"Quite fancy."

"You get used to it," he said. "Life here's simpler than in Savannah."

"Rufus, how long you going to stay? Don't you miss your congregation?"

"Don't know. Yes, I miss work, and my congregation, but I've decided to wait until my church is rebuilt. Don't want to impose on Reverend Patterson any further. Hopefully, Third Baptist will be rebuilt by sometime in May. I get occasional reports. But then I think, I'd rather be here during the summer. So I don't know. I just don't know."

CHAPTER 37

———

— FRIDAY, FEBRUARY 17

IT WAS STILL DAYLIGHT WHEN Polly and Abigale reached the Savannah
dock. With two suitcases to carry, Abigale planned to rent a carriage
for the ride to Liberty Street. To her surprise Jane met them at the
dock.

"Didn't expect to see you here. Is everything all right?"

"Yes," Jane replied. "I decided to come and help you. Mother gave
me money to rent a carriage. How was your trip?"

"Excellent," said Abigale. "Jekyll is a beautiful island. You should
go sometime."

"One reason I came is to alert you."

"Alert me? About what."

"Not just you, but Polly also."

"What are you talking about?"

"Polly's sister Lucy came to our home yesterday. With her four-
year old son Sam."

"Lucy at da house?" exclaimed Polly. "What be da matter?"

"Everything seems fine. She said her husband went off with the
army, and that she's being relocated to one of the islands where she
can do farming and raise chickens. She has some papers that allow her to travel at government expense to get there. I think it's St.
Catherine's Island. Polly, she wanted to see you before she goes, and
I didn't want you two to walk in and be surprised. So I came to pick
you up."

250

"They are staying with us?" asked Abigale.

"Yes, Mother said they could stay in Polly's room."

"Dat be nice. The boy Sam, he behavin'?"

"A nice boy," said Jane. "Doesn't cause any trouble."

"Well, we'll have to get all this sorted out when we get home. Thank you for coming, and arranging a carriage."

"One more piece of news."

"Yes?"

"Mayor Arnold has asked mother out for an evening of entertainment. To a local play tomorrow night."

"He has?" Abigale was genuinely surprised.

"Yes, he wrote that he had two tickets, and his note said "I request the pleasure of your company." Our mayor seems to be a cultivated gentleman."

"She's going, I hope?"

"Oh, yes, she's quite excited about it. A New York company is performing, and the play is called *Our American Cousin.* Apparently it's a popular play up north."

"We've been away two days, and seems lots has happened. Anything else?"

"No, nothing else. But tell me about your trip. Tell me everything."

———◆———

Lucy wanted more than just to visit Polly. She wanted Polly to move with her to St. Catherine's Island.

At first Polly said no, of course not. But Lucy picked up where her husband had left off: mild intimidation. "My Digby was right. You still just a house slave."

Polly objected. "I ain't a slave no mo'. At least I gots what to eat, and dis' here roof over my head. What you got at da islands?"

"Freedom."

"I is free, here."

"Sister, let me see what dey is payin' you."

"You knows dey not payin'. Why you and Digby keep pokin' so?"

"Well, I gets twenty five dollars for moving, and all the land I can farm. If you come, you gets some money too. And I sure could use the help. We be eatin' our own food. There's talk dey give us a mule, too."

"And dey gives you a place to live?"

"Dat's a promise. Dey say da president hisself ordered it so. We is goin' to an old plantation da white folks done left behind. Lots of places to live dere."

"When you leavin'"

"Anytime, sister. I waits for you to makes up yo' mind. You go tell Miss Abigale."

"I don't know what's right no mo'."

Polly felt conflicted over forces. Desire for true freedom, versus… all the negatives of leaving Savannah, which were several. *What Miss Abigale gonna say? What kind of living gonna be on the island? What if Rufus comes back soon? I should be here for him.*

— Saturday, February 18

"Miss Abigale, can we talks for a minute?"

"Of course, Polly, what about?"

"Lucy wants me to go to da islands wi' her and Sam."

"Is that something you really want to do? They're pretty, those islands, but living could be hard, you know that."

"I knows that, but now I's free, can do what I want."

"And what do you want?" Abigale was prepared for this conversation, one she knew would come eventually. She was careful to appear kind, but also determined to retain Polly's services.

"I wants to be wi' my sister and Sam, and to be free."

"Polly you are free."

"I don't make no wages."

"We'll pay you." *There, I said it.*

"Dat be nice, Miss Abigale. But den I gots to pay for da room and da food?"

Abigale was prepared for this question as well, but paused for effect.

"No. We'll pay you in addition to the room and the food. And here's something else, Polly. You already have Sundays off. You can also take off any afternoon during the week, if you like, after your morning chores. Now, let's discuss the wages. We'll give you five dollars a week, paying it to you each Saturday, starting today."

"Did you say today?"

"Yes, five dollars today. That will be for the past week. Then next Saturday you will get another five dollars. The only condition is that you agree to stay on. You can't take the five dollars and then go with Lucy to the islands. That wouldn't be fair."

"Oh, I'd never do nothin' like that. If'n I stay, I stay. Now my head is spinnin'. Done told Lucy I'd go, but you make it so I stay. Now gots to tell her."

"Where is she, down in your room?"

"Dat's where I left her, to come talk to you."

"Here is a suggestion. I give you the five dollars, you show it to her, tell her you are staying, that we are going to pay you every week."

"Dat be good idea. I gives her the five dollars, to buy Sam some clothes and such, and dat make her happy. Oh, Miss Abigale, you sho' are a nice mistress."

— SUNDAY, FEBRUARY 19

On Sunday, February 19, the boat left Savannah for St. Catherine's Island, with Lucy and Sam, but not Polly. Abigale felt satisfied. Polly was secure in their home, the affair with Rufus was behind her and it had ended in the manner of her choosing. She noted his church was being rebuilt by volunteers, and trusted he would return soon to the city to begin life anew.

Most importantly, she could pursue a relationship with Major Sanford. Was that what she really wanted? She listed the pros and cons in her mind.

Pros: He's young, handsome, strong; loves music and plays the piano; is an attorney in civilian life, therefore can be a good provider; has no children to support and would want to have them.

Cons: He is a Yankee, certainly at odds with the southern culture she grew up in; he is an officer in the very army that killed her father and husband; he would likely not want to live in Savannah -- could she be happy living in New York? And he smokes cigars. Could she break him of that habit?

So there they were, the good and the somewhat worrisome about this Yankee. Should she wait and hope for someone else? And who might that be? Another soldier from the war, a Confederate, perhaps battle-scarred or disabled? An older man like Mayor Arnold? News reports indicated that up to a third of all Southern soldiers had died since 1861. Up to a third! She hoped and prayed Johnny would get home safely. Estimates of how long the war would last went from a day to another year.

Sanford is here now. He could be transferred up north any time. I will not wait.

Abigale decided to accept his invitation from earlier in the month, to have dinner with him, but in her house. She would invite him and have her mother invite Mayor Arnold. She broached the plan to her mother.

Mrs. Gordon did not like the idea. "Oh, we can't have Yankee soldiers here. Johnny is off fighting them, and we're going to invite one for dinner? I don't think your father would approve."

"Mother," replied Abigale, "he's asked me to dinner. He's an excellent pianist, and I want you to meet him. Yes, he's fought with the enemy, but Savannah has accepted defeat, and our own Mayor has said we are part of the Union and should cooperate. In fact, my idea is that you would invite Mayor Arnold as well."

"Oh, dear."

Jane chimed in. "It's a wonderful idea, Mother. After all, I had a nice relationship with that young Yankee captain before he left for Carolina." Jane never mentioned, and her mother never asked, exactly what type of relationship.

"But what if our Johnny comes home, and finds him here? Oh, my, what a scene that would be."

"He's not coming home this weekend," said Abigale. "We would have heard something for sure. Mother, we can't be enemies forever. I worry about Johnny as much as you do. I wish he was home. But he's not, and we have to live our lives. Please, let me invite him, and you invite the mayor. I think Dr. Arnold likes you. We'll have a wonderful time. Jane and I, along with Polly, we'll do all the work to prepare."

Jane nodded to show agreement.

"Well, I suppose so. Do you think Dr. Arnold will come?"

"You can ask. I think he will," said Abigale. *And he'll see I have another, much younger interest, which will be good.*

The dinner was planned for the following Saturday. As Abigale expected, both men readily accepted the invitation.

———

CHAPTER 38

— MONDAY, FEBRUARY 20

AT TEN IN THE MORNING a note arrived from Mrs. Susan Tate. Unlike the last note, this one was not a request for a meeting, but a demand. And not in Abigale's house. "Please, visit me at No. 13 York Street, where I am staying with my sister-in-law. It is only a short walk from Liberty Street. I will expect you later today or tomorrow, and will be waiting. There may be no excuse, young lady."

Of course Abigale could think of several excuses, or she could simply refuse to appear. But she sensed a certain imbalance in the woman, borne out of Franklin's death, that could cause trouble and must be dealt with. But how?

Abigale walked over after lunch, arriving around one o'clock. She dressed as always when out and about, with skirt, blouse, head scarf and jacket against the winter chill. The address was a townhouse of similar design to her own.

She knocked and the front door opened quickly. The other Mrs. Tate stood in the doorway wearing a dark smock, with a black shawl over her shoulders. "Come in, come in, Abigale. I am glad you could make it this afternoon."

Abigale entered the living room. "Thank you, Mother Tate. What is this meeting about?"

"Oh, you needn't call me Mother Tate. I am no longer a mother. Call me Susan."

She made no objection to calling her Mother Tate when we last we met. 'No longer a mother' means me she is bitter. I must brace myself.

"Come, sit down in the parlor," said Susan, "and let's talk. Just you and me." Abigale did not know if anyone else was in the home. Susan directed Abigale to a chair while she sat on the sofa.

"Now that the odious Sherman has left Savannah," began Susan, "I came back to visit, to see my sister-in-law and pick up on the latest news. When we last met I told you what her friends had relayed to me. They are not spies. They are not seeking you out, I assure you. But they see and hear things, and they know my situation. When they come over here to visit, they tell me what they see and hear, not to hurt my feelings but merely to educate me. They know the importance of family, of—"

"Please, Susan, no more. I know what you are going to say. It sounds like these people *are* spying on me. This is most unethical, if I may say."

"I am sorry you see it that way. It is not spying, but observing. And here is what they have observed." Susan pulled out a sheet of paper from a deep pocket in her smock and began reading.

"First Ogeechee Colored Baptist Church. Second Ogeechee Colored Baptist Church.

Third Ogeechee Colored Baptist Church. You have visited all three at one time or other, without any mourning clothes. A sacrilege, in my opinion, but there is more."

Abigale stared at her inquisitor and did not respond.

"You have recently visited the coastal islands with your negro maid. What for, I do not know, and it's none of my business. But, again, no hint of mourning clothes on this long journey. Yet the boarding area on the river is a very public place. People see you, they notice things. They tell me, out of courtesy. And they ask, 'Why is Abigale not in mourning dress, and what are you going to do about it?' What they relate offends me and I cannot abide. Next thing I hear you will be courting a Yankee, God forbid."

Abigale felt both disheartened and relieved at Susan's accusations. That someone could be so petty and irrational about her choice of dress was disheartening. It only confirmed her impression of Susan's imbalance, of her inability to focus on living life, as opposed to observing death. But at the same time there was nothing in the accusation about Rufus, or of Sanford. Susan didn't even seem curious why Abigale visited all *three* Ogeechee Colored churches. Wouldn't an intelligent person ask? No, this unfortunate woman's focus was solely on mourning clothes and local gossip, and no amount of talk or explanation would change her obsession.

"I don't know what to say," said Abigale, which was true enough.

"Well, Abigale, these women feel I should act, should do something and not just sit back and ignore the effrontery."

"Do something? What are you thinking of?"

"They suggest I prepare a formal written complaint to your own church, which I know is the First Methodist. And also, write a letter to the newspaper, telling how you besmirch the memory of a war hero. In a word, they think I should go public and try to shame you into wearing proper dress."

"That would be a mistake."

"Oh? Why so?"

"It would draw attention to you as well, and to Franklin." *It could also affect my relationship with Sanford. And perhaps reveal what has gone on between me and Rufus. I must stop this woman, somehow.*

"Franklin is a war hero," continued Susan. "You cannot besmirch him."

"I would never. You are making this very difficult for me. I have lost my father and my husband. My brother is still at war, the city is occupied, the economy is hurting and…and I am now to be threatened by you for not wearing black dress? I will not have my own reputation besmirched by you. I could just as well write letters about you, about your spying and your extreme pettiness in this matter."

Susan's took a big sigh. "Then you don't understand, my dear Abigale. I have nothing more to lose. I have already lost the one thing dearest to me in life. You will find another husband. I will never find another son."

I have to contain her. She is unstable and unbalanced. But I cannot wear a black dress just to satisfy her.

"Think hard before you seek publicity, Susan. It will draw attention to yourself. Not everyone agrees with these women who spread gossip. We are now occupied by Yankees, who do not care for our southern customs. And the more attention you receive, the less sympathy will eventually come your way. Publicity may not be to your liking. Short term satisfaction, perhaps, but long term it is *you* who will be the focus of attention. And I have an advantage you have not considered."

"What, pray tell, if I may ask?"

"I can leave Savannah. For good. Is that what you wish?"

"You will wear black."

"I will not."

The two women stared at each other for perhaps half a minute, then Abigale spoke.

"I have a compromise, a suggestion." It came to her quickly, out of desperation.

"Yes, what is it?"

"In deference to you and your wishes, when out in public I will wear a black arm band for the next three months. Not a full dress, but an arm band, and then only on one condition."

There was no immediate response. Abigale looked into her eyes and could feel the woman's contempt. *I trust she feels my resolve. I will not yield.*

"Only an arm band?" asked Susan. "That is a widower's convention, not a widow's. You insult me further."

"Mores are changing. I have seen women wear arm bands. If you persist, you risk pushing me out of the city. Then it is I who will have nothing to lose. And I assure you, if I leave I will first let it be known how you threatened me, a poor war widow. I shall start with the Mayor, whom I know personally, then proceed to the pastor of your church and then the newspapers. Then we'll see about your reputation the next time you visit Savannah. The gossip may not be in your favor."

The woman in black remained silent.

"I am not haughty, Susan, not at all. I will admit some traditions don't hold me as they do you. But I hold great respect for what Franklin did, and can honor him in other ways, through thoughts and prayers. I just cannot dress as you do. I am sorry."

"A black band, as you say?"

"Yes, and only on one condition, which is very important to me."

"What is your condition?"

"Simply this. Whatever you hear, you will keep to yourself, as long as I wear the black arm band in public."

"What would I hear?"

"I may choose to seek a male companion."

"Oh? So soon?"

"Franklin died almost six months ago. I am lonely and would not pass up an opportunity to marry again, should it present itself."

"Again I must ask. So soon? Can you not contain your desires? I know you were faithful when Franklin was in the army. And that was for almost two years."

"It is soon in your mind, perhaps. It is not too soon for a woman of marriageable age. But really, the elapsed time is beside the point. If you hear gossip that I am keeping company with another man, that is my business, not yours. You will keep it to yourself. There must be no more meetings, no more demands, no more threats of writing letters, if I keep my part of the agreement."

"He is not dead six months!" Susan began to cry. Abigale did not flinch, or move to comfort her.

"I am sorry, Susan, but those are my conditions. I will wear an arm band outside my home, and you will not seek to make a public cause about me, no matter what you may hear. I may go to every black church in town, I may associate with Yankees even, and you will not bother me again with demands, or write anything against me. I must have my freedom not to be spied on. As long as I wear the arm band, my business is mine, no one else's."

"You drive a hard bargain, Abigale."

"Do we have an agreement?"

"A hard bargain." Susan repeated, this time in a whisper.

"It is a fair bargain. Very fair. Do you agree?"

"It is not fair, but I will agree. If you wear the arm band. And may God take pity on your soul."

CHAPTER 39

— *TUESDAY, FEBRUARY 21*

THERE WERE SEVERAL BLACK ARM bands in the house, a large one for wearing over the arm of a jacket, a smaller one for a dress sleeve. They were common on the streets of Savannah, although as Susan had pointed out, much more so for widowers.

As Abigale was now known for abandoning mourning clothes, she pondered what questions it might raise.

"Why now, Abigale?"

"What made you change your mind?"

"Is it for Johnny – was he killed?"

Her mother and Jane were first with the questions; they knew no details about the meetings with Susan. She had told them the December meeting was benign, just a chance to reminisce. The one in January she did not even report. As for the arm band, she said "I see a few widows wear them. I just thought it would be appropriate for me to do so."

"Something made you change your mind," insisted Jane. "What was it? His mother, I wager."

"Let it go, Jane," said Abigale. "Let it go."

Abigale decided to walk to the main market and see if her arm band made any difference. She went with Polly. Fortunately the weather was good and they found Ellis Square crowded with shoppers. Several men tipped their hat in deference, but no one stopped to ask questions. She blended in with the other women quite nicely.

On the way home, a block from the market, she saw a familiar figure walking toward them – Gustav Heinz. Initial alarm dissipated when she noticed he was holding the arm of a woman, a rather stout person whose age and dress suggested she was not one of his prostitutes. They seemed a happy couple. As Gustav and the woman passed by, he tipped his hat in recognition, but said nothing. Abigale thought she detected a smirk on his face; if so, she reasoned, it would be in character.

Polly made the first comment. "Dat be da German from da church?"

"I believe so, Polly."

"Looks like he got hisself someone, don't be botherin' you no mo'."

"Let's hope so, Polly. Let's hope so."

— SATURDAY, FEBRUARY 25

Sanford arrived to Liberty Street first, dressed in civilian clothes. As an officer in the enemy army, he and Abigale both agreed wearing his major's uniform would be offensive to her mother. She explained to him on arrival, apologizing for greeting him with a prohibition, that smoking was not permitted in the house. To her surprise and delight, he replied he surmised as much and did not even bring any to light up, so it was not an issue with him.

"So you're the young man who plays the piano," said Mrs. Gordon. "Abigale has told me so much about you. I played when I was younger, but no longer. I taught my children to play. Perhaps you'll play something for us?"

"Not now, mother. After dinner, perhaps."

Jane appeared. "And this is my younger sister, Jane."

"How do you do?" she said.

"Glad to meet you, Miss Gordon. Abigale has told me all about you. I understand you went out with one of our captains last month."

"Yes, Jason Broderick. Do you by chance know where he is now?"

"No way to know. I assume in either South or North Carolina, with General Sherman."

Mayor Arnold knocked on the door and Jane went to open it. "Come in, Mr. Mayor."

Entering the foyer, he remarked, "Oh, remember, you can call me Arnold. But watch those questions, young lady." They both laughed.

Dinner was festive, with food prepared by Polly and Jane. Conversation steered toward the future, not the past, and Johnny's name wasn't mentioned.

Polly's was.

"Polly's a fine servant," said Sanford, after she had retreated to the kitchen. "I am glad she has not left you. Many other negroes have run away from their former masters."

"Why would she run away?" asked Mrs. Gordon.

"Henrietta," said Mayor Arnold, "I'm sure a lot of your acquaintances treated their former slaves with much less civility than you have treated Polly."

Jane laughed.

"What's so funny, young lady?" asked the mayor.

"I'm sorry. It's just…you have a funny way of saying things. I don't mean to be rude, oh, please excuse me, I'm embarrassed."

"No, no, not at all, you're not being rude. Please, explain what I said that's so funny."

Jane laughed again, in a school girl sort of way. Abigale stared, not sure where this was heading.

Sanford cleared his throat. "Here, let me help," he said. "Instead of saying, 'treated their slaves poorly', you said 'much less civility'. So, with all due respect, it must sound awkward to a young person. Is that right, Jane?"

Jane nodded.

"That is funny," said Mayor Arnold. "It's the politician in me. Always giving speeches. Why, Mrs. Gordon, it is incumbent on me to express my profound pleasure of your company, and to this magnificent repast which you have so generously bestowed upon your guests."

Sanford laughed and Abigale applauded. "Mother, our mayor has a fine sense of humor. Jane, thank you for bringing this up. Now Dr. Arnold, to answer your question, we have begun paying Polly a small sum each week, and she gets an extra afternoon off each week. This was in response to her intention to leave us and go the islands with her sister. I assure you, she did not really want to go, but felt obligated, until we made the counter offer. So, she is truly free to do as she pleases, and has decided to stay with us."

Abigale could tell Sanford was pleased, which was her whole point. To show him she was not a die-hard Confederate seeking to preserve bondage no matter what. *I have been through this with Rufus. I can handle a Yankee officer just as well, if not better.*

After dinner Sanford played the piano, followed by Abigale. Dr. Arnold listened, and at one point made a showing of holding Henrietta's hand.

As Sanford prepared to leave, and away from the others, he asked Abigale when he could see her again.

"I am free anytime."

"I cannot wait. Tomorrow? How about dinner at Pulaski House?"

"Is that where you are boarding?"

"Yes, they have an excellent restaurant."

"That will be fine."

"I will arrive for you up at six, then?"

I should tell him now, not surprise him. "I will be wearing a black arm band. A traditional mourning band."

"Oh? I didn't see you wearing one before. Why now?"

He is surprised. This is so awkward. Damn Mother Tate! "It is a promise I made to my dead husband's mother. I can explain better at dinner. I assure you it will have no effect on our relationship." *What am I saying?*

"As you say. Six o'clock, then?"

"Yes." *I am ready for him.*

— Sunday, February 25

She wore the black band on her jacket sleeve. When Sanford arrived for the date he commented immediately.

"I am thankful you warned me. Lately I've seen many women in black dress or with arm bands. I am sure they are prevalent up north as well. I'm only surprised at your sudden switch. I believe your husband was killed last September?"

"Yes. Let me explain at dinner. I hope it is not offensive."

"It's not offensive, but may draw attention."

And it did, more than they wished, during dinner at Pulaski House. Even as she related the story of her meetings with Susan Tate, patrons in the large dining room – other army officers, plus several locals and civilians from up north – seemed to stare at their table. The black band, now round her dress sleeve, signaled she was in mourning, while Sanford's uniform advertised he was a Yankee officer. This was an odd combination in occupied Savannah, so of course people would take notice.

Abigale pondered her dilemma. Abandon the band and risk a public calling out from an imbalanced Susan Tate, which could lead to much unwanted attention. Or wear the damn thing and hope it did not derail her new relationship.

"Perhaps I'm imagining it," she said, "but I think people are talking about us."

Stephen looked around. As he did so, eyes looking their way quickly averted.

"Ignore them," he said.

"I'll try." Which she did, but the meal was uncomfortable, and they hurried to finish.

"Abigale, let's get out of here. Go for a walk."

"Yes, a good idea. I do need some fresh air."

They walked across the street to Johnson Square. The park was lit with gas lamps, providing some illumination on the paths. He led her away to an interior section, near a large oak tree.

"Are you cold?" he asked.

"No, it's nice to get out of there."

He held her, hesitated briefly, then placed his lips on hers. She relaxed and kissed him with a great deal of passion, in a manner to show she wanted more, would accept more. All he had to do was ask.

Thus their affair began with a simple question under a Johnson Square tree. "Abigale, will you come to my room with me?"

And a simple answer: "Yes."

They returned to the hotel, walked quickly to his room, entered and shut the door. There was no coyness, no hesitation. Two mature adults, each with the experience that previous marriage afforded. He was prepared with protection; she was prepared with desire. More than just physical desire, also a wish to prove she was not in mourning, that she was a free and independent woman.

Naked, in his embrace, Abigale felt freer than ever before. She succumbed readily, joyously. She conveyed to him that which could not be spoken, for it would sound trite: *I am a woman. I want you, I need you. I am yours.*

When they were done, he spoke music to her ears. "Abigale, you are someone very special. I have not been so happy in a long time."

"You read my mind. My own thoughts about you," she replied.

Abigale did not stay with him the whole night, as she vowed to always return to her own bed, but they made plans to meet again in Pulaski House – his room, not the restaurant. Though not nearly as busy as in January, the hotel still afforded some anonymity, as long as she and Sanford avoided the restaurant. If someone took umbrage that she was in the company of a Yankee, she didn't care. Susan Tate, if she found out, could not complain.

———

CHAPTER 40

THE MONTH OF MARCH PROVED a strange interlude, with good and bad news for Savannah, and for the Gordon household.

Both Savannah newspapers had resumed publication, albeit under Yankee editorial control. The *Republican* kept its name but the old *Morning News* was now the *Daily News and Herald*. Of course it did not matter who controlled the papers; the war news was all bad for the South. You didn't lose Atlanta, Savannah, Charleston and Columbia and expect to prevail.

Columbia was a horror story – much of the city burned to the ground on February 17. The Confederates blamed General Sherman and his vengeful troops. The Yankees blamed rebels fleeing the city, claiming they purposely burned anything the bluecoats might find useful.

Savannahians absorbed the news with a sense of relief, that they had been spared this fate. But the news also confirmed the view of many about Sherman. He was the devil in a blue uniform. Explanations for Savannah's benign treatment abounded.

"Too lovely to burn."

"Hardee skedaddled, no one for Sherman to fight against."

"Sherman was just tired from marching, needed a quiet place to sleep."

Slowly, Savannah seemed to be recovering, in part from northern generosity. Several ships from Boston, New York and Philadelphia had docked in previous weeks, bringing much needed food from those cities. Most impressively, after Julian Allen's visits up north with a boatload of rice, these cities *donated* the food in a show of magnanimity. In February citizens of Boston printed out a detailed report of this charity.[16]

More than food came from the north. Carpetbaggers arrived, two or three a day, seeking to reinstitute trade and make their fortune. The port began flourishing, providing an increase in employment and circulating greenbacks.

Yet there remained abundant poverty, and most stores on Broughton were still boarded up. Black troops patrolled the streets, affronting the sensibility of many citizens. Confederate money was worthless, and most people took to bartering or using whatever greenbacks they could earn working for the Union Army or northern enterprises.

The Gordon-Tate household was not immune to economic adversity. Abigale worked as a substitute teacher at Drayton School, earning a few valuable dollars each session. If she and Jane did not find steady work, or marry, their mother would soon run out of money. The family had bartered all their silver and fine linens, and used up most of the inheritance left by Colonel Gordon. Reluctantly, Abigale eyed the piano as an item of value, which could be sold to a Yankee and transported up north.

Yet Mrs. Gordon had never been happier, or so it seemed to Abigale. She assumed, but never asked, that her mother and Mayor Arnold had by this time shared a bed, though like Jane, Mrs. Gordon always came home at night to sleep.

Even Jane seemed happy. With Jason away, Abigale did not think Jane had another man, and she did seem content with waiting for her captain. So content, Abigale wondered if she could be...*no, that's not likely. I am sure they used protection.*

— WEDNESDAY, MARCH 8

Abigale and Stephen began to meet regularly, every few days, in his hotel room. No more public dining, not with his uniform and her arm band. The room smelled of cigar smoke but there was no lit cigar; he had agreed not to smoke in her presence. This was a compromise she would live with. At some point, perhaps, she would try to get him to quit altogether.

Their affair was remindful of her situation with Rufus Simms, though with one major difference. Simms risked murder by white renegades if the affair had been discovered. Abigale knew blacks were sometimes lynched for supposed impositions on white women, consensual or not. For her, ostracism or outright banishment would have been a likely punishment.

With Sanford, the only sin lay in the fact he was a Yankee soldier and she a southern belle, one whose family had fought *his kind*. If people learned of the affair there would be gossip and perhaps verbal calumny, but no violence. Not wishing to test the reaction, they chose to remain as private as feasible, and Abigale always spent the night in her own bed. Their lovemaking occupied the early evening hours. Once home, Abigale would eat a late evening meal before going to sleep. That was her plan for this Wednesday as well.

"I have a surprise," said Stephen.

"Oh? I like surprises. Sometimes."

"Room service. We're going to order food from the hotel's kitchen, delivered right to our room."

Abigale immediately saw a problem. "For two? Or do I eat the leftovers?" she joked.

"I suspect the staff know I have a guest. It's common, and they are very discreet. There is no concern there. You would be surprised what goes on in this place." Actually, thought Abigale, with what she knew about Jane's affair she would not be surprised.

"Fine dining in room 174," she said. "What a wonderful idea."

"Are you hungry now? We can order first."

"I'll leave it up to you."

"Stephen fingered the one-page hotel menu, then said, "Let's eat afterwards. That makes more sense. Otherwise, I would probably rush through the meal, wanting you for dessert"

"How crude!"

He moved his eyes up and down her torso. "How beautiful."

"Oh, Stephen."

They quickly undressed and rolled into bed. A half hour later they dressed and he gave her the single-sheet room service menu. While she looked it over, he went to the dresser, opened a drawer and brought out a bottle of Old Madeira wine and two glasses. "To go with our dinner," he announced. He poured the wine and handed a glass to Abigale. They each took a sip.

"Splendid," she said. "As for food, there are several choices here. Have you decided?"

"I think I'll order the mutton, if they have it," he said. "And you?"

"I'll try the turkey. They must be getting it from up north. We don't have any turkeys around here anymore. We did at one time, but they all got killed during the war. Like the men."

Stephen frowned.

"I am sorry," she said. "I can't help myself sometimes."

"I understand," he said. "I would rather you speak your mind than keep these thoughts bottled up. I have much to learn about you."

"Yes, it works both ways." She thought what little she did know about him. He hailed from Maine; his father, a widower, still lived in Portland; he had one younger brother, a soldier in New York; before the war, Stephen worked as an attorney in Manhattan; he was skillful in handling rogues like Ignatius; and, of course, he played the piano.

He knew more about her, she reasoned. After all, she had opened her home to him, he had met her family. Still, she sensed one part of her life about which he must be curious, and hoped he wouldn't ask. He did, though, just after room service left with their dinner order. The question came while she sat in the room's padded chair, and he lounged upright on the bed.

"I hope you don't think me intrusive, Abigale, but I think this is a fair question. What was your relationship with Rufus Simms?"

Outwardly she did not flinch or show surprise. Inwardly, she fretted about how much to reveal. "Why do you ask?"

"Why? Count it curiosity. Count it the fact his name kept coming up in my interrogation of Ignatius Gardner and Gustav Heinz. They seemed to have a morbid interest in your movements about town. Ignatius noted several visits to First Ogeechee Colored church, apparently to see Simms. He said you always went in the back, where the office is located. So not to pray, I assume."

"What do you think it was?"

"Common sense informs me you met him for counseling, of the type a minister might give members of his flock."

"And what does uncommon sense tell you?"

He paused.

"Yes, Stephen?"

"That you were lovers."

"Really?"

"Though if confirmed," Stephen continued, "I would find it hard to believe. I've heard many tales of plantation owners fathering children with their slaves, but not of a white woman taking advantage of her male slaves. But I admit to ignorance of true plantation life."

"He is not a slave. Never was."

"No, I understand. Just used plantation life as an example."

"Honestly, Stephen, does it matter?"

"Only that there should be no secrets between us."

"Did you ever cheat on your wife?"

"Madam! Talk about changing the subject at hand." He sat upright on the side of the bed, as if ready to do battle. "Your honor, counsel's question is tangential to the primary question before the court."

"Your honor," replied Abigale, drawing out her words to affect a deeper southern accent than she normally spoke, "my question is not tangential, but direct and pertinent. Opposing counsel is seeking private information which may affect our relationship. If I am to answer, surely I am entitled to similar information about his background." Then, in a faux-male voice, she said, "So ruled. Mr. Sanford, you must answer the question."

He smiled. "Now I know why I love you. You are the smartest woman I've ever met."

Not those words again! "Strange. I think I've heard that before. It is more like a curse than a compliment, I fear."

"You don't take it as a compliment, then?"

"I suppose it is. But's it not always a good thing."

"Oh? Even if it attracts me?"

"It is not what attracts you, dear Stephen."

"Oh, and what then?"

"Do I have spell it out? My intellect, such as it is, may pique your interest, but it is the frosting, not the cake."

"You have a way with words. As I said, the smartest woman. So I am not the first to make that comment. Perhaps Mr. Simms, before me?"

"Did you ask him about me?"

"Did I ask him about you? No, it was not part of my purview and would have been inappropriate at the time. But other testimony has left me curious."

"As am I," said Abigale. "About you."

"Well, then, for the record, the answer is no. I stayed faithful to the end, but do admit to some lustful urgings the last months of her illness. A difficult period for me, as you can imagine."

"What is worse? A sudden loss or a protracted one?"

"A protracted one," replied Sanford, without hesitation. "Far more painful, I believe. So I have bared my soul. Your turn."

"I forgot the question."

"Your relationship with Rufus Simms?"

"Oh, yes. That one. What do you think?"

"Up until ten minutes ago I thought it nothing more than an unusual friendship, a white woman perhaps receiving counsel from a black minister. I wondered if there might be more, but doubted it. Now I am changing my mind."

"Now you're thinking...what?"

"There was more to it. That you *were* lovers."

Abigale smiled, the coy smile of someone who knows the answer and is deciding whether to offer it.

"Well?" he asked. "I'm waiting. Patiently."

Abigale took another sip of wine. "Take away the difference in race, and we might still be together. He is a most remarkable person. But our relationship could not continue, so whatever its nature, the thing is over, of that I promise, as God is my witness."

"So you affirm?"

"I affirm, and pray it does not matter to you."

Sanford paused, causing some alarm to Abigale.

"Does it?" she asked.

"It would concern most men, most Yankees, to tell you the truth. For all their grandstanding about slavery, I think most of them are prejudiced against the black race. A woman with such a history – involvement with a black man, even though the extent be unknown – would make them pause before initiating a relationship. Even for a woman as beautiful as you."

"Stephen, you are scaring me. I don't care about most men. I only care about one. Let's get this out in the open. If my womanhood is to be judged by a past indiscretion – no, that's not the right word – by a past dalliance with a negro, tell me now."

Stanford gave a half smile. "Forgive me, it was on my mind. You've answered my question."

"But you haven't answered mine. Does it matter to *you?*

"No. Not at all. It is over, as you said."

CHAPTER 41

—*Sunday, March 12*

Four days later Abigale and Stephen met again. While still in bed, before dressing for her return to Liberty Street, she spoke up. "Stephen, do you think you could ever give up the cigars?"

"I promised not to smoke them around you. Now you wish me to quit altogether?"

"It is just a question. I am not making any demand."

"Great men smoke cigars. They say you never see General Grant without one between his lips."

"Oh yes, General Grant. A great man if ever there was one. Highly revered in these parts."

"Where did you get your sarcasm from? It is most becoming."

"What makes you think I am being sarcastic?"

"My mother always warned me not to get involved with a southern woman who was beautiful and smart and could tie me in knots during casual conversation."

"Your mother was extremely prescient, I see."

"I give up. You win."

"About the cigars?"

"No, no, not that. About this inane conversation."

"Just tell me you'll consider quitting."

"I will consider quitting. Just no promises."

"That makes me happy."

"Good. Any more questions?"

Abigale paused for a moment. "Actually, yes, one I've been meaning to ask."

"Please do."

"You enlisted in the army? You weren't drafted?"

"That's right. I entered as an officer, so it's not like you join up and become cannon fodder."

"Well, my father did the same, so I understand. He entered as a colonel. And I suppose the two of you had similar motives, to preserve a way of life."

"That would be arguable. I wanted to preserve the Union, and abolish slavery. I doubt those were your father's goals."

"Father was never big on slavery. We only had one, Polly. For him the conflict came down to a matter of states' rights. If the colonies could break away from England, why couldn't the South break away from the North?"

Sanford leaned over on his side and stroked her hair. "I'll tell you why, and I want you to listen very carefully."

She didn't respond, but braced herself for what promised to be a political harangue. *Oh, I have made a mistake bringing this up.*

"Are you listening?" he asked.

"Yes."

"Then here's my answer. You are a beautiful woman, smart and engaging. If you think I'm going to let our differences in political philosophy affect our relationship, then you are mistaken and misguided."

"And that's why the South couldn't break away from the Union?"

"Precisely."

"You are the devil, Stephen!"

"And you are a princess. Kiss me."

— SUNDAY, MARCH 19

Abigale felt secure with Sanford. Unlike her previous situation, this relationship had real possibility. There was nothing to hide, both being white, unmarried and mature. They did not flaunt their love, but if they had, no one – excepting, perhaps, Susan Tate – would have cared.

She had been able to put aside Sanford's Yankee-ness, and the fact that it was his army who killed her father and husband, and might yet kill her brother. *Am I a traitor? Of course not, that's a foolish thought. I am a woman in need of love and he is a very loving man. That's all there is to it. Still, I wonder if other southern women could adapt so easily. Am I unique?*

She occasionally cried in bed; he would ask "what's wrong?" and she would answer "Nothing, just happy to be here."

Tonight, when they were done and still naked in bed, she burst into tears.

"Did I do something wrong?" he asked. "You certainly seemed to enjoy it."

"I…am…so happy…and I don't have a right to be," she sobbed.

"Nonsense, that shouldn't make you cry."

"I can't help it. They are tears of joy. And I have forebodings. I can't help it. I don't want to lose you."

He kissed and caressed her, then asked, "Why would you lose me?"

"Life is too short. We don't know what will happen, the next minute or hour or day, do we?"

"Abigale, you are being needlessly philosophical."

"I can't help it. Stephen, I LOVE YOU!" She put her face in his chest and cried. He held her tightly until she stopped.

"I'm sorry. I'm being foolish. Please forgive me."

"Abigale, there is nothing to forgive."

As they dressed for the ride back to her home, Abigale pondered that she had not been entirely honest with Stephen about her emotional outburst. No lies, of course. She just didn't explain what was in her thoughts: that his lovemaking transcended all previous experience. She knew about a woman's 'orgasm' and thought she'd had it with Franklin a few times, but was never sure. He had always seemed to come at the height of her pleasure, and then they were done. Now she was sure, and this was her secret, one she wished to keep forever private.

Four months ago she was in the depths of melancholy. Rufus had brought her up from hell, but his lovemaking was quick, perhaps withholding for fear of offending his white treasure. What he gave her was sufficient, and she was thankful, but she always knew there should be more. Now, with Sanford, she felt like a complete woman, emotionally, physically. *Truly happy.* That's why she cried so hard. With Sanford she felt *liberated.*

Abigale wondered about other women, if orgasm was common or rare. One day, perhaps, she would ask a married friend. Or her mother? No, she could never. Jane? Perhaps, but if Jane answered something snotty, like 'Yes, of course, all the time, how about you?' she would feel foolish. On this subject Abigale realized that her teenage sister, despite obnoxious and occasional childlike behavior, may actually be more experienced than an older, married woman. No, Abigale would not ask.

— *Friday, March 31*

Friday evening again brought Major Sanford and Mayor Arnold to the Gordon home. Henrietta and the mayor were seeing each other regularly, which greatly pleased both daughters. They liked Richard Arnold, but would probably favor any man who could drag their mother out of the house and into the world of normal social interaction.

Dinner talk concentrated on the winding down of the war and the state of Savannah. Sanford emphasized the Union's valiant efforts to feed and house the thousands of ex-slaves who had followed Sherman to the city. At one point he asked Polly, as she served the main course, "Abigale told me your sister moved to St. Catherine's Island. What do you hear from her?"

"I hear she be doin' good, dat girl. Dey's workin' hard, plantin mo' rice. It be hard work, I hear, but nobody complainin'."

Sanford knew some Union soldiers patrolled the island, to make sure no whites interfered. "That's good," he said. "I know your husband went north with General Sherman. With the war almost over, maybe he can come home soon and join you on St. Catherine's. That certainly was General Sherman's wish, for all the negroes who signed up, to return home and work the land."

"Dat be good, for sho'. Dey certainly could use some men's help out dere."

"And maybe other soldiers can leave also," interjected Jane. "Stephen, what do you hear from Captain Broderick? Surely you can get hold of him now, since the war, as you say, is almost over."

"No way of knowing for sure, Jane. I think his regiment is still in North Carolina. You've sent him letters?"

"Yes, several, but I have to address all of them to the War Department in Washington."

"That's right," said Sanford. "From there they are sent to wherever the troops are, but sometimes as you can imagine it takes weeks or longer to catch up. Has he replied to you?"

"Not a single word have I received. It's frustrating."

"Well, I'm sure it is."

"But surely, Stephen," continued Jane, "you have a way of contacting his unit?"

"Jane," Abigale interrupted, "Stephen said he doesn't know where the captain is. Why do you keep persisting?"

Jane ignored her sister and looked at the major. "Well, if you do make contact, please tell him he's going to be a father."

Forks dropped. Henrietta looked at Jane as if something of high importance yet unintelligible had just been uttered. Abigale stared at her sister, understanding everything immediately.

Only Mayor Arnold accepted the statement as obviously good news. "Congratulations, young lady. New life is what we need more of in Savannah. I'm sure your captain will be very pleased."

"How do you know?" asked Abigale. "You were only with him a few weeks, in January."

"Jane?" asked Henrietta. "Did you two do...you know what?"

"Mother, stopped being so dense," scolded Abigale. "Of course. That's not important. Please, let me handle this." In her periphery Abigale noted Arnold and Sanford smiling at each other. Everyone stopped eating.

"How do you know?" asked Abigale.

"I have not had my monthly since he left."

"How many have you missed?"

"Abigale, this is not polite table conversation in front of the men," admonished Henrietta.

"Mother, one is a doctor and both men have been married. I don't think they are embarrassed or concerned. Am I right?"

The men commented at the same time, in effect, 'No, that's fine. Doesn't bother me'.

"See? How many, Jane?"

"Two."

"Are you having any feelings of nausea or pelvic cramping?" asked Mayor Arnold, now sounding clinical.

"Yes," replied Jane. "I believe you call it morning sickness. For several days. Nothing serious, it passes."

"Well," said Arnold, "I believe the young lady is probably correct."

"But Jane," retorted Abigale, "I thought you said you used protection."

"Abigale!" yelled Henrietta. "Stop this now. This is not dinner conversation."

"It is now, mother."

"Then I shall return when we are back to civilized society." Mrs. Gordon got up to leave the room.

"Wait, wait," said Mayor Arnold, I'll come with you. Looking at Abigale, he said, "The conversation, I assure you, bothers me not at all, but I think your mother could use some company at this point."

"Thank you Richard," said Abigale. "I agree. You are most kind."

"I'll go too," said Stephen and he began to rise from his chair.

"NO! I mean, no, please stay, I beg you," said Abigale. Sanford sat down.

With the three now seated, Abigale again looked at Jane. "I thought you used protection."

"Sometimes, not always. I didn't think this would happen. But I am not unhappy. I just want him to know. So he can return." She began to cry.

"Stephen," asked Abigale, "is there any way to get him the message? Surely, you can exert some influence in this matter."

"Yes, I'll see what I can do. First thing in the morning. But even if we can reach him with the news, there's no guarantee he will be able to leave the army to return to Savannah."

"No, we understand that," said Abigale. "But it would give him information to begin planning what he must do. That would be great help and comfort."

"Yes, I will do everything possible to get him the message. One warning, though. These messages are not private. It will be read by several layers of staff before reaching him. He could receive some ribbing or worse from fellow officers, about leaving a pregnant woman in Savannah. Are you sure you want me to go ahead?"

Abigale looked to Jane for the answer.

Jane nodded, stifling tears, then in a whisper, "Yes, please. Please."

CHAPTER 42

— *SATURDAY, APRIL 1, SELMA, ALABAMA*

GENERAL FORREST'S NEW HEADQUARTERS TOOK only a day to set up. At five p.m. Forrest's commanders assembled in his tent, along with aide-de-camp Johnny Gordon.

"I ain't gonna lie to you," said Forrest. "The situation is bleak. We lost a lot of men up at Montavello. Now we have to defend Selma, with only 2000 men, against Wilson's 12,000, or more. And he's still got those damn repeating rifles."

"And we still have none," noted General Frank Armstrong.

"And no word from President Davis. I don't think we'll ever see them repeaters. Word is Richmond is trying to manufacture them, but they ain't gonna get here in time even if they do. My hunch is, even if they did get them out, Lee would have first crack at 'em. He's holed up against Grant in Virginia. Boys, we fight with what we've got."

"Where is Wilson now?"

"North of here, maybe five miles," said Forrest. "I think we can expect an attack in the morning. Here is my plan."

— *APRIL 2, 1865, SELMA, ALABAMA*

"Here they come!" yelled Forrest.

"Jesus Christ! There's a lot of em," murmured Johnny.

The rebels fought bravely, but men in blue easily overran the thin Confederate line, leading to hand-to-hand combat. More bluecoats arrived and rebels began retreating, but not Johnny. He stayed firm, first on his horse, then dismounted, out of ammunition, with only his weapon a bayonet.

Sons of bitches, I'll die fightin' if I have to.

He gorged several rushing bluecoats and would have killed them all, given the chance, but the numbers were too great. They just kept coming.

A bayonet slashed at his coat, ripping it open. He saw blood. Superficial, he thought. He moved back to avoid another slash, when his attacker took a bullet, from god knows where.

That was lucky for me.

His luck did not hold. Only fifty yards distant came another on-slaught of Yankees.

"Get out of here!" screamed Forrest to the few remaining men still able and willing to fight. "That's an order"

Johnny turned to look at his commander.

"I don't want you dead, son. Retreat to our rear line!"

Reluctantly, Johnny obeyed. He walked backwards, fast. He could not find his horse. Only smoke, confusion. He stumbled over two fallen comrades and looked down. One of them had no head. Then he felt a sharp sting in his leg. *I'm hit. I'm hit.*

Johnny fell to the ground. Forrest stopped his horse, leaned over to lend a hand.

"Get on my horse. Now!" Johnny felt hurt, in agony. *If I don't get on that horse I'm dead meat.*

Another bullet whizzed by.

Johnny grabbed the outstretched hand and with great effort mounted the horse.

"Giddyup!" Another bullet grazed Johnny's ear and grazed Forrest's right shoulder.

The two wounded men galloped hard for half a mile, until Forrest felt confident they were no longer in shooting range.

The North won the Battle for Selma. Over half of Forrest's men were dead or taken prisoner and Selma's armory, its gun factories and arsenal were now in Union hands.

What Forrest and his men did not know was that on this same day, President Jefferson Davis abandoned Richmond, the Confederate capital. That fact would have only confirmed the reality of their situation: the war was about over, and they were the losers.

———

Only one surgeon attended Forrest's cavalry, a colonel whose well-deserved nickname was 'Doc Cut-em-off'. He patched Forrest's shoulder, fortunately only a superficial wound.

Johnny's leg proved more complicated. The bullet went through the lower leg and just missed fracturing the tibia. The bone remained intact, but the wound oozed. The doc packed it with gauze, over which he poured alcohol.

"I won't minimize this, son," said the surgeon. "You are at great risk of infection. We should take off this lower leg, right here." He pointed to an area just below the kneecap.

Johnny, in pain, at first did not fully grasp the words.

"What you mean, take off the leg?"

The surgeon drew his finger below Johnny's kneecap.

"You talkin' amputation?"

"To save your life, son."

Now the pain took a secondary position to this sudden reality. Not just the medical advice, but that he might have no choice. He had seen other men refuse and be forcibly held down while the surgeon operated. If an army surgeon decided to amputate, four or five men could be summoned to hold the patient and let the thing proceed.

Johnny would fight back. "General Forrest! General Forrest!"

The surgeon stared down at his patient, lying on dirty army cot outside the hospital tent. "Son, stop your screaming."

Johnny grew desperate, tried to move, which only caused more pain. "General Forrest! General Forrest!" Other men in the vicinity looked at Johnny but did not interfere.

Finally, the general appeared. "What's all that yellin'?"

"Oh, thank goodness," said Johnny. "Please sir, do not let the doctor take off my leg. I would rather die. Let me heal, please, sir. Or let me die. Please!"

Forrest looked at the surgeon. "What is it?"

"Bad leg injury sir, open to infection, which I fear could prove fatal. We should amputate."

Johnny shook his head, pleaded with his eyes.

"Leave him be. The boy has made up his mind."

"But if he gets infected—"

"That's an order, colonel. Treat the wound. No saw. I may need him back in battle some day."

"Yes, sir. I'll fix him up with soldier's joy, give him some relief of pain. That dressing's got to be changed twice a day."

Soldier's joy: a combination of whiskey, beer, morphine. No knife. Johnny cried as if just reprieved from a death sentence.

Now I have a chance. Got to get back on my feet.

— APRIL 3, ON THE ROAD TO GEORGIA

Johnny could not walk but he could ride. The surgeon splinted his leg, and gave him a crutch so he could hobble around on one leg.

"If you don't get infection, the thing might heal in due time, though you'll probably have a limp. If you do get an infection, well, can't say I didn't warn you."

Johnny didn't answer, just thankful to be out of the grasp of Dr. Cut-em-off.

What remained of Forrest's cavalry began their march to Georgia, some still on their horses, some in ambulance wagons, but most only on their feet. His men were spent, no longer a fighting force. Forrest spoke privately with Johnny.

"We've got a number of injured. I'm going to send all of the sick and wounded on to Augusta, which has a hospital. Seeing as how the war is winding down, don't think the Yankees will care at this point, that is, if you run into any. They'd rather not have to feed you."

"Yes, sir," said Johnny.

"We'll part here. When you get to Savannah, and meet like-minded people yourself, mention you were in my outfit. I believe my reputation will help in your adjustment. It's going to be a new order."

"A new order?"

"A new situation. Things is going to be different, at least on the outside. But maybe not so much on the inside. You get my meaning?"

"I think so."

"We may be losing the war, but we haven't lost the hearts and minds of our countrymen, those of us who are left. I'm counting on you to keep the flame burning."

"Yes, sir. And general?"

"Yes, son?"

"Thank you for helping me out yesterday. You saved my life. Twice. I won't ever forget what you did."

"Twice?"

"Yeah. Second time from doc's saw."

Forrest nodded, smiled and walked away.

CHAPTER 43

— *WEDNESDAY, APRIL 12*

ABSENT A TELEGRAPH LINK BEYOND Hilton Head, South Carolina, news from up north reached Savannah slowly. It came by ship from Boston, New York or Fortress Monroe, Virginia. With the war over, steamships loaded with cargo and passengers plied the Atlantic coast daily. Before reaching Savannah they usually stopped at Hilton Head, where important news could be telegraphed ahead to the Savannah newspapers.

Robert E. Lee's surrender of the Army of Northern Virginia, at Appomattox on April 9, was truly important, though not unexpected. By the time the news did reach Savannah on April 12, it was common knowledge that Lee's army had been greatly weakened by battlefield losses and large-scale desertions. All through March and early April, letters home from soldiers still with General Lee, as well as those who had defected to Union lines, told the same tales of woe: soldiers without shoes, without enough to eat, without hope. Savannah more or less expected the final capitulation.

Local newspaper headlines on April 13 blared LEE SURRENDERS AT APPOMATTOX, WAR IS OVER. Of course, it was not yet over; there were still thousands of Confederates in uniform, mostly in North Carolina, but also pockets scattered throughout the South. A few more battles would yet be fought by troops ignorant of the surrender and, regrettably, there would be war casualties after April 9.

Johnny, now home several days and recuperating, did not comment on the war news, and his family did not engage him. To Abigale, the situation was like that of an old uncle who has just died after a long illness; all the relatives who had lived with his illness knew he was dead. Why discuss it further?

Abigale also did not want to upset her brother. She could feel his silent, seething anger over the outcome. Once, as he walked past the newspaper and glanced at its large-type headlines, she heard him say, in a manner more suggestive of retribution than resignation, "I fought for this?"

— MONDAY, APRIL 16, 1865

A quiet routine brought Abigale to Sanford's Pulaski House room twice a week. There was no impediment, no more demands from Franklin's mother and no gossip, at least none that reached her ears. Perhaps, she thought, God was now on her side.

Providentially, her affair with Rufus had dissipated without scandal. It had flourished for a short interval during the occupation, when soldiers and plantation negroes crowded the streets, turning Savannah from a blockaded, inward-looking port into a cosmopolitan city. It was a time when people could hide if they wanted to. Neighbor was not so focused on neighbor, but more so on the occupying enemy and on wondering how the war would end. Before Sherman's arrival, Abigale thought, her affair would have been impossible. "I have been lucky," she said to herself more than once during these early spring weeks.

She continued to worry about Johnny, but he was not the only veteran to throw a shadow against her happy situation. There came, over the weekend, an unexpected message from Maurice McPherson. She had known him as Morrie, a classmate of Franklin's and among the group that enlisted together after the war broke out. She knew at least a dozen Savannah boys who fought in the war; counting Franklin, four were killed. Morrie's name never appeared in the papers, and until his note arrived, she never thought of him.

> *Mrs. Abigale Tate*
> *Dear Abigale,*
> *I have just returned from the army. I am well, fortunately. I was with Franklin at the end. I wish to come pay my respects to you and your family, and relate what he told me before he passed. Would tomorrow be appropriate for me to come to Liberty Street?*
> *Yours,*
> *Maurice (Morrie) McPherson*

She stared at the request. Her first reaction was to say no, lest his visit rekindle painful memories. But to tell him no would be cruel and only serve to raise questions. How could she deny meeting her husband's war buddy? She could not, but her home was not the right place. *Stephen will somehow come up in conversation with my family. And Johnny is unpredictable. Does Morrie have designs on me? Is that his motive?*

She felt foolish over the last thought. *I should not prejudge. I will meet with him in some public place.*

She replied her mother was not feeling well (never a total fabrication) and that it would be best if he did not come to the house. She would meet him Monday afternoon in Forsythe Park, suggesting 2 p.m. By return message he affirmed her request.

At the appointed hour Abigale and Maurice sat together on one of the wooden benches surrounding Forsythe Park's fountain, a baroque structure in full bloom with its jets of water spraying in every quadrant. April was always pleasant in Savannah, and today the sky was blue, the air a comfortable temperature. Maurice came dressed in civilian clothes. Abigale wore a full skirt and the black arm band. At this juncture of the war – over but not quite over – women in mourning were common, with all manner of black dress displayed.

They exchanged greetings, agreed to call each other by their given name. Maurice is quite handsome, she thought. As was Franklin.

"I see you're still wearing a mourning band, Abigale."

"Yes, I wore the full dress for a while, but now this is acceptable," she explained. For the first time Abigale was thankful for the band. It made her situation more credible. "I am happy you escaped unharmed."

"So how is your family? I hope your mother is not seriously ill. And I heard Johnny made it back. I was hoping to see him if I came over."

"As I wrote, Mother is not well. Nothing serious, but her mood varies. You know father was killed at Gettysburg."

"Yes, I know. Franklin informed me."

"And Johnny was wounded in the leg just before the war ended, but he is recovering. He has a limp. I do feel it best if I alone receive whatever message you bring, and not increase their suffering over our losses."

"I understand," he said.

"When did you get back?"

"Oh, just a few days ago."

"And your plans? What will you do now?"

"I am interviewing for a teaching position up north. A boy's boarding school in Philadelphia. Do you remember Samantha Higgins, about your age?"

"Not really. Did Franklin know her?"

"Yes, she was in our circle."

"He might have mentioned her, back then. Why do you ask?"

"I courted her before enlisting. She waited for me, and now we are engaged."

"That's wonderful, Morrie." *He is not after me. That is good.*

"Abigale, I was with Franklin when they carried him off the battlefield, on a stretcher. He was severely wounded but could still talk."

"Please, Morrie, you don't have to do this."

"No, Abigale, I do. I promised."

She began to cry, sensing what was coming.

He hesitated. "I am sorry if I upset you, Abigale." He took her hands in his. She did not pull back.

"I walked beside the stretcher. He said, 'Morrie, if you make it out alive, please tell Abigale I love her, and I will always love her. Tell her she must live her life and not mourn for me. Tell her, please Morrie, promise?' Abigale, those were his last words."

With no warning of how she might react to whatever message he came to deliver, she collapsed into his arms. Tears flowed.

He held her gently and whispered, "I'm sorry, Abigale. I had to tell you. I hope you understand." She pressed her lips to his shirt to muffle her sobs.

A middle-aged couple stopped by the bench. The man asked, "Is she all right?"

"Yes, yes," said Maurice. "Just some bad news. No, I mean some good news. She will be fine. Please." The couple moved on.

Though being held, and in a public space, Abigale felt alone. For the moment she was not in the park, not in Maurice's arms, but in heaven, searching the sky for Franklin. He was nowhere to be seen. No matter. Surely he could read her mind. *Oh, Franklin! Please, please, please forgive me.*

Maurice comforted her for a few minutes, until her crying abated. She pulled back from his chest. He gave her a cloth from his pocket and she wiped the tears.

"There is no reason to be sorry, Maurice. I understand. You promised him. Did you expect a different reaction?"

"I don't know what I expected. I only know I did what I had to do. Will you tell your family?"

"Yes, and that you have offered your condolences."

"That will be appreciated, Abigale."

Abigale took his cloth and walked a few yards to the fountain. Maurice followed her. She reached over the metal railing and managed to catch a few drops of spray to moisten the material, then wiped her eyes again.

"There, that's better. Sorry I came apart like that. The past can be painful."

"Abigale," he said, "I'll tell you a secret. I myself cried for two days after he died. And I still cry at night, sometimes, when alone, as I think about him and that battle and this war. We are all victims."

We are all victims. That's what Rufus always preached. So true.

She felt genuine affection for Maurice McPherson. Had she not met Stephen, and had Maurice not had Samantha, she could see them together somehow. He was a young Southern gentleman who made it through the war, not emotionally scarred like her brother. *Why does this thought even come into my head? I have Stephen, and am happy for that. It is time to go.*

"You have been most kind, Maurice. Now I must return home. Under the circumstances, I think it best if I walk back alone."

He nodded.

"Abigale, call on me if I can be of service. I will likely be in town at least another month."

"Thank you. And I wish you best of luck in your new position, and happiness with your bride to be."

He took her hands in his, as a final parting gesture.

She stood on her toes and kissed him on the cheek, then turned and walked back toward Liberty Street.

Her mind swirled. *God, please let me be! Let me be!*

— WEDNESDAY, APRIL 18

The next telegram from Hilton Head brought news wholly unexpected — President Lincoln's assassination. He was shot in Ford's Theater Friday evening, April 14, and died the next morning, but the news did not reach Savannah until the evening of April 18. The *Savannah*

Republican staffer accepting the message from Hilton Head read it twice and immediately telegraphed back: PLEASE CONFIRM! PRESIDENT LINCOLN DEAD?

Confirmation came a few minutes later. The telegrapher jumped from his chair and ran through the building, yelling the "President Lincoln was shot. He's dead!" From there the news spread quickly throughout the business district – to saloons, hotels, wherever groups gathered.

In those first hours there were still precious few details. More details arrived when the ship from Hilton Head reached Savannah at 3 a.m., carrying northern newspapers. Their stories were copied and a fuller picture appeared in the Savannah papers on April 19. The assassin, John Wilkes Booth, was still free, presumably in Maryland. There were several co-conspirators. Secretary Seward was also attacked, but lived. Andrew Johnson was the new president.

The news greatly saddened all the colored, plus the Unionists and even some Confederates. The way Sherman, and then Stanton, had handled the occupation spoke of a compassionate administration, one that would work with the Confederates and not treat them as mortal enemies. For the negroes, the news was particularly devastating. Lincoln, their friend and emancipator, was gone. What would happen to the promised "40 acres"?

Many whites, of course, welcomed the news. Cries of "he deserved it!" and "Booth is a hero" echoed in Savannah's streets throughout Wednesday. Among those gladdened by the news, though he made no demonstration, was Johnny Gordon.

———◆———

Homecoming had not been easy for Johnny. He was glad to see his mother and sisters, to be back in his own bed, free of battle. But apart from losing the war, recent events at home left him bewildered, angry. One word best described his feeling as the days unfolded — *betrayed.*

Betrayed by Jane's pregnancy, unmarried *and* carrying the child of a Yankee soldier. On more than one occasion he asked "You swear you wasn't raped?" followed by, "That son of a bitch better come for you and his child. When he does, you gonna have to move up North."

Betrayed by Abigale's relationship with Major Sanford. "We're just friends," she lied, knowing Johnny could become explosive if he thought they were intimate. He could not abide one sister sleeping with the enemy; the thought of two would be unbearable.

Betrayed by Polly's freedom, and the fact she now received a weekly stipend. "Father would never have approved," he said over and over, and plotted ways to reverse the decision. Equally galling, Polly now had at least one afternoon off a week, in addition to the customary Sunday. And her attitude didn't suit him. Not deferential, as before the war. Now, if inclined, she could walk away.

Betrayed by the family's finances. From direct questioning he learned their father's inheritance had dwindled to the point that getting a job would soon be a necessity. But what work could he do? He could walk now, without a crutch, but certainly could not do his old job on the docks. He limped and his leg still ached if he stood too long. Dwindling inheritance and no job prospects raised the specter of even selling the house.

There was one more betrayal that ate at him — his own Confederate army. Johnny first learned of Orville Bradley's death after coming home. They had been to school together, hunted together and enlisted together. Johnny's way with horses landed him in Bedford Forrest's cavalry. Orville's way with a rifle landed him in The Army of the Tennessee and defending Fort McAllister the previous December.

And then there were the circumstances of Savannah's defeat, how General Hardee had skedaddled across the Savannah River with his troops just a week after McAllister surrendered. Why had General Hardee not evacuated the fort before Sherman's assault? Surely he knew Sherman would go after the fort with overwhelming numbers, and that defense was impossible. In Johnny's mind Hardee sacrificed 230 good men…all now dead, wounded, or prisoners. And for what? His friend Orville didn't have to die. He died because of official incompetence.

The god-damned war, he thought over and over to himself. *We have lost practically everything.*

———◆———

The surrender at Appomattox meant Lee's soldiers could go home, but that took time, and only now were Confederates returning to Savannah in sizable numbers. They mixed and connected with those already in town, the ones injured and released early like Johnny, or who, for whatever reason – illness or willful desertion – did not leave Savannah with General Hardee's army on December 20. A few men of this last group had a particular interest in Johnny Gordon.

CHAPTER 44

— WEDNESDAY, APRIL 26

LATE IN THE MORNING CALEB Jenkins came to the house, and in Polly's presence introduced himself to Johnny as "Captain Jenkins."

"We need to talk," he said

"About what?" asked Johnny.

Caleb eyed the servant, still within hearing distance. Johnny motioned for Polly to leave them, and she walked away.

"I can't stand long periods, so let's sit," said Johnny. They retreated to the living room and sat on opposite ends of the couch.

"Captain in what regiment?" asked Johnny.

"Third Savannah Regulars. I know you soldiered under Bedford Forrest. That's why I'm here."

"How'd you know that?"

"We got sources. I know you came down from Augusta over a week ago. And I know you sympathize with our cause."

"What cause might that be?"

Jenkins explained how he heard about Johnny's homecoming from a runner in Augusta, and of his service as Forrest's aide-de-camp. The general's groundwork in setting up a resistance movement had spread to several southern cities. Forrest didn't give a damn if some of its members were deserters. The war was going to be lost. The cause for which they fought should not be.

Caleb wanted Johnny to join his group. It would mean some night rides. He would be given a horse.

Johnny liked the message, but did not care for the messenger. "Yeah, I see your points, but can't work with no Confederate deserters, not after what I seen. Don't mean to be disrespectful, but men died while you was lollygagging about Savannah."

"Johnny, we don't look on ourselves as deserters. The army deserted us. They wasn't planning to put up any fight to keep Sherman out. We know'd they were going to skedaddle out of town long before they did so. Savannah is lost, and I don't mean just to Sherman and the Yankees. We've lost our culture. Our women are cavorting with black men, slaves is talking back, taking over plantation houses. You've only been home a short while. You'll see what's happening, then you'll join us."

What Caleb said had some truth to it, Johnny could already see that. "Let me think about it. You say you'll give me a horse?"

"If you can ride with that leg."

"Oh, I can ride. How would I get hold of you, with you hidin' out south of town?"

"We have an inside man who lives in town. Name's Ignatius Gardner. He's been to army headquarters, they tried to recruit him to turn us in for the award. He's on our side, our eyes and ears in Savannah. You go to him, tell him you want to meet, he'll bring you. He's a good man."

"Don't know him. Got his address? Ain't saying I'm joinin', just having some second thoughts working with deserters."

"You'll change. Savannah is lost if we don't do something bold."

———————

Caleb left Liberty Street and rode to find Ignatius, who lived over on East Broad, only a few blocks away. His boarding house was one of several East Broad tenements, three stories each, and about as run down as any Savannah housing inhabited by whites. Caleb knocked three times and Ignatius opened the door.

"Get your ass out of bed," he said, jokingly.

"I'm up. What brings you here so damn early?"

"It's noon, in case you didn't notice."

"Well, I go to bed late."

"We might have another recruit. Says he wants to think about it. Told him to contact you when he changes his mind. You'll bring him to us."

"Name?"

"Johnny Gordon, lives over on Liberty Street. Just home a few days, served in Bedford Forrest's unit."

"Liberty Street, you say, do you know the number?" Ignatius knew that street well, and wondered, just wondered.

"Yeah, twenty-seven."

Ignatius froze inside, but did not display any emotion to Caleb. "He got family, or live by hisself?"

"I'm sure he got family. Has a nigger maid. Big townhouse. Why does it matter?"

"Secrecy. Too many people know, word gets out."

"I don't think he's gonna tell people he might go night-ridin' with us."

"What makes you think he's gonna join up?"

"Just a hunch. I could see it in his eyes. Already seething about Savannah."

— SATURDAY, APRIL 29

After a week Johnny felt back to his old self. Though he still had a limp, he could now get around town without the crutch. On occasion he borrowed a neighbor's horse, which gave him some mobility.

As he had not had a woman in quite a while, he decided to visit Savannah Gardens. There he met Gustav Heinz. As per usual practice,

Gustav made enquiry of his new customer. Who are you, where do you live, what did you do in the war?

"My name's Johnny Gordon. From right here in Savannah. Fought with General Nathan Bedford Forrest. Wounded in Alabama. What you got for me?"

The Gordon family of Liberty Street? This is a gift. "Are you related to a young woman, Jane Gordon, perhaps?"

"My sister."

Gustav raised his eyebrows. *Can't let him see my surprise.* He quickly softened his facial expression to one of indifference, but a bit too late.

"How do you know my sister?" Johnny asked, in a manner Gustav felt accusatory.

"Oh, I met her in church, along with your other sister. Let me see, I think her name is Abigale Tate. I believe she is a war widow."

"That's right. So, they friends of yours?" Gustav sensed an edginess to the question. *This young man is bomb about to go off. Now perhaps get my moment of revenge. Oh, Providence!*

"Not friends, just people I have met. I know lots of people in Savannah. I met them in black church, they came with your mother to hear negro minister speak. He talk about war, very excited Mr. Sherman was coming to town."

"My family went to hear a nigger preacher? What are you saying?"

"Oh, don't be angry with me. I am a foreigner, not a Yankee. You have a lovely family. Your older sister, Abigale, became very friendly with the minister." Gustav rolled his eyebrows slightly upward, to give a hint of intrigue. "His name is Rufus Simms. She visited him several times." *This is good. Look how angry he is becoming.*

Angry indeed. Johnny grabbed Gustav's shirt with his fist, twisted the cloth around the buttons. "Come again? What are saying?"

"Please, Mister Gordon, I don't want any difficulty. I just explain how I met your sisters. Please, you are young, strong man, I mean no harm. Please, let go. I cause no problem." *I could squash this stupid rebel if I had to. A punk.*

Johnny let go. "I ain't gonna hit you. I just want to know more about this nigger minister you say my sister visited 'several times'. Rufus Smith?"

"Rufus Simms. Free colored. Third Ogeechee Colored Baptist. She visit, no secret. Common knowledge. She grieved by loss of husband, sought solace and comfort. So, many visits to his office."

"Say, ain't that the church that burned down?"

"Yah. You heard?"

"I heard."

"After that fire," explained Gustav, "the preacher, he moved over to another church, First Ogeechee Colored Baptist. One, two, three, maybe four of these Ogeechee Colored Baptist churches, I don't know. I know nothing more, just that they met many times, privately. I am not suggesting anything. Please, I mean no harm, just telling you because you insist."

"Then how come you know so much? How come you so interested?"

"Not my business. But beautiful young widow goes to black church, people take notice. Start talking. I get many customers here, they talk and talk. About the war, about the politicians, about the things they see on the street. I listen, but none of my business. Still, can't help but hear what I just tell you. Like what you say in your country, 'common knowledge'.

"So, you fucking immigrant, are you suggesting my sister has been hugging a nigger?"

"Oh no, no, no. I am not suggesting anything. Only that they met many times in his church office. Please. I don't know if she's still seeing him, this was back in the winter, busy time after Sherman arrived with all his troops. Most are gone now, not so busy, I don't hear no more."

"But you still see her at his nigger church, whichever Baptist it is now?"

"No, no. I myself no longer go to any church. I know nothing really. Just what I tell you, what I heard." *And what Ignatius saw with his own eyes.* "Please, Mr. Gordon, because you are a war hero, no charge tonight for your first visit. Fair?"

"Fair," agreed Johnny. "Yeah, that's fair. Let's see who you got."

"I have something very special for you, a young black girl."

"Whoa, you think I'm gonna fuck a black bitch?"

"They say she mighty fine. My soldiers pay extra. Exotic, from Africa. For you, free."

Gustav noted a change of expression form disdain to anticipation. *He is excited, yes, I can see. The idea he likes much. He will have her. His lust will make him think about his sister and Rufus, yes. This is good. Very good. Will lead to my revenge. Rache!*

—————◆—————

CHAPTER 45

— TUESDAY, MAY 2

FOR JOHNNY, THERE WAS TOO much going on he didn't like, and didn't understand. Home barely two weeks, he found the situation increasingly difficult. Not only was the city under Union control, but many of the Yankee troops were colored. He'd heard scuttlebutt in the army about mobilizing negroes for the South, but nothing ever came of it. Not so the North which, he knew, had thousands of black troops. And, as if to put knife to a wound, someone in Washington figured a good place to send them would be Savannah.

Then there was Polly, no longer under his thumb. She still did her chores, but on her own time, and always with the implied threat of walking away if she wanted to. If she wanted to! And there was nothing he could legally do about it. Worse, Abigale was paying her to work! He would put a stop to that, for sure, he just didn't know how to do it without upsetting the apple cart. He would bide his time on that issue, then strike.

And his own family. Jane pregnant by one Yankee soldier, Abigale being courted by another. And now, the most damning news that he could not shake: Abigale may have had an affair with a black preacher.

He had to fight back, and Caleb's entreaty now seemed reasonable. Deserter or no, he had spoken the truth. Johnny remembered Caleb's prediction. "We've lost our culture. Our women are cavorting with black men, slaves is talking back, taking over plantation houses.

You've only been home a few days. You'll see what's happening, then you'll join us."

In the late afternoon Johnny went to find Ignatius. He was not home and his landlady suggested the Broughton Saloon and if not there, she named two other bars. "If you miss him, he should be home before midnight, 'drunk as a skunk'."

The Broughton Saloon was new to Johnny; didn't exist before he went away. A narrow room tucked beneath the Marshall hotel, it hosted ex-Confederates and Union soldiers alike. With the war over, drinking became a great unifier of once-opposing soldiers; they now mingled freely where just weeks before they were trying to kill each other. Johnny made enquiry and the bartender pointed him to a short, wiry man standing at one end, drinking alone.

Johnny approached. "Is you Ignatius Gardner?"

"Who might be asking?"

"My name is Johnny Gordon."

Ignatius blinked his eyes, looked around, then grabbed Johnny's arm. "Let's you and me go outside." Johnny couldn't tell if he was drunk or just acting that way, to get outside without drawing much attention.

They reached the sidewalk. "What you want, Mr. Gordon?"

"Caleb Jenkins said to look you up."

"For what purpose?"

"If I want to go meet him in the swamp."

"Well, it ain't exactly a swamp, but it is hidden. Not really far from here, but woods south of the city is dense, and they got a piece of it. No Union ever go that way. Anyway, if he sent you, I figure you ain't no spy."

"I was in the army. Got injured just before Lee surrendered, sent home. That's why the limp."

"I hadn't noticed. I was in the army, too, guess you heard. Got sick the night they left town over the bridge. Never caught up with them."

A deserter just like Jenkins. Never mind.

"You'll take me to him?"

"Not tonight. Too late. Tomorrow, though. You got a horse?"

"No, he said you'd get me one."

"He says a lot of things. I ain't got one of my own. I rents them when I need them. I'll rent one for tomorrow. We's gonna have to ride together, then when you get there, he'll give you one. Think you can ride with me for a few miles?"

"If I have to. Why can't you just rent two?"

"Then we gotta bring one back without a rider. Raises suspicions. See, here's the thing. The federals is looking for this bunch. Anything that don't look right, they stop, ask questions. Oh, where you been with that extra horse? That kind of shit."

"You burned those churches Caleb told me about?"

"Me? Hell, no. I don't ride with them. Too risky, for my blood, but I helps them out. We all on the same side."

"Caleb said you had a run-in with Union Army headquarters. How'd that happen?"

"Yeah, they picked me up on suspicion of being a Confederate deserter. Did he tell you, they tried to recruit me to help them find the arsonists?"

"Somethin' like that. Yanks must think we're all stupid."

"Yeah, big award. That kind of shit. For my money, we still fightin' them sons of bitches."

"Yeah, I been back just two weeks, and place is goin' to hell," said Johnny. "Niggers taking over."

"You don't tell your family nothin, right? They got spies everywhere. Can't say nothing to no one."

"I got two sisters. Don't tell them anything."

"You didn't tell 'em you was comin to see me?"

"Of course not. What I do is my own business."

"You can't say nothin' to no one. Not your sisters, no one. Can't never mention my name, or where I'm gonna take you, or anythin' else about what we do. Got to have you swear on that, or we can't get involved. Too much risk for me. Got to have your word."

This made sense to Johnny. "You got my word. I never mention your name, or anything else."

"Good. Yeah, Savannah goin' to hell. White folks been visiting black churches, even. Caleb and his men, they fightin' back."

"What do you mean, white folks visiting black churches?"

"Oh, goin' to the services. Hearin' all kids of slander against our kind. That's why they burned them churches."

"So I heard. Caleb told me about it."

"Serves 'em right. Not just attending nigger churches but meeting with the ministers afterwards, in private."

"Who?"

"White folks. White women."

"Wait, you talkin about my family?"

"I ain't talkin about your family, just all kinds of rumors, you know, young women don't got their menfolk around, been keeping company with niggers. That's just all the talk."

"Yeah, I heard that, too. Something about women being with a Reverend Simms. Any truth to that?"

"Yeah, his was the first church they burned. Rumor is a young widow used to go there every week, then followed him over to another church when his burned down. Just a rumor, you know. Never would have happened before Sherman came. Next thing you know we be having mixed marriages."

"You know her name, this woman?"

"Don't know, just hear about a young, beautiful war widow."

Johnny didn't respond or ask any more questions. He did wonder at the coincidence of hearing the same story from two different sources. Were the war widow's meetings with this Mr. Simms such common knowledge that everyone knew the same rumors? *What has Abigale been doing?*

"Can you bring the horse to my house, and we leave from there? I live on Liberty Street."

"Not safe. I avoid all main streets. We just go the back ways. Liberty Street's got too much traffic."

"That makes sense. Then I'll see you at your place tomorrow night. What time?"

"Better get here around eight o'clock. I'll have us a horse."

They shook hands and Johnny limped home.

— WEDNESDAY, MAY 3

It was a very secret place, in the sense no road went there. Just a cabin in the woods, down a narrow, rutted lane. Yet it could be reached in less than half an hour by horseback, riding due south of Forsythe Park. Johnny never fully appreciated how civilization dropped off just a few miles from his house.

In the cabin Johnny met Caleb Jenkins and two other men, learned that all three worked various jobs during the day, but retreated to the cabin at night. Before bedtime they installed trip wires to alert if anyone approached. He marveled at their arsenal, enough guns to ward off a regiment.

Behind the cabin was a stable for several horses, plus a pen with pigs and chickens. The outlaws were all ex-Confederates, expert with guns, hunting and horses, and could survive in these woods, if need be, without ever entering the city.

The five men, Ignatius included, swapped war stories until midnight. The fact that only Johnny had been honorably discharged and served under Nathan Bedford Forrest engendered his rapid acceptance into their ranks. Indeed, they all wanted to know about Forrest as a commander, if he had said anything about Fort Pillow, and did he plan to come to Savannah after the war. In the space of a couple of hours Johnny bonded with these men because of his war experience, and a shared antipathy to the new culture overtaking Savannah.

Caleb did not make the connection between Abigale Tate and Johnny Gordon. All he knew was that back in January, while sitting in First Ogeechee Colored Baptist listening to blasphemy, he had enquired who the white folks in the front bench might be, and was told only, "Mrs. Tate, a war widow, and her family." The "Gordon" name wasn't mentioned. And when he came to meet Johnny on Liberty Street, Abigale was not there.

Ignatius, for his own reasons, said nothing about Abigale. Whenever "white folks" came up in the context of negro sympathizers, Johnny never asked for any names.

Close to midnight, with the men yawning and slightly loose from imbibing, Caleb said, "we want to go after another church, Johnny. Think you can help us?"

"What do you have in mind?"

"There's an old run-down nigger church, no more than one or two Union men guarding it as near we can tell, should burn quickly." Caleb looked at Ignatius, who nodded to acknowledge the intelligence.

"You interested? We only want to use two riders."

"Burn a nigger church?" asked Johnny. "Wouldn't want to miss it. How we going to get past the guards?"

"With this." Caleb showed him a Spencer rifle. "And here's the best news. They're nigger guards. We take 'em out if we have to, set the torches, and be on our way."

"Sounds good. I'm in."

"Good. We ride Friday night, then."

After a few more minutes of planning, Caleb took Johnny out back and gave him a horse and saddle, as promised. Then Johnny and Ignatius galloped back to Savannah. They parted where Drayton Street intersected with the lane behind Johnny's house. Johnny trotted down the lane to his stable, put the horse away and went inside the house. It was one in the morning and everyone was asleep.

— FRIDAY, MAY 5

Caleb Jenkins and Johnny Gordon rode their horses fast. A block from their destination, around midnight, a half moon and a single kerosene street lamp outlined the Ebenezer Methodist Church.

"I just see one tent on the lawn. The coons must be sleepin'," said Caleb. "Soon as you see one, shoot." Johnny didn't need prodding. The hood he wore left big holes for his eyes, and his vision was excellent.

The horsemen bypassed the tent, rode to the far side of the rectangular building where they could not be seen. They hurled two torches through the glass windows, sending a smashed-glass sound into the night air.

Soon a black man in soldier pants but no uniform top came running around the side of the building. Johnny heard "What the hell?" and saw the soldier raise his rifle. Instinctively Johnny raised his own and fired one shot. The black man fell. Just then another negro soldier, similarly half-dressed, came running round the church. Seeing his compatriot on the ground, and Johnny on the horse with rifle in hand, the soldier ran back toward the tent.

"I'll get him," yelled Caleb, and he galloped away. "Make sure the church is burning."

Johnny peered through the church window to assure sure some part of the interior was on fire, then rode to catch up with Caleb.

"Catch him?" asked Johnny.

"Nah, he disappeared in the darkness. The flames started?"

"Yeah, getting nice and cozy inside. Let's get our asses out of here."

———

CHAPTER 46

— SATURDAY, MAY 6

SAVANNAH'S THIRD BLACK-CHURCH FIRE OCCURRED too late to make it into the Saturday papers, but the news nonetheless spread by word of mouth, especially among Polly's network.

By mid-morning on Saturday Polly could relate the news to Abigale. "Dey done burned another church. Da Ebenezer Methodist. Hear tell one of da soldiers got hisself killed. Don't know much mo'. Da army all over da place, dey say, lookin' for clues."

"When you say the army, Polly, did they mention any names, who is looking for the clues?"

"No, jus say da army."

In fact the army had one clue. While the surviving soldier, Sergeant Billings, could not describe the culprits, since it was dark and they wore hoods, he did get a good look at the horses, especially the horse of the man holding the shotgun when it galloped past him. He noted a large white circle on its rear end, almost a foot in diameter. His description could be a vital clue, so the army made sure it went into the next day's papers.

— SUNDAY, MAY 7

The *Savannah Republican* came to Liberty Street early. The lead story carried three headlines.

EBENEZER METHODIST BURNED BY ARSONISTS.
Negro Sergeant Shot, Killed.
Army Looking For White-Spotted Horse's Ass.

Abigale had never paid much attention to Johnny's new horse, no need to. She asked where he got it and he said only "a friend," and she did not enquire further.

She had noted he was not home the night of the Ebenezer church burning, and that he came in sometime after midnight. Yes, he had been out often at night, with "my war buddies," but this latest coincidence gave her pause.

Pause turned to concern Sunday morning, when she read the paper just after it arrived. Polly had not mentioned anything about a horse description, but now there it was, in bold-faced print.

Does Johnny's horse have a white mark? *He's still sleeping. I'll go look.*

She took a lantern. The stable was locked but she had a key. If he caught her inside the stable she would confront him with the news article. That would be better than not knowing. She unlocked the door without hesitation. *I have to find out.*

The horse whinnied. She hoped no one in the house could hear it.

"Steady, boy," she said. She patted his side and walked behind him, careful to stay a few feet away in case he started kicking.

There it is! A large white splotch. Oh, my god!

She scanned the small space beside the horse, looking for the saddle. It lay against the wall. She carefully opened the pouch to rummage inside, pulled out a damp woolen cloth and unfolded it: a hood, with openings for a man's eyes and mouth.

She put the hood back in the saddle, locked the stable door and returned quickly to her room. Still dressed, she plopped on the bed and stared at the ceiling.

Oh Lord, I am doomed. Do you even exist? God is supposed to be good and just. No just god would allow a war to take our men and slaughter them like cattle. First my father, then my husband, and now – though he yet lives – my brother.

I don't deserve this! You put me in the arms of a black man, and I accepted that. Then you put me in the arms of a Yankee soldier, and I accepted that. But now you have put a killer in my house, my blood kin. And my lover would like to find him, see him hung.

Abigale cried silently with this last thought.

Do I sacrifice my brother to justice? Do I jeopardize my love – to protect a murderous brother? Why, or Lord, why do you do this to me?

I am done. I see no way out. No way.

There is no god!

I can't believe I'm thinking that. Now, who will help me? Who? There is no one.

Her mind turned to a more immediate consideration.

What if Mother or Jane see the paper, and they want to go look in the stable? What will they say or do?

A loud knock on the front door reverberated upstairs.

Who is that? The police, coming to arrest Johnny? Sanford, coming to hang him?

Abigale got up, but before she could go downstairs noted Jane had already opened the front door.

The visitor was loud. "I have to talk to Johnny," he said, with anxiety obvious to Abigale.

"He's still sleeping, I think," said Jane.

"Well, you got to wake him."

"No need," came Johnny's voice from the top of the stairs. He was half dressed, pants and undershirt, no shoes, and did not see Abigale who was now partially hidden behind her bedroom door. "What you got so early in the morning?"

"We need to talk," yelled the man.

"Well, come the hell upstairs," said Johnny. The visitor bounded up the stairs, as Abigale hid behind the door. They disappeared into Johnny's bedroom. A few minutes later they emerged, Johnny now dressed. Abigale could hear him announce to Jane, "We're going out to the stable, be back in a few minutes."

It was all so obvious to Abigale. Should she go downstairs and tell Jane what she knew? No! Her sister was pregnant, she should be kept ignorant about their murderous brother.

Abigale walked to the head of the stairs, called out to her sister. Jane climbed the stairs and asked Abigale if she had heard Johnny and Caleb.

"I heard. They went out back?"

"Yes, what do you think is going on?"

"I don't know. They're up to something, but Johnny is hard to read. Been acting strange lately. I think the war has touched him a bit." *This is good and vague. Who can argue with that assessment?*

"I suppose so."

A few minutes later Jane and Abigale heard a banging from the stable. In another ten minutes Johnny returned, without Caleb.

Both sisters came downstairs. "What was that all about?" asked Jane.

"Oh, that was Caleb Jenkins," replied Johnny. "He left some stuff in my saddle, came to pick it up. Some tools he needs for work today. That's why he came early."

"Oh, what was all the banging?"

"The damn lock's broke. Nailed the door shut with a two by four so my horse can't escape. I'll get it fixed later today."

Oh, Johnny! You lie so well.

Abigale predicted what would happen next, she just wasn't sure when. Just after sundown Caleb returned to the house, on horseback. He and Johnny went to the stable, then Caleb rode off – on Johnny's horse.

— MONDAY, MAY 8

Abigale did not predict the next visitation. On Monday two Union soldiers, carrying rifles came calling. This time Johnny opened the door. The bluecoats introduced themselves, stated there were authorized to look at every horse in the neighborhood, and would he take them to the stable behind the house.

"Why of course," Johnny said, "right this way."

———◆———

Abigale had plans to meet Sanford at Pulaski House that same evening for dinner and lovemaking, but should she go? The question vexed her from the minute she saw Johnny's white-marked horse.

She longed to be held and caressed. They had not shared a bed for almost a week. Her physical self was ready, but not her emotional one. He would see through her, sense her anxiety about something. She could hear his mellow voice as he stroked her. 'What's bothering you Abigale? You can tell me'.

But she could not, would not. *I know what will happen. I will cry or mope or act sullen. I can lay there, pretend, let him have me, and he will – men are like that – but he will sense a change, and that will be a threat. No, I cannot meet him tonight. I must beg off.*

As much as she did not want to put anything in writing, she wrote a note, and paid a messenger to deliver it "in person, to no one else but Major Stephen Sanford." No salutation, no signature. Her message would identify the writer:

Not tonight. Sorry, am not feeling well. Nothing serious. Should be better soon.

CHAPTER 47

— TUESDAY, MAY 9

ALL WEEKEND AND THROUGH MONDAY Johnny had been mostly absent from the house, coming in late at night to sleep, then leaving mid-morning. Abigale was thankful for his absence; she did not want the temptation of confronting him with what she knew. What good would it do? Yet the knowledge caused her constant turmoil. *My brother is a hoodlum…if Stephen finds out…*

Tuesday, Johnny decided to join the family for dinner. His foul mood permeated the room. Not a good time, Abigale thought, to confront him with the evidence she found in the stable.

Mrs. Gordon tried to make light conversation but Johnny would not participate.

"Where's your nigger maid?" he asked. "How come she's not serving us?"

"I told you she has the afternoon off," replied Abigale, "for bible study and such."

"She's off on Sundays. And now Tuesday also?"

"She gets an afternoon off when she wishes, once a week. Her choice."

"Yes, but it's almost dark already. Shouldn't she be here waitin' on us? What's this world coming to?"

"Johnny," replied Jane, "she's free now, and you know we pay her something. She's very loyal, so don't go making things hard for her."

"If it was up to me, she'd still be a slave. Damn those Yankees!" His words did not bother Abigale – she'd heard them before – but his stare did. Every time their eyes met he stared, as if trying to bore a hole through her skull, she thought. *He is making this a most unpleasant meal.*

Finally, near the end, she could sit no longer. "I'm not feeling well," she said. "I'm going to sit on the couch. Jane, if you're finished, perhaps you could come also. We can do the dishes in a bit."

"Oh, dear," said Henrietta.

Johnny snickered. "Must be Abigale's time of the month. Jane don't get them now. She's a got a baby growing inside. A Yankee bastard."

"Johnny," admonished Mrs. Gordon, with all the emphasis of a wet sackcloth.

Abigale and Jane retreated to the living room couch, so their conversation could not be heard.

"What's got into him, Jane? I don't like the way he's behaving. He scares me. The army has changed him so."

"Oh really? Seems to be the same old negro-hating boy we knew so well. I'm surprised Polly stays around, quite honestly."

"I am, too. I think it would be intolerable if she was still a legal slave. At least now she has some afternoons off, and I think she's saving money. Her sister keeps sending messages for her to come to the islands, but you know what?"

"What?"

"I think she's afraid to, afraid of the hardships. She likes living here, knows it would not be comfortable on the islands with Lucy. And certainly the weekly payment helps in her decision."

"You're probably right."

Johnny entered the room, still scowling.

"You girls going to leave the dishes for Mother to clear? Or wait for the nigger to get home?"

"You could help," said Jane.

"Not man's work, dear sister. Not man's work." He stared at Abigale.

"Johnny, why do you keep staring at me?"

"How you doing with that major friend of yours, what's his name, Sanford?"

"He's fine."

"You gonna end up with a Yankee, like your little sister here, who done got herself knocked up by one?"

Abigale smoothed her dress, to dry off a sweaty palm. "Johnny Gordon, if you're going to talk like that you can leave the room." *Should I confront him now, challenge him with what I know? No, it will just make things worse.*

"Though I must admit, he's a better catch than some lowlife nigger."

Abigale felt sweat from every pore. She could see where he was heading, and did not respond. Nor did Jane.

"What's the matter girls, cat got your tongues?"

"Johnny, if I didn't know better, I'd think you've been drinking," said Jane. "Abigale, did Mother serve wine tonight?"

"Nah, I ain't drunk. I'm just hard up for women. You understand? And you know where men go when they get that way?"

"Stop it Johnny, stop it now!" Abigale stood to leave the room.

"Oh, I wouldn't leave just yet, unless you want me to get some answers from that army major of yours. Maybe he knows someone named "Rufus".

Abigale froze.

"Do you deny it, sister? Ever heard of Gustav Heinz? Ever heard of Ignatius Gardner? Do you deny it?"

Jane looked at Johnny, then Abigale, but did not speak.

"Johnny, if you've got something to say, say it! Stop playing games with me."

"Do you deny it? Do you deny this black preacher was your lover? Oh, not now, maybe, but a short time ago. DO YOU DENY IT?"

Both sisters remained silent. Jane, sworn to secrecy, turned away so as not to look at Johnny.

"You got something to hide, Jane?"

Jane remained silent.

Johnny took a step toward Abigale. "Tell me. SWEAR ON OUR FATHER'S GRAVE THAT THIS NIGGER WAS NOT YOUR LOVER, THAT HE NEVER PLACED HIMSELF INSIDE YOU. SWEAR!"

"You're crazy, Johnny. Just crazy. You make things up, then you put me on trial. I've had enough of this nonsense. Jane, let's go." Abigale grabbed her sister's arm and they began walking to the dining room. Johnny ran in front of them, held up his hand. He spoke calmly, yet his flaring nostrils and wide open eyes conveyed sheer menace.

"Just one more thing, Abigale, and I'll be done. I did not risk my life fighting for what we've become. Nigger lovers. Lovers of niggers. Real, honest-to-god lovers of niggers. Well, I'm here to put a stop to that. You can kiss your Rufus goodbye. He's dead meat." Johnny walked quickly to the closet, pulled out his coat and left through the back door.

"Abigale, aren't you going to stop him?"

"How can I stop him? He's crazy, on a mission."

"But he could kill Rufus, can't you do something?"

"I'm not concerned about Rufus, at least not at this moment. He's on Jekyll Island. Nothing's going to happen to him tonight. I am far more concerned about Johnny. He's in deep trouble, in with the wrong people, I fear." *And if Sanford knew, I would lose both him and Johnny.* "Tonight he might burn down Rufus's house. If caught, he's going to hang. And honest to God, I don't know what to do about it. Let's not alarm Mother."

Affecting calmness, the two sisters entered the dining room. "What was Johnny yelling about, Abigale?" asked Mrs. Gordon, still seated. "He sure seems upset about something."

"Nothing, Mother," said Abigale. "Nothing to worry about."

———◆———

Polly came home an hour later, just after sunset. She found the table cleared, the sisters putting away the dishes. She seemed in a good mood.

"How was your bible study?"

"Oh, it be good, Miss Abigale. An hour with Reverend Patterson's deacon."

"My, you've been gone all afternoon, and then some. Did you go to the market?"

"No ma'am. Went to see Reverend Simms, to see how he be doin'."

Abigale dropped a dish. It broke into myriad pieces.

"What did you say? Reverend Simms? He's back in Savannah?"

"He done returned over a week ago. Gettin' over de doldrums from his wife's passin'."

"Why didn't you tell me?"

"Oh, he not preachin'. Just moanin'."

"He's alone in the house?"

"'Cept when I be there."

"You've been to his house before, I mean since he came back?"

Abigale noted a change in Polly's demeanor, as if she might be embarrassed by something.

"A time or two."

Jane, silent to this point, uttered "Oh my God!"

"What be goin' on, you two? Looks like you done seen da ghost."

"Polly, does he have a gun?" asked Abigale.

"Why would da reverend need a gun?"

"Never mind. Jane, come with me now. Polly, wait here. Don't leave. We'll be right back."

"I'll sweep da pieces off da floor."

"Oh, thank you."

Abigale and Jane retreated to the living room. Abigale spoke. "Johnny will kill him. I know it. I've got to get over there."

"You should let the authorities deal with this. Go find Major Sanford, he'll take care of it."

"Why, and see our brother hang? We've lost father and Franklin. Johnny's blood kin, Jane."

"So what can you do? Johnny's on a rampage."

"I've got to stop him!"

"You? Alone?"

"I've got to get there before Johnny does. If he's not there already."

"Does he even know where Rufus lives?"

"I'm sure he does. If he found out about us, I'm sure he made such enquiries. Can't take the chance."

"Same question. Alone?"

"No, I'll take Polly."

"At night?"

Abigale returned to the kitchen, Jane following right behind her. The floor was clean.

"Polly, Rufus is in danger. Real danger. Some men want to do him harm. We've got to warn him."

"How you know dis?"

Jane answered. "Johnny's threatened to kill him because… because—"

"Because we were lovers!" blurted Abigale. "At one time, for a short time."

"Lawd Jesus," said Polly, "I knowed dat from da first. From da first."

"You did?"

"Lawd Jesus, yes, it be on your face. No talking gonna do da good dat I seen the reverend done fo' you. You was like a new woman. Now *he* the one need da comfort he gave to you. I jus' glad I can help him in dat way."

"Polly, what are you saying?"

"Man's got to have comfort. Polly's no spring chicken, but I knows what to do when a man is down w' da dumps."

"You've been…you've been…"

"Lordy, Jesus, look at you. You'd think only white folks knows how to do da thing. Now why's we wasting time? We gots to get over dere, keep your brother from doin' harm to the reverend."

Abigale hugged Polly. "Oh, you're wonderful."

"You better go," said Jane. "Abigale, is there a gun in the house? Didn't father leave one somewhere when he joined up?"

"I have no idea, and if there is one, I wouldn't know how to use it. No, I've got to use my wits to prevent a calamity."

"You two go," said Jane. "I'm going to look for Major Sanford. He's got to get his men there."

"They'll kill him! Please, leave him out of it!"

"And Johnny will kill Rufus, and possibly you and Polly as well. He's my brother, too, and he scares me. You're going to need help. Just tell me, where do I find Major Sanford? And when I do, where does Rufus live?"

"I can't. I can't!" cried Abigale.

"You must! If you won't, I'll stop the first soldier I see and make enquiries. Then you'll have the whole army looking for him."

Just then Mrs. Gordon entered the room. "What's all the noise? Is Johnny in any trouble?"

"No, mother," replied Jane. "Abigale, me and Polly are going for a walk. It's stuffy in here and we want some fresh air. We may be out a while, so please don't wait up for us."

Abigale went to the front closet to get her coat.

Polly turned, her back to Abigale and whispered to Jane. "Over on West Boundary, in Yamacraw. Number fifty-two."

———

CHAPTER 48

As soon as Abigale and Polly left the house, Jane put on her coat and went looking for Major Sanford. But where?

Is he at Pulaski House? I know they've met there. Was it just for dinner or does he live there? Or someplace else?

She realized the hotel could be a waste of precious time if he wasn't there. Where were the closest soldiers? Were they still camped at the Old Colonial Cemetery, where she had met Winston back in December? Surely there must be guards there, she thought. Or perhaps not, since so many troops had left the city since war's end. She decided to try the cemetery and turned left to walk up Abercorn Street.

The cemetery looked deserted. She saw no camp fires, no soldiers.

Damn! Where is everybody?

As if an answer to her question, under the street lamp she noticed a soldier on the corner of Abercorn and South Broad.

He's a colored soldier. Lot of them here, lately. Doesn't matter. I will ask him.

She walked quickly toward the sentry. "Excuse me, do you know where I can find Major Stephen Sanford?"

"Ma'am, what are youse doin' out here alone at night? Are youse in trouble?"

A northerner. Some of them talk so strange.

"No, no. I just need to find Major Sanford. Can you tell me where he might be?"

"Don't know no Major Sanford. But you can ask my captain. He's right up yonder in Oglethorpe Square."

"Are soldiers camped there?"

"Yes ma'am, the colored regiment. They don't give us no regular housing."

"Thank you. I'll go there. Who is your captain, I mean, his name?"

"Captain Joe Randall. I'll take you there. You shouldn't be wandering out here alone."

In the moonlight she could see the entrance to Oglethorpe Square just a short block northward, but couldn't make out any soldiers. As they came closer she saw camp fires and a few men milling about. On the way to Captain Randall's tent she noted all the men were colored.

"Wait here, ma'am. I'll go tell the captain."

A young man came out of the tent.

Oh, good, he's white.

"I'm Captain Randall. You are?"

"Jane Gordon. I live over on Liberty Street. Can you tell me where I can find Major Stephen Sanford?"

"Ma'am, what's this about? Sergeant Johnson said you were walking the street alone. You'll have to tell me."

She burst into tears. "Please! Someone is going to be killed, maybe my sister!

Please, I need Major Stephen Sanford to help. Can you reach him? Oh...I think I'm going to faint."

Randall grabbed an arm to steady her. "Sergeant, help me bring her inside the tent."

They put her in a chair. "Would you like some water?"

"No, no. Please, I need to get to Major Sanford. My sister's on her way to Yamacraw. They're going to kill someone. Please, help me."

"Just relax, ma'am. Why don't you start from the beginning? I'll do what I can to help, but I've got to know what in heaven's name you're talking about."

Jane pulled herself together. If this captain couldn't help, the situation seemed hopeless. She could not go on walking aimlessly around the city. *I don't think I can even walk home.*

She explained the situation, omitting anything about Abigale's affair with Simms. She emphasized her brother's stress from the war, said he wasn't thinking right and that he just had to be stopped from harming Abigale...and Rufus Simms.

Captain Randall listened patiently. She explained how her sister knew this Major Sanford, and how he must be located to save Abigale from harm. She kept repeating the same names: Abigale, my sister... Johnny, my brother...Major Sanford.

Finally the captain said. "Yes, Major Stephen Sanford, I do know him. I'll see what we can do. Meantime, you'll stay here, Miss Gordon. "

———◆———

Polly and Abigale approached Simms' house cautiously, looking up and down the street for any men on horseback.

"Well," said Abigale, "if Johnny's coming, he's not here yet."

"Dat's good."

They climbed the few stairs to the porch and Polly banged on the door. "I reckon he be in bed already."

"It's only been dark an hour," offered Abigale.

"Master Simms, you get yourself up," Polly yelled.

"Why do you call him Master Simms?"

"Oh, dat be between me and him. We jokes about it."

A lantern came on inside and the door opened slightly.

"Polly, what are you doing back here?" asked Simms.

"Youse gonna let me in, or we gonna' freeze to death outside?"

He opened the door, revealing Abigale as well.

"Abigale, you too? What's going on? Why are you two here in the middle of the night?"

"Ain't the middle, da night jus' started," said Polly, moving inside with Abigale. "Get yourself dressed, we gotta move outa here."

"Hold your horses, woman. You have to explain what's going on."

Their easy familiarity with one another impressed Abigale. Looking back, her own relationship with Rufus seemed more formal, as if they were always on guard, especially with language.

"Rufus," said Abigale, "do you remember me mentioning my brother, the one in the army?"

"Vaguely, yes. Why? Polly told me he's home now. Is he causing trouble?"

"Yes, unfortunately. He came home last month, with a leg injury from a bullet wound. He's got a limp, but I think the whole experience has touched his head. He cannot accept the changes in Savannah. Or in our own home. He's promised to do you harm. Tonight."

"Ten thousand negroes in Savannah and he's come to harm me? Could it by chance have something to do with what went on between us?"

"You two's gonna hash out your doin' this and doin' that, we's gonna be in a heap of trouble. Rufus, get some shoes on and a coat. You's comin' wi' us tonight."

Abigale ignored Polly's entreaty. "Yes, indirectly. He can't abide that we had a relationship."

"You told him?"

"Of course not. He inferred it, most likely from that fellow who was following me around."

"Now, I'm lost. What fellow?"

"Never mind, it's not important now. My brother's in a state of rage, and I'm afraid can't be contained. I think he's coming to hurt you. Maybe kill you."

"Which is where we started," blurted out Polly. "Are youse two done talkin'? We gots to be moving on."

"To where? This is my house," objected Simms.

"Me and Miss Abigale done decided. To da colored hotel over on West Bryan. Miss Abigale is payin' fo' you to stay da night."

"What she means, Rufus, is we're going to walk over to the Bryan Street Hotel, only a few blocks from here. It's run by the Freedmen's Bureau, and I've heard good things about it. You can stay there until the danger blows over. It's the safest plan."

"If your brother's coming to get me, he's not coming alone."

"I don't know. I really don't know."

"He'll come with the men who burned my church."

"Rufus, please, I just don't know."

"And if I leave, they'll burn my house, too. I'm not leaving."

"Oh, my," said Polly, as if suddenly resigned to a bad outcome.

"Rufus, do you have a gun?"

"A gun? No, I don't keep a gun."

"What's we gonna do, Miss Abigale?"

"I'll think of something. Do you have neighbors who can help, who might have a gun?"

"Abigale, I'm not going to place my neighbors in harm's way if your brother is a renegade. And I don't think they have guns either. But if you're here, and your brother shows up, perhaps you can talk to him. It is hard to believe the brother of Mrs. Abigale Tate could have none of her rational qualities."

"Oh, my goodness," said Polly. "What are youse two talkin' about?"

"Then I have no choice," said Abigale. "I will bed down on your couch until the sun rises, then we can better assess the situation."

"As you wish, Abigale. Will it bother you if Polly waits in my bedroom?"

"Of course not. I am pleased you have found each other."

CHAPTER 49

———————

— *TUESDAY, MAY 9*

ABIGALE SETTLED ONTO RUFUS'S COUCH. Only then did she notice the house smelled, from what she could not tell. 'Musty' came to mind. Maybe this is how all the Yamacraw houses smell, she thought. A lone kerosene lamp provided light. The furniture seemed worn, the drapes dirty. *This is his home. A free negro's home.*

The house had just two rooms, the living room, where she sat, and the bedroom. Apart from the couch the living room had a desk and chair, and one large case filled with books. There was an unlit fireplace with a side-arm kettle for boiling water. She saw no kitchen, and assumed there was a cooking shed out back. She knew this was common in poorer areas, due to the risk of fire in frame houses and intense heat that made these houses uncomfortable in the summer. The privy would be in the back as well.

The door to the bedroom remained open and Abigale could see Rufus and Polly sitting on the edge of the low bed. Their conversation was indistinct, with some of it in Gullah dialect.

She thought of the war and how her life – and the lives of all the war's survivors, at least the ones she knew – had been upended, twisted in ways unimaginable a short while ago. She remembered studying wars in school, particularly the American Revolutionary War and the Battle of Waterloo. None of her studies ever mentioned the families of soldiers killed and wounded. Books always seemed to focus on victorious or losing generals, or the number of soldiers killed or wounded, or proclamations and treaties – but never about the families left behind and how the war affected them. Nor was there mention of soldiers who made it home but could not adjust, whether because of battlefield infirmity or emotional disturbance. Surely, she thought, Johnny can't be the first soldier to lose his way after coming home.

She dozed. For how long, she did not know, perhaps only a few minutes. The clatter of hoofs awoke her. She got up, grabbed the lantern. She opened the front door and went out to the porch.

Oh my God!

In front of the porch were three horsemen, each wearing a white hood. The man in front held a rifle, the other two held lighted lanterns. As she took in the scene, the lantern carriers dismounted, placed their lanterns on the ground and looped the horse reigns to a porch post.

The lanterns, plus the moon, gave ample light to make out the figures. She had no trouble recognizing the rifleman still on his horse – her brother Johnny.

"Take the hood off, Johnny. You're not fooling anyone."

He took it off, scowling with evident disgust.

"I knew it was you," she said.

"Put the hood back on," yelled one of Johnny's partners, standing at the foot of the porch steps. "We don't take it off except for a real emergency. And this ain't one."

Johnny donned his hood. "Abigale, get out of the way. You shouldn't a come."

"I'm not moving. You'll have to kill me first. Reverend Simms has done nothing to hurt you or these men. Go home, and forget this."

"Goddamn it, Johnny, you gonna let that bitch get in our way?" growled one of his partners.

"Watch your tongue. She's my sister."

"Jesus Christ! Your sister? Then she's the one—"

"Shut up!" yelled Johnny. "I'll take care of this. Abigale, I ain't stopping these men from doin' what they gotta do. We didn't ride all this way for nothin'."

"Johnny, please, you can't go in there. Leave him be. Mr. Simms didn't do anything to you."

"Oh, ain't you being fancy. Now he's Mister Simms, not Rufus. Well, he molested a white woman. My sister, goddamit. How could you ever—"

"We're going inside," said one of the other horsemen, and both bounded up the porch and brushed past Abigale. From inside, Abigale heard a scream, then a thud.

In less than a minute the two men, still wearing their hoods, came onto the porch holding Rufus by his arms. Across the street, a couple of lanterns suddenly lit up behind windows. One elderly man exited his front door, then quickly went back inside. Some window curtains brushed aside, but no one came out to help.

"What the hell happened inside?" Johnny asked. "Who screamed?"

"His wife tried to stop us. Gave her a good slap, and she's down."

"Polly! What did you do to Polly?" yelled Abigale. She vacillated between checking on Polly and staying outside with Rufus.

"We should kill him now, Johnny, then let's get the hell out of here."

"No! I've got to ask him some questions, watch him squirm before he's shot."

"Leave him alone, Johnny, please! He didn't do anything to harm you. Just go now. If you do something crazy the Army will hunt you down. Johnny, please…"

"You gonna tell your Yankee major about me?" asked Johnny. "Or have you already? And as for your nigger preacher here – hey, mister, what did you do to my sister? My friends want to kill you now, but I want some answers first." Johnny pointed his rifle at Rufus's chest. "What did you do?"

Rufus stared at his tormenter and spit.

"Who you spittin at, nigger boy?" yelled one of the men, as he pushed Rufus down the porch stairs. Simms landed face down, a few feet from Johnny's horse.

"Start running, nigger boy," yelled Johnny, his rifle still aimed at Rufus.

Abigale rushed to Rufus, threw herself on top of him.

"Boys, get my sister off him. God knows what they be doin' next."

The two men jumped from the porch and bodily lifted Abigale off the prostrate Simms.

"Gentle, boys, don't want to hurt her."

"Johnny, no!" she screamed. Another lantern lit up across the street.

"Run, boy, run," yelled Johnny. "Run for your life!"

Rufus got to his knees, paused a few seconds, then stood and faced Johnny.

"Mister, I ain't runnin'. Do what you have to do. And may God rest your soul."

"You goddamn nigger. You—"

A rifle shot pierced the air. Then another and another.

Abigale stared in horror at Rufus, who showed no movement. Then she jerked her head toward Johnny, still sitting upright on his horse. Only now the rifle that had been aimed at Rufus pointed at the ground. Then it fell out of his hand. A few seconds later, his balance gone, Johnny fell, head first, onto the dirt.

Johnny is shot! Not Rufus! Oh, my God!

"Johnny!" she cried, and ran to her brother. "Johnny! Johnny, don't die, please don't die!"

She cradled his head, gently turning it to look into his eyes.

"Abigale...I just wanted to protect...your honor. Don't you know...". His head fell back, eyes wide open, no longer perceiving. The open eyes of sudden death.

"What the hell?" said one the henchmen.

Both hooded men turned to gaze across the street, where the shots appeared to come from. "Not what, but who," replied the other man. "Who the hell is that?"

"Can't tell for sure. Men on horseback. If I didn't know better, I'd say they's nigger riders." The men pulled pistols out and fired, but the targets were moving and their pistols were no match for Spencer rifles at that distance.

One, two, three, four, five rifle shots pierced the air. Both men went down.

Polly appeared at the doorway, rubbing her head.

"Stop your firing!" screamed one of the approaching riders.

"What be goin' on?" yelled Polly. "Lordy, where's Rufus? Miss Abigale, what you doin' on the street? Oh, my goodness."

A group of five Union cavalrymen stopped in front of the house, their rifles aimed at the downed men. They dismounted and checked all three hoodlums for signs of life. They found none.

"You all right, ma'am?" a sergeant asked Abigale.

"You killed my brother!"

"Oh, Miss Abigale," shouted Polly. "What jus' happened?"

"I don't know who he is, or was, ma'am, but from what we could see, he was about to kill this here man," the sergeant replied, pointing to Rufus. "And maybe you also."

Abigale did not respond.

Polly ran to Rufus, hugged him. He gently moved her aside, walked over to Abigale and helped her stand. "I'm so sorry, Abigale."

Before she could answer, the sergeant spoke. "Are you Mr. Simms?"

"Yes, Rufus Simms."

"Glad to meet you. I am Sergeant Thomas Billings. That was your church they burned down awhile back?"

"Yes. Third Ogeechee Baptist."

"And two others, if I'm not mistaken. Outside one of them, my partner was shot and killed. A United States Army soldier."

"I...yes, I heard, but that was not at my church."

"No, I know. It happened at Ebenezer Methodist. Well I'm glad we got here in time. From what I could see, you were going to be the next victim."

"How...how did you know to come?"

"That was our orders. Seems this woman's sister found our camp, alerted our commander and he ordered us here. Cavalry of the 103rd Regiment, United States Colored Infantry. With orders to shoot to kill if you were in any danger from hoodlums. From what we could tell, you were."

"Colored cavalry," said Rufus, almost inaudibly. "There is a God."

"Sir?"

"Nothing. Just ruminating. You have...my eternal gratitude."

"Yes sir. Thank you." Rufus walked over to Abigale, who was now sitting on the porch steps, head in hands, weeping.

Billings followed him toward the porch and asked, "You know this woman?"

"Yes, we've become friends."

Abigale wanted to yell out 'No, it was more. We were lovers' but she said nothing.

"The man on horseback you killed was her brother," said Rufus.

"Well, I am sorry," replied Billings. "Killing is never easy. We did what we had to do. We'll have to take these men to the morgue for identification, file a report, then arrange for their burial. Mr. Simms, do you and your wife feel able to stay here tonight, or would you like us to take you someplace?"

"No, we'll stay here tonight. But if you could escort Mrs. Tate home when you're ready, that would be most appreciated. She lives on Liberty Street."

Johnny is dead. Rufus lives. Why doesn't he say Polly's not his wife?

"Her sister is at our camp," said Billings. "I'll bring Mrs. Tate there and we'll escort both of them home."

Abigale turned sharply to look at the sergeant "My sister? She's at your camp?"

"Yes, ma'am. She showed up, alone tonight. Told our captain about your brother, asked him to help. He sent us. Why don't you wait inside with Mr. and Mrs. Simms? We've got to get three dead men on horseback so they can be moved. I'll come get you when we're ready to leave."

My father. My husband. And now my brother—all dead. Killed by this war. Oh, mother! Will you survive the news? I am back in that dark period... when I first met Rufus.

Abigale did not want to go inside. She wanted to yell and scream and pound Billings' chest and beat him up, this black man who just killed her brother. Why did they have to shoot? Would Johnny really have killed Rufus, who was utterly defenseless? Or was Johnny just pretending, to give him a scare? Could he really kill a man just for being black? *I will never know.*

Another thought crept into her mind, one she tried to keep out. *And if Johnny had killed Rufus? Would I feel as empty as I do now?*

She gave Billings one last stare, then stood and entered the house with Polly and Rufus. Once inside she felt overcome with exhaustion and that she might faint. *I need to sit down.* She sat in the middle of the worn couch. Polly sat on her right, Rufus on her left.

"I so sorry, Miss Abigale," said Polly, taking hold of Abigale's hands. "I knows me and Johnny didn't see eye ta eye, but I hates to see anyone killed."

"That's kind of you, Polly. I'll be all right. I think Rufus needs your attention more than I do."

"Abigale," said Rufus, "Polly told me everything, and about your sister Jane. You risked your life to come here. You could have avoided Yamacraw altogether, and still called for the army. You didn't have to come. I too am so sorry how this turned out. There will always be love between us."

"Amen," said Polly.

Rufus gave Abigale a big hug, and Polly did the same. For a brief moment she felt good, and loved. But the moment was fleeting, and then she felt awkward. *What am I doing here?*

"Polly, why don't you sit next to Rufus? Please, I know he needs your comfort."

Polly did not argue the point. She stood and Abigale shifted to the end of the couch. Polly moved next to Rufus and they held hands. Abigale turned to look away, to think and hide her tears. *How will I tell mother? Will she survive yet another death? This must be what hell is like. Yes, I am in hell. Oh, Lord, rescue me from hell.*

Ten minutes passed, then the sound of approaching horses, and a voice from outside.

"Who goes there?" yelled Sergeant Billings.

"It's me, Sergeant. Captain Randall."

"Oh, yes, didn't recognize you, sir. The situation is under control. Who are you with, sir?"

"Major Stephen Sanford."

Sanford and Randall stopped in front of the house and dismounted.

"Sergeant, I am Major Sanford. We met before, after the Ebenezer arson. Are these men—?"

"Dead, sir. I think we got here just in time. Their white hoods made them easy targets for our Spencers."

"And Mr. Simms? And the women? Did they make it here, coming from Liberty Street?"

"They're in the house. Unharmed. The white woman was outside when the shooting took place. I'm afraid she's shaken up a bit, but not harmed. Apparently her brother is one of these men."

The front door opened and Abigale stepped onto the porch. Sanford ran up the stairs and held her tightly.

"They killed Johnny," she sobbed. "They killed my brother."

"I know. I'm sorry."

She did not speak, but went limp and collapsed against his chest. He lifted her up, asked Captain Randall to open the door, then carried her inside. Rufus and Polly stood up to help.

"I've got her," said Sanford. "I'll lay her on the couch."

As soon as he put her down Captain Randall came in. "Is she going to be all right, Major?"

"I trust so," said Sanford. "This has been quite a shock." He held Abigale's hands between his and rubbed them gently. "I'm right here, darling. You don't have to speak, just nod that you hear and understand me."

"What happened?" she asked, her voice weak. "Did I faint?"

"I believe so," replied Sanford. "Just lie here for a while. You will be fine."

She stared into his eyes. "No, I won't be fine. My brother has just been killed."

Before Sanford could reply, Captain Randall interrupted. "Sir, my plan is to bring her back to our camp on Oglethorpe Square, then escort her and her sister to their home. That is, if you think she can be moved."

"Give me a few minutes with her, then I'll decide."

"Yes, sir." Randall left to join his men outside.

Sanford stroked Abigale's hair, and whispered. "I'm here. It will be all right. Captain Randall told me the whole story. Jane walked over to Oglethorpe Square, found him. Captain Randall did the right thing, sending over his cavalry. Based on what Jane told him, he thought you were in mortal danger. Not just Simms, but you, darling. If something had happened to you, I don't know what I would have done, but under the circumstances I—"

"Don't say anything, please. If it had been you with that rifle, no matter how justified, we could never be together. Take me home, please. Don't speak about this now. I've got to tell mother."

"I understand. Let's see if you can walk. I'll put you on my horse, in front. It's a short distance. First, though, we have to pick up Jane. I want to bring both of you home together. I'll have Captain Randall accompany me."

"Oh, my god," said Abigale. "I've got to tell Jane also."

"I'm afraid so. Unless you want me to."

"No, she has to hear it from me."

Just then Captain Randall re-entered the house. "Major Sanford, could I see you a minute? This won't take long. I'll wait for you outside."

"I'll be right back, Abigale. Please don't try to get up until I return."

Sanford met Randall outside, standing next to the dead men's horses and Sergeant Billings.

"What is it?" asked Sanford.

"Sir, Sergeant Billings thinks these three dead men are the arsonists, the ones who have been burning down churches."

"I thought so myself, but how do you know for sure, Sergeant?"

"This horse here," said Billings, pointing, "belonged to the man who killed my partner outside Ebenezer Methodist."

"It's got a white mark?"

"The same one. The mark was hiding under a horse blanket when we got here. I just uncovered it."

"Let me see this."

They moved behind the horse in question. Johnny's body lay strapped over the top, but the horse's rear remained uncovered.

"I'll be damned," said Sanford. "Just as you described."

"Yes, sir, same horse. No doubt about it."

"So my hunch is confirmed, Sergeant. There are probably accomplices out there yet to be captured. We can't let them know what's happened here tonight, at least not yet. I want you in my office tomorrow morning, nine a.m., Army headquarters on Bay Street. We'll file a formal report. In the meantime don't talk about this episode to anyone. When we have it all wrapped up I'll see that you get a commendation, which you richly deserve."

"Major Sanford," said Randall, "standard procedure is the cavalry gives me their report, and I send it to the War Department. Are you saying to forgo that procedure?"

"That's exactly what I'm ordering. I'll stay in charge for now, so any reports will go directly to me. I will issue that directive in writing, for your files, so you should have no concern."

"Yes, sir," said Captain Randall.

"And also tell your men not to report anything about this raid to anyone at camp."

"Understood."

"Good. Now I'll go get Mrs. Tate, and we'll head back to camp."

"Sir?" asked Billings, "the man I shot, on the horse with the white mark, is he really that woman's brother?"

"I'm afraid, so, yes."

"What was she doin' here? She seemed to be trying to protect Mr. Simms."

"I don't have an answer for you. Just want you to know, you did the right thing."

"Thank you, sir."

CHAPTER 50

———

— *FRIDAY, MAY 12*

THE THREE DAYS BETWEEN JOHNNY's death and his funeral were difficult for the family. Jane handled the news about as well as could be expected, ever thankful Abigale had escaped harm. Mrs. Gordon, oblivious to the surrounding circumstances, simply did not believe Johnny capable of doing mischief. After an initial breakdown, which left her bed-confined for twenty-four hours, she made clear her assessment: that the U.S. Army must have wanted him killed because he had saved the life of General Bedford Forrest.

Abigale fought self-recrimination, by rationalizing her brother had no chance the moment he stormed out of the house, intent on killing Rufus. She obsessed over every permutation, and just when she thought she was done, the 'what-ifs' kept recurring in her mind. She tried to play the piano, but never got beyond the first measure of Chopin before she got up, moved to a chair or walked the room, to think again about the tragedy.

Had she not intervened, and Johnny been successful, there is no way she could hide the information from Sanford – unless she abruptly ended their relationship, an action which would surely suggest she knew the perpetrator. The note she sent Sanford cancelling their May 8 meeting was suspicious enough, though Sanford did not ask her more about it. If he suspected she *knew* Johnny was one of the arsonists, he did not ask. And she would not admit it, if he did ask. She vowed to keep that secret forever.

What if Johnny and his men had killed Rufus, Polly *and* her, and escaped? Surely, she figured, Jane's quest for help would have led to a massive manhunt, Johnny's eventual capture and hanging.

And if Rufus had listened to them and run from the house? What then? Again, Jane's quest would have led to Johnny's capture as a suspected gang member, interrogation and, Abigale had no doubt, the same result.

Over and over Abigale pondered the pathways, and each time Johnny ended up a hung man. Thus could she reconcile both her own actions, and Jane's as well.

Jane, for her part, offered no remorse to her sister. "They could have killed you, Abigale. From what I heard, the two men riding with Johnny were thugs, through and through."

"Heard? From whom?"

"Polly."

"Strange, I never felt personally threatened."

"You don't know. You were there, a witness. Johnny may not have been able to stop them. First you, then Polly. They were a crazy bunch. I did the right thing. Johnny left us no choice. I think he had a death wish. There is no other way to explain it."

"Really? A death wish? I never thought of that," replied Abigale. *I had my own death wish once.* "Perhaps you're right."

———◆———

Both Savannah newspapers reported the event sparsely, offering only the official Army report and no interviews. At first General Grover wanted to have a big story— ARSONISTS CAUGHT IN ACT, KILLED—but Sanford convinced him publicity could hurt the investigation.

"There are other conspirators, and if we tip our hand, they may flee," he explained to Grover. "Also, it's not clear, if we find others, that we can have a military trial. President Johnson might countermand the military trying civilians for civilian crimes. The man who killed the sergeant is dead, so all we have are civilian crimes to prosecute."

"What do you recommend?" Grover asked.

"Report the events as a robbery gone bad. Three men caught in the act of robbing a home in Yamacraw. Don't even mention Mr. Simms or Mrs. Tate. Only that our roving army unit came upon the men breaking into a house, a gunfight ensued and they were killed. Give their names, nothing more. No mention of church arsons, or the near murder of Rufus Simms."

Reluctantly, Grover agreed, so the story of three hooded horsemen shot dead by Union cavalry, soldiers' race omitted, appeared on the inside pages of Savannah's newspapers.

———————

Only a few people attended Johnny's funeral: his immediate family, their neighbor Joseptha Morgan, Mayor Arnold and Major Sanford. Polly did not attend, spending the day instead with Rufus.

A local minister conducted the brief graveside service. He made no mention of Johnny's terror activities, or of how he came to die. Instead, he eulogized Johnny as a war hero, one who would find peace in heaven.

Leaving the graveside, Mrs. Gordon remarked to Abigale, "Johnny was a good boy. A good boy."

Abigale did not argue. *She will never acknowledge what Johnny did, or why he was killed. It is just as well. It helps her cope.*

— Sunday, May 14

In the evening Major Sanford came to Liberty Street to pay his respects to the family. By mutual agreement, he and Abigale had decided to forgo meeting at Pulaski House, at least for a while. "It won't feel right," she told him. "Let me get over Johnny's death."

Stephen spent a few minutes with Mrs. Gordon and her daughters, and when all was said that needed saying, Abigale asked to be alone with him. Dutifully, Jane and her mother left the living room. Abigale and Stephen sat on the couch, a couple of feet apart.

"It was nice of you to come over, Stephen."

"Words are never enough, but sometimes the gesture does help. And of course I wanted to see you."

"You are very tolerant of mother and the way she sees things."

"There is no point arguing with her. She thinks the army was out to get Johnny because he saved the life of General Forrest. I am surprised she doesn't throw me out of the house."

"That's how she deals with the situation," said Abigale. "I don't push the truth on her, either. It would make things worse. She hates your army but likes you. Which makes me think she really doesn't believe what she says."

"Which proves a point I've long argued. Women are inscrutable. You've seen the newspapers?"

"Yes, and I am ever thankful my name is out of it. They didn't even attempt to interview me or Jane."

"They damn well better not. Or General Grover will be on their rear ends."

"Umm, that's nice, Stephen, but don't you believe in freedom of the press?"

"Absolutely. And I also believe in protecting my own interests."

"Such as?"

"You, for starters."

"So, just as I thought, the army still controls the press in Savannah?"

"Well, let's just say General Grover has some sway. It's going to change, very soon, though. President Johnson is going to pull all the troops out, probably sometime this year, then your press will be truly free. Which it should be. It's in the constitution."

"I know, and I know the situation will get better. One thing still bothers me though, and I have been reluctant to bring it up. Something I can't let go of."

"What is it?"

"I have reconciled Johnny had no future once he decided to kill Rufus. But what led him to that decision?"

"To preserve your honor. I thought we had this discussion after the funeral?"

"No, I mean yes, but how did he know we had even been together, had an affair?"

"You tell me."

"That evening, when he started with his hateful accusations, asking me to deny this and deny that, he called out the names Gustav Heinz and Ignatius Gardner. They obviously told him something, though how he got to them I don't know."

"Can you keep a secret?"

"Absolutely."

"I mean, tell no one until we release a formal report for the papers, which might not be for a few days."

"My lips are sealed."

"Ignatius is in custody. He was in with the other arsonists, though he didn't participate in the burnings. He is the one who brought Johnny to their hideaway, where the night riders lived."

"So Ignatius spread the rumor. It makes sense because he followed me around Savannah. But where does Gustav come into the picture?"

"Ignatius denies ever meeting with Johnny in Gustav's presence. So I interviewed the German again. This won't be flattering, but your brother visited Savannah Gardens and met Gustav there."

"I am not surprised. He probably knew all the brothels in town. What did Gustav tell him?"

"He denies telling Johnny anything. He admits he knew Johnny was your brother, but swears he said nothing about you. He's lying, of course, but no way to prove it."

"Did Johnny pay for one of his girls? I don't blame him, but I find the business repulsive."

"Do you want the truth?"

"Of course. What a silly question."

"Gustav offered him a negro girl. For free, because he said Johnny was a war hero. Gustav actually bragged about it."

"I'm listening. I fear there is more."

"Johnny readily accepted, or so Gustav says."

"Am I to believe this? You already said Gustav's a liar."

"He gave me her name, said I could ask her myself."

"Did you?"

"No."

"You believe him?"

"Yes. I have a way of knowing when Gustav is lying and when he's telling the truth."

"So my brother had a negro girl. Then a few days later he wants to kill Rufus because of my past affair with him? Do you not see the irony?"

"Honestly, I don't think Johnny thought about it for a moment. And if he did, if someone had thrown the irony in his face, he would probably have brushed it off, just said 'It's different for a woman'. I never met your brother, but I've encountered men like him."

"Perhaps. Men can be awful creatures, sometimes."

"Affirmed."

"Oh, stop it, Stephen. You don't have to agree with me."

"Very well, then. Denied."

"You're impossible."

He reached for her hands and held them. "Not impossible," he said, "just a bit lonely."

She wanted to kiss him but resisted. Instead, she gently withdrew her hands. "I understand. Please be patient."

"I am patient, darling. I know what you've been through."

"Can you bear a few more questions? I am still puzzled."

"Yes, but I may not know the answers."

"If neither Gustav nor Ignatius ever saw me in Rufus' embrace, how could they tell Johnny something they really knew nothing about?"

"Again, my hunch is, they inferred it, and incited Johnny, to get back at you."

"For what?"

"I don't know. For thwarting their voyeurism. For being interrogated in my headquarters. For being a beautiful woman beyond their reach. For all three."

"Will Ignatius hang?"

"Possibly. It depends on the jurisdiction for his trial, and right now it's not clear."

"What about Gustav, can't you arrest him?"

"On what grounds? For being a scoundrel? Because he spread rumors? Or because he runs a whore house?"

"Well, isn't that illegal in Savannah?"

"Yes, technically, but it's also under civil jurisdiction, so we really can't interfere."

"Oh Stephen, you sound like a judge."

"One day, perhaps."

"Seriously, Gustav gets away with this behavior? I'm not vindictive, but the situation now seems clear. Without him and Ignatius, Johnny would have learned nothing about me, and might be alive today."

Stephen did not respond, but looked away.

"What's the matter? You always have the answer. Am I not right?"

"He would not have been killed that night, in Yamacraw, I agree. But his joining up with the hoodlums had nothing to do with Gustav or Ignatius. He was recruited for a lost cause by another man, who is also in custody. This gang was going to be caught sooner or later. Gustav just gave Johnny an excuse to act against Simms. If not caught that night, it would have been another night, another location. We now have a fairly complete picture of these arsonists. Johnny was one of them."

Abigale pondered his explanation, and found nothing to challenge. "I see. So Gustav does not have to answer for his odious behavior?"

Sanford smiled. "Well, there is something we can do. And it would be justified."

— *MONDAY, MAY 15*

Two Union officers approached Savannah Gardens at 7 p.m. Sophie welcomed them in, a captain and a lieutenant, both dressed in uniform. Sitting at the lobby desk, she asked, "May I help you?"

"Mr. Gustav Heinz, please," said the captain.

"I can help," she said. "We open for business at eight, but if you are in a hurry we can make accommodations."

"We are not here as customers, ma'am, but on orders from the United States Army. Please fetch Mr. Heinz."

She got up from her desk and rushed to the back. In a minute Gustav appeared. Strands of spaghetti and dabs of red sauce dripped from his shirt.

"Gentlemen, Gentlemen," effused Gustav. "Officers of the army. How can I help you? Please, you are early, but we have women for you, no problem."

"Mr. Heinz," spoke the captain, "we have orders to designate an official off-limits to your establishment for our soldiers. Savannah Gardens is a fount of venereal disease, which is infecting our troops. Therefore it is henceforth off limits to all army personnel, colored and white. This order does not affect civilians who may come and go, but only army personnel."

"Vat? Vat? Vat venereal disease. Vat you speak? There is no disease in my establishment. Leave, go avay. Go avay!"

"We will establish a sentry during normal business hours, who will screen all customers. Any army personnel will be forbidden to enter. If you interfere with our sentry you will be subject to arrest."

"But, but—"

"Gustav," interrupted Sophie, "don't fight them. Not so many soldiers like we used to have."

"But…but…others will see this. Not true. Who tell you I have venereal? No, not me, this place. Who sent you? Who? Vat is going on? Vere is Mayor Arnold? The police? I pay the police. Mein Gott! Vat is going on here?"

"Here is the order Mr. Heinz," said the captain, and he placed a single sheet of paper on Sophie's desk. "The army ban will begin this evening and stay in effect until further notice."

———

CHAPTER 51

— *FRIDAY, MAY 26*

MAJOR SANFORD AND MAYOR ARNOLD came to the Gordon home for dinner. Abigale arranged it, the first social event for the household since Johnny's funeral. Mrs. Gordon still wore black. Being at home, Abigale did not wear the arm band.

Before dinner began, Arnold pulled Major Sanford aside in the living room. "Stephen, that's quite a stunt you pulled at Gustav's place, posting a sentry on the pretense of venereal disease. Rumor has it he may close down Savannah Gardens. He's already lowered his prices, and is giving out free condoms to all customers who want them. He's been to my office twice, demanding I do something about your sentry. Do you know what it's like to confront an angry German?"

"Good riddance, I say. If you enforced your own laws, this order wouldn't be necessary."

"Oh, come now, Stephen, there's half a dozen other houses around town, if not more. They all keep the police well fed. And besides, I see just as much disease from the other establishments. Why target only Gustav?"

"Let's just say he played host to some of the arson gang, and knew more than he let on. He was not a conspirator, but in some ways a facilitator. And the fact is, President Johnson's going to pull out the army anyway, probably soon. So with a ban on our troops or no ban, Heinz will be back to where he started, with his old crowd of Confederate ne'er do wells. It's really a small punishment to fit a misdemeanor, if you will."

"So you're saying he was involved with the arsonists, but wasn't?"

"Well put, your honor. Affiant further sayeth naught."

Mayor Arnold shook his head. "Well, it's no secret those men Johnny rode with were the arsonists, though the newspapers don't mention it. Were they the only men involved? Did you find other accomplices?"

"Given your position, I suppose you have a right to know, and you'll read about it soon. We've already picked up two others. One of the dead men had a receipt from Tanner's Mill, a grainery about four miles south of here. We checked it out, learned of a remote cabin nearby, and raided it early this week. Got one man, sleeping, named Caleb Jenkins. Found his hood and other incriminating evidence. He's locked up, will go to trial. We'll release his name after we're done with our interrogation."

"Well, I'm surprised he stuck around. Didn't he think you'd come after him?"

"Apparently not. When the men who went to Simms house that night didn't return, the next morning this Jenkins fellow rode into town, found out what happened from all the Yamacraw gossip, and figured his friends died too quick to tell us anything. Figured we had no reason even to know he existed. Which would have been the case, but for that receipt."

"Who is the other man? You said there were two."

"An ex-Confederate and army deserter named Ignatius Gardner. He served as the gang's front man in Savannah. For all their smarts, they were pretty dumb. Found his name in a notebook Jenkins kept."

"Dinner's ready, ya'll, please sit down," called out Mrs. Gordon from the dining room.

"That is interesting," said the mayor. "Though I disagree with your action against Gustav Heinz, I must say you've helped make Savannah a safer place."

"Well, thanks. Now, let's eat. I'm hungry."

Everyone took their seat at the dining table. Polly did the serving, assisted by Jane until most of the dishes were on the table.

"Now that we're all seated," said Abigale, "Stephen has some good news."

"Oh?" asked Mrs. Gordon. "We could use some good news." All eyes turned on Sanford.

"Yes, I've located Captain Broderick. He's on his way to Savannah, and should be here in a few days. Jane, he asked me to give you this message, which I just received this morning." He handed over a folded piece of paper.

Jane read the note.

"What's it say?" asked Abigale.

"None of your business," Jane answered with a broad smile, while refolding the note. "He's coming home. We're going to get married."

"Well," retorted Abigale, "your announcement is very much our business, wouldn't you say so, Mother?"

"Yes, and very good news," replied Mrs. Gordon, rather flatly. She paused, then added, "I'll have a Yankee son-in-law. Oh, my."

"And we have some more good news," said Abigale.

"Oh?"

"In the future you will have two Yankee sons-in-law."

"Abigale!" screamed Jane. "You two are—"

"Yes, we are. Stephen's put in his discharge papers, and as soon as they're approved, we're moving to New York, where we'll get married."

Polly, just bringing in one last dish from the kitchen, said "Dat's real nice, Miss Abigale. I am mos' pleased to hear dis."

"What about you Polly?" asked Abigale. "You and Rufus?"

"Now don't go be pushin' what ain't got to be pushed."

Noticing a puzzled look on the Mayor's face, Abigale offered, "Polly's been seeing Mr. Simms quite regularly. You never know."

"I certainly learn much coming here," replied Mayor Arnold. "This is the place for news of the day."

"New York? Why New York?" asked Mrs. Gordon, turning the conversation back to her family. "Your home is here, Abigale."

"It has to be New York, Mother. Stephen's old legal partners are there. He cannot profitably practice here in Georgia. And as much as he loves our charming city, he's finding the heat a little bothersome, and he's heard too much about our mosquitos."

Abigale did not hear whatever comment ensued. Instead, she began thinking. *Stephen would set up practice here if I insisted, but New York is my wish as much as his. More so, even. I must get away from this place. Marrying within a year of Franklin's death is sure to cause gossip. His mother may yet come back to taunt me. I escaped my affair with Rufus and in hindsight it seems so utterly reckless. But God knows what Ignatius may babble before he is hung? And Gustav, that odious creature. He will find a way to spread rumor. Inevitably, there will be questions, chatter. 'Abigale, there is talk that you and Mr. Simms...' 'Abigale, is it true...?' I love Savannah but it is small and provincial, and I have violated our traditions. I will miss my family, true, but leave I must. No one will care in New York.*

"Abigale" said Mrs. Gordon, "you seem to have wandered off. Are you all right?"

"Oh, yes, mother. I am sorry. I was just thinking about all we have to do before moving to New York. I do hope we don't have much problem with mosquitos up north. Stephen will be sorely disappointed."

"Well, I admit the situation can be a bit unpleasant here in the summer," said Mayor Arnold. "But Stephen, you really should consider living down here. I've been to New York and it's too congested. The living is so much easier here."

"Thank you, Richard. We'll certainly return for visits. But to live here, no thank you. I do think Abigale will love the hustle and bustle of the big city. Anyway, we'll certainly be around for a while. I assume Jane and Captain Broderick will be married soon, and we wouldn't want to miss their wedding."

"But why can't you two marry in Savannah?" asked Mrs. Gordon.

"Yes, why not" chimed in Mayor Arnold. "You know, as mayor I do perform marriage ceremonies. I could do a double ceremony, if you prefer. Have not done one of those for a while. A double wedding would be splendid."

Abigale and Stephen looked at each other.

"Well," Abigale said, "I suppose we never thought of the possibility."

"You owe it to your mother, Abigale," said Mrs. Gordon. "If you're going to move up north, at least start your married life in Savannah. I insist."

Stephen shrugged his shoulders, suggesting 'a double wedding is fine with me'.

"Well," said Abigale, in a manner wishing to show agreement but not outright commitment, "Jane and I would have to agree on a date."

"The sooner the better," Jane said, and made a show of patting her abdomen.

Marry here, in Savannah? Not a year after Franklin's death? Not a month or two after Johnny was murdered? And to a Yankee officer? I don't want to confront the naysayers and the gossipers. The only way feasible would be for us to embark on our honeymoon the very day of the ceremony. Or the next day at the latest. Yes, marry here to please mother, then leave. That is my plan.

"Wait a minute," said Stephen. "I wish to marry as a civilian. Too many things can go wrong if I am still in the service. The war is over, yes, but you never know what orders might come down. So we'll have to wait on the discharge papers."

"As a practical matter," asked Mayor Arnold, "how long do you think the orders will take?"

"Oh, given my relationship with General Grover...and the fact the war is over, and that I am not career military...it could take up to...a week."

"Oh, Sir, you had us in great suspense," joked the mayor. "Then it's settled. A double ceremony. At no charge. In my office. Abigale and Jane, give me the date when you know for sure."

"Oh, dear," said Mrs. Gordon. "Can we have wedding ceremonies so soon after we've buried Johnny? And still in mourning?"

"Actually," said Mayor Arnold, "you can. Happy ceremonies are always to replace sad ones, the sooner the better. It's a mayoral decree."

Everyone laughed except Mrs. Gordon, who merely smiled.

"Mother," said Jane, "you should be happy."

"Oh, I am. I just wish Abigale would stay in Savannah."

"Mrs. Gordon, we promise to return after the baby is born, and visit for several days," said Stephen. "When *is* that baby coming, Jane?"

"Dr. Arnold says the baby should be born around the end of September."

"Well, yes," said Arnold. "My estimation is based on the information you've provided."

"So let's see," said Sanford. "A lot is happening. Two weddings here, hopefully within the month, and a baby born in September. Any other big news coming soon?" He looked at Henrietta Gordon, whose face remained impassive.

Abigale looked at the mayor, who glanced at her mother but said nothing.

"Mother?" asked Jane.

"Mother?" echoed Abigale.

Mrs. Gordon looked past her guests, as if peering into the future, and said only, "Oh, my."

EPILOGUE FOR MAJOR
HISTORICAL CHARACTERS

———————

RICHARD ARNOLD, MD (AUGUST 19, 1808 – July 10, 1876) served out his fourth non-consecutive one-year term as mayor on December 11, 1865, and did not run again. Nor did he ever remarry. He later served as president of the school board, until his death, at age 68. He is buried in Savannah's Bonaventure cemetery.

General Nathan Bedford Forrest (July 13, 1821 – October 29, 1877) was considered by both Generals Sherman and Grant as one of the South's most formidable officers. He famously said that the way to win is "to get there first with the most men." After the war he became an early member of the Ku Klux Klan, but was not a founder. He later turned against the methods used by the Klan, and before his death fully renounced his involvement with the KKK.

General John Geary (December 30, 1819 – February 8, 1873) was served two terms as the Republican governor of Pennsylvania, from 1867 to 1873. On February 8, 1873, less than three weeks after leaving the governor's post, Geary was stricken with a heart attack and died at age 53.

Charles Green (1809, in Shropshire, England – 1881) entered the insurance and shipping business in Savannah after the war, and remained wealthy throughout this life. He died in Maine. His son inherited the Savannah home, where General Sherman stayed in 1864-65. In 1892 it was sold to Judge Peter W. Meldrim. The mansion has since been known as the Green-Meldrim house. In December 1943 the Meldrim family sold it to St. John's Episcopal Church, situated immediately across the street, and the former kitchens, servant's quarters and stable now serve as the rectory for the church. The home was designated as a National Historic Landmark in 1976, and is now open for tours on selected days throughout the year.

General Cuvier Grover (July 24, 1828 – June 6, 1885) was a career officer in the United States Army and a general when he headed the Savannah occupation from late January through the spring of 1865. He is buried in West Point Cemetery.

General William Joseph Hardee (October 12, 1815 – November 6, 1873) left Savannah with his troops December 20, 1864 and made his way to North Carolina, where he took part in the Battle of Bentonville in March 1865. In that battle his only son, 16-year-old Willie, was mortally wounded. Hardee surrendered along with General Joseph E. Johnston on April 26, 1865, at Durham Station, NC. After the war, Hardee managed his wife's two plantations near Demopolis, Alabama. In February 1866, he moved to Selma, Alabama, to take the position of president of the Selma and Meridian Railroad. In 1868, along with co-author John Francis Maguire, he published *The Irish in America*. In 1873 he became ill at his family's summer retreat and died in Wytheville, Virginia. He is buried in Live Oak Cemetery, Selma, Alabama.

General William Tecumseh Sherman (February 8, 1820 – February 14, 1891) remained in the army after the war, and when Ulysses Grant became president, was promoted to Commanding General of the United States Army. He was one of the first generals to write his memoirs (first published 1875), which were revised in two later editions. He was considered a potential Republican candidate for president in the election of 1884, but said "I will not accept if nominated and will not serve if elected." Sherman has long been vilified in the South for his infamous march through Georgia and South Carolina. However, his benign approach to Savannah during the occupation, and the city's current preeminent position as an historic tourist site, have led some to consider him Savannah's first preservationist.

Edwin Stanton (December 19, 1814 – December 24, 1869) served as Secretary of War under President Johnson. He opposed Johnson's lenient policies to the rebel states, and the president tried to have him removed. This attempt was one reason Johnson was impeached by the Congress. After retiring as Secretary of War, Stanton returned to his law practice. In 1869 he was nominated to the Supreme Court by President Grant. Stanton died four days after his nomination was confirmed by the Senate.

———◆———

Polly and **Lucy** are fictional sisters, but representative of Savannah's newly-freed slaves in the immediate post-war period. Some blacks chose to stay on with their previous masters at a stipulated wage. Others accepted the government's offer to relocate to abandoned plantations on the coastal islands. There is much controversy about Sherman's Field Orders No. 15, which granted forty acres to all negroes who met certain qualifications. Sherman always viewed his directive as a war measure only, subject to modification and/or dissolution by Congress or the president. Which is just what happened. In late 1865 President Johnson rescinded Field Orders No. 15 and returned abandoned plantations to their original owners, as long as they signed a loyalty oath to the Union. By that time some 40 thousand ex-slaves had settled on the islands.

On their return to the abandoned plantations, the newly re-enfranchised owners could hire ex-slaves at an agreed upon wage, which required "contracts." These contracts were often handled by the Freedman's Bureau, a government agency set up to help ex-slaves, almost all of whom were uneducated, adjust to the new order. There was much conflict over this situation, with some blacks refusing to be part of any contract, while others forcibly tried to keep the white owners from returning.

Polly would likely have continued working for the Tate-Gordon household. Lucy may have stayed on her assigned plantation at a wage negotiated for her by the Freeman's Bureau. Her husband Digby would have returned from the army to help work the planation.

What happened to Lucy, Polly, Digby and other characters during the period of reconstruction could fill another novel.

APPENDIX: HISTORIC DOCUMENTS

———

NOTE: THE KINDLE E-BOOK EDITION of *Liberty Street* allows for one-click access to the websites listed below if your reading device is internet-connected. The e-book is enrolled in the Kindle Unlimited program, and is also free for those who buy the print edition from Amazon.

1. **December 17, 1864: General Sherman's demand for the surrender of Savannah**

   https://archive.org/stream/warrebellionaco35offigoog #page/n746/mode/2up/

   HEADQUARTERS MILITARY DIVISION OF THE MISSISSIPPI
   IN THE FIELD, SAVANNAH, GEORGIA, DECEMBER 17, 1864

   General William J Hardee, commanding Confederate Forces in Savannah.
   GENERAL: You have doubtless observed…that sea-going vessels now come through Ossabaw Sound and up the Ogeechee to the rear of my army, giving me abundant supplies of all kinds, and more especially heavy ordnance necessary for the reduction of Savannah. I have already received guns that can

cast heavy and destructive shot as far as the heart of your city; also, I have for some days held and controlled every avenue by which the people and garrison of Savannah can be supplied, and I am therefore justified in demanding the surrender of the city of Savannah, and its dependent forts, and shall wait a reasonable time for your answer, before opening with heavy ordnance…I am prepared to grant liberal terms for the inhabitants and garrison; but should I be forced to resort to assault or the slower and surer process of starvation, I shall then feel justified in resorting to the harshest measures, and shall make little effort to restrain my army—burning to avenge the national wrong which they attach to Savannah and other large cities which have been so prominent in dragging our country into civil war.

I have the honor to be your obedient servant.

W. T. Sherman, *Major-General*

2. December 17, 1864: General Hardee's reply to General Sherman's surrender demand

https://archive.org/stream/warrebellionaco35offigoog #page/n746/mode/2up/

HEADQUARTERS DEPARTMENT OF SOUTH CAROLINA, GEORGIA AND FLORIDA
SAVANNAH, GEORGIA, DECEMBER 17, 1864

Major General W. T Sherman, commanding Federal Forces near Savannah, Georgia.

GENERAL: I have to acknowledge the receipt of a communication from you of this date, in which you demand "the surrender of Savannah and its dependent forts," on the ground that you "have received guns that can cast heavy and destructive shot into the heart of the city," and for the further reason that you "have, for some days, held and controlled every avenue by which the people and garrison can be supplied."

...Your statement that you have, for some days, held and controlled every avenue by which the people and garrison can be supplied, is incorrect. I am in free and constant communication with my department.

Your demand for the surrender of Savannah and its dependent forts is refused...

W. J. Hardee, Lieutenant-General

3. **December 21, 1864: Mayor Richard Arnold's letter of surrender**

   https://books.google.com/books?id=n8QtAAAAIAAJ&printsec=frontcover#v=onepage&q&f=false

   [Page 772]

Savannah, *December 21, 1864*

Maj. Gen. W.T. Sherman,
Commanding U.S. Military Forces near Savannah:

Sir: The city of Savannah was last night evacuated by the Confederate military and is now entirely defenseless. As chief magistrate of the city I respectfully request your protection of the lives and private property of the citizens and of our women and children.

Trusting that this appeal to your generosity and humanity may favorably influence your action, I have the honor to be, your obedient servant,

R. D. Arnold,
Mayor of Savannah

4. **December 21, 1864: Savannah Republican editorial just prior to Union occupation**

    http://georgiainfo.galileo.usg.edu/thisday/ownwords/
    12/21/savannah-newspaper-announced-surrender

Savannah Republican
December 21, 1864
Citizens of Savannah:

By the fortunes of war we pass today under the authority of the Federal military forces. The evacuation of Savannah by the Confederate army, which took place last night, left the gates to the city open, and General Sherman, with his army will, no doubt, to-day take possession.

The Mayor and Common Counsel leave under a flag of truce this morning, for the headquarters of Gen. Sherman, to offer the surrender of the city, and ask terms of capitulation by which private property and citizens may be respected.

We desire to counsel obedience and all proper respect on the part of our citizens, and to express the belief that their property and persons will be respected by our military ruler. The fear expressed by many that Gen. Sherman will repeat the order of expulsion from their homes which he enforced against the citizens of Atlanta, we think to be without foundation. He assigned his reason in that case as a military necessity, it was a question of food. He could not supply his army and the citizens with food, and he stated that he must have full and sole occupation. But in our case food can be abundantly supplied for both army and civilians.

We would not be understood as even intimating that we are to be fed at the cost of the Federal Government, but that food can be easily obtained in all probability, by all who can afford to pay in the Federal currency.

It behooves all to keep within their homes until Gen. Sherman shall have organized a provost system and such police as will insure safety in persons as well as property.

Let our conduct be such as to win the admiration of a magnanimous foe, and give no ground for complaint or harsh treatment on the part of him who will for an indefinite period hold possession of our city.

In our city there are, as in other communities, a large proportion of poor and needy families, who, in the present situation of affairs, brought about by the privations of war, will be thrown upon the bounty of their more fortunate neighbors. Deal with them kindly, exercise your philanthropy and benevolence, and let the heart of the unfortunate not be deserted by your friendly aid.

5. December 22, 1864: General Sherman's telegram to President Lincoln

http://www.lakesidepress.com/Savannah-CivilWar/ sherman-telegram.html

Savannah Georgia, December 22, 1864
To His Excellency President Lincoln, Washington, D.C.:

I beg to preset you as a Christmas-gift the city of Savannah, with one hundred and fifty heavy guns and plenty of ammunition, also about twenty-five thousand bales of cotton.

W.T. Sherman, Major-General

6. December 23, 1864: General Sherman's orders for occupation of Savannah

http://georgiainfo.galileo.usg.edu/thisday/ownwords/ 12/23/shermans-orders-for-occupation-of-savannah

SPECIAL FIELD ORDERS NO. 139
HEADQUARTERS MILITARY DIVISION OF THE
MISSISSIPPI, IN THE FIELD, NEAR SAVANNAH, GEORGIA,
December 23, 1864.

Savannah, being now is our possession, and the river partially cleared out, and measures have been taken to remove all
obstructions, will at once be made a grand depot for future
operations.

1. The chief-quartermaster, General Easton, will, after giving the necessary orders touching the transports in Ogeechee
River and Ossabaw Sound, come in person to Savannah, and
take possession of all public buildings, all vacant store-rooms,
warehouses, &c., that may be now or hereafter needed for any
department of the army. No rents will be paid by the Government of the United States during the war, and all buildings must be distributed according to the accustomed rules of
the quartermaster's department, as though they were public
property.

2. The chief commissary of subsistence, Col. A. Beckwith,
will transfer the grand depot of the army to the city of
Savannah, secure possession of the needful buildings and offices, and give the necessary orders, to the end that the army
may be supplied abundantly and well.

3. The chief engineer, Captain Poe, will at once direct
which of the enemy's forts are to be retained for our use and
which dismantled and destroyed; and the chief ordnance officer, Captain Baylor, will, in like manner, take possession of all
property pertaining to his department captured from the enemy and cause the same to be collected and carried to points
of security. All the heavy sea-coast guns will be dismounted
and carried to Fort Pulaski.

4. The troops, for the present, will be grouped about the
city of Savannah, looking to convenience of camps, General
Slocum taking from the Savannah around to about the

seven-mile post, on the canal, and General Howard thence to the sea. General Kilpatrick will hold King's Bridge until Fort McAllister is dismantled and the troops withdrawn from the south side of the Ogeechee, when he will take post about Anderson's plantation, on the plank road, and picket all the roads leading from the north and west.

5. General Howard will keep a small guard at Forts Rosedale, Beaulieu, Wimberly, Thunderbolt, and Bonaventura, and he will cause that shore and Skidaway Island to be examined very closely, with a view to finding many and convenient points for the embarkation of troops and wagons on sea-going vessels."

Source: U.S. War Department, *The War of the Rebellion: A Compilation of the Official Records of the Union and Confederate Armies* (Washington: U.S. Government Printing Office, 1893, reprinted by The National Historical Society, 1971), Series I, Vol. XLIV, pp. 793-794.

7. **December 26, 1864:** *New York Times* **article announcing General Sherman's Christmas present to President Lincoln**
    http://www.nytimes.com/1864/12/26/news/savannah-ours-sherman-s-christmas-present-official-dispatches-generals-sherman.html

SAVANNAH OURS; Sherman's Christmas Present. Official Dispatches from Generals Sherman and Foster. WHAT SHERMAN FOUND. 150 Cannon, 200 Cars and Locomotives, 3 Steamers, 800 Prisoners, and 30,000 Bales of Cotton. Twenty Thousand People in the City Quiet and Well Disposed. ESCAPE OF HARDEE'S ARMY. The Rebel Iron Clads Blown Up and the Navy-Yard Burned. AN ALMOST BLOODLESS VICTORY. News from the Wilmington Expedition. [OFFICIAL.]

WAR DEPARTMENT, WASHINGTON, Dec. 25 -- 8 P.M.
To Maj.-Gen, Dix, New-York:

A dispatch has been received this evening by the President from Gen. SHERMAN. It is dated at Savannah, on Thursday, the 22d inst., and announces his occupation of the city of Savannah and the capture of one hundred and fifty guns, plenty of ammunition, and about 25,000 bales of cotton. No other particulars are given.

An official dispatch from Gen. FOSTER to Gen. GRANT, dated on the 22d instant, at 7 P.M., states that the city of Savannah was occupied by Gen. SHERMAN on the morning of the 21st, and that on the preceding afternoon and night, HARDEE escaped with the main body of his infantry and light, artillery, blowing up the iron-clads and the Navy-yard. He enumerates as captured 800 prisoners, 150 guns, 13 locomotives, in good order, 190 cars, a large lot of ammunition and materials of war, three steamers and 33,000 bales of cotton. No mention is made of the present position of HARDEE's force, which had been estimated at about 15,000.

The dispatches of Gen. SHERMAN and Gen. FOSTER are as follows:

SAVANNAH, Ga., Dec. 22.
To His Excellency, President Lincoln:

I beg to present you as a Christmas gift, the city of Savannah, with one hundred and fifty heavy guns and plenty of ammunition, and also about twenty-five thousand bales of cotton.
(Signed,) W.T. SHERMAN, Major-General.

STEAMER GOLDEN GATE, SAVANNAH RIVER, 7 P.M., Thursday, Dec.23.
To Lieutenant-General Grant and Major-General H.W. Halleck:

I have the honor to report that I have just returned from General SHERMAN's headquarters in Savannah.

I send Major GRAY of my staff as bearer of dispatches from General SHERMAN to you, and also a message to the President.

The city of Savannah was occupied on the morning of the 21st. Gen. HARDEE, anticipating the contemplated assault, escaped with the main body of his infantry and light artillery, on the morning of the 20th, by crossing the river to Union Causeway, opposite the city. The rebel iron-clads were blown up, and the Navy-yard was burned. All the rest of the city is intact, and contains twenty thousand citizens, quiet and well-disposed.

The captures includes eight hundred prisoners, one hundred and fifty guns, thirteen locomotives in good order, one hundred and ninety cars, a large supply of ammunition and materials of war, three steamers and thirty-three thousand bales of cotton safely stowed in warehouses.

All these valuable fruits of an almost bloodless victory have been, like Atlanta, fairly won.

I opened communication with the city with my steamers to-day, taking up what torpedoes we could see, and passing safely over others. Arrangements are made to clear the channel of all obstructions. Yours, &c.,
(Signed.) J.G. FOSTER, Major-General.

8. **December 26, 1864: President Lincoln's thank you note to General Sherman for gift of Savannah**
   http://www.lakesidepress.com/Savannah-CivilWar/sherman-telegram.html

EXECUTIVE MANSION
WASHINGTON, Dec 26, 1864
My dear General Sherman
Many, many thanks for your Christmas gift - the capture of Savannah.

When you were about leaving Atlanta for the Atlantic coast, I was anxious, if not fearful; but, feeling that you were the better judge, and remembering "nothing risked, nothing gained," I did not interfere. Now, the undertaking being a success, the honor is all yours; for I believe none of us went further than to acquiesce; and, taking the work of General Thomas into account, as it should be taken, it is indeed a great success. Not only does it afford the obvious and immediate military advantages, but, in showing to the world that your army could be divided, putting the stronger part to an important new service, and yet leaving enough to vanquish the old opposing force of the whole, Hood's army, it brings those who sat in darkness to see a great light. But what next? I suppose it will be safer if I leave General Grant and yourself to decide. Please make my grateful acknowledgments to your whole army, officers and men.

Yours, very truly,

A. LINCOLN

9. **December 26, 1864: General Sherman's orders for governance of Savannah**

https://books.google.com/books?id=eAMYgEeIKJ8C&pg =PA98&lpg=PA98&dq=Sherman+special+field+orders+no.+14 3&source=bl&ots=wrVicVxxDR&sig=lokyYB_xr-QcDM9t6Fr5 wMwYoaI&hl=en&sa=X&ved=0ahUKEwih89bE45LTAhXCSS YKHcj2Ang4ChDoAQggMAM#v=onepage&q=Sherman%20 special%20field%20orders%20no.%20143&f=false

SPECIAL FIELD ORDERS NO. 143
HEADQUARTERS MILITARY DIVISION OF THE MISSISSIPPI, IN THE FIELD, NEAR SAVANNAH, GEORGIA, December 26, 1864.

The city of Savannah and surrounding country will be held as a military post, and adapted to future military uses, but, as it contains a population of some twenty thousand people, who must be provided for, and as other citizens may come, it is proper to lay down certain general principles, that all within its military jurisdiction may understand their relative duties and obligations.

1. During war, the military is superior to civil authority, and, where interests clash, the civil must give way; yet, where there is no conflict, every encouragement should be given to well-disposed and peaceful inhabitants to resume their usual pursuits. Families should be disturbed as little as possible in their residences, and tradesmen allowed the free use of their shops, tools, etc.; churches, schools, and all places of amusement and recreation, should be encouraged, and streets and roads made perfectly safe to persons in their pursuits. Passes should not be exacted within the line of outer pickets, but if any person shall abuse these privileges by communicating with the enemy, or doing any act of hostility to the Government of the United States, he or she will be punished with the utmost rigor of the law. Commerce with the outer world will be resumed to an extent commensurate with the wants of the citizens, governed by the restrictions and rules of the Treasury Department.

2. The chief quartermaster and commissary of the army may give suitable employment to the people, white and black, or transport them to such points as they may choose where employment can be had; and may extend temporary relief in the way of provisions and vacant houses to the worthy and needy, until such time as they can help themselves. They will select first the buildings for the necessary uses of the army; next, a sufficient number of stores, to be turned over to the Treasury agent for trade-stores. All vacant store-houses or dwellings, and all buildings belonging to absent rebels, will be construed and used as belonging to the United States, until such time as their titles can be settled by the courts of the United States.

3. The Mayor and City Council of Savannah will continue to exercise their functions, and will, in concert with the commanding officer of the post and the chief-quartermaster, see that the fire-companies are kept in organization, the streets cleaned and lighted, and keep up a good understanding between the citizens and soldiers. They will ascertain and report to the chief commissary of subsistence, as soon as possible, the names and number of worthy families that need assistance and support. The mayor will forth with give public notice that the time has come when all must choose their course, viz., remain within our lines, and conduct themselves as good citizens, or depart in peace. He will ascertain the names of all who choose to leave Savannah, and report their names and residence to the chief-quartermaster, that measures may be taken to transport them beyond our lines.

4. Not more than two newspapers will be published in Savannah; their editors and proprietors will be held to the strictest accountability, and will be punished severely, in person and property, for any libelous publication, mischievous matter, premature news, exaggerated statements, or any comments whatever upon the acts of the constituted authorities; they will be held accountable for such articles, even though copied from other papers.

By order of Major-General W. T. Sherman,

L. M. DAYTON, Aide-de-Camp

10. December 28, 1864: Resolutions proposed by Mayor Richard Arnold and passed at town hall meeting

Northern Relief for Savannah during Sherman's Occupation. John P. Dyer, *The Journal of Southern History*, Vol. 19, No. 4 (Nov., 1953), pp. 457-472

http://www.jstor.org/stable/2955087

At the call of the Mayor of Savannah, a public meeting was held in that city December 28th, 1864, which unanimously adopted the following preamble and resolutions:

Whereas, by the fortunes of war, and the surrender of the city by the civil authorities, Savannah passes once more under the authority of the United States; and whereas we believe that the interests of the city will be best subserved and promoted by a full and free expression of our views in relation to our present condition, we therefore, the people of Savannah, in full meeting assembled, do hereby Resolve —

First, That we accept the position, and, in the language of the President of the United States, seek to have peace by laying down our arms, and submitting to the national authority under the Constitution;" 'Heaving all questions which remain, to be adjusted by the peaceful means of legislation, conference, and votes."

Second, That, laying aside all differences, and burying bygones in the grave of the past, we will use our best endeavors once more to bring back the prosperity and commerce we once enjoyed.

Third, That we do not put ourselves in the position of a conquered city, asking terms of a conqueror; but we claim the immunities and privileges contained in the Proclamation and Message of the President of the United States, and in all the legislation of Congress in reference to a people situated as we are, and while we owe, on our part, a strict obedience to the laws of the United States, we ask the protection over our persons, lives, and property recognized by those laws.

Fourth, That we respectfully request his Excellency the Governor to call a convention of the people of Georgia, by any constitutional means in his power, to give them an opportunity of voting upon the question, whether they wish the war between the two sections of the country to continue.

Fifth, That, Major-General Sherman having placed, as military commander of this post, Brigadier-General Geary, who has, by his urbanity as a gentleman and his uniform kindness to our citizens, done all in his power to protect them and their property from insult and injury, it is the unanimous desire of all present, that he be allowed to remain in his present position ; and that, for the reasons above stated, the thanks of the citizens are hereby tendered to him, and the officers under his command.

Sixth, That an official copy of these resolutions be sent to the President of the United States, the Governor of Georgia, General Sherman, and to each the Mayors of Augusta, Columbus, Macon, and Atlanta, and to Brigadier-General Geary.

11. January 5, 1865: New York Times story of the Savannah occupation

http://www.nytimes.com/1865/01/05/news/savannah-details-military-occupation-judicious-orders-gen-sherman-important.html?pagewanted=all

FROM SAVANNAH; Details of the Military Occupation. JUDICIOUS ORDERS FROM GEN. SHERMAN. Important Action of the Citizens. They Resolve to Return to Thei Allegiance. SCARCITY OF FOOD IN THE CITY. Revival of Trade and the Press. Popular Feeling in the City? Strong Undercurrent of Unionism? Wife of Capt. Morris Sent North? Suffering Among the Poor? The Approaching Campaign? A Newspaper Transformation? Savannah Merchants Coming North. The New Regime in Savannah? The Temper of the Citizens? Revival of Trade? The Cotton Question. IMPORTANT ACTION OF THE CITIZENS OF SAVANNAH. PROVISONS FOR THE PEOPLE OF SAVANNAH. THE

PROVISIONS NEEDED. AFFAIRS IN SAVANNAH. REVIEW OF THE TWENTIETH ARMY CORPS. CITIZENS AND THE AMNESTY OATH. ARRIVAL OF A POSTMASTER. THE SHAD SEASON. Casualites in the Twentieth Army Corps, in Operations Before Savannah. SEVENTY-THIRD PENNSYLVANIA VOLUNTEERS. James Quinn, Co. C-severe. SAVANNAH, Saturday, Dec. 31, 1864.

Quiet reigns in Savannah. With a good sense and judgment that contrasts favorably with the conduct of the New-Orleans Secessionists, when that city was first occupied by Gen. BUTLER, the citizens here submit gracefully to the rule of the successful invaders, and from the first hour of the occupation by our troops till now, have wisely abstained from every kind of aggressive demonstration. To the praise of our soldiers, it should also be recorded that they have exhibited the utmost consideration toward the people of the city, and have, one and all, studiously refrained from every act that could be possibly construed as an affront to their sensitive and wounded pride. The natural consequence of this mutual forbearance is witnessed in the pleasant spirit of cordiality, and even fraternity, that begins to exist between the "invaders" and the citizens, and from which we hope for the best results in the future. It shows that the "undying Southern hate" for Yankees, which rebel papers love to prate about, is a ferocious delusion, that exists only in rebel print.

I would not be understood to say that the spirit of secession is wholly dead in Savannah, but only that a strong Union sentiment is gradually winning its way among the citizens. They have seen the folly of rebellion. The Sodom apples of secession have been pressed to their lips, and turned there to bitter ashes. The occupation of their city gives them the opportunity to repent, for which a large number have long signed and looked with eager expectations. Of course, there, are many individual cases of confirmed apostacy from the Union, and the worst of these it is deemed necessary to send out of the city. One of the most haughty and violent is the wife of the celebrated corsair MORRIS, commander of the late privateer Florida. This lady will go North by the next steamer, with the intention of proceeding to England, where she hopes to join her husband.

Savannah is suffering, just now, from a deplorable scarcity of provisions. There is an absolute want of the necessary means of subsistence. Rice abounds in immense quantities, and is almost the only kind of food within the reach of the great mass of the citizens. Of course, they cannot subsist entirely on rice; and they propose, I understand, to send an agent to New-York to barter a quantity of this commodity for other articles of food. The matter will be placed in the hands of Col. JULIAN ALLEN, who has been authorized by the Mayor of the city and by Maj.-Gen. SHERMAN, to proceed North for this purpose. It is to be hoped that he will be successful in his mission. Meanwhile, the military authorities are doing their utmost to alleviate the sufferings of the poor of the city, among whom the commissary stores left behind by the rebels, in their hasty evacuation of the city, will be judiciously distributed.

I have no active military operations to record; but on every side I see evidences of immense preparations of renewed activity. Gen. SHERMAN is not the man to rest on his laurels. Like a soldier of the true Christian stamp, he turns his back on the past, and presses forward to new fields of battle and conquest. Where and when he will strike his next blow at the power of the staggering rebellion, it is not in my power to inform you; but in the army every man talks of a grand and overwhelming march on Charleston, and every man is eager for the ensuing campaign to take this direction. Perhaps Gen. SHERMAN will not disappoint their expectations.

12. January 11, 1865: General Sherman's reply to Salmon P. Chase regarding treatment of negroes

https://sherman150.wordpress.com/2015/01/11/january-11-1865/

TO SALMON P. CHASE
Headquarters Military Division of the Mississippi, In the Field,
Savannah, Jan. 11, 1865
Hon. S. P. Chase. Washington D.C.
My Dear Sir,

I feel very much flattered by the notice you take of me, and none the less because you overhaul me in the negro question. I mean no unkindness to the negro in the mere words of my hasty dispatch announcing my arrival on the Coast. The only real failures in a military sense, I have sustained in my military administration have been the expeditions of Wm. Sooy Smith and Sturgis, both resulting from their encumbering their columns with refugees. If you can understand the nature of a military column in an enemy's country, with its long train of wagons you will see at once that a crowd of negroes, men women and children, old & young, are a dangerous impediment.

On approaching Savannah I had at least 20,000 negroes, clogging my roads, and eating up our subsistence. Instead of finding abundance here I found nothing and had to depend on my wagons till I opened a way for vessels and even to this day my men have been on short rations and my horses are failing. The same number of white refugees would have been a military weakness. Now you Know that military success is what the nation wants, and it is risked by the crowds of helpless negroes that flock after our armies. My negro constituents of Georgia would resent the idea of my being inimical to them, they regard me as a second Moses or Aaron. I treat them as free, and have as much trouble to protect them against the avaricious recruiting agents of New England States as against their former masters. You can hardly realize this, but it is true.

I have conducted to freedom & asylum hundreds of thousands and have aided them to obtain employment and houses. Every negro who is fit for a soldier and is willing I invariably allow to join a negro Regiment, but I do oppose and rightfully too, the forcing of negroes as soldiers. You cannot Know the acts and devices to which base white men resort to secure negro soldiers, not to aid us to fight, but to get bounties for their own pockets, and to diminish their quotas at home. Mr. Secretary Stanton is now here and will bear testimony to the truth of what I say. Our Quartermaster and commissary can give employment to every negro (able bodied) whom we obtain, and he protests against my parting with them for other purposes, as it forces him to use my veteran white troops to unload vessels, and do work for which he prefers the negro. If the President prefers to minister to the one idea of negro Equality, rather than military success; which as a major involves the minor, he should remove me, for I am so constituted that I cannot honestly sacrifice the security and Success of my army to any minor cause.

Of course I have nothing to do with the Status of the negro after war. That is for the law making power. But if my opinion were consulted I would Say that the negro should be a free race, but not put on an equality with the whites. My Knowledge of them is practical, and the effect of equality is illustrated in the character of the Mixed race in Mexico and South America. Indeed it appears to me that the right of suffrage in our Country should be rather abridged than enlarged.

But these are all matters subordinate to the issues of this war, which can alone be determined by war, and it depends on good armies, of the best possible material and best disciplined, and these points engross my entire thoughts.

With sincere respect & esteem,

W. T. Sherman, Major General

13. E.D. Townsend's affidavit regarding minutes of January 12, 1865 ministers' meeting in General Sherman's army headquarters, the Green Mansion

http://www.freedmen.umd.edu/savmtg.htm

WAR DEPARTMENT, ADJUTANT-GENERAL'S OFFICE, Washington, February 1, 1865.

I do hereby certify that the foregoing is a true and faithful report of the questions and answers made by the colored ministers and church members of Savannah in my presence and hearing at the chambers of Major-General Sherman, on the evening of Thursday, the 12th day of January, 1865. The questions of General Sherman and the Secretary of War were reduced to writing and read to the persons present. The answers were made by the reverend Garrison Frazier, who was selected by the other ministers and church members to answer for them. The answers were written down in his exact words, and read over to the others, who, one by one, expressed his concurrence or dissent, as above set forth.

E. D. TOWNSEND,

Assistant Adjutant-General

14. Answer to the third question at January 12, 1865 ministers' meeting, in General Sherman's army headquarters, the Green Mansion

http://www.freedmen.umd.edu/savmtg.htm

...<u>Third Question:</u> State in what manner you think you can take care of yourselves, and how can you best assist the Government in maintaining your freedom.

[Garrison Frazier] The way we can best take care of ourselves is to have land, and turn it and till it by our own labor-that is, by the labor of the women and children and old men; and we can soon maintain ourselves and have something to spare. And to assist the Government, the young men should enlist in the service of the Government, and serve in such manner as they may be wanted...We want to be placed on land until we are able to buy it and make it our own.

15. January 26, 1865: General Sherman's orders for distribution of land to ex-slaves.

https://en.wikipedia.org/wiki/Sherman%27s_Special_Field_Orders,_No._15

SPECIAL FIELD ORDERS NO. 15
HEADQUARTERS MILITARY DIVISION OF THE MISSISSIPPI, IN THE FIELD, NEAR SAVANNAH, GEORGIA, January 16, 1865.

1. The islands from Charleston south, the abandoned rice-fields along the rivers for thirty miles back from the sea, and the country bordering the St. John's River, Florida, are reserved and set apart for the settlement of the negroes now made free by the acts of war and the proclamation of the President of the United States.

2. At Beaufort, Hilton Head, Savannah, Fernandina, St. Augustine, and Jacksonville, the blacks may remain in their chosen or accustomed vocations; but on the islands, and in the settlements hereafter to be established, no white person whatever, unless military officers and soldiers detailed for

duty, will be permitted to reside; and the sole and exclusive management of affairs will be left to the freed people themselves, subject only to the United States military authority, and the acts of Congress. By the laws of war, and orders of the President of the United States, the negro is free, and must be dealt with as such. He cannot be subjected to conscription, or forced military service, save by the written orders of the highest military authority of the department, under such regulations as the President or Congress may prescribe. Domestic servants, blacksmiths, carpenters, and other mechanics, will be free to select their own work and residence, but the young and able-bodied negroes must be encouraged to enlist as soldiery in the service of the United States, to contribute their share toward maintaining their own freedom, and securing their rights as citizens of the United States. negroes so enlisted will be organized into companies, battalions, and regiments, under the orders of the United States military authorities, and will be paid, fed, and clothed; according to law. The bounties paid on enlistment may, with the consent of the recruit, go to assist his family and settlement in procuring agricultural implements, seed, tools, boots, clothing, and other articles necessary for their livelihood.

3. Whenever three respectable negroes, heads of families, shall desire to settle on land, and shall have selected for that purpose an island or a locality clearly defined within the limits above designated, the Inspector of Settlements and Plantations will himself, or, by such subordinate officer as he may appoint, give them a license to settle such island or district, and afford them such assistance as he can to enable them to establish a peaceable agricultural settlement. The three parties named will subdivide the land, under the supervision of the inspector, among themselves, and such others as

may choose to settle near them, so that each family shall have a plot of not more than forty acres of tillable ground, and, when it borders on some water-channel, with not more than eight hundred feet water-front, in the possession of which land the military authorities will afford them protection until such time as they can protect themselves, or until Congress shall regulate their title. The quartermaster may, on the requisition of the Inspector of Settlements and Plantations, place at the disposal of the inspector one or more of the captured steamers to ply between the settlements and one or more of the commercial points heretofore named, in order to afford the settlers the opportunity to supply their necessary wants, and to sell the products of their land and labor.

4. Whenever a negro has enlisted in the military service of the United States, he may locate his family in any one of the settlements at pleasure, and acquire a homestead, and all other rights and privileges of a settler, as though present in person. In like manner, negroes may settle their families and engage on board the gunboats, or in fishing, or in the navigation of the inland waters, without losing any claim to land or other advantages derived from this system. But no one, unless an actual settler as above defined, or unless absent on Government service, will be entitled to claim any right to land or property in any settlement by virtue of these orders.

5. In order to carry out this system of settlement, a general officer will be detailed as Inspector of Settlements and Plantations, whose duty it shall be to visit the settlements, to regulate their police and general arrangement, and who will furnish personally to each head of a family, subject to the approval of the President of the United States, a possessory title in writing, giving as near as possible the description of

boundaries; and who shall adjust all claims or conflicts that may arise under the same, subject to the like approval, treating such titles altogether as possessory. The same general officer will also be charged with the enlistment and organization of the negro recruits, and protecting their interests while absent from their settlements; and will be governed by the rules and regulations prescribed by the War Department for such purposes.

6. Brigadier-General R. Saxton is hereby appointed Inspector of Settlements and Plantations, and will at once enter on the performance of his duties. No change is intended or desired in the settlement now on Beaufort Island, nor will any rights to property heretofore acquired be affected thereby.

By order of Major-General W. T. Sherman,
L. M. DAYTON, Assistant Adjutant-General

16. February 15, 1865: Savannah and Boston. Account of the supplies sent to Savannah: 1865

https://archive.org/details/savannahandbost00arnogoog
(Quoted herein is small portion of 43-page report)
REPORT OF COMMITTEE SENT TO SAVANNAH
To Messrs. William Gray, E.R. Mudge, John A. Blanchard, Nathan Crowell, William T. Glidden, Executive Committee, &c.
The Committee appointed by you to proceed to Savannah in charge of the supplies contributed by the citizens of Boston for the relief of the people of that city, having delivered the same in accordance with your instructions, beg leave to submit the following Report : —

The value of the supplies placed in our hands at the time of our departure was about twenty-five thousand dollars, about thirteen of which were shipped on board the steamer "

Greyhound"' which sailed from Boston on Saturday, January 14th; and the balance, on the United-States transport "Daniel Webster," which sailed from New York on the Monday following. Two members of the Committee took passage on the "Greyhound," and the other on the "Daniel Webster." It was hoped the voyage from Boston would not occupy more than four days, and that we should have the satisfaction of landing the cargo in Savannah, and relieving the wants of the people, without delay; but, owing to a succession of accidents which have already been reported, the "Greyhound" did not arrive until the 25th, and even then, owing to the movements of the army, and difficulty in obtaining assistance, we were not able to commence discharging the cargo until the 30th. The "Daniel Webster" experienced similar delays, and arrived on the same morning with the "Greyhound;" but, being needed for special service by the Government, the goods were discharged immediately.

While the vessels were aground in the river, the Committee proceeded to the city, and waited upon General Sherman. He at once approved of the enterprise, and gave orders to General Grover, the Post Commander, to render us all needed assistance; and we take pleasure in acknowledging the kindness with which he received the Committee, and the prompt manner in which he acted by detailing one of his staff. Lieutenant Chariot, to co-operate with the municipal authorities in the distribution of the stores. The address which you requested us to present to the Mayor was then delivered, and subsequently published in the papers of the city.

The steamer "Rebecca Clyde" with the New York contributions had arrived before us, although she did not leave that city until the day after we sailed from Boston. Her small size and light draft of water enabled her to pass directly up the river, and the supplies on her were being discharged when we arrived.

The contributions, on being landed, were immediately placed in an adjoining store-house, and protected by a guard. From the store-house they were removed to a store in the central part of the city for distribution...

END of APPENDIX